I0600765

DARK ANGELS

HUBERT E. DEVINE

Dark Angels
Copyright © 2017 by Hubert E. Devine All rights reserved.
Second Edition: October 2017

ISBN for print book: 9780993817342
ISBN for ebooks: 9780993817359

No part of this book may be reproduced, scanned, or distributed in any printed or electronic
form without permission. Please do not participate in or encourage piracy of copyrighted
materials in violation of the author's rights. Thank you for respecting the hard work of this
author.

This is a work of fiction. Although inspired, in part, by actual events and real people, any names
and characters used in the book, and any events or incidents depicted, are either the product of
the author's imagination or used in a fictitious manner.

The first edition of Dark Angels was published in 2016 by Three Dogs Press.
ISBN for print book: 9780991979349
ISBN for ebooks: 9780995048508

WHAT READERS ARE SAYING ABOUT DARK ANGELS, BY HUBERT E. DEVINE

"Not a typical book I would have selected for myself. However, once I began to read it, I could not put it down. It's the story of insight into a young man's mind – his battles, challenges, emotions, development and growth. It's shocking and nail-biting, but, at the same time, it transports you to beautiful Halifax. You can smell the salty air, touch the trees and hear the seagulls. An exciting story! I highly recommend it."

– M. Rewerenda Wright, Tucson, Arizona

"So well written ... plot is enthralling, characters are vivid, and the tensions leave you with a sense of wonderment. Loved every page."

– B. Keddy, PhD, Professor Emerita, Dalhousie University

"Immediately drawn in ... it's well-paced and there's always a sense that something else is about to happen, so it makes you want to keep reading. I found these guys to be mostly likeable and I genuinely cared about them, despite their being anti-heroes"

– B. Ross, Yarmouth, NS

"Exceeded my expectations. Conclusion is surprising without being unbelievable."

– J. Doherty, Canadian Motorcycle Hall of Fame, Dartmouth, NS

"A great insight into the world of biker clubs that will keep you hanging on to each chapter ... intertwines between doing what is right, doing what you want to do, what you should do, or what is expected of you. You won't be able to put this down."

– R. LeBlanc, Yarmouth, NS

To the yearning for adventure and belonging
that stirs in every awakened soul ...

*"Our acts our angels are, for good or ill, our
fatal shadows that walk by us still."*

—*John Fletcher*

PART 1

DARK ANGELS

THE CORNER LEAPT AT HIM like a hungry panther hiding in the murky shadows of thick pines lining the roadside. He shot a glance at the white-faced speedometer. Its black needle vibrated between 80 and 90 miles per hour. He snapped the throttle shut with a flick of his right wrist, jerked in the stiff clutch with his left hand, and kicked the transmission down into third gear. As he dumped the clutch, the bike shuddered and the big motor howled in protest.

He cranked the snorting steel dragon over to the right, throwing it hard into the turn. The Harley twitched and wobbled, bouncing its smooth leather seat against his tailbone, trying hard to buck him off. First the footpeg and then the outer edge of the chrome exhaust pipe kissed the coarse asphalt, sending a shower of white-hot sparks dancing behind and inscribing a perfect arc through the corner's apex.

Look through the corner! Look through the corner, he reminded himself.

He willed his eyes to find the end of the corner, not to look down where he was but ahead where he wanted to go. Softening his grip on the throttle, he pushed a little harder against the left handgrip, and the bike began to come back up, pointed straight at the spot where the corner straightened.

He was back hard on the gas. As fast as the turn had sought to devour him, he now broke free of its bounds. "**EIGHTY! – NINETY! – ONE HUNDRED!**" he screamed into the hurricane of road wind that blasted over and around him, flattening his denim jeans and jacket tight against his young, muscular body, and blowing his shoulder-length dirty-blond hair straight out behind. The motor wailed a machine-gun burst of high-compression explosions – 80 **KA-BOOMS** crammed into each crazy second.

He sucked the fragrant June air bursting with succulent, moist pine deep into his lungs. Colours and shapes whizzed by. The noise of the wind and motor choked out all other sounds. The handlebars and footpegs buzzed through his hands and feet, sending tingles of electricity skittering along happy nerve pathways to his pounding heart and wild-eyed brain – and skittering back again in a tango of yearning to see, and touch, and feel, and *be* to the core of his being.

He shot out of the shade into Waverly's evening sun. He raced on, rolling on and off the gas, feeling light as he crested hills and heavier on the descent. He leaned left and right into turns, seeing the earth tip and turn, and angle up and then down, absorbing the intoxication of g-forces against his body.

He closed upon Barry's place faster than expected and had to hit the brakes hard and hammer the transmission down through its gears to avoid overshooting the driveway. He came to a stop at the foot of Barry's driveway. *Only one bit of tricky riding left*, he told himself – 200 feet of gravely, rutted climbing.

He coaxed the bike up the hill in first gear, holding the throttle steady and feathering the clutch. Up, up he went, climbing higher than the tops of the trees that grew along the side of the highway below. He aimed at a place to stop among the other bikes parked in front of the house and steered his bike into the spot.

He sat there letting the motor idle, the tempo of the notes now synchronized with the beating of his heart. He savoured the moment – the heated air wafting up from the motor to his face, the jacked-up exhilaration and thrill of the ride, the contentment of being in perfect connection with time, place, and fate. He let the clutch lever slip from his fingers. The bike lurched ahead a few inches and stalled. He let it coast backward the inch or two it took before the engaged transmission prevented further movement. He then pushed the sidestand out with his left heel and let the bike fall against its stand with graceful ease.

From among the crowd of bikers assembled on the verandah above him, Shotgun nodded in his direction and made his way down the steps. Grinning as he approached, he pushed clumps of black greasy hair from his forehead, moving his gangling limbs in all directions until he stood next to him.

"Good ride? I was starting to think you weren't going to make it." He grabbed Will, giving him a beer-drenched kiss of brotherhood on the lips, and pushed a bottle of beer against his chest.

"I had to work late." He took a long drink from the bottle. "Bike's working great, but I still find it top-heavy. Feels like it's going to fall over in the corners. Not much ground clearance either when you got it cranked over. Not like the Bonnie."

"Well, that's a Harley for you, son. They handle like pigs, but you gotta love that torque." Shotgun scratched his temple. "You could always extend the front forks a few more inches. That'd give you more than enough ground clearance to strafe corners. But it'll never handle like a Triumph. You just gotta get used to that."

Up on the verandah, Barry, Stumpy, and several other Dark Angels milled about, drinking beer and watching the bikes rumble up to the house. Music spilled out from inside the house through the open front door. Stumpy stared at Will and Shotgun. He pulled at his matted hair and coarse beard, cleared his throat and spat on the weather-cracked boards of the verandah floor. He elbowed Barry, and then crossed his tattooed arms against his massive chest.

"That kid gives me the creeps." He tipped his head toward Will and scrunched his face into a somber frown.

"Will?" Barry peered down. "Why do you say that?"

"Why? Look at him! He don't even shave yet, does he? What will people say when they see some pretty-boy punk kid flying our colours? I mean, shit, Barry, we got a reputation to think of. Where the hell was I anyway when you guys voted him in?"

"How the hell am I supposed to know where you were? Most likely fixing that orange piece of junk you call a bike or still in jail. He's been around for a while. If you came to meetings, you'd know what was going on."

"Well, you idiots must've all been stoned. That's all I can think."

Barry turned to face him. "Shotgun's known him for about a year, and Frantic says he's okay. We'll keep an eye on him. And if he screws up, well, we'll get rid of him. No big deal."

Stumpy shifted his bulk from side to side. "Ain't that just peachy-keen. I didn't join this outfit to be no babysitter for no choir boy. I'm tellin' ya right now, he's gonna have to look after his fuckin' self."

Barry shrugged.

Will and Shotgun left the bikes and headed up the verandah steps. Stumpy turned away as they passed him on their way to the front door.

Once inside – a chaotic cauldron of sweaty high energy, sweet marijuana smoke, and pounding music – Shotgun motioned for Will to follow him to a corner at the far end of the living room. On a low wooden table, he unfolded a scrap of tinfoil containing two brownish pills.

"Do you want a whole one or just half?" he asked in Will's direction, straining to be heard over the music.

"What is it?"

"Acid. Really good shit. No other crap in it." He broke one pill in half. "Here, try half now. I'll save the other half for you for later in case you want it."

Shotgun washed a whole pill down with his beer. Will took the half Shotgun held out. He popped it in his mouth and finished off his beer.

"I'll get us more beer," Shotgun said, heading off to the kitchen behind them.

Will sat on the table and surveyed the roiling brew of the party that bubbled all around him.

"It's like a garbage dump," he said to a thin girl leaning against the wall beside him.

She frowned. "Wha …?"

"I mean, all the people are different and they're all doing different things, and the music is always changing. But it all makes up a party and not something else. It's like garbage. Garbage is made up off all kinds of different things, and everything in it changes, and nobody controls any of it. And all together it's just garbage. But no matter what's in them, all garbage dumps smell the same and more or less look the same, and you can't mistake them for anything else. See what I mean?"

She narrowed her eyes. "Ohhh, yeah," she said, after a pause. "That's deep, isn't it?"

He heard a commotion at the door and turned to see Stumpy and Barry push their way inside. Stumpy headed to the kitchen, plowing a gaping hole through the crowd as everyone stepped aside or was nudged out of the way. Barry stopped in the middle of the living room. Shotgun returned to Will's side with more beer. Soon, a group of people began to form a rough circle around Barry, whose voice began to rise above the music.

"Okay, the cops will always feel in your boot tops, right? So you don't put the knife there." Barry stroked his black moustache and goatee, made more room for himself in the middle of the crowd, and settled into a relaxed, professorial stance.

Shotgun shook his head and rolled his eyes. "It's one of his favourite routines," he said to Will. "Lots of new people here tonight, so he's got to play it up."

Barry fished down the front of his jeans, pulled out a brown leather pouch that resembled the amputated finger of a glove, and held it up for everyone to see. A small metal hook was attached to the top of the pouch and inside was his ebony-handled switchblade.

"See, the knife goes in the pouch, and you hook the pouch on the inside of your jeans or on your belt. It'll hang down on the inside of your zipper. I mean, the heat's not going to grab the front of your crotch and say, 'Hey, man, what's that hard thing? Unzip your fly'. They pat but they don't squeeze, right?" His audience chuckled and nodded.

He put the pouch and knife into position inside his jeans. "When you're in a scrap, you don't want to be searching around for your blade. You want to be able to get at it fast, and you don't want the stupid dude you're hoping to slice up to figure out what you're up to."

He tightened his face, its dark handsomeness made more interesting by the deep acne scars it bore, and pulled his lips back into a sinister sneer. The muscles in his sinewy arms tensed. He looked like an animal ready to pounce, the whites of his eyes framing huge pupils that shone black. "You just grab it by the top, slip it out, and swing it back like you're getting ready to pitch a ball underhand." His voice became more urgent and more of a snarl. "That gives you a second to feel for the button and get a good grip. Then you bring it up open, right in that sucker's face." He whipped the knife from the front of his jeans and stabbed at the air with a deft thrust. "**LIKE THIS!!**"

People jerked away, crashing into one another, laughing and hooting.

"That's pretty cool," Will said to Shotgun.

"Yeah, Barry's cool. Least he works hard at it. You just have to watch him, that's all."

"What do you mean?"

"What I mean is that with Barry it's all about image, about acting out some kind of Hollywood-biker part. You know, the posing, the long hair, all the right tattoos, all the one-percenter crap, all that tough-guy, look-at-me bullshit. Listen, I knew him when he was a kid. He was a screwed up nerd then and he's still screwed up. He's the twistiest, most-manipulative prick you'll ever come across. If he can't order you around, he'll find some way to suck you in or con you to do what he wants. That's all."

"But he's the president of the club."

"Yeah, so what? Just because he's screwed up and paranoid doesn't mean he's not the best guy for the job. You gotta be warped to want to be in charge of this bunch of rejects. Besides, nobody else wanted to do it."

He grabbed Will by the arm. "But to hell with him. You're a smart kid. You'll figure him out quick enough. Come on, I want you to do something with Stumpy for me."

Will pulled back. "Uh, I don't think so. I think it'd be best if I stay away from him. I don't know what I did, but he's been evil-eying me ever since he first saw me."

"Ah, that's nothing. Stumpy lets on like he doesn't like anybody. He doesn't know you yet, and he's the suspicious type. Once he knows you're okay, he'll back you up against the world. It's just that right now he can't see past your lovely complexion and your cute school-boy ways, sweetheart."

Will laughed as Shotgun strong-armed him into the kitchen and pushed him into the crowd that had formed around the kitchen table. He saw Stumpy sitting at the narrow table on a wooden chair. Barry bound into the kitchen behind them and pushed past, hopping up on another wooden chair on the opposite side of the table. He looked around the kitchen at everyone, and then held his arms out from his sides.

"Okay, listen up," he commanded, as the chatter died down. "What do you weigh now, Stump?" he asked, looking down at Stumpy.

"I don't know – 265, 270, I guess," Stumpy said, looking bored as he scratched at his beard.

"No takers tonight? Too bad. I was hoping for a chance to bet against you."

Stumpy put his meaty palms on the top of the table and began to push himself up. "Yeah, jerk, guess tonight's not your night."

"Whoa, not so fast!" Shotgun blurted out. "We got a taker." He waved Barry off the chair. As Barry hopped off, looking dismayed, Shotgun pushed Will down into the chair.

"No, no!" Will protested. He tried to stand, but both Shotgun and Barry pushed on his shoulders from behind and he sank back down.

Stumpy glanced up at Shotgun, then at Barry. He lowered himself back onto the chair, glaring across the empty table at Will.

"What do *you* want?"

"Um, I don't know. Nothing. It's not my idea." He turned and looked back up at Shotgun and Barry.

"He wants a turn to arm-wrestle you," Shotgun said, grinning.

Stumpy arched back and roared with laughter, as did many others around the table.

"No, not really," Will mumbled.

"What'd you say, you little turd? Speak up!" Stumpy said.

"No, it's okay. We don't have to do it. I'm not that good at it. It's probably not a good idea."

Stumpy stared at him. "I don't know. Maybe it *is* a good idea. Let's see, I could break that chicken-shit arm of yours. Or, wait , we'll do a bet." His eyes brightened, and he shifted his weight. "Yeah, that's it, even better – a bet! Let's say, yeah, let's say that if I win, you give me those colours off your back, kiss Barry's hairy balls – if he's got any – and get your scrawny ass outta here."

Everybody but Will, Shotgun, and Barry laughed.

"And what if *he* wins?" Shotgun asked.

Stumpy's jaw tightened and a deep line creased his brow. "You're kiddin' me, right? You know he ain't gonna win. So it's a stupid fuckin' question."

"No, he's right," Barry interjected, his eyes sparkling. "It's not a bet unless Will's got a chance to get something out of it too."

Stumpy looked down at the table and shook his head. He leaned back and looked Will in the eyes. "Okay, kid, what d'ya want if one of these losers shoots me while this is goin' on and my arm falls down on the table under yours?"

Will shrugged and remained quiet.

"Come on, say something! You stupid, too?"

"Well, if I win," Will said, smiling, "You have to give me a big hug and tell me you love me." He straightened his back, leaned forward, brought his right arm up, and positioned his elbow on the table. He opened his hand toward Stumpy.

Stumpy gawked at him and again burst out laughing. He slammed his thick hand down on the tabletop, jarring it and startling the onlookers before they had time to laugh. He then banged his right elbow down onto the table and opened his hand toward Will.

"I know what we should call you, kid – Squeaky. That's what we should call you because you're so squeaky-clean and tight-assed, that's why. Look at you – your hair's so friggin' clean it shines."

Will held his arm in place and smiled. "You're quite attractive, too. I mean in a cave-man, beastly sort-of-way. Like King Kong meets the Incredible Hulk, just a little less human on both counts."

Everyone howled and laughed, and a faint smile stole across Stumpy's face.

"What do you weigh – about 150, 160?" Stumpy asked.

"About that."

"Barry? Shotgun? Come on, gimme a break," Stumpy said.

Barry pulled at his goatee and smiled. Shotgun reached down and dropped a 20-dollar bill on the table next to Will's arm. Others began putting money on the table.

"I can't believe I'm doing this," Stumpy said, shaking his head.

He leaned forward into the table and clasped Will's right hand with his own.

Will took up the tension of their grip. With their heads now no more than six inches apart, he looked into Stumpy's eyes.

"You ready?" he asked.

ELEMENTS OF SURPRISE

STUMPY SHOOK HIS THICK HEAD like a Rottweiler with a toy poodle in its mouth. He reached under his shirt with his left hand and pulled out a huge, yellowed fang that dangled on a tarnished chain hanging from his neck. "Grizzly. Killed it myself," he said to Will. "I'm gonna chew you up and spit you out, pretty boy."

Shotgun laughed. "Don't listen to him. He bought that from a drunk Russian when he was in the navy. I was there."

Stumpy growled and fired a menacing look in Shotgun's direction. He began to pull against Will's arm. Will held firm. Like two boxers testing the waters in the first round – the champion not wanting to show his stuff and the challenger not knowing quite what to expect – the contest was on, and the opposing forces in their grip grew second by second. The crowd squeezed in all around them shouting, clapping, urging them on – lusting blood. Stumpy pulled harder. Will's arm shook but he held firm. Stumpy sucked air in through his clenched teeth and pulled – and pulled. Will's arm didn't move.

For what felt like an eternity to Will, they rocked the table back and forth and ground its legs hard against the floor. He glanced up at Stumpy's swollen, red face. He crooked his wrist with a quick, hard snap and leaned his shoulder completely over it, bending Stumpy's wrist back and out of shape. Straining with all the strength he could summon, he watched in disbelief as Stumpy's arm began to sink inch-by-excruciating-inch toward the tabletop. He felt Stumpy's hot breath on his forearm, heard his quick, strained panting, and smelled his sour, sweaty exertion.

"PULL! PULL! PULL!" everyone screamed.

Will glanced up at Stumpy and locked onto his eyes. The desperate eyes that met his – the raw, gut-churning fear – startled him. His mind flashed back to a time his grandfather had taken him hunting in the deep woods outside of Yarmouth, where they came upon a live bear caught in steel leg-trap. He jerked his elbow up off the table.

"HEY! HEY!" Stumpy shouted, shaking his hand loose. "You got your elbow off the table! You gotta do this right!"

Suddenly, it was over and an orgasmic release of tension washed over everyone.

"Sorry, Stumpy, I couldn't hold you any longer. Felt like my arm was going to snap."

Barry came up behind Stumpy and slapped the side of his head. "You mean you were really trying? You *really* couldn't put him down? I can't believe it. And here I thought you were just being nice for a change and taking it easy on him. Sweet Jesus, you must be losing it big guy. You disappoint me, Lawrence. Maybe we should make young Will here our sergeant-at-arms."

Stumpy jerked up from the table and bulldozed his way through the crowd to get to the refrigerator. He looked back at Barry. "Don't fuckin' call me Lawrence. You know I don't like that." He reached in the refrigerator and grabbed two bottles of beer. "You do what you want, asshole. You always do. Don't matter to me." He turned and stormed out the back door.

Will glanced at Shotgun. "Is he okay? I didn't think that would happen."

Shotgun ran his fingers through his hair, slicking it back behind his ears. He draped an arm across Will's shoulders. "Yeah, he'll be okay. You did good, real good! It's okay that you brought him down a peg or two. You could've beaten him, couldn't you? Why didn't you?"

Will shook his head. "Didn't seem right. Reminded me of something bad." He turned to head back to the living room. He looked around, noticing that the walls, the furniture, and all the objects and people around him were beginning to shift and change.

Shotgun grabbed his arm from behind. "That's how you'll fit in here – one classy move at a time. You just gotta be who you are. There's only one thing that'll get you into trouble with the other guys and that's being a phoney. You can go to church and worship Jesus, or you can fill yourself with hate and worship Hitler. You can be an idiot or a depraved, freakin' maniac. None of it matters. All that matters is being real."

Will nodded. "There are only two things that matter to me in the world right now. One is being in this club. The other is my bike out there."

"That *is* all that matters, son. And that's more than most people have. Everybody's trying to figure out the rest of it – who we are, why we're here, what it all means, if it means anything – all that existential shit."

Will nodded and smiled.

"I'm gonna get some air," Shotgun said. "Goin' outside to mess with my bike. Coming?"

Will shook his head. "Stumpy's probably out there roaming around. I'll hang back here for a while. Chill out and listen to the music or something. Acid's coming on."

Watching Shotgun disappear through the front door, he plopped down onto the sofa in the living room. All the characters and scenes that had been *something* when he arrived were becoming other things or things he couldn't picture clearly. Time slowed or sped up. He couldn't be sure which. The fuzzy black throw that covered the sofa was turning into a bug-infested furry hide. The people moving around in front of him were becoming animalistic beings – Speedy a bulldog, Barry a cobra, Frantic Fred a gunslinger, Frenchy Jack a wolf – predators all. The dancing became a jerky pantomime – cuckoo-clock figures moving about to music in images of flashing, patterned colour.

He looked down at his body – his torso, his arms, hands, and legs – all he could see. Nothing seemed to shift or change, yet he couldn't tell what or who he was. He tried to recall who he was, who he had been, but he could conjure up no clear thoughts or images. It was like a dream in which he was the main character and everything seemed familiar, and yet it was not exactly him. It was like seeing a picture of someone he knew and should easily recognize. But the more he strained to find something known and familiar, the more it slipped away into a misty uncertainty. All he could see was thick fog, the cool mist of nothing and nowhere. All he could feel was a wind that blew in every direction and no direction.

From somewhere, from nowhere, a girl rushed into the house screaming. "BARRY!! BARRY!! SHOTGUN'S TAKING HIS BIKE OUT!!"

Will saw it was Kay, Shotgun's girlfriend. He heard the words and felt the panic in her voice but couldn't fathom why she would be freaking out because Shotgun was taking his bike out.

Barry charged outside followed by most people in the house. After the stampede had passed, Will stood up and guided his body out to the verandah. He saw Barry and some others circling around Shotgun down among the bikes. *Vultures circling a creature seeking to embrace life or death,* he thought. Shotgun sat motionless on his bike in the darkness, facing the bottom of the rocky driveway.

Gravity and curiosity pulled Will down the steps and across the hard earth until he was standing next to Shotgun on the opposite side of the bike from Barry and Stumpy.

"What do you think you're doing?" Barry asked.

Shotgun settled into the bike. "You know what I'm doing. I'm going for a ride."

Barry laughed. "Sorry, you know I'm not going to let you do that."

"Who are you, my fairy godmother? Why not?"

Barry looked around at the crowd. "Did he do acid tonight?"

Several people nodded.

"You're not going. No discussion."

"Ah, Christ, don't be such an asshole. I'm fine. I'm going down to the Texaco station to get some gas. We're going out when it gets light and nothing's open then. You know that."

"I said you're not going. If you need gas we can drain some from a few of the other bikes. Now, get off that bike."

Shotgun looked away and stared down the driveway. He reached out and grabbed the Harley's high handlebars.

"Come on, Shotgun, get off the bike. I'm getting tired of your little games."

Shotgun sighed. "Screw you."

Barry paused and looked around. "I'm going to give you one more chance. If you don't get off that bike right now and come inside, I'm going to get Stumpy to knock you out. You know he wouldn't mind doing that after the way you set him up tonight."

Shotgun didn't look up. "Screw you – both of you."

Barry smiled across at Stumpy. "This is it, Shotgun. Get off!"

Shotgun said nothing.

"Okay, Stump, if that's what he wants, go ahead. Take him out."

Stumpy lurched toward Shotgun. Everyone flinched and pulled away. But Stumpy just leaned forward and wrapped his big arms around Shotgun from behind.

"No, Barry, we don't have to do that," he said. He spoke to the side of

Shotgun's head. "Listen, you little jerk, you know we're not going to let you do anything stupid. Now come inside. We'll do our ridin' in the morning."

"When ya going to think for yourself, Stumpy, and stop being Barry's bitch?"

Stumpy looked down at Shotgun. His body began to shake. He released one hand from around Shotgun's waist, wiped his brow with it, and then relocked his bear hug. He began to lift and pull Shotgun. Shotgun clung hard to the bike, his arms and legs all spidery. Stumpy pulled and twisted and lifted but couldn't pry Shotgun off. Within seconds, the bike began to slide sideways in the dirt, stirring up gravel and dust.

"WAIT!" Will screamed.

Everyone jumped and stopped in their tracks, then stared at him wide-eyed.

"Sorry. I didn't mean to yell so loud."

He stepped up to Shotgun's bike, knelt down, and felt around under the gas tank. He found the high-tension wire that ran from the bike's coil to the sparkplug of its rear cylinder. He pulled the pencil-thick wire off, stood up, and held it out to Barry. "Here, he won't go anywhere now."

Barry smirked, looking more disappointed than satisfied. He snatched the plug wire from Will and stuffed it into the back pocket of his jeans. The others glanced from side to side, looking confused.

"You coming inside, now?" Barry asked Shotgun.

Shotgun righted himself with an indignant look. He stared down the driveway – eyes fiery and defiant, brow furrowed – to a place beyond its darkness, to a place he alone could see.

"Suit yourself," Barry said.

"I think we should leave him alone," Stumpy said, beginning to herd people back toward the verandah.

"That was pretty smart," Barry said to Will, once back inside. He hugged Will, kissing his neck as he did. "What made you think of taking his wire?"

"I don't know. I didn't think about it. It just sort of came to me. But I don't get it. What was the big deal about Shotgun taking his bike out? Lots of the guys ride when they're drunk or stoned."

Barry pointed at his partially-built bike, sitting off to one side of the living room against a wall. "Last fall, Shotgun's bike was tit's up and we were at a party like this. So Shotgun says he wants to go for a ride and wants to take my bike. And I say 'Sure, go ahead,' not knowing he's stoned. So he's gone all night. We go out in Frenchy Jack's truck looking for him but can't find a trace of him. Around seven in the morning, he comes walking up my driveway with that stupid toothy grin on his face. He's all torn up and can't remember a thing. So we go out again in the truck and drive around most of the morning looking for the bike. Around noon, we see this funny hole in a bunch of alders off that tight corner just before the railroad tracks when you get closer to Sunnyside. We dig through the bushes and there it is."

Will caught himself laughing. "Sorry."

"It's okay. Makes for a good story, I guess. That's Shotgun for you. If he can't buck against the greasers or the cops, he'll find some way to buck against us. Anyway, he sure thought it was funny. Still does, I'm sure."

There was a break in the pounding music as they began to thread through the crowd toward Barry's bike. Suddenly, Barry stopped in his tracks and cocked his head to the right. "Listen!" he said. They both strained to hear. "What the hell is that? It's not a Harley. Sounds like a big single."

"Sounds like a Velocette or, um, maybe an old Norton," Will said, closing his eyes to listen harder.

Barry hesitated. "Or could be a – GODDAMN!" He bolted for the front door and charged outside with Will and everyone else following in his wake. They jostled for position on the verandah, straining to see the dim outline of a bike and rider at the bottom of the driveway. They heard the motor chugging and rasping in a rough idle. The revs began to build, a growing momentum of off-tempo, thumping intensity.

From the bottom of the driveway, Shotgun glanced up at the house and the throng of screaming black shapes. He thrust the middle finger of his left hand into the darkness, and then took off in a blur, rocketing through the gears down on the highway below the house. First in one direction, then back the other way, he flew back and forth with no headlight – the booming of the motor's one firing cylinder and the taillight that blinked on at the end of each pass the only clue to his exact location. While Barry paced and shook his head, and the rest of the crowd peered down at the highway through the trees and cheered and clapped, Shotgun completed three full-rip passes in each direction.

All of a sudden, he braked hard and turned into the driveway. Will and the others heard the motor die.

"Good. He stalled it," Barry said to Will.

At that moment, they saw the brake lights of a car speeding from the same direction blink on and heard its tires screech on the asphalt. They saw the car's back-up lights come on. As the car began to turn in the direction of the driveway, they heard Shotgun's bike cough to life once gain. They heard the revs rise to a howl.

APPARITIONS AND APPEARANCES

T HE CAR LURCHED INTO THE driveway, its blinding high-beams illuminating Shotgun, his bike, and a plume of rocks and dirt spewed up by his spinning back wheel. The bike heaved and fishtailed, bouncing Shotgun in all directions. Close behind, the car heaved and bucked, churning up even more dirt and dust, and scraping its undercarriage on the driveway's center ridge.

Wild-eyed and grinning, Shotgun closed fast and hard upon the parked bikes, the Dark Angels, and all the other party-goers frozen in place. Taunting disaster, he jammed on his brakes and slid his bike in among several others. Before his bike's motor had chugged its last stroke, he kicked the sidestand out and took off at a full run into the tangle of bushes and trees behind Barry's house.

The final bellowing of the bike's motor hung in the air, and its motor clicked and clacked from intense heat as the machine – guided as if by an invisible hand or knowing somehow what to do itself – fell to the left against its sidestand. At the same moment, the RCMP cruiser ground to a crunching stop. The door flew open and a lone Mountie jumped out.

The Mountie stopped short, scanning the crowd and bikes. He felt for his gun and unsnapped the strap that held it in its holster. He flicked on a long flashlight that he gripped with his left hand and angled it back and forth in the direction of the people and bikes in a jerky, swiping motion. He squared the broad shoulders of his compact body and took a few tentative steps toward the bikes.

Barry moved out from among the crowd and sauntered up to him.

"Where's the owner of this place?" the Mountie asked.

"That'd be me," Barry said. "Let me guess. Um, you came to join our party, right Constable – Constable ...?"

"Jackson. Peter Jackson. Not that it should matter." He shone his flashlight up at Barry's face. "I'm not here for any party. I want the guy driving that motorbike over there." He pointed at Shotgun's bike.

Barry smiled. "I like that bristly haircut you got there, man. Is that a brush-cut under that hat? Don't see many of those these days." He reached for the Mountie's hat.

Jackson pulled his head back. "Easy," he said, nudging Barry's arm with his flashlight.

"Peter Jackson – like the cigarettes?" Barry asked, grinning. "You know, Peter Jackson cigarettes. I like that brand. So we're off to a good start, right?"

Jackson took the flashlight beam off Barry's face. "Yes, the same name."

Barry snickered. "Right. Okay, where were we? Oh yeah, well, there's no one driving that bike. It's sitting there all by itself."

Those nearby chuckled.

Jackson reached up and tugged at the bill of his hat, pulling it down tighter against his head. "Funny. Very funny. I mean, of course, the guy that *was* driving it a few minutes ago."

"Well, okay, Pete. May I call you Pete? First, we have to get our terms straight. You see, you don't *drive* a bike – you drive a car. A bike you *ride* – like a horse. Know what I mean? The other thing, Pete, is that the machine you pointed at over there is not a *motorbike*. Motorbikes are those little ring-a-ding things with two wheels they make in places like Italy and Japan. The ones girls ride. *That*, Pete, is *gen – eew – wine* Milwaukee steel, a Harley-Davidson, a classic Knucklehead to be exact. And definitely *not* a motorbike."

The crowd of bikers laughed as Barry turned to face the verandah. "Hey, Stumpy, why do some people call them motorbikes?"

Stumpy scowled down at him. "How am I supposed to know, Barry? You're the genius here, remember? I guess it's because they don't know no fuckin' better, that's all."

Jackson spoke up. "Thanks for that little lesson. But it doesn't change anything. I want that guy."

"You're right, Pete. Okay, so you say you want the guy you say was riding that Knucklehead. Why's that?"

"I came up behind him riding down on the highway without any lights on. I was *right* on his tail and saw him fly up here. This is 1970, not the old west. You boys can't expect to be running like a bunch of wild hooligans, doing whatever you please. We got laws and regulations."

Barry brought his hand down across the front of his face, replacing what had been an impish grin with a solemn face of stone. "Pete, I don't know how to tell you this without hurting your pride, and I sure don't want to be hard to get along with, but you must be mistaken. You see, we've all been drinking way too much and doing drugs. And, as the president of this club, I'd never let anyone ride in that condition or ride a bike that wasn't properly equipped with lights and all. Why, I'd punch him out personally before I'd let that happen. Matter of fact, the guy who owns that bike is quite stoned on acid. We think he's lost somewhere in the woods out back. We were just going to call you guys to help us look for him. He's officially a missing person."

Jackson shook his head and pursed his lips. "You really do think you're funny, don't you? A real comedian. Ha, ha, ha – tell me when to laugh." He widened his stance. "But I know what I saw. It was a skinny guy with long black hair, and he had those crests on his back. And that *is* the *motorbike* I saw – right over there." He shone his light on Shotgun's bike.

Barry hesitated. "Looks like we got ourselves to what they call an impasse, Pete. What do we do now?"

Jackson took out a notepad and pen from the breast pocket of his short-sleeved shirt, wet with sweat around the armpits. "Okay, who did you say owned that bike?"

"I didn't say. But it's Shotgun."

"Shotgun? What's his real name?"

"That's it. I shit you not. That's really it. Shotgun – S-h-o-t-g-u-n."

"I know how to spell it!" He pointed his pen at Barry. "Listen to me Mr. President of the Dark Angels, this has been all cute and entertaining, but I'll tell you what I'm going to do. I'm going to call Ace Towing and have that motorbike towed the hell out of here and brought to where we lock up seized vehicles. When Mr. Shotgun finds his way out of Sherwood Forest, get him to come talk to me if he wants his bike back."

"C'mon, Pete," Barry said, his tone becoming more serious. "Even though you've made an unfortunate career choice, I'm quite impressed – all alone like you are up here with us bad guys, and making threats to do this and do that. I really do like that. I do." He paused, staring into

Jackson's eyes. "But I have to tell you, Pete, you can check out Shotgun's bike all you want. You can even shine it up and take a picture of it. But you have to understand there's no chance in hell of you or Ace Towing taking it anywhere."

He slid his hands into the pockets of his jeans and relaxed his shoulders. "Come on. It doesn't have to be this way, man. All you gotta do is take it easy. Come inside and have some fun."

Jackson shifted his feet but stopped short of moving ahead. He looked around again.

Stumpy approached Barry from one side and held a lit cigarette out to him. Barry took it and dragged on it. He held it out toward Jackson.

Jackson shook his head. "Don't smoke."

"Kind of ironic, don't you think? I mean, you not smoking." Barry rounded his lips and blew two smoke rings up over Jackson's hat. "Think about it, Pete. It's a good proposition. We've got some seriously-good drugs and some seriously-hot chicks in there. They'd probably get off doing a young, clean-shaven guy like you in a Mountie uniform – pretty blue eyes and all. They're probably tired of getting banged all the time by us dirty oil-soaked bums. Bring your handcuffs and nightstick, man. We sure won't tell anybody."

Jackson cleared his throat and waved the smoke away. "No, that's not going to happen. But I *am* going to check out that bike and take down the serial number." He stepped to the side to go around Barry.

"Are you sure that's the one? I mean, shit, there's a lot of bikes here and they all look about the same in the dark."

Jackson headed toward the bikes, picking his way through the crowd of bikers. Speedy, Frantic Fred, and a few others began to form a line to intercept him.

"No!" Barry called out. He shook his head and waved them aside with a forceful swat of his right hand. He made the same gesture at Shotgun, who skulked in the background at the corner of the house.

Jackson stood behind Shotgun's bike and wrote down the license plate number. He moved around to the right side of the bike, where the two gleaming exhaust pipes snaked back from the motor, hugging the contours of the bike. He studied the two pipes –one above the other, about eight inches apart – then licked the fingers of his right hand and bent forward at the waist. He looked back at Barry.

"This is the right bike," he said, as he tapped his moist fingers against the upper pipe, which ran back from the motor's rear cylinder. But, then, his whole body twitched as if attacked by a huge shiver, his eyes owled wide, and he jerked upright. "What the …?" he muttered. He looked around and again reached down to tap the pipe. Then squeezed it. "Cold. It's cold," he muttered, looking off to one side.

"What? What, Pete? What's the problem now?" Barry asked. He caught Will's eye and winked.

Jackson said nothing. He began to wander from bike to bike, feeling their exhaust pipes. Within seconds, a wave of quiet laughter rippled through the crowd of bikers.

Jackson walked with slow, distracted steps back to Shotgun's bike. He put his notepad and pen back into his shirt pocket, and then slipped his flashlight into a side pocket of his navy trousers. "I was sure it was that one," he said to Barry.

Barry shook his head. "Honest mistake, man. Like I said, it's real dark and all these damn *motorbikes* look the same, right? But listen, we may still need help to search for Shotgun."

"Not my job. Call Ground Search and Rescue. Their number's in the phone book." He turned away from Barry and began to walk back to his cruiser, rubbing his right temple with his index finger.

Will's breath caught in his throat when Jackson stopped, swivelled around, and headed straight back to Shotgun's bike. Without hesitating, he again bent toward the motor and squeezed the lower pipe coming from the front cylinder.

THE MASK

"YYYOOOWWWLLLL!" Jackson screamed, shaking his hand as if trying to whip it off his wrist. He lunged toward his cruiser.

The Dark Angels jumped back.

"JESUS, PETE," Barry called after him. "GET A GRIP, BOY! YOU SCARED THE SHIT OUT OF ME!"

Jackson clambered into the cruiser. He slammed the door, and twisted his body to the right and across the steering wheel to reach the ignition key and start the car with his left hand. He used the crook of his right elbow to shift into reverse, while still trying to shake the searing pain from the palm and fingers of his right hand. He shot backward down the driveway, in rocking-horse fashion, as fast he had come up.

Shotgun ambled up next to Will. They both watched as the RCMP cruiser sped away down the dark highway. The air was heavy with acrid smoke from the car's motor and dust from the driveway. "Running rich," Shotgun said.

Will nodded. "Air filter probably needs to be changed."

"Sparkplugs, too, most likely."

"May even need new plug wires."

Barry approached them and hauled Shotgun's plug wire from his pocket. He offered it to Shotgun. "You owe me, shithead."

When the sky to the east behind Barry's house began to change colour from black to dark blue, Will and Shotgun went down and sat among the bikes, smoking chunks of hash Shotgun impaled on a straight pin and lit with matches. When the first probing rays of sunlight splintered through the trees, Shotgun reattached his sparkplug wire.

"Time to roll," he said, throwing his body into the air and heaving down on the kick-start pedal. The snake-like exhaust pipes crackled and snarled, scattering birds and rustling leaves.

Will, Stumpy, Frantic, and the rest of the Dark Angels wiped dew from their bikes and kicked life into their motors. Will noticed that the wild roses at the edge of the steep hill were coming into bloom. He sniffed the air and caught a faint whiff of their sweetness intermingled with the smoky exhaust gases of the Harleys.

They eased the bikes down the driveway and stopped in a jumbled group at the bottom. They looked up and down the highway.

"See anything?" Barry shouted from the back of the pack.

Shotgun shook his head. "No, all clear. He's long gone." He turned onto the pavement and blasted away.

Like jets taking off from the flight deck of an aircraft carrier, the others followed. Will accelerated through the gears. The blast of cool wind sent shivers through every fiber of his body, causing his eyes to water and instantly blow away the tears. He passed Stumpy on the inside of the lane and tapped his shoulder as he flew by. He glanced back to see Stumpy smile a little. He then jammed in front of Frantic, on the back of whose bike sat Barry, gesturing like a master-of-ceremonies while trying to light a cigar with a Zippo lighter.

Will and the others jockeyed for position in a rough, staggered formation – passing one another and being passed, blowing past cars and trucks, and whistling through any narrow opening to raise the stakes. Every taut muscle in Will's body quivered. He wove through the bikes to the front of the pack, then leaned forward and kissed the bike's blood-red gas tank.

With each passing mile, they slowed, and slowed some more, until they were cruising at a snail's pace, free and easy under the bright Nova Scotia sun – the line of bikes stretching out a few hundred feet.

As they neared Grand Pré, Shotgun sped to the front of the pack, pointing at his gas tank. They turned into an Esso station in the village.

"Man, I gotta eat," Stumpy said, screwing the gas cap back on his tank after filling it. "How about we go over there?" He tipped his head in the direction of a small roadside diner on the other side of the road.

Barry nodded. "Looks like it's open."

Will sat with Shotgun and Frantic Fred in a high-backed booth constructed of plywood and layered with dulled amber shellac. He folded his hands on the pale-green arborite tabletop and stared down, mesmerized by the tiny silver flecks embedded in its surface. He felt a wave of exhaustion wash over him. The warm air in the diner and the aroma of toast and frying eggs and bacon coaxed him to rest his back against the booth. He felt his head bob.

"You okay?" Frantic asked.

He snapped to. "Yeah, crashing pretty hard, that's all." He saw that the waitress was standing at the side of the table.

"What do you want to eat?" Frantic asked him.

He shrugged. "I don't know. Nothing. I don't think I have any cash."

"Don't be an idiot. We got money. Order something."

"Toast," he said, looking up at the girl. His eyes lingered on her pretty face, the bright reflected light of day bouncing off her golden hair bound in a high, tight bun. "I'll have toast and black coffee."

"Toast?" Frantic said, raising his eyebrows. "You want toast?"

"Yeah, toast."

"That's no breakfast for a man." Frantic smiled at the waitress and pointed to an item on the laminated menu. "He'll have this. Me, too."

"The Eighteen-Wheeler Special," the waitress said, scribbling on her pad. "Two?"

"Three," said Shotgun.

"How do you want the eggs?"

"Not runny," said Frantic. "Don't care otherwise." Will and Shotgun nodded.

"And the rib steak? Comes with rib steak."

"Dead and greasy," said Shotgun.

Will didn't realize how hungry he was until he started eating. It made him smile to see all the Dark Angels wolfing down their food without speaking – clinking knives, forks, and spoons against plates and saucers with manly purpose. He watched the young waitress move with graceful confidence from table to table, wasting not a step and missing no cues.

"You're really good at what you do," he said, when she came back to their booth to offer more coffee.

Smiling, she reached across the table to refill his cup. "I try. I'm just here for the summer. My folks own this place so it's not just a job for me."

"It shows."

She paused and smiled again, remaining at the side of the booth. She brought her free hand to the side of her head and fondled her left earlobe. "I heard about you guys." She tilted her body back to see the crests on his back. "Dark Angels. You guys don't seem so bad. Not like what I heard."

"You're right, sweetheart'," Shotgun said, smiling. "We're the good guys. But don't tell anybody." They all laughed.

Frantic leaned toward her. "Um, so I guess it would ruin everything now if I said you had great tits?"

She tapped the side of her cheek with a forefinger and looked up to her left, a coy smile on her face. "Nahh, probably not." She reached out and tousled Frantic's scraggly curls, then whirled away and disappeared through swinging doors into the kitchen.

"Got enough to leave her a big tip?" Frantic asked Shotgun.

"Ten? I got an extra ten."

"Yeah, that'd be good. Man, she's beautiful."

"And cool," Shotgun said.

Back on the open road, they headed northeast toward the city. Soon, bikes began to peel off – lone riders, small groups of two or three – headed in different directions. Will split off from the few remaining bikes where the Bedford Highway enters Halifax. He gave them a thumbs-up and turned onto Windsor Street, and then onto Robie Street.

Minutes later, he slowed in front of Sadie's Lodge – the stately tan and burgundy Victorian rooming house that had seemed like a mansion to him when his mother had inherited it from the real Sadie six years earlier – and turned into the driveway directly across from the grassy expanse of Halifax's North Common.

He stopped short when he saw Sid's Ford Falcon in the driveway up in front of the garage. His abdomen tightened with a quick spasm and a chill shot through his body. He took a deep breath, killed the bike's motor and dismounted. He pushed the bike up the driveway and off to the side of Sid's car. He waited a few moments, listening, then stole up the back steps. He eased the aluminum screen door open, then the hardwood back door, and slipped into the back porch. Peering around the edge of the doorway leading into the kitchen, he found his mother standing in front of the stove.

She looked across at him and put a finger to her lips, a faint smile crossing her face. "Shhh, he's still in bed."

Will approached her and kissed her cheek. "You look tired. Everything okay?" He slid a straight-backed walnut chair away from the round table in the center of the kitchen and lowered himself onto the chair's caned seat. He folded his hands on the cream-coloured table cloth embroidered with pink roses – *the kind of pretty things she likes*, he thought.

"I wish you'd call when you're not going to come home. You know I worry. A little consideration would be nice." She bustled from the stove to the refrigerator and back again, not looking at him. "I don't ask for a lot from you."

"Sorry. I rode out to Barry's after work. He doesn't have a phone. I stayed there last night."

She sighed. "Well, next time call before you do anything like that. It's not just that I worry, Sid gives me fits when you don't come home."

"Where is he? I thought he'd be at work."

"What's wrong with you? It's Saturday." She sighed again. "Do you want breakfast?"

"Ah, sure. I'm not too hungry but that'd be great. I love your cooking." He smiled and leaned back in the chair. "Hey, guess what! I saw a girl at a restaurant this morning who reminded me of you. You know, pretty and blonde with a nice smile. Good at what she does, too."

Her face softened, and she brushed strands of air away from her temples. "I don't feel too pretty these days, but I guess I could turn a head or two not too many years ago. Your father's head for sure." She smiled, finally looking at him. "He used to come into Sadie's Restaurant in the Valley when I worked there. He liked vanilla milkshakes, but I think he just came to watch me. I told you before."

"I know. But I always like to hear about it – about all the things that happened back then"

She smiled. "He was smart and well-built, like you. Proud and straight. Heavier than you, but not as tall. I wish he could see you now." She sighed. "He used to tell me all the time how pretty I was."

He nodded. "You're still pretty. Everybody says so." He plunked his elbow down on the table. "And as for me, I'm now stronger than your friendly neighbourhood Spiderman. Want to arm-wrestle?"

She laughed, and the sound of her soft laughter told him her mind was at peace, at least for the moment. She tossed several pieces of thick ham into a cast-iron skillet and then cracked three eggs, the whites bubbling the instant they hit the hot pan. She took two slices of white bread from a Ben's Bread bag and popped them into the toaster. Within seconds, the sweet aroma of maple-flavoured ham filled the small kitchen.

"How did you learn to cook?"

"Sadie taught me a lot. Mom wasn't much of a cook. But she liked to bake and everybody liked her blueberry pies. The hardest thing about cooking is the timing of things." She slid the ham and eggs from the skillet onto a plate and turned for the toast. "Things don't cook at the same speed. So you have to know how long to cook your vegetables or anything else before you start your meat, so everything you're going to serve is finished at the same time. That's the hardest part. Sadie used to say no good cook was a stupid person."

She took her coffee and sat across from him as he began to eat. "I was hoping I'd see you this morning." She glanced back over her shoulder. "When I was going through one of the old trunks in the basement the other day, I found a picture of your father. I forgot I had it. I don't think you've seen it before." She reached down into her apron and pulled out a small black and white photograph. She held it out to him. "I put it in that plastic envelope to protect it."

He laid his knife and fork down and took the photo. "I've only ever seen one picture, the one you gave me in Petawawa – the one where he's wearing his beret. I've got it in the garage."

"That one was taken right after he enlisted. He was 19 – same age as you are now."

"He looked older than 19."

"Everybody seemed to look older in those days. Life was more serious, with the wars and such."

Will turned it to the light.

"I'm pretty sure this one was taken at Fort Lewis, in Washington," she said. "Not long before he shipped out. See the mountains in the background?"

He studied the image of his father, a young soldier in army fatigues.

He stood straight and tall between two other soldiers, his arms draped over their shoulders. The sun shone from behind them, casting long, sharp shadows that jutted down to the right.

"He looks happy," Will said. "Smiling and relaxed, right? Looks like he was in good shape."

She nodded. "I got letters from him when he was in Fort Lewis. He said they had to march up and down the mountain in full battle gear as part of their training."

"Thanks, I'll take care of it." He paused, still staring at the photograph. "I wonder if he ever thought he would never come back."

His mother came behind him and looked over his shoulder. "I imagine he thought of it. How could you *not* think of it? But he was the kind of person who would have figured he'd be coming back home. He'd never believe it could turn out any other way."

He slid the picture into his shirt pocket, letting his fingers rest against it for a moment.

"Juice?" she asked.

He nodded.

When his mother turned to the refrigerator, he closed his eyes and pressed the picture against his chest. Though he tried to continue to eat, it became hard to swallow.

They both fell silent.

"I wonder what things would have been like if he had come back," he said. "Do you ever think about that?"

She hesitated. "All the time. I was supposed to go meet him in Vancouver. He wanted us to get married there as soon as he got back ..." Her voice trailed off, and her body stiffened at the sound of footsteps approaching from the next room.

"Who's getting married?" Sid asked, stomping into the kitchen wearing only crumpled khaki boxer shorts. He leaned back against the kitchen counter and scratched at his dark two-day growth of beard and then at his crotch. He looked at Will without expression.

"It's nobody you know," she began. "It's ..."

"Never mind, Celeste," Sid interrupted. "Do you really think I give a damn about some fool getting married? Look where it got me." He glanced across at Will. "When you finish waiting on our star boarder here, maybe you can find time to get me some breakfast."

He leaned toward the refrigerator, opened it, and snatched a glass bottle of milk from inside. He pulled the top off and guzzled from the bottle. Milk spilled out the sides of his mouth, splashed down the smooth, hairless skin of his pasty chest and splattered onto the black and white tiled floor. He clanked the empty bottle onto the countertop and forced a burp. "Ahhh, that's better. Goddamn whiskey dries me out every time." He stepped around the milk on the floor and plopped down in a chair across the table from Will.

He again looked at Will, waiting for a reaction. "What're you gawkin' at? My manners not up to your standards, or what?"

Will turned his head slightly to avoid Sid's putrid breath. "Matters not to me."

"Hmphh, just stopped by for another free meal, eh, Joe? One thing about you is you're predictable."

"He does give us money for room and board, Sid. You know that."

Will looked down at his plate and moved the food around with his fork.

"Oh, yeah, right. I almost forgot," Sid continued. "Well, that's great. I don't see none of it though, do I?" He snapped his fingers to get Will's attention. "It's so funny, everybody thought you'd sail through school and end up some kind of big shot earning lots of money. Then you go and drop out of college and go to work with a pick and shovel. It's so rich. Makes me laugh. And then you start running with those dirty hippie biker bums. Yeah, you had the world by the ass, but I knew you wouldn't amount to anything."

"Please, Sidney. You don't have to do this. It's no way to start the day," Celeste said.

"Am I talking to you? Did I ring a bell or rattle your chain, woman? Yeah, I *do* have to do this. Somebody's got to talk some sense into the boy, Celeste. You're too soft on him. That's not doing him any good. He needs some discipline. Spending some time in the army would fix him up. You Goddamn-well know I'm right, don't you, Joe?"

"Yes, you're right, Sid," Will said without emotion. "Being in the army really worked miracles for you. You've got a lot to be proud of."

Sid smashed his first on the table. "Don't you smart-mouth me you ungrateful punk!" The words spewed from his lips in a stream of foul spit. He jumped to his feet and started to pace around the kitchen. "If your mother wasn't here, you'd be flying out that door right now with my size twelves up your ass. I'm telling you, Celeste, if I grab him it won't be pretty. He's been pushing his luck for a long time." He circled the table, gasping and grunting like a spurred bull. "I'll tell you something, momma's boy, I was a sergeant in the Fourth Royal Canadian Horse Artillery, which is a *big* accomplishment, considering I didn't get any of the breaks you did. You've had it too easy. *That's* your problem."

"Sid, stop. Please," Celeste pleaded.

"It's okay, Mom. I've got to go anyway."

Will grinned at Sid with disdain. He got up and put his dishes next to the sink. He kissed his mother on the cheek. "See you, Sid," he said, as he squeezed past him to the back door.

Sid stomped to the door behind him. "Kiss my ass, punk." He flung the door shut, rattling the dishes in the sink and on the counter.

"I'm telling you, Celeste, that boy's headed for big trouble. Running with that trash, doing nothing good with his life. And you're not doing him any good by letting him live out there in that stinking garage and mooch food off me. And I'll tell you something else, I'm done taking his lip. After all I did for him and put up with all these years, I'm just not going to take it." He held up his fist. "Him and me, we're going to tangle before long. I can see it coming."

Celeste turned to leave the kitchen, but Sid grabbed her by the arm. She winced. "Don't. You're hurting me."

"Don't you turn away from me! I'm trying to have a conversation with you." He stared into her eyes, then shoved her toward the stove. "Ah, shit on you and that little bastard of yours. Neither of you is worth my time. Just get me my Goddamn breakfast." He slammed his fist against a cupboard door and shook his head. "Jesus H. Christ, my headache's even worse now, thanks to you two morons. Go get me some Aspirin."

Celeste hurried into the bathroom off the kitchen and opened the medicine cabinet above the sink. She reached in and grabbed a half-full bottle of Aspirin. She peered into the glass bottle, then glanced in the direction of the kitchen. She emptied all the white, chalky tablets into the toilet and flushed it. Staring with a blank expression at the pills swirling in the forming vortex, she drew in her breath and called out, "Sorry, Sid, there's no Aspirin left. The bottle's empty."

Will headed to his bike and threw his leg over it. He started it and sat motionless on the vibrating machine, looking down at the gas tank. He sighed deeply and then turned the motor off, dismounting the bike at the same time. He went into the garage and grabbed a roll of heavy duct tape hanging on a nail in a post near the side of his cot. He brought it out to the bike and tore off four short strips, then took the photo of his father in its soft clear-plastic envelope and taped it with care to the top of the gas tank just below the speedometer.

He returned the tape to the garage, yanked down the large metal door peeling of burgundy paint, and climbed back on the bike. He again kicked it to life. Reaching for the clutch, he paused and looked up at the kitchen window, hoping to see his mother's face, to see her wave good-bye to him as she usually did. But it wasn't her face he saw. Instead, Sid's mean-spirited scowl bore down on him. It was the same contorted mask of anger and hate that had haunted his days and dreams since childhood – the sullen expression, the cruel, shifting eyes always searching for another reason to be angry. Not even the steam from the sink as it crept across the inside of the window or the dirt-encrusted bug screen could hide Sid's disgust.

Will tapped the bike in gear and idled down the driveway to the street.

PART 2

JACQUES' CREW

WILL INCHED CLOSER TO THE edge of the concrete slab – 12 floors high in the partially-finished office tower on Duke Street, nothing between him and the rush-hour traffic below but open air. He pushed his hardhat back and wiped grimy sweat from his forehead. He shielded his eyes from the intense glare of the late-afternoon sun with the back of his hand. *What's that down on Argyle Street?* He strained to make out the three bikes and riders below. He watched the trio stop close to where his bike had been parked since early morning, and then walk around his bike, each looking from side to side as if expecting to see someone.

He could see they flashed crests on the back of their jackets, but because of the sun and the distance couldn't tell if they were the Dark Angels' colours or another club's. They lingered there longer than he liked. *Probably nothing*, he told himself, trying to quell the uneasiness that crawled up his spine and gripped the muscles in his neck with tentacle-like fingers. After five minutes, the riders remounted their bikes and rode off, heading south down Argyle Street.

Clouds of dust billowed up under a sweltering August sky and trucks, backhoes, and other machinery spewed choking diesel smoke in all directions as he made his way down to the construction-site office at four-thirty. He trudged to the flimsy screen door of the office and flung it open. He stepped inside and felt a wave of cooler air smack into the back of his sun-burned neck as the door slammed shut behind him.

"Hey, boss," he said, "Thought this day would never end."

Harry glanced up from behind the drafting table he used as a desk and squinted at Will through Coke-bottle-thick glasses perched on the end of his plump nose. "You're looking a might wilted, son," he said, smiling and shaking his glistening bald head.

Will nodded. "Spent the last couple hours on the twelfth floor stacking all the jacks, four-by-fours, and three-quarter plywood." He plopped down onto a stool to the left of Harry's desk.

Harry pushed himself up and turned to a metal cash box sitting on a battered file cabinet behind him. "Well, you got a break coming up, deserved or not." He flipped the lid of the cash box open and rifled through a stack of pay envelopes. "We'll need you back in November." He looked over his shoulder at Will. "You're coming back, right?"

Will nodded. "If you want me back, I'll be here."

Harry turned and tossed Will his pay envelope. "Yup, we'll need you. There'll be lots of work. I'll give you a call when the time comes."

"Thanks, Harry." Will shoved the envelope in his back pocket and reached forward to shake hands. He looked the older man in the eye. "I have to admit I can use a break from shovelling wet concrete and hauling steel jacks around all day."

Harry grabbed Will's hand and smiled. "Don't doubt that. No honest man should have to do hard labour like this. Look what it did to me. I used to be as handsome as I am smart." He pushed his glasses closer to his eyes, puffed up his chest, and grinned from ear to ear.

They both laughed.

"Lots of new crews on site now," Will said.

Harry moved back behind his desk and sat down. He gripped the wooden arms of his chair and leaned back, draping his right calf on the edge of the desk. "Yeah – plumbers, electricians, bricklayers, interior finishers – they'll put flesh and clothes on that concrete skeleton you guys put up. When it's all done, the business suits will move in and put their feet up in their swanky offices, and they'll call it the Duke Tower or something fancy like that."

Will shook his head. "They can have that kind of life. Doesn't appeal to me."

Harry looked over at the *Playboy* calendar hanging on the plywood wall to his right. Again, he squinted. "Yup, if we stay on schedule with plans for that new student residence at Saint Mary's, I'll need you around early November. You got anything lined up till then?"

"Sort of – just some house painting. It's not much money. But I know this guy – Frenchy Jack we call him." Will chuckled. "Frenchy Jack's crazy as hell. He's got a pretty good system going, though. Says he did the same thing in Montréal for years." He paused, taking off his hardhat and running his fingers through his hair. "You can't say anything, Harry, but what he does is he drives around looking for houses in need of a few coats of paint – especially ones, you know, the ones you can tell old people live in. And he goes to each one and offers to scrape and paint the house with high-quality paint for a low, low price. Hundreds of dollars less than you'd expect to pay."

"How the hell does he do that?"

Will leaned forward and stood up from the stool. "Well, he has a panel truck and he steals all the paint and supplies he needs. And he only pays each of our guys exactly $11 a day. But he pays in cash every day and our guys like that. It helps keep them out of trouble with the law, and it gives them enough money to keep their bikes on the road and go to the tavern. Meanwhile, Frenchy Jack's rolling in tax-free cash." He turned toward the door. "Anyway, all the guys have to do is show up. Jack supplies everything, and it doesn't even matter to him who shows up, long as he has a crew."

Harry shook his head and laughed. "Jesus Christ, ask him if he needs a partner."

Will paused at the door and laughed. "For sure. See you in a few months."

Harry nodded. "You stay out of trouble till then."

"I'll give it a try," Will said, glancing back with a mischievous smile.

His body felt heavy as he made his way to the lunch shack. He caught a faint whiff of salty sea-air and noticed it was already beginning to cool down. A brown rat scurried across his path on the hard dirt and dove into a week's worth of lunch garbage heaped on the ground around a 45-gallon drum a few feet from the shack's door. *Good luck, friend*, Will said to himself, *it's all yours now*. He couldn't wait to get home, throw off his dirty, sweaty work clothes and wash the grime from his body.

Not slowing to talk to any of the other men, he rushed into the shack and snatched his leather jacket and canvas knapsack from one of the two dozen pegs that stretched above a long wooden sitting-bench. He tossed his hardhat onto the bench and watched it bounce and tumble to the worn plywood floor with a plastic, clattering *whap, whap* sound. Hurrying toward the door, he tossed the knapsack from one hand to the next as he jammed his arms into the sleeves of his jacket and pulled it up onto his shoulders.

He picked his way through the jumble of machinery, building materials, and construction debris, moving faster and faster to the pangs of hunger that tightened his belly and the smell of leather that rose to his nose and thrust him toward his bike. He darted across Duke Street, dodging cars coming from both directions. By the time he reached his bike parked on Argyle Street, he was breathing hard.

He walked around his bike, examining it from all sides. He knelt next to it and peered at the motor. "Didn't touch it," he muttered to himself. Straightening up, he tugged the knapsack open and hauled out his denim cut-off jacket that bore the crests of the Dark Angels on its back. He threaded his arms through the sleeve openings and pulled the jacket tight against his leather jacket. Taking another deep breath, he threw his leg over his bike and dropped to the seat. Moments later, he was blasting up Duke Street with the lowering sun hot on his face and road wind evaporating the sweat clinging to every inch of his body.

Splitting lanes of traffic and riding up the center lines of the westbound streets, he made it home in a few minutes and pulled into the driveway, happy to see that Sid's Ford Falcon wasn't there.

His mother opened the screen door as he jumped off his bike and bound up the back steps. "Whew, hot, eh? I was keeping my fingers crossed you wouldn't get here until he left for work." She threw her arms around his neck and kissed him on the cheek. "He was *ugggly*. Hung over again and didn't want to go to work."

"Uh, huh," Will said, as they moved into the kitchen. "Patty here?" he asked, glancing around.

"No. Out running around with her friends. He's wound up about her, too." She shook her head. "Your sister's like him. Everything's a fight with that girl. *Everything*! Once school starts again in a few weeks, it'll be even worse."

He sat at the table as his mother heaped a plate with spaghetti and meat sauce from the stove and put it in front of him. He leaned forward to wriggle out of his jacket.

"She'll grow out of that, don't you think? She's only 14, right?" He reached for the knife and fork his mother held out to him.

She shrugged. "Maybe in ten years. They'll be the death of me before then." She turned toward the refrigerator. "What do you want to drink?"

"Doesn't matter."

She placed a bottle of Graves Apple Juice and a beer glass on the table in front of him. "Now, she wants her father to get her a job at the Halifax Shopping Centre. He has her believing he's in charge of the place, instead of hiding in the security office like he does, drinking like a fish. He always looked good in a uniform, I'll give him that. Only reason he got that job as far as I can see. Anyway, she wants to work in a clothing store or a record store." She paused, shaking her head. "What about you? You're finished working at that building downtown now, aren't you?"

Will nodded. "Uh, huh. Finished with construction work – for a while at least. They'll have something else for me in November. We'll be starting work on a new building at Saint Mary's. I'm going to work painting houses in the meantime."

"Saint Mary's?" She sighed and sat in the chair across from him. "I'll never understand why you didn't stay in school there. Hoping you'd do good is what's kept me going all these years. You could still be there instead of doing labour work or painting houses."

He shrugged. "I know it's hard for you to understand, and it's hard for me to explain."

She fingered the edge of the tablecloth resting on her legs. "I suppose you're going out tonight?"

He smiled and shook his head. "I don't think so. I'm really wiped. I'm just going to get cleaned up and take it easy. Maybe read a bit." He reached for the apple juice, unscrewed the bottle top and began to fill his glass. "Actually, I have to find Frenchy Jack in the morning to start painting."

She nodded and forced a weak smile. "Better that you stay busy, I guess."

Cruising through fog-shrouded streets in the city's south end early the next morning, he scanned from side to side looking for Frenchy Jack's truck or Dark Angels' bikes. Turning onto Tower Road, he spied three bikes – Stumpy's, Speedy's, and Frantic's – parked at the curb in front of a large Victorian home with leaded glass windows and peeling paint. He saw the guys standing in a circle in the driveway. Parking his bike beside theirs, he walked up to join them.

"You're late," Speedy said, holding a smoldering joint out to him.

"Hey, my mother cooked breakfast for me. How could I refuse? Plus, took me a few minutes to find this place." He shook his head. "No thanks, too early for me. It'll make the day seem way too long."

"You still living there with your parents?" Stumpy asked.

"Not exactly with them. On the property. I stay in the garage. Got everything I need there except running water. It's like my own place."

Speedy smirked. "He's still living with his mommy and daddy." He made a cradle of his beefy arms in front of his short, thick body and rocked them back and forth.

"Man, you gotta move out of there," Frantic said. "It don't look right for no outlaw biker to be living with his parents."

Will shrugged and prodded at a few rocks in the driveway with the toe of his boot. "I know. I'll probably move out once I get back to construction work in the fall. But, for now, I want to stay there to keep an eye on my mother."

"Ah, what a nice little boy. Looking after his mommie," Speedy said.

"Ain't nothing wrong with that as far as I'm concerned," Stumpy said, frowning at Speedy. "That's enough talk. Let's get going so we can get this dump finished by the end of the day. We been working at this job long enough. There ain't a whole lot more left to do here."

Speedy flicked away what little was left of the joint, sending a quick flash of hot ash across the pavement. They went to the shed behind the house, took out the paint and other supplies and got to work.

When Frenchy Jack arrived in his truck later in the afternoon, they were putting lids on the paint cans and cleaning their brushes with turpentine.

"*Bon travail, mes frères.* Jacques like these work," Frenchy Jack said through the open window on the driver's side. Looking at himself in the truck's rear-view mirror, he dragged a comb through greasy black hair as thick and jarring as his accent. He hopped from the truck and trotted up to Will, grabbing him in a wrenching headlock with anaconda-like arms. "*C'est bon, très bon,* you here, too, Willie. You work good, *oui?*"

"*Mais* friggin' *oui*," Frantic said. "He workee good. What about the rest of us?"

"Yeah, you good, too. Maybe, I think so," Frenchy Jack said, reaching into his pocket and pulling out a roll of cash as big around as a baseball. He squatted in the driveway on legs like coiled steel springs and began to count out fives and ones, laying them in the dirt in four neat piles.

"Jesus, you'd think he'd give us a little bonus or something," Frantic said, winking at the others. "Least we'd be able to get some food with our beer."

Stumpy held his right hand out toward Frenchy Jack and rubbed his thumb against his first two fingers. "Come on, Frenchy, we finished this job right on time."

"Yeah, if you weren't such a cheap French-fried prick, we wouldn't have to ask," Speedy added.

Frenchy Jack paused and squeezed his dark brown eyes into narrow slits. He smiled, sticking the tip of his tongue out through the gap of his missing front teeth. "Ah, you guy try pull wool on Jacques, *oui*. Funny guy. Okay, I give some more dollar. *Cinq*, okay? That five more. Jacques happy *aujourd'hui*." He peeled off four more five-dollar bills and passed one to each of his crew.

"That's more like it, happy Jacky," Frantic said. "Now you can call me your brother."

They loaded all the paint and supplies into the truck and strapped the ladders onto its roof.

"We go tavern now, hey boy?" Frenchy Jack asked.

Frantic nodded. "Seahorse. Let's roll."

They headed downtown – Will and the other riders on their bikes with Frenchy Jack following behind in his truck. As they neared the harbour, Will could smell the salt water. The thundering exhausts from the bikes hung in the heavy air between the downtown buildings, drowning out the screeching of gulls and the steady background hum of the busy seaport.

They settled into wooden armchairs in the Seahorse Tavern, behind a long, heavy table whose surface was scarred over almost every square inch with dents, scratches, and knife-carved names and messages. Shotgun, who was already there, joined them. "Beer!" Stumpy shouted at the grizzled waiter slouching behind the bar. "Lots of it and keep it comin'. And fish and chips all around when ya get time."

"What kind of fish is it?" Frantic asked.

"What do you mean?" Stumpy asked, his face scrunched up. "It's just fuckin' fish. It's all the same. Fish and fuckin' chips."

"You fool," Frantic said, laughing. "You don't even know they use different kinds of fish, do you?"

Stumpy scowled, not taking his eyes off Frantic as the waiter clunked beer after beer down onto the top of the table. Stumpy grabbed a mug, threw his head back and drained it in one long gulp. "You ain't so smart yourself. Even that dumb-ass frog is smarter than you." He burped and nodded toward Frenchy Jack. "If you were smart as you think, you wouldn't be working for a toothless idiot that don't even talk our language."

"Hey," Frenchy Jack said, sitting up straight, "*Non, non.* Jacques talk good language."

"Yeah, right, 50 percent English, 50 percent frog language, and 50 percent idiot language" Stumpy said, bursting out with a loud guffaw.

Frantic coughed out his own deep belly laugh that vibrated across the dimly-lit room. "You really are a moron. That's not possible. That's 150 percent. That's like saying half English, half French, and half idiot language."

Stumpy paused. "What do you mean that's not possible? That's exactly right." He turned to Will. "I'm right, aren't I, Will?"

Will smiled. "Made sense to me when you said it."

"God, don't be siding with him," Frantic said, grinning. "Your IQ will drop 50 points just by sitting next to him." He grabbed his beer mug, stood up and moved away from the table. "Going outside."

Stumpy looked at Will. "He just insulted me again, didn't he? Friggin' big words." He paused. "What's an IQ anyway?"

"Well, um, it's – well, it means intelligence quotient."

Stumpy blinked.

"It means how smart you are or, in your case, how smart you aren't," Shotgun said. "You get a number, like 100 or 120. A hundred's about average. So you're about 70, on a good day." He laughed and flicked his hair away from his eyes.

"What's so funny about that? I don't see nothin' so funny about that," Stumpy said straight-faced. He snatched another beer from the table and guzzled it down. "How do they decide what number you get?"

"You do some tests, like exams in school," Will said. "You probably did some when you were in school. You don't pass or fail, you just get a score."

"Who knows what your score is?" Stumpy asked, looking concerned.

"Teachers. School people – that type."

"What's yours?"

"I don't know. It doesn't matter for anything. Don't worry about it."

Stumpy leaned back. He looked at the last few drops of beer in the bottom of his beer mug. "What's yours, Shotgun?"

"Oh – let me think – about 165, as I recall. That's around genius level."

Stumpy narrowed his eyes and scratched his head. "That explains it."

"Explains what?"

"Why you got no dink." Stumpy slapped the table and roared with laughter. "God gave you brains instead of a dink. Yup, sucked that thing up into your skull and now you got a two-inch dick."

They all broke into riotous laughter, pushing one another and banging the top of the table with their fists. Out of the corner of his eye, Will noticed Frantic waving from the front door for them to come. Before he had a chance to move, Frantic screamed. "HERE! NOW!"

The Dark Angels jumped up and hurried to Frantic's side. They crowded together and jostled one another to peer out the door, which Frantic held open several inches. They saw four riders on bikes parked on the opposite side of the street. The riders sat there, bikes idling, looking across at the Seahorse Tavern and the Dark Angels' bikes parked in front.

"Assholes," Shotgun said.

The Dark Angels walked out onto the sidewalk, their eyes fixed on the other bikers.

"What do they think they're doing?" Frantic asked.

"Pushing their luck," Shotgun said.

Stumpy crossed his arms against his chest. "I told you guys we shoulda put 'em in their place the first time we saw them. Soon as they started that Mickey Mouse club. But no, you guys had to sit back to see what'd happen. Well, here you go. Here they are rubbing our noses in their armpits."

Shotgun pulled his pants up and notched his belt one hole tighter. "I suppose we could go over and give them a little advice."

"*Tête-à-tête*," Frenchy Jack said.

THE DEVIL'S CHAIN

STUMPY LOWERED HIS ARMS TO his sides, puffed out his chest and stepped off the curb. Followed by the other Dark Angels, he strode to the nearest bike.

"Put 'er in gear and roll out," he said.

The biker held his hand out toward Stumpy. "Hey, bro', that's no way to treat a friend. We were hoping you'd let us buy you a round."

Frantic moved in beside Stumpy. "Don't push your luck. You ain't no brother or friend. Move out."

The biker lowered his hand and shrugged. He looked to the side at his friends and reached into his jacket pocket, pulling out a small business card. He held it out to Frantic.

Frantic snapped it out of his fingers and studied it. He read aloud, "We are the Devil's Chain. We are the Devil's links. Through us, Satan drives his noble work forward." Frantic looked up. "Ooooo! Lah-dee-fuckin'-dah! That's so cool."

"Come on guys, lighten up," the biker said. "We're on the same side, right?"

Stumpy stepped closer, while Frenchy Jack reached to grasp the claw hammer that hung from a carpenter's belt encircling his waist.

"You fools stupid?" Stumpy asked. "You got no IQ, or what? Coming down here, showin' those Mickey Mouse colours."

"If we'd wanted to lay eyes on you or drink with you, we'd have got word to you," Shotgun added.

"Like we said, get your stupid asses out of here before you lose them," Frantic said, his face turning deep red.

The biker shook his head. "You gotta relax, man. We're not trying to prove anything. Only want a beer. Last time we checked, this was a free country." He grinned at his biker friends.

Frantic's body stiffened. He looked down and brought his left hand up to his head. He clutched a handful of his thick curly hair, trying to work his fingers through the knotted tangles. He stepped closer to the Devil's Chain bikers. "Don't ever tell me to relax," he said in a flat, even tone. "I'll relax when I'm dead. I don't know *how* to relax. That's why they call me Frantic."

The biker he faced laughed. "Good one, man."

Frantic began to move his right hand in under his jacket, reaching to the left across his stomach.

"No, Frantic," Stumpy said. He stepped in front of Frantic, no more than two feet away from the nearest biker. He squared his body in front of him as Frantic, Will, and the others also moved closer.

"No respect," Stumpy said to the biker. "That's dangerous. Didn't your mother ever teach you respect?"

The biker began to speak. Before he could complete one syllable, Stumpy spun his body and back-handed him across the side of the jaw, sending him flying off his bike. In an instant, the other Dark Angels swarmed the remaining bikers like wild hornets, throwing them to the ground and raining kicks and punches upon their bent and heaped bodies.

Frenchy Jack turned to their bikes with his claw hammer, pounding dents in the gas tanks, cracking engine cases and sending glass from headlights and mirrors clinking and scattering across the pavement in vicious, splintered protest. In seconds, the Devil's Chain members were battered and bloody. The Dark Angels turned in silence and marched back into the Seahorse Tavern.

"I'll be right back," Frantic said, pulling Will aside as soon as Stumpy and the others were distracted ordering more beer. He headed outside, Will following about 20 feet behind.

Out on the street, the bikers were helping one another get up and beginning to push their bikes away, aided by a few bystanders. Frantic ran toward the lead bike. He caught up to it and grabbed the biker by the arm.

"Don't got as much to say now, do you, man? What's your name?"

"Go to hell," the biker said, spitting blood at Frantic's feet, as Will came up next to them.

Frantic reached under his jacket and pulled out his Smith and Wesson .44. He cocked the gun and placed the end of its barrel against the biker's temple. "I asked you a question. What's your name?"

"Chief," he sputtered.

"No – your real name. What's your real name?"

"Ha … Harvey."

Frantic twisted the barrel of the gun against the biker's temple. "Harvey, this ain't no movie. It's real life. Your game's done. You drag your sorry asses outta here and go tell all your girlfriends that the Dark Angels don't ever want to see those colours anywhere in this city again. Understand?"

The biker nodded.

"I asked you a question, Harvey. Don't test me."

"Okay, I fucking understand."

Frantic tipped his head toward the tavern, signalling Will to walk away. He released his hold on the biker and slid his gun back into the holster strapped under his left arm. He caught up to Will and flung his arm around his neck. "Thanks."

"For what? I didn't do anything."

"Yeah, you did. You had my back, right?"

Will laughed. "Right. Like you needed it."

"That's the thing about back-up. You never know if or when you'll need it."

Back inside the Seahorse, they returned to their chairs and dropped onto them.

"Shoulda done that months ago," Stumpy said, with a satisfied grin on his face. "Told you all back then." He tapped the bottom of his beer mug against the tabletop.

"What do you think they'll do now?" Will asked.

Stumpy shrugged. "Who knows?"

Frantic patted his gun and smiled. "Who cares? They got the message."

Shotgun shook his head. "Too easy. This isn't over."

Around midnight, Shotgun eased his bike up next to Will's. "Keep your eyes open," he said, looking around and blipping his throttle.

Will nodded. "You, too."

He rode home at a sedate pace, not wanting to attract attention – looking from left to right and back over each shoulder along the way.

He killed the bike's motor and lights a few hundred feet from the foot of the driveway at Sadie's Lodge and coasted to a stop, hearing only the hum of the bike's tires on pavement and the greased clicking of its drive chain against the teeth of the sprockets. He waited under a leafy maple tree, shaded from the streetlights nearby. He waited – and watched – and listened. He dismounted and took slow, steady steps up the driveway until he was in front of the garage. He tilted his head trying to hear any sound and then looked all around. He turned, walked back down the driveway and pushed his bike up.

He spent the next morning cleaning and shining his bike. The solid feel of the bike's metal and the flowing, seductive beauty of its lines pushed aside the phantoms of the preceding night. The crystal-bright sun that shone in the open sky above the North Common and the chirping of songbirds that came to him in the warm air made the slithering apprehension of the Devil's Chain feel distant and unreal. It was hard not to be happy and at ease.

In the late afternoon, he headed out and rode in the direction of the harbour, downtown to Granville Street. He came to a stop in front of the Dark Angels' clubhouse, a store-front space with windows painted flat-black and boarded up from the inside, inconspicuous among so many other derelict buildings in the oldest, most-neglected part of town. He backed the bike into the curb and waved to Stumpy and Speedy as they came through the open door and down the building's granite steps.

"You guys ready?" he asked.

"Damn it!" Speedy said. He paced around Stumpy's orange Harley 45 Flathead, and pulled a bottle of pills from his pocket. "Don't know about this." He unscrewed the bottle, tilted his head back and shook a bunch of pills into his mouth. He chewed them with quick, piston-like movements of his jaw.

"Speed freak," Stumpy said to Speedy, with a scowl. He looked over at Will. "He's scared to come with me."

"It's not speed," Speedy protested. "Just diet pills. No worse than candy."

"Hurry up. Get your ass on back," Stumpy said, swinging his leg over his bike.

"ON WHERE?" Speedy shouted, bouncing up and down in his cowboy boots. "You got no damn back seat. No back footpegs or sissy bar. What am I supposed to do, wrap my arms and legs around your fat, ugly body?"

Stumpy shrugged. "Don't matter none to me. Stay here if you want. And, Jesus H. Christ, stop vibrating like that you short-assed freak."

"You can ride with me," Will said to Speedy.

Speedy hesitated. "Nah, that's okay. I seen how you ride."

He sighed and turned to Stumpy. "If I tell you to stop before we get to Barry's, you better fuckin' stop."

"Or what?"

"Or I'll piss up your back, that's what." Speedy threw his leg over Stumpy's back fender and wriggled against it. "Wait!" he said, hopping off and bolting into the clubhouse.

"We're leaving," Stumpy said after him. He leaned to his left and kicked down hard against the kick-start pedal with his right foot – once, twice, three times. The motor barked to life with clouds of blue smoke billowing from the slash-cut exhaust pipes.

Speedy came running from the clubhouse, clutching a small cushion. He placed it against the back fender of Stumpy's bike and climbed on. "Better," he said, smiling. He grabbed the sides of Stumpy's jacket and positioned his left heel on the primary case and his right on the kick-start pedal.

Stumpy looked back at him. "You ready, now?"

Speedy squeezed his knees together, digging them into Stumpy's hips. "Yee-haw! Go Trigger!"

Stumpy jerked up and away. He twisted his head back and glared at him. "Don't you be squeezing me between your legs like that, you little pervert. You know I hate that fruity kind of shit you do." He eased back down into the seat, still looking back at Speedy.

"Cute couple," Will said to them. "Real cute."

They pulled away from the curb and the other bikes still parked there. They rode up from the downtown, up Sackville Street, headed west. Will followed behind Stumpy's bike, laughing to himself as the old Harley sputtered and belched smoke, straining to haul almost 500 pounds of Dark Angels up the steep grade. Once on the flat of Bell Road, they began to gather a little more speed.

They stopped at the Willow Tree intersection, and Stumpy pointed at the Shell gas station across on Quinpool Road. He tapped his gas tank. Will nodded.

When the light changed, they crossed the intersection and Stumpy pulled into the station, while Will swung around the corner, making a sharp right onto Parker Street. He got off his bike but left it idling. He could hear Stumpy's bike echoing in the gas station. He heard the motor shut down.

He glanced to the west and noticed the sun had lowered to the top of Saint Patrick's High School. He removed his sunglasses and began to clean them in his shirt, lost in thought.

He heard Stumpy's bike start up again. Then, he heard the sound of other bikes roaring into the station. *One, two, three, four – maybe five*, he counted to himself. He walked to the station and inched his head around its concrete corner. He counted seven Devil's Chain members on five bikes. He hurried back to his bike and jumped on. As he smacked it into gear, Stumpy and Speedy came chugging out of the station and headed up Windsor Street, ignoring the Devil's Chain bikers spilling out behind them. Speedy glanced over at Will and waved for him to follow. Will nodded, sitting motionless on his bike. He watched Stumpy and Speedy ride away.

Like hyenas smelling an easy kill, the Devil's Chain riders closed in around Will, their hungry eyes wide with surprise. They twisted at their handlebars and contorted their bodies trying to lever their bikes to block him in. Before they could, Will cracked his throttle wide open, dropped the clutch and tore the back tire loose from the pavement.

PLAYING IN TRAFFIC

SMOKE PLUMED UP FROM THE back wheel of his bike as he punched a hole between the front wheels of the two bikes angled in front of him. He shot down Parker Street, slammed the bike around the 90-degree corner on Welsford Street and made a hard right again onto Robie Street. He rocketed south on the three-lane street, hammering the transmission up through the gears – a flash of red and chrome, faded denim, and come-get-me bravado.

He stole a glance in the mirror mounted on the handlebar near his left wrist and saw the Devil's Chain in hot pursuit. He scanned the road ahead. Traffic was stopped at the intersection of Robie and Spring Garden Road. His mind raced. *Going to be blocked in again*!

He jammed on the back brake. The tire screeched and the back of the bike whipped from side to side. When the bike was almost stopped, he swung his weight to the left and cocked the handlebars to the right. The back of the bike swung around 180 degrees to the right and snapped to a stop, facing the opposite direction. He cracked the throttle, painting a long black stripe up the center of the street, heading in the wrong direction against traffic. He flew past his pursuers head on, hearing their tires screech as they braked hard and tried to swing their bikes around.

Slicing through lanes of traffic, running through red lights and riding on the edge of the abyss, he raced toward the waterfront and the Dark Angels' clubhouse – with the Devil's Chain, a grimy cacophony of heat-seeking missiles trailing hot behind him, single-file.

He careened around the corner onto Granville Street. Glancing back to his left, he saw they had slowed and were turning right onto Barrington Street, headed in the opposite direction. He looked up ahead and saw

Shotgun and Frantic standing near their bikes in front of the clubhouse. Stopping in front of them, he backed into the curb.

"What're you doing back here?" Shotgun asked.

"Ran into some of those Devil's Chain guys." He got off his bike. "Up at the Shell station. We stopped for gas."

Shotgun looked across at Frantic, then back at Will. He pushed his hair behind his ears. "What do you mean exactly?"

"Well, Stumpy had to gas up, so we stopped at the station and they came down on us. I thought there'd be no way Stumpy could outrun them, especially with Speedy on back, so I split off. I thought if I gave them a chance, they'd come after me instead. We played in traffic all the way down here. No big deal." He smiled. "Worked, right?"

Frantic shook his head. "Bad move. You should've stayed together no matter what."

"Come on, Frantic. It wasn't even close. Just a little excitement and some wild riding."

"It *is* a big deal, smart-ass," Shotgun said. "Seriously, if they'd caught you, they'd be roasting your hide and pissing on your colours right now."

Will put his hands in his pants pockets. "Seemed like a good idea. Not like I had a lot of time to come up with a plan."

"It's not something you have to think about," Frantic said. "Stick together. That's all there is to it."

They heard another bike in the distance decelerating down Duke Street. Moments later, Stumpy and Speedy chugged around the corner and came rolling up the street.

"What's with you running away like that?" Stumpy asked, slowing to a stop and scowling at Will.

"I didn't run away."

"Looked like running to me. You damn well didn't stay with us."

"I know, I know," Will said. "I already got that lecture."

Speedy slid off the back of the bike and tossed his seat cushion at Will. "We could've taken them on."

"I didn't *run*. I was just, you know, just trying to get them to chase me – sort of for fun. And like a diversion away from you guys." He picked up the cushion and flung it back at Speedy. "They could have caught up to you two on foot."

Stumpy grunted.

"For *fun*?" Speedy blurted out. "Gettin' my teeth kicked out and my colours ripped off don't sound like no fun to me."

"I been sayin' all along he's weird. But does anybody listen to me?" Stumpy asked with a guttural growl. "No. Course not. I'm stupid, right? Nobody listens to me." He pointed at Will. "You better start listening to me from now on or else ..." He paused and looked skyward.

The others waited. "Or fuckin' what?" Speedy asked, exasperated. "Why you lookin' up there? The 'or what' ain't up in the sky."

Stumpy looked at him. "I was tryin' to think of the right words. You in some kind of a fuckin' hurry?" He turned to Will. "Or there'll be trouble. That's what."

Will and the others burst out laughing.

"He got that brain wave from his buddies in outer space," Frantic said.

Shotgun trotted into the clubhouse and returned a minute later cradling several bottles of Ten-Penny Old Stock Ale in his arms. He began snapping off the caps with a flathead screwdriver and passed the bottles around.

"You better get yourself some extra protection," he said to Will. "They got a bead on you now. You made them look bad on top of what's already been done."

Will nodded.

"Do they know where to find you?"

"I don't know. I don't think so."

"Only a matter of time if they feel inclined to figure it out. Like I said before, keep your eyes open. My guess is they'll keep looking for a chance to get back at us."

When he left the clubhouse at midnight, Will wasted no time riding home. Once more, he eased with light foot and serrated senses upon Sadie's Lodge and up the driveway to the garage. He tiptoed in through the side door, then opened the big garage door and guided his bike inside. He hurried to lock the doors. He began rooting through boxes of old parts and motorcycle odds and ends. He pulled a length of hemp rope from one box and used it to secure the doors to the wooden frame of the garage. Standing in the darkness, he listened and waited, then took a deep breath and lay down on his cot.

He tried to relax, to settle his tight body. He took another deep breath, inhaling the comforting smells of motorcycle steel, gasoline and used oil, tools, old magazines, and even older books – all the parts and debris, all the present flotsam and jetsam of his life. He breathed in the cleansing smell of the garage's dry wood. He put his hand to his heart and felt it beating. Slower – and slower. The pulsing sound of blood moving through his head and ears began to fade. As the warmth of sleep crept up through his body, his mind turned to what protection he might find for himself at dawn's first light, and he drifted off.

He awoke early to the sounds of a bird tapping on the roof of the garage. *A woodpecker or flicker*, he thought. He threw on his clothes and again began to search through boxes of used parts. He found an old Harley primary chain in an oil-soaked Tide detergent box – a triplex chain, about two inches in width, machined of close-fitting hard-steel links. He grasped the chain by one end with his right hand and let it hang to the floor. Its heaviness made him smile.

He washed the chain clean in a basin of kerosene, then dried it in an old towel. He took a can of fresh Castrol 30-weight oil and emptied it into a large coffee can. He coiled the primary chain into the can and let the oil soak into the chain for a few minutes. Then, he pulled the chain out, dripping of oil, and hung it on a nail against the wall at the back of the garage.

While the oil dripped from the chain and pooled on the floor, he went to his toolbox, fished through it and found the switchblade and pouch Barry had given him in June. He wiped the knife clean, sharpened it and oiled the release mechanism. He inserted the knife into the pouch and slid it down the front of his jeans, attaching the pouch's metal hook to the waistband of his jeans.

He returned to his primary chain. Taking it down, he began to wipe off the excess oil. Over and over, he stroked the length of the chain with heavy rags, changing rags as each became saturated with the glistening oil. Soon, the old chain took on a greyish metallic sheen in the dim morning light.

He slipped the chain through the belt loops of his jeans and drew it tight around his waist. He held out the excess chain and counted the unneeded links. Using the grinder mounted on his workbench, he ground through the ends of the rivets at the right spots and popped them out with a hammer and counterpunch. He threaded what would now be his primary-chain belt through his belt loops and used a master link to connect the ends together.

Hearing the back door of the house open, he scrambled to untie the rope from the garage doors.

"Will?" his mother called. "Will, you there?" She knocked on the side door.

"Yup. Just a second."

He threw the rope aside and looked around, then pulled his sweatshirt down, making sure it covered his new belt. He unlocked the door and pulled it open. His mother stepped inside, looking instinctively back over her shoulder at the house.

"I didn't think you were here. I didn't hear you come home last night."

"I shut the bike off up the street. You know, so I wouldn't wake you guys up."

"Don't do that. I'd rather know you're home. I don't care what time it is."

"But Sid …?"

She shook her head. "He's usually passed out long before you get here. I can't sleep unless I know you're here or where you are if you're not here."

Will smiled and shook his head.

"It's not funny."

"I know. But I'm 19. You've got to stop worrying like that."

"Nineteen. You think that makes you old? Or that it means you know what you're doing?" She shook her head. "You have no idea. I can't help but worry about you. I think it's all I know how to do, on top of having to put up with Sid and deal with Patty."

He began to move around the shed, picking things up. "You don't have to worry about me. I can take care of myself."

She looked at him and fidgeted with the rings on her fingers. "You'll see what it's like when you have kids of your own."

He moved to the side and leaned back against his bike. He looked down at his father's picture taped to the gas tank. "I suppose."

His mother sighed. "I'm sorry. I know you don't like it when I talk about these things. It's just that …"

"What? What is it? Is it Sid again?"

She sat on the edge of his cot. "When is it ever *not* about Sid?" She smoothed her apron against her legs.

"If it's because of me, I can leave. I've got friends I can stay with. I don't want to make things worse by being here."

She shook her head. "No, that's not it. Nothing would ever please him. If it wasn't about you, it'd be something else. It's always something."

"What then?"

She began to tremble. "When your father went overseas – the minute he told me he enlisted – I got this bad feeling. It made me sick to my stomach. I couldn't believe it. I said to him, 'Why'd you go and do that? How can you think of leaving me and going to war?' I had no clue where Korea even was. And I didn't know I was pregnant with you."

She lowered her head and tears fell from her cheeks onto the pink roses adorning her apron. "I knew deep down it was all bad. I had a feeling right then and there he'd never come back, no matter what he said to make me feel better. That feeling never left me." She looked up at him. "And I was right."

"Mom," he began.

"Be quiet." She wiped her eyes. "I got that same feeling about you now. What you're doing. It's just like with your father. It's that same sick feeling in my stomach, the very same. That feeling I'm going to lose you. That you're going to leave one day and never come back."

He sat next to her. "I'm not going anywhere." He looked into her eyes, seeing them brimming with tears and reddened from exhaustion. He took her hand in his.

"You've already gone – somewhere," she whispered. "Somewhere I don't know."

She pushed her tears away from under her eyes, wiping her fingertips on her apron. "It's funny. You start off with all kinds of hopes and dreams, and you turn around a few times and all of a sudden life goes flying by. And you look and all you got are worries and regrets. How does that happen? I'm only 39 – *39*, Will. I'm not old yet, am I? But I feel old."

He shook his head and squeezed her hand. "No. You're not old. You look really young. Everybody says so."

She sighed and smiled. "Maybe with some make-up on and my hair done."

"No. You're always pretty."

She patted his thigh and pushed herself up. She reached out and stroked the side of his head. "You always said that, even when you were a little boy. You liked it when I wore dresses and put lipstick on. You'd say, 'Mommy, you look pretty today.' That meant more to me than anything anybody else in the world might say."

"I remember." He smiled at her. "Jeez, I better get a move on."

"Where you going? It's Sunday."

"I have to meet Frenchy Jack and the other guys. We're going to start a new job the first of the week – Monday or Tuesday, I guess – once he gets all the paint and stuff. We're going to check it out this morning. See what we need."

"What about breakfast?"

"I'll be back later or get something downtown. We shouldn't be too long."

He went to his bike. "I'll push it up the street before I start it."

"Doesn't matter. He didn't come home last night. Don't know where he is."

"I wondered. Didn't see his car."

When his mother was back inside the house, he rolled the bike into the driveway, then returned to the garage and finished dressing. Once on his bike, he felt at his waist and crotch, repositioning the weighty, solid comfort of his weapons. He pulled away and rode in the direction of the south end. He shivered as the cold air wrapped around his body. It felt cooler than usual. He looked up and saw grey mushroom clouds folding in upon one another from the east. *Rain on the way.*

He found Frenchy Jack's truck parked on Inglis Street, down near Barrington. *What a character,* he thought, seeing Frenchy Jack standing in front of the truck, puffing hard on a cigarette and cranking his head from side to side, looking up and down the street. Frenchy Jack began to wave, gesturing for him to hurry up.

Before Will came to a stop near the truck, Frenchy Jack bound into the street, flicking his cigarette aside.

"*C'est* okay? Willie okay?"

Will laughed and cut his motor. "I'm okay. What's going on?"

"Chase you, eh? Those guy."

"It was no big deal. I was on my bike so I was able to outrun them."

Frenchy Jack cocked his head to one side and smiled, sticking the tip of his tongue between the gap in his front teeth. "Ah, *bon*, you like that guy from USA. How you say – Eebel Kneebel?"

"Evel Knievel?"

"*Oui*, heem. You jump over car, too?"

"Next time."

Frenchy Jack began to laugh, then his face tightened. "Beeg meeting tonight, eh? Barry call you, *oui*?"

Will shrugged. "Barry? No."

"*Oui*, beeg, beeg meeting. All guy must come."

"What's going on?"

At that moment, they heard the sound of bikes thundering down the street in their direction.

BUSINESS RELATIONS

BEFORE WILL COULD GET OFF his bike, Frenchy Jack dove toward the truck and skidded to a stop at the driver's door. He flung the door open and whipped a three-foot-long crowbar out from the cab. Will hopped off his bike and reached to his waist. At that second, Stumpy and Frantic shot into view.

"*Merde*!" Frenchy Jack said to Will, tossing the crowbar onto the driver's seat. "Make me shit my pant."

"I know what you mean."

Stumpy and Frantic rolled off the gas and made a U-turn. They pulled up next to Will's bike. They killed their motors, remaining seated on the bikes.

"Did he tell you?" Frantic asked Will.

"About the meeting? Yeah."

"Tonight at the clubhouse. At seven," Stumpy said. "Barry wants everybody there."

"What's up?"

"Devil's Chain. Didn't just run at us. Went out to Barry's last night – all the way to Waverly."

Frantic laughed. "A bunch of them hung down on the road below his place, calling his name and revving their bikes. Jesus, you know how paranoid he is. A couple of girls there got spooked and wanted to call the cops." He shook his head. "That would've been funny, eh? The president of the Dark Angels calling the cops for help."

"Get to the point," Stumpy said.

"Yeah, so anyway, Barry goes and gets his 12-gauge and blasts a few shots through the tops of the trees. That scattered them."

The others laughed, with the exception of Stumpy.

"Barry called me and we talked about all this shit, and we said this thing is gettin' away from us. So we called a meeting to set the guys straight. No more playin' around." He looked over at Frenchy Jack. "We finished here for today or what?"

"Old lady, she no home. *C'est* okay. Jacques know what need to make good painting on house. Come back *demain*. You boy, too, eh?"

"What the hell did that frog just say?" Stumpy asked.

"Come back tomorrow. We'll start painting," Will said.

"Why the hell didn't he just say that?" Stumpy asked with a growl, looking askance at Frenchy Jack.

"Eight in morning," Frenchy Jack added, holding up eight fingers.

Stumpy shot his middle finger at Frenchy Jack.

By the time Will made it back home and pushed his bike inside the garage, rain had begun to patter on the roof, the big noisy drops creating a staccato-like rhythm. He shed his heavy riding clothes and went to his cot, picking up a tattered hardcover book from the floor next to it. He lay back on the cot and looked at the cover – *Outlines of the History of Greek Philosophy* by Edward Zeller. He began to thumb through the pages, reading passages here and there. He felt his breathing slow and his body begin to feel less tight. His mind drifted, finding pockets of peace in the solidness of the words on the page and the exactness of the ideas and concepts they wove together.

A knock at the side door jarred his mind. He sat up, realizing he hadn't noticed the rain had stopped.

"Will, open the door for me. I've got some supper for you," his mother called.

He sprang from his cot to the door.

"It should still be hot," she said, handing him a plate covered with another placed over it upside down to keep the food warm. "It's baked chicken with Syrian pepper – Sadie's recipe. And salad with some mint, with just oil and vinegar. That's the way you like it, right?"

"Uh, huh. Thanks."

She reached into her apron and handed him a knife and fork. "Do you want me to get you something to drink? I never thought."

"I'm okay for now. You didn't have to do this."

"I like to cook for you. At least you appreciate it."

"Sid show up yet?"

She shook her head. "No. He'll show up when he's good and ready. Same as always. I'm not surprised. He said he was going to celebrate because he got the shift he wanted at the mall." She rolled her eyes. "The overnight shift. Said he had it made now because he wouldn't have to deal with people at all because the mall would be closed when he worked. Just means he'll be able to drink more, far as I can see."

"Just as well he didn't come home if he's on a binge."

She nodded and glanced around. "You really should clean this place up a bit. Not safe with all the things here that could catch fire." She paused. "Funny for you to be here all afternoon. Everything all right?"

"Yeah, there was nobody home at the new painting job. We didn't do much. It might not even have been the right house. You never know with Frenchy Jack." He began to dig into his food. "I have to meet the guys again tonight. It's just a business-type meeting."

She raised her eyebrows. "*Business*? I can imagine."

He smiled. "Well, you know, the painting business – business relations – that kind of thing."

The setting sun began to poke through the heavy clouds and the streets were beginning to dry as he rode toward the clubhouse. Turning onto Granville Street, he saw that the street in front of the clubhouse was already clogged with bikes and cars, while only a few people stood on the sidewalk. He squeezed his bike in among the others and hurried inside.

He passed Stumpy in the hallway. "Members only," Stumpy grumbled to a group of people he was herding toward the door. "You all gotta wait outside 'till were done," he said to them. "You can keep an eye on the bikes while we have our powwow. That'd be good. Won't be too long."

Will pressed his body against the wall, allowing them to get past.

"About time you got here," Stumpy said to him. "They're all down in the big room." He tilted his head back and looked down at him. "You ain't been screwin' around have you? Where you been anyway?"

"Home. Taking it easy."

Stumpy frowned. "Right. Don't you be doin' any more stupid moves, thinkin' I'm gonna be lookin' out for you."

"No. No stupid moves. Not me." He smiled.

He made his way to the big living room at the end of the hall and sat on the floor cross-legged. Shotgun handed him a beer and dropped down on one knee next to him.

Barry and Stumpy moved to the center of the floor. Stumpy signalled to Speedy to pull the plug on the blaring music coming from the big chrome jukebox off to one side.

"Okay, listen up," Barry began. "This Devil's Chain thing – this has gotten way out of hand. We've been playing this wrong. Acting like it's business as usual, while they're taking it real serious. It's time to change our strategy."

"Barry and me talked this out," Stumpy joined in. "We figure we all got to be thinkin' this is a war. No more pansy, chase-me games. Floyd – you know, dope-dealer Floyd – well, Floyd called me up and said they been goin' around Spryfield and all over the place, roundin' up greasers and punch-out artists, and gettin' them all wound up to come at us. He's happy to sell them dope, but he wouldn't steer us wrong."

"Lots of losers we rubbed the wrong way one time or another who've been waiting for a chance to come at us," Barry said. "These guys have been building this little army and now they're calling us out."

Frantic stepped forward. "No harm done yet, except to them. They might have the numbers but they got no experience or fighting smarts. We seen that, right? They don't know what to do even when they got the drop on us. We got strength to the core." He patted his gun. "Time to dust off them lead-slingers, boys, and put an end to this."

Everyone began to chatter and shift about, the whole room vibrating with nasty energy.

"Quiet!" Barry commanded. "Starting right-fucking-now, these are the rules. First, you don't ride alone – no time, nowhere. Second, you make sure you're always ready to fight and that you've got the weapons you need. And don't wait for them to go first. You go first."

Speedy raised his hand. "Is that still part of number two – I mean, hittin' them first – or is that number three?"

Barry glared at him. "Third, think ahead. I know that's hard for most of you idiots, but always look around wherever you go and have a plan, a back-up plan, and a way out."

"There's one more rule, Barry," Stumpy said. "It's my sergeant-at-arms rule, and it's if you act stupid and they get your colours, you better hope they put you in the hospital – 'cause if they don't, I will."

Shotgun stood up. "We can let this drag on or we can end it fast. It's good they're coming at us. Good for us and bad strategy for them. The heat will see they're the ones causing trouble so they'll be on them more than on us."

"So no more fun and games. Is that what I'm hearing, Barry?" Frantic asked.

Barry nodded. "No games."

"Are we done the talking part of the meeting, then?" Frantic asked.

Barry looked at Stumpy and they nodded in unison. While the others milled about and slapped palms and the noise level spiked again, Frantic and Speedy tore aside a Hell's Angels poster pinned with thumbtacks to the plaster of the back wall. They disappeared through a jagged opening into a crawl space littered with bricks, plaster, and other debris and emerged a minute later, each carrying two long canvas sacks. They flopped the sacks onto the floor and loosened the cords cinching the tops. Reaching inside, they began pulling out handguns, sawed-off shotguns, and other weapons.

"And if they get themselves some guns," Stumpy said, "we'll haul out the plastics and shape them up like, like – what d'ya call them things – them depositories? And shove 'em up their asses."

Shotgun looked at Will with a blank expression, then at Stumpy. "Depositories? Do you mean *suppositories*?"

"Yeah, that's it. That's what I meant to say. We'll customize them some special suppositories and blow their assholes to fuckin' Sunnyside."

"How about to George's Island?" Barry asked, smirking. "Sunnyside's a little too close to where I live."

"Don't matter to me where they land," Stumpy said, letting loose a deep belly laugh.

Frantic stood up and moved next to Will. "What do you want? Better grab one." He pointed at the pile of guns beginning to disappear from the center of the floor.

Will shrugged. "A gun? I don't know. I don't think I need a gun." He lifted his shirt to show Frantic his chain and knife.

Frantic chuckled. "You're going in the right direction, but that's not any kind of real protection you got there." He whipped out his Magnum.

"You see, with a gun like this, you'll probably never have to use it – though it's a bitch of fun when you do. Most guys – if they got any brains at all – will split soon as you point a gun like this in their direction. It's like a little nuclear bomb. It's all about deterrence."

Will nodded. "I understand what you're saying."

"You gotta think about it, Will. Like, what'll you do if they're in a car or truck and you're on your bike and they try to run you down? I mean, *really* try. Who knows? It can happen, right? No chain or knife is gonna keep them off. But let them look up the barrel of a beauty like this or, even better, drop a slug or two in their motor and I guarantee you won't see them for dust. It's only common sense."

Will smiled. "It's hard to argue with common sense. Kind of like arguing with Stumpy, right? But ..." he hesitated. "But I wouldn't want to take a chance of actually killing somebody. Know what I mean?"

Frantic stared at him. "Hmmm, yeah, I get it about not wanting to waste anybody. Cranks the heat way up, right?" He paused and scratched his beard. "Look, how about this, then?" He knelt down and began to pick through the remaining guns. He plucked a chrome western-style gun with an inlaid-pearl handle from the pile. He held it out to Will. "Check this one out. It's only a .32 – a little showpiece more than anything. It won't hit that hard, especially from any distance, but it still looks like a big gun – I mean, from a distance and if you don't know a whole lot about guns. Too pretty to be scary but it at least looks like the real thing, right?"

Will took the gun in his hand, feeling its weight and looking at it from different angles. "It feels really balanced. I didn't know they fit your hand this way." He felt a warm rush flow through his body. "Feels really good – like it belongs there."

Frantic put his arm around his shoulder and kissed his neck. "Yup, I'll have you swinging a Magnum in no time. Wait and see." He knelt to the floor again and searched through the sacks. He pulled out boxes of cartridges, one after another, glancing at each box. "Here we go. These aren't that easy to come by." He eased the gun out of Will's hand and loaded it with six of the cartridges He passed the gun back to Will along with the box of remaining cartridges. "Safety's on."

Will took the gun and slid it into his belt. "Thanks."

"I'll help you make a holster for it later. Shoved down your pants ain't the best place for a gun." He looked at Will and laughed. "Jesus, man, you got a shitload of metal around your waist now."

Will grinned, noticing that others were standing nearby waiting for Frantic's advice. As he moved aside to give them room, Shotgun joined him. He opened Will's jacket to look at the chrome six-shooter.

"What did you get?" Will asked.

"Nothing. Don't need one of those things. I'm no gun freak like Billy the Kid." He nodded at Frantic.

Frantic peered at Shotgun through a gap in the wall of onlookers standing in front of him. "One of these days, you'll wish you had one of these when the Grim Reaper's got you by the tail. Maybe we should call you Slingshot or Pea Shooter or something like that. You don't deserve to be called Shotgun."

Shotgun shrugged. "Wouldn't matter to me. I don't need a special name or a big gun to make me feel like something I'm not. Like you do." He nudged Will's shoulder. "Look at him. He still hasn't figured out that flashing that canon around will never make him as tall, smart, or good looking as me." He blew Frantic a kiss and grinned from ear to ear.

"You'll see I'm right one of these days," Frantic said, his expression darkening.

"Hurry up, Frantic," Barry said, pushing his way in, Stumpy not far behind. "This isn't show 'n tell. Just pass them out." He turned to Stumpy. "Soon as he's finished, hide those sacks again and put things to right. Then you can go let the people out front back inside."

Will and Shotgun moved to a nearby sofa and sat back, beers in hand, soaking up the electric atmosphere. They watched Stumpy march to the front of the clubhouse and yank open the heavy front door. A kaleidoscopic collection of girlfriends, hippies, drug dealers, and other misfits flooded in as fast as rough iron filings drawn to a powerful magnet – Kay among them.

She flitted across the room and slid onto the sofa next to Shotgun. She smiled and squeezed his knee. "Everything okay, now?"

"We'll see."

"What are you guys going to do?"

"Be prepared, I guess."

"Barry and Stumpy are calling the shots, now," Will said.

"Oh, there she is," Kay said, looking toward the hallway.

"Who?" Shotgun asked.

"Gloria – that blonde girl – the pretty one there. See her? She's a friend of mine." She nudged Will in the ribs with her elbow. "What do you think?"

"About what?"

"Gloria. She's really pretty, don't you think?"

"Yeah." He hesitated. "She looks familiar."

"Guess what. She wants to meet you."

"Me? Why?"

Shotgun tapped Will's head with his knuckles. "To talk about guns, why else, genius?" He shook his head. "Jeez, man, were you born yesterday?"

"Leave him alone," Kay said. "He's a little naive, that's all. Girls like that. It's sweet." She patted Will's cheek and pushed herself up from the sofa. "Come with me. She thinks you're cute and wants to meet you – that's all." She grabbed his hands and pulled him up. "She doesn't know anybody here, and I already told her about you – that you were quiet and nice. Not like the rest of these obnoxious animals."

They weaved their way across the crowded room. Kay took Will's shoulders from behind and positioned him in front of the girl. "Will – Gloria, Gloria – Will," she said. "There, I've done my part. The rest is up to you two." She giggled, turned on her heel and sashayed back to Shotgun, waving and smiling at them as she dropped back onto the sofa at Shotgun's side.

PART 3

THE REAL TRUTH ABOUT THINGS

WILL AND GLORIA'S EYES MET. "Hi," she said. A confident smile slid easily across her face. She held her hand out to shake his.

Will looked down and clasped her hand, noticing the sweet smell of her perfume. *Jasmine or honeysuckle*, he thought, as he gently squeezed her warm hand.

"It's okay," she said. "It won't break. And I don't bite."

"Sorry." He quickly pulled his hand away. "Would you like a beer? I don't know if we've got anything else. Um, I could check." He forced a quick smile.

"I can drink from yours. I mean, if that's okay." She coyly pointed at his beer.

"Ah, sure, that's fine. I thought you might want your own." He passed her the bottle.

"I think most of my germs are harmless."

He smiled to see how she drank with bold, thirsty gulps.

"Oops. Looks like we're going to need another beer," she said, looking at the label on the stubby bottle. "Schooner – is that your favourite?"

"No. Well, I don't know. I'm not fussy." He paused. "Come to think of it, I don't have very refined tastes when it comes to beer – or much else, I guess."

"What about girls?"

"Girls? Umm, probably fussier." He felt his face warming. "I'll get us another beer."

He darted into the kitchen and returned moments later with two bottles. "You can have your own or we can keep sharing. Your choice." He smiled, then glanced down as he felt his cheeks getting hot again.

"Let's share." She touched his arm with her fingertips. "It's almost like kissing, isn't it?"

He took a drink and passed her the bottle. "You're not shy, are you?"

"No. What's the point? What about you – introvert or extrovert? Probably introvert, judging by how you blush. Kay said you were quiet."

"Introvert, I guess. Never thought about it much."

She touched her earlobe and laughed. "You're staring at me. It's okay. I just thought you might want to know."

"Oh, sorry. It's strange. You look familiar. It's like I know you from somewhere."

She tilted her head a little to the right and smiled. "It was a few months ago. I waited on you once – breakfast – remember?" She paused. "In Grand Pré."

His eyes widened. "No way! Was that you?"

"Uh, huh. I guess you made more of an impression on me than I made on you."

"No, really, I remember you. I was tired, though. We had a long night." He retrieved the beer from her and took a quick sip. "You don't work there anymore?"

"No. Not right now. I go home for the summers and work there. The diner belongs to my parents. It's mostly to help them out. I can make more money here."

"What are you doing here?"

"You mean in the city?"

"Uh, huh."

"Right now, getting ready for school. That's how I met Kay. I moved in with her and a couple other girls last week, up by Dalhousie. Some coincidence, eh?"

He nodded and passed her the beer.

"I wasn't too sure about coming here. But I met Shotgun through Kay, and he seemed like a nice guy." She took a long drink. "So I said to myself, 'Okay, you're bored. Go check it out.' Plus, when Kay described you, it got me thinking, 'I wonder if that's the cute guy from before in the diner?' And, holy cow, it was."

"So you go to school here?"

"Dalhousie – second year science." She shrugged and rolled her eyes.

"I still don't know what I want to do. Veterinary medicine maybe. My parents want me to go to law school." She shook her head. "Who knows why? Can you picture me as a judge in those robes, sitting up there behind a big bench?"

He grinned. "Nobody would be able to concentrate on the court cases or the criminals."

"Just like all the legal types that come into Ginger's now." She shook her head.

"Ginger's Bar?"

"Have you been there? I've never seen you there."

"No. You go there?"

"I work there. Pays my tuition and what it costs to live in the city – my share of the rent and food and things like that. My parents help, too."

"You *are* a good waitress. I remember that."

She smiled, her lips closed, crinkling the corners of her mouth and eyes. "I dance there. And serve drinks."

"You get paid to dance there?"

"Uh, huh. To dance and take my clothes off. Most of the money's from tips, though."

"Sorry, I don't mean to be so, um, so dumb," he stammered. He reached to take the beer from her. "So, you work as a, umm, a ..."

"Stripper? Uh, huh." She reached and squeezed his hand. "It's fine, you're allowed to say it. You don't have to blush. You're not the one getting naked in front of strange men. At least I hope you're not because that would probably change everything, unless you had a good explanation." She laughed.

"I just wasn't thinking."

"It's okay. Appearances can be deceiving, I know. Everybody looks at me and thinks I'm so sweet and innocent. Most people look down on strippers. But I like it. I like the power." She took the beer from him and swirled the remaining liquid around in the bottom of the bottle. "When I'm dancing, I'm in control. All those men gawking at me – no matter how young or old, or rich or poor, or weak or powerful they are – they're in the palm of my hand. I can look them in the eye and feel I *got* them. I don't think there's any other way girls my age can do that."

"I never thought of it that way but I understand what you're saying." He chuckled. "You know, it's funny what you were saying about appearances being deceiving. I was reading about this ancient Greek philosopher who said you can't really trust your senses. So you can never know the real truth about things by how they appear. Another coincidence, right?" He paused.

"Go on."

"Well, he said for everything you *think* you know based on what your senses tell you, there's an opposite way of sensing and thinking about the same things. So you really can't know *anything* for sure. That's where the term skeptic came from."

She crossed her arms and tilted her hips. "Hmm – interesting. Where did you say you read that?"

"An old book I picked up. The philosopher's name was Sextus Empiricus."

"You're pulling my leg, right?" She frowned.

"No." He paused. "Sorry, I didn't mean to get weird on you. I know most people find this stuff pretty boring or strange."

She continued to frown at him, then burst out laughing. "Just teasing. But, God, that's an erotic, manly name for sure – Sextus Empiricus. I can guess what the Sextus part has to do with, but what about Empiricus? No, wait, I know. He was a male exotic dancer, right? Some old Greek stripper dude."

"No doubt," Will said, laughing.

She took another drink and looked into his eyes. "What do you do?"

He hesitated. "As in, what do I do besides being a member of the Dark Angels? What do I do for work?"

"Uh, huh."

"Right now, I work with some of our guys painting houses. But, in a few months, I have a job coming up at Saint Mary's. I'll be going back to work with a formwork company that's building the new student residences. The main building will be quite high, I think. My boss said there'll be an observatory on the top with a big telescope. I work with the concrete crew, pushing wet concrete around in wheelbarrows and shovelling it in place to make floors and columns. Nothing fancy, that's for sure."

"Sounds like hard work."

"I suppose. But – here I go sounding strange again – I like hard physical work."

She reached and squeezed his right bicep. Then, with both hands, felt his shoulders. "Is that how you got these hard muscles? Impressive."

"Oh, man." He shook his head and looked at the floor. "You do say what's on your mind, don't you?"

"Only when I'm in the company of people who interest me. Otherwise, it's not worth the bother. By the way, girls don't like soft men. If they say they don't like to look at muscles or feel them, they're lying. Did you know that?"

"I guess so, but I never heard a girl actually say it."

"And when men say they don't care if their wives or girlfriends get fat and stop making themselves pretty because they just love them big bunches for who they are ..." She paused and raised her eyebrows. "Right, they're lying, too. I hear it all the time at Ginger's. That's why they're there looking at me."

She took his hand. "Can we go sit down with Kay and Shotgun? You can talk more of that philosophy talk to me if you want. I won't think you're too weird. It's kind of sexy in a tangled, strange way."

They worked their way across the clogged room – dozens of people gyrating to music or clustered in groups shouting above the music. Shotgun moved two visitors off the sofa so they could sit. They lowered themselves down and Gloria wriggled her body between Kay and Will, snuggling in next to him.

"Okay?" she said, squeezing his thigh.

"You bet." He smiled and opened the next beer.

Sitting next to her on the sofa, her energy oozed through him like an inviting, warm bath. He drank in the sweet scent of her skin, feeling his senses tingle with each breath. Unable to take his eyes from her mouth and lips, he hung on the words floating effortlessly from them like the lyrics of a perfect song. He pictured her dancing – naked, confident, and at ease. The frenetic energy around them became muted white noise and *she* became all he could clearly sense. Then, time itself disappeared.

"I should get going soon," Gloria said, breaking his trance. "Can you take me home? It's after midnight already."

"Sure. Have you been on a bike before?" He stood up and held his hand out to her.

"A small one," she said, taking his hand. "A dirt bike at home."

He held her hand as they made their way outside. "Right here," he said. "This one." He pointed to his Harley.

"Wow – nice bike."

He nodded, swung his leg over the bike and settled into the seat. He turned toward the back of the bike. "Your ass goes here," he said, tapping the back pillion seat. He pointed at each of the footpegs. "And your feet go here." He turned to face the front. "And, when you get on, you hold on to my waist."

"I think I can manage that."

She climbed onto the bike without hesitation, positioning her body as directed. "What now?"

"A little more instruction." He reached back and put his hand on her leg. "If I lean left or right, just relax and go with the bike. Don't lean away or fight it. And, if I say hold on, I really mean *hold on*. Hold on to me."

"Got it."

"Don't worry, I won't go fast."

"I'm not worried. Maybe I'll want to go fast."

He looked back at her. "I should have known that."

He reached under the gas tank and opened the gas petcock, then bent down to the right and rotated the circuit breaker cap clockwise to retard the ignition spark. After closing the choke on the carburetor, he stood up, straddling the bike and leaning his weight on his left leg. He pushed against the kick-start pedal. Then, heaving up, he dropped the weight of his body down onto it. The motor barked to life.

"I like that," she said above the rumbling of the exhausts and the mechanical clatter of the motor's internals. "It's like a start-up ritual. Do this, do that, do the other thing, before you can even start it."

"Exactly." He sat there, letting the motor idle and settle into a smoother rhythm.

"What are you waiting for?"

"Letting it warm up."

"Another ritual?"

"Uh, huh."

"I hope you treat your women that well."

He looked down, shook his head and accelerated away from the curb with authority. "DO YOU CARE WHERE WE GO?" he shouted back to her.

"NO." She wrapped her arms around his waist and pressed her body against his back. "SURPRISE ME."

He rode through the near-deserted downtown streets, cruising slowly, gliding past stop signs and through intersections with flashing traffic lights. He climbed Citadel Hill and looped around the top, descending on the western side and continuing on toward the residential center of the city.

"CAN WE GO FAST NOW?" she shouted, when they turned onto Connaught Avenue with its wide boulevard.

"I DON'T WANT TO SCARE YOU."

"I WANT YOU TO."

He nodded and rolled the throttle on. They flew down Connaught Avenue toward Chebucto Road and on toward Windsor Street, Gloria screaming with delight in his ear. Before reaching Windsor, he turned onto the darkened side streets – rocketing from one to another, braking and accelerating, accelerating and braking, dragging the footpegs around every corner – on and on, the booming exhaust echoing off sleepy houses and stoic apartment buildings.

He began to slow down. "SHOULDN'T PUSH OUR LUCK TOO MUCH," he shouted back.

She hugged his waist harder and gave two quick squeezes with her knees against his hips, sending a tingle up his spine.

"YOU CAN TAKE ME HOME NOW – LEMARCHANT STREET, CLOSE TO DAL."

Near the southern end of LeMarchant Street, she pointed to a large house with clapboard siding and a prominent turret. He slowed to a stop in front of it and cut the motor.

"Nice place," he said.

"A professor owns it. It's all rented out, mostly to students."

"So was it okay?"

"The ride? Uh, huh. Fabulous." She climbed off the bike and tried to smooth her hair. "Must look quite wild."

"No, looks great."

"Can we do it again sometime?"

"Sure. Should I call you? Or would you want to meet me somewhere?" He paused. "Maybe I could come see you dance."

She smiled. "Ah, no. I wouldn't want that. If you are going to see me dance, I'd rather it be a private performance." She took a step toward the house. "I'll find you the next time – like I did tonight. How would that be?"

"If that's what you want."

She nodded and walked up the stone walkway to the house. When she reached the front steps, she stopped, turned, and walked back to him.

"Can I ask you something? You don't have to answer if you don't want."

"Sure. Anything."

"Why do you have that God-awful big chain around your waist and that gun? It's hard not to notice things like that. It *is* a real gun, isn't it?"

"Yeah, it is." He hesitated. "Uh, we're having some trouble with another club. It's a little extra insurance. In case they decide to get cute. Well, maybe more than a *little* insurance." He smiled.

She crossed her arms. "I suppose it's a good idea to plan ahead. Do you think you're actually going to need it?"

"I doubt it. At least Frantic doesn't think so, and he knows a lot about these things." He looked into her eyes and took her hand. "Are you sure you want to be a part of this? You know, this Dark Angels' stuff?"

"Compared to what? Being around boring college boys whose idea of fun and excitement is to drink beer from a bong until they vomit. Or horny middle-aged men with big mortgages, bellies that hang over their pants, and no asses – who think you really like it when they paw at your tits. I don't think so. Remember, I'm not a scaredy-cat. I just like to know the score, straight up." She leaned down and kissed his forehead. "One last question. Why do you have that, there?" She pointed to the picture taped on his gas tank.

"It's my father. I never knew him. He was killed in Korea when I was a baby. I keep it there for good luck."

"I'm sorry." She patted his cheek. "But I like that you've done that. Kay was right about you."

He watched as she walked to the house and let herself in, waiting until he saw a light come on in one of the top-floor dormers. He took a deep breath, started his bike and rode off.

He rode to the end of LeMarchant Street and headed down University Avenue to Robie Street. In no time, he was across from Sadie's Lodge. He slowed, then pulled over to the right side of the street. The bike shook beneath him. He felt for the gun at his waist and slipped it out. He studied it, squeezing its hard sensuality with his hand. He held it out, pointed away from his body, aiming it across the North Common. He sighted down the barrel and noticed a pin-point sparkle of light glinting off the chrome. Glancing up, he saw a delicate sliver of crescent moon suspended in the sky above the Common, as if hooked on the inky-blackness of space. He raised the gun and aimed it at the moon.

"Bang," he whispered.

He slid the gun back into his pants and prodded the transmission into gear. He rode north and then west, curious if the Devil's Chain might still be up and about – and interested in discussing the real truth about things.

ERRANT ANGEL

H E RUMBLED THROUGH THE PARKING lots of the west-end shopping centers and out past Spryfield's gas stations, pizza joints, and late-night drinking holes. He rolled back into Armdale and Fairview – past all the places he thought the Devil's Chain might still be hanging around. For an hour, he rode and searched and tried to lure a bite.

On Dutch Village Road, he saw a few bikes parked up ahead in front of Arnie's Fish and Chip's. As he neared them, his motor sputtered. He pulled over and screwed off the gas cap. He squinted to look down into the tank, rocking the bike from side to side. He screwed the cap back on and reached under the tank to the left, twisting the petcock to the reserve position. The bike's motor immediately smoothed out. He turned and headed home.

Arriving at Sadie's Lodge, he saw that Sid's car was still not in the driveway. He motored up to the garage.

As he lay on his cot in the heavy stillness a few hours before twilight, he found sleep to be as elusive as the Devil's Chain. His body felt tired and stiff, but his mind raced. Images of Gloria's sensual feline movements, her teasing voice, and her warm, scented touch collided and fought with images of cold steel guns, blatting motorcycle exhausts, and the sweaty, violent maelstrom of bikers splashing bright red blood onto warm pavement. His mind flitted and roamed and could settle on nothing, nor let go of anything.

At dawn, he dragged himself out of bed and crept into the house to shower. He finished quickly, wrapped a towel around his waist and tip-toed back outside, carrying his clothes. When he pulled his jeans on, he set his primary-chain belt and switchblade on his cot and found his old leather belt, which he slipped through the belt loops. He took his gun from under his pillow and slipped it into his belt. Snatching the chain, he wrapped it upon itself in a tight coil and slid it and the knife under his pillow.

He shivered as he dried his upper body and hair. He glanced around but could see no kindling to use to start a fire in the cast-iron stove tucked in the far corner of the garage. He pulled on a T-shirt and a sweatshirt, then grabbed his leather jacket. A few minutes later, he was ready to leave.

As he mounted his bike and leaned his weight forward to coax it down the driveway, he heard a quick tapping coming from the kitchen window. He looked up and saw his mother gesturing for him to stop. She hurried out the back door, carrying a paper bag.

"What's your rush? It's not even eight o'clock yet."

"I didn't want to wake you. We're starting that new job on Inglis Street."

"So? Can't take time for breakfast? You need to eat to work."

"I know. I'll get something later."

She held the paper bag out to him. "Take this. It's a tuna sandwich and a few other snacks. I made it for you last night. Guess you didn't see it on the counter."

"I was trying to hurry." He unzipped his jacket, took the bag and eased it down inside his jacket. "Not too warm this morning."

She pulled her housecoat snug around her body. "September in a couple days. Be winter before we know it." She stood still, looking at him.

"What?"

"Nothing. You should go, I guess."

He hesitated. "No big rush. It's not like it's a job at the Royal Bank. Come back inside the garage." He dismounted and they went into the garage through the side door.

"You're going to need your stove soon," she said, rubbing her hands together.

"That's what I was thinking."

"Sid's convinced you're going to burn the place down."

He passed her a blanket, which she wrapped around her shoulders. "He show up yet?"

"He got back last night – reeking of liquor and perfume. Stayed long enough to change his clothes and take off again."

"Did you say anything to him?"

"About what – him drinking and chasing around? What's the point? Just leads to more trouble." She paused and bit at her bottom lip.

"What? What happened this time?"

"I made the mistake of telling him Patty went out on her bike looking for him, which was the truth because she was worried he was going to be driving the car drunk again. He got wild and told me I was a lousy mother and should be doing a better job of controlling her." She pulled up the sleeves of her housecoat and held her wrists out toward him. "He didn't like that. I should've kept my mouth shut. You'd think I'd know better by now."

He took her hands and examined the purplish-blue bruises that encircled both wrists and extended half way up her forearms. He took a deep breath. "I'm going to kill him!"

She shook her head. "Don't talk like that. It scares me. I'd just lose you and he'd win again, dead or alive."

"You've got to do something. Get away from him. It's not like you've got small kids anymore. Any kind of life would be better than this. It's so crazy. *He's* so crazy!" He began to pace, his breathing tight and fast.

She sighed. "Where would I go? This place is all I've got. When Sadie left it to me, I told myself I could never let it go. Because, then, I'd really have nothing – nothing besides you and Patty." She shook her head. "And he'll never leave. Why would he? He's got everything he wants right here and doesn't pay one red cent. If he ever did take off, Patty would probably go with him." She took a deep breath and exhaled loudly. "When I first found out I was pregnant with Patty, I knew then and there I'd never get away from him."

Will looked down at his hands. He clenched and released his fists and glanced around the garage. His eyes fell on an old poster from Calquhoun's Motorcycle Shop. "Swing into the Saddle of a Harley-Davidson and See the World!" urged the words in bold letters across the top of the poster.

"Maybe I could persuade him to leave."

She stared across at him. "Don't talk so foolish. If you try something like that it would just cause more trouble – a lot more." She began to flick her right thumbnail against her fingernails. "Best thing is for you to steer clear of him."

He said nothing.

"Will? You listen to me. Keep clear of him. Promise?"

"Uh, huh. No problem. You don't have to worry about me."

Within the hour, he was leaning an aluminum extension ladder against the back of an old house on Inglis Street. Looking up, he saw peeling grey paint and more damaged shingles than good ones. "Frenchy Jack's got a winner here," he said to Stumpy and Speedy, both clinging to ladders as they scraped at the loose paint. "These shingles really should be replaced."

Speedy laughed. "Frenchy Jack says to slap on the oil-based paint. Says that'll be enough to keep them in place."

"He don't give a shit," Stumpy said, shaking his head with disgust. "Just some old broad livin' here all alone."

Will watched clouds above the house thin through the morning as he scraped the old paint away and brushed primer on the bare wood. He noticed the leaves on the chestnut trees were already beginning to wilt and turn brown. *Early for that,* he thought. His mind drifted, thoughts coming and going, tumbling and spiraling away like flakes of paint falling to the ground. He looked up beyond the roof and the tops of the trees, noticing that the sky was blue and the sun shining. *When did that happen?* he wondered.

"Jeez, must be time for lunch," he heard Speedy say to Stumpy.

Stumpy looked at his watch. "Yeah, I suppose."

They climbed down the ladders and began to brush flakes of paint and dust from their clothes and hair. "I don't know why you guys don't wear coveralls," Speedy said, unzipping his. "Makes things a lot easier. You don't have to worry about getting all that paint and crap on your clothes."

"Each to his own," Stumpy said. "You find some to fit me and maybe I'll wear 'em."

"Frenchy Jack says a good painter doesn't need to wear any special painter's clothes," Will said. "He claims if you pay attention and work smart, you shouldn't get any paint on yourself." He paused "Well, he didn't say it exactly like that but that was the idea. Who knows, maybe he'd get us some coveralls. Want me to ask him?"

"Forget it," Frantic said, as they headed toward the shed at the back of the property, still brushing off their clothes. "He's so cheap, he'll say something like 'No, no boy, no money for workey pant'. Unless he can steal them somewhere. Cheap prick."

"No, we oughta ask him," Speedy said. "Mine are almost worn out."

"Give it up," Stumpy said, sneering. "Looks fuckin' stupid, anyway. Look, you got 'em rolled up about six times. You look like one of them Snow White dwarfs. Yeah, that fuckin' Dopey one." He laughed.

"What're you talking about? Fuck right off. They're only rolled up twice." He wriggled the coveralls off his shoulders, pushed them to the ground and stepped out of them. "I had to get them long to fit my Tarzan chest."

They stood in front of the shed looking up at the back of the house. Frantic patted his jacket pockets, then hauled out an Export "A" cigarette package. He flipped the top open and pulled out a thick joint. Speedy rustled through his pockets. He pulled out a box of matches. He struck a match against the box and cupped it in his hands, holding it out for Frantic. Frantic dipped the end of the joint into the flame and sucked hard. He filled his lungs with the sweet smoke and passed the snapping, crackling joint to Stumpy.

"Goin' pretty fast," Stumpy said, looking at the back of the house again.

Frantic blew the smoke out hard and took a breath. "Too fast, I'd say. We better slow it down. All we do by working fast and finishing quick is make more money for Frenchy Jack."

Stumpy nodded as he dragged on the joint. He exhaled and passed it to Will. "Damn right. He comes to our friggin' country and all of us who been here all along end up slavin' for him for 11 lousy bucks a day." He looked at Frantic. "How much do you figure he makes."

Frantic stared at him. "Our country? What fuckin' country do you think he comes from?"

Stumpy looked at him. "That place where they talk that frog language – Kweeebeck, or whatever it's fuckin' called," he sputtered. "Not our country. Not friggin' Nova Scotia, that's for sure."

Frantic, Will, and Speedy broke out laughing. "You idiot," Frantic said. "Nova Scotia and Québec aren't countries. They're two different provinces, but they're both part of the same country – Canada. Christ, they teach you that in grade six."

Stumpy frowned at him. He turned to Will. "Is he shittin' me? I don't remember learnin' that in grade six."

Will nodded. "He's right, Stump."

Stumpy shook his head. "Holy shit, I can't believe it – Frenchy Jack's really a Canadian?"

"I figure he clears about 600 or 700 bucks for each house we paint," Will said.

"At least all the money stays in the country, eh Stump?" Frantic said, still laughing.

As Will began to drag on the joint, the back door of the house swung open. He whisked the joint behind his back. A well-dressed, elderly woman – her white hair in a tight bun and her glasses hanging below her neck on a gold chain – stepped gingerly onto the back landing. She carried a tray piled high with sandwiches in one hand and a pitcher in the other. When she got her bearings, she looked up and smiled at Will and the others.

"Yoo-hoo," she said in a sing-song voice. "Mildred, here. I could use a little assistance, gentlemen – if you don't mind."

Stumpy rushed across the backyard and up the steps. Will butted out the joint against the sole of his boot.

"Thank you, young man," she said, passing Stumpy the tray and pitcher. "There are chicken salad, egg salad, and tuna sandwiches – even a few peanut butter and jelly. And cherry Kool-Aid. I know how you young people like Kool-Aid." She looked down at Stumpy's midsection. "Now, they're not all for you, young man. They're to share."

Stumpy turned and walked down the steps, smiling. The woman followed him, moving both feet to each step before stepping down to the next.

"Look. They're all cut into little triangles," Stumpy said, as he joined the others.

By the time the woman reached them, they had begun to devour the sandwiches and were taking turns drinking from the pitcher.

"Oh, my. I forgot glasses," she said.

"Don't matter ma'am," Stumpy said. "We don't need 'em."

She looked at each of them. "Well, seeing as how we're outside and it's rather like a picnic, I suppose it's acceptable. But, if we were inside, well, that would be a different matter."

"This is really nice of you, ma'am," Will said. "You didn't have to go through all this trouble."

"Oh, it was nothing. I like to watch hungry boys eat and it gives me something to do. Reminds me of when I used to have picnics out here with my own boys." She turned her pointed nose to the air and sniffed. "You boys weren't smoking cigarettes were you?"

They all shook their heads.

"I certainly hope not. Stunts your growth, you know." She lifted her glasses to her eyes and looked Speedy up and down. "I always expected my boys to have good manners and to follow the rules and regulations and not smoke or drink. My late husband, Wilber, died three years ago from cancer of the bowel. Very messy it was. Well, Wilber used to say, 'Mildred, you're going to make those boys rebellious with all your harping about rules'. But he was wrong – rest his soul. My boys all turned out good. John's a lawyer in Saint John, and Alec's a vet up in Cape Breton. And the youngest one, Eric, well, he married into money. Cosmetics. They live in New York City." She took a breath. "Yes, they have all done very well indeed. Though, I must say, I don't see much of them or the grandchildren. They tell me I've even got great-grandchildren, but I expect I'll be senile before I see them."

"So it's just you living here, Mildred?" Frantic asked. "It's a big house."

She nodded. "Yes, only I." She paused. "What's your name, dear?"

Frantic glanced at the others. "Um, it's an unusual name, ma'am. It's Frantic Fred."

"Hmm. Yes, you're right. It *is* unusual." She paused and smiled. "But, now then, I wager you have a nickname?"

"Um, yes ma'am, I guess I do. It's, ah ..."

She waved her hand at him. "Oh, don't worry about it. If you tell me, I'll just forget by the time I see you again." She giggled and looked across at the house. "You boys are doing a wonderful job. I was watching you all morning. I'm more than pleased. Mr. Jacques was telling me you were very good workers. He was right." She sighed. "Oh, such a charmer that one. And that French accent – *oohlala*! Makes me wish I was 50 years younger."

"Frenchy Jack?" Stumpy whispered to Will. "She talkin' about Frenchy Jack?"

Will nodded.

"Bastard," Stumpy whispered. "He's probably casing the place out to rob her blind."

"I'll let you finish your lunch in peace," she said, turning to leave. "Shall I bring you some tea and cookies later? You will take a break later, won't you?"

"Tea!" exclaimed Stumpy. "Do you have any of that grey tea? My mom used to make that grey tea for me all the time when I was a kid."

"Grey tea, dear? I don't think I know that kind."

"Earl Grey? Is that what you mean, Stumpy?" Will asked.

"Yeah, that's friggin' what it was – Earl Grey." He looked at Mildred. "Oops, sorry ma'am. I didn't mean to say friggin'."

She smiled. "No harm done." She again brought her glasses to her eyes and looked at each of them in turn. "You know, you boys wouldn't be bad looking if you shaved, got nice haircuts and cleaned yourselves up. I always used to tell my boys that mannerly and clean-cut young men get ahead in the world. Even Wilber had to agree with me on that count."

She ambled across the yard and back up the steps, disappearing inside the back door.

"She's cool, ain't she?" Stumpy said.

The others nodded.

When all the sandwiches were gone and the pitcher of Kool-Aid drained, they sat in a circle in the tall grass at the far side of the shed, out of sight of the windows at the back of Mildred's house, and smoked the remaining half of Frantic's joint. "Let's pace ourselves to get half of the back painted today," Frantic said.

The others nodded.

At two-thirty, Mildred again emerged from the back door. "Yoo-hoo," she called, waving at Stumpy, painting on the lowest ladder. "Help, please."

Stumpy climbed down, placed his paint pail and brush on the ground and hurried up the back steps. Mildred passed him a large silver tea pot and a silver tray rounded with chocolate-covered graham cookies. "Come back and get the cups and saucers, dear," she said.

Following behind Stumpy, Mildred toddled across the back yard. "Oh my, where's my brain?" she said, shaking her head. "I should have brought a blanket for all of us to sit on."

"That don't matter, Mildred," Stumpy said. "We don't mind sittin' on the grass." He lowered himself clumsily at her feet.

She patted the top of Stumpy's head, then passed out delicate porcelain teacups and saucers.

"You can pour, Francis," she said to Frantic, gesturing at the tea pot.

With a grin on his face, Frantic filled the cups, with Mildred teetering above them offering milk and sugar.

"Wilber – did I tell you about my late husband, Wilber? Poor soul.

Died last year from cancer of the throat. Couldn't talk in the end. God bless him. Wilber used to say, 'Mildred, you should never skimp on china or linen. A family should have good china and linen because these are things you use every day.' Yes, he'd say, 'Mildred you should use the best things every day, and not save them for special occasions.' And, you know, I believe he was right about that."

Frantic leaned toward Stumpy and Will. "This could get out of control," he said, bugging his eyes wide.

"You watch your mouth," Stumpy warned, scowling at him.

As the afternoon ground on, Will felt his calves beginning to tighten and cramp from standing on the ladder. He tried to shift his thoughts away from the discomfort and monotony of the work, tried to get lost in thoughts of Gloria, or deep philosophical questions, or the war brewing with the Devil's Chain – anything but flakes of paint, and Mildred smiling and waving from each window.

"Hey, Stump, what time is it?" he called, beginning to think it might be better to go back and ask Harry if he knew where he might find a construction job.

Stumpy glanced at his watch and nodded. "Yeah, we can stop now. Frenchy'll be here soon."

"I'll catch up with you guys later," Will said, as they walked down the driveway to their bikes after putting the supplies away in Mildred's shed.

"Where you goin'?" Stumpy asked. "If you're not around when that frog shows up, he'll try to gyp you out of your money."

"Just have to go home and check on things."

"Be sure to hook up with us at the Seahorse," Frantic said. "If we're not there, we'll be at the clubhouse."

Will nodded and started his bike.

"Want us to get your money from him?" Speedy asked.

Will shook his head. "He won't screw me around."

Stumpy frowned at him and grabbed his arm before he could pull away. "Don't get lost."

Will smiled. "See you in a couple hours."

As Stumpy released his grip, Will rolled the throttle on and accelerated up Inglis Street. Slicing and dicing through the thickening rush-hour traffic, he headed west, retracing his route from the previous night.

THE EUPHORIA OF RISK AND POWER

H E LOOPED THROUGH SPRYFIELD AND Armdale and on toward Fairview. He rumbled up Dutch Village road in first gear, looking left and right, scanning every parking lot and peering up every driveway. Approaching the Dairy Queen, off to his right, he saw five bikes parked side-by-side in the parking lot, up close to the restaurant. He slowed to a stop at the curb. He sat looking at the plate glass windows. He waited. Then, he rolled his throttle on, pounding the motor up close to redline, and holding it there as windows in the vicinity began to rattle and people began to stop and stare. In seconds, several bikers tripped over one another, jamming through the Dairy Queen's doors and bolting to their bikes.

He watched them throw themselves onto their bikes, smiling to himself at their herky-jerky bloodlust. "That's it, you amateurs, that's it," he whispered to himself, unable to hear his words over the roar of his bike. He pulled away and headed up Dutch Village Road. He watched in his mirror as they took off at full speed – hot on his tail.

They were closing fast – 400 feet back – 300 – 200!

Now!

He hit the brakes and screeched to a stop, smack in the middle of Dutch Village Road. He popped the transmission into neutral and placed both feet flat on the pavement. He reached to his left, drew out his gun and twisted his body to face them. He raised the gun and pointed it at them. They bore down on him. He didn't flinch. Holding the gun straight out at arm's length, he cocked the hammer with his thumb.

Time and space collapsed onto the end of the gun's chrome barrel. He heard his bike thudding under him – KA-BOOM, KA-BOOM, KA-BOOM. *Ahh, that sweet, peaceful noise.* He saw his hand – steady as a concrete slab – holding the gun. Beyond his hand and the gun, he tried to find their faces. He looked for their eyes, wanted to know if they saw their fate. *How can human beings be so stupid?* They kept coming. He felt a warm rush shoot through his body. *God! What now?*

He aimed high and felt his finger squeeze the trigger – **CRACK**. The gun snapped back in his hand as the barrel jerked up.

The bikes screeched to a stop, jamming in upon one another like a jumbled train wreck.

He sat motionless on his bike, still holding the gun straight out at arm's length. He watched the bikers turn around in clumsy arcs and peel away. He lowered the gun and looked around, seeing that cars had stopped, their drivers staring at him with stunned, horrified expressions.

He slipped the gun back into his pants and rode off, noticing that his heart was pounding with rapid, exhilarating thuds. He headed south on Howe Avenue, then angled east toward home. *Frantic was right.* He felt as if he had become someone else – *but who?*

In a daze, he slowed in front of Sadie's Lodge and turned into the driveway. His stomach churned when he saw Sid's Falcon parked in the middle of the driveway. He hesitated, then maneuvered close to the house to squeeze past the car. He parked his bike in front of the garage, hopped off and slipped inside through the side door. He sat on his cot, took a deep breath and held his hands out over his knees, palms down. His hands were steady, his head clear, his senses satiated — the rhythms of his body telling him to be calm.

He took his gun from his pants and slid it under his pillow. He lay back, feeling the hard weapon against the back of his head. He listened for any worrisome noises coming from the house, but everything was quiet, so he allowed his heavy eyes to close as his breathing slowed. He remembered the feel of his gun, the hard steel caressing his hand. He saw himself poised on the Harley, sighting down the chrome barrel of the lovely .32, ready to strike – to make the Devil's Chain understand reality.

A violent pounding on his door jarred him awake. He found himself engulfed in darkness, unsure if it was morning or night.

"Little pig, little pig – let me come in. Or I'll huff and puff and blow your shack down," he heard Patty call out in a girlish voice.

"Hold on." He jumped up, shook the grogginess from his head and went to unlock the door.

As soon as he turned the lock, Patty flung the door open, barged in and brushed past him. "Whatcha doin'?"

"Damn it, Patty, you didn't have to pound on the door like that. I was asleep."

"I do it just to bug you. Guess it works, eh?" She blew a bubble with her gum, took it from her mouth and eyed it before placing it back in her mouth and chomping down on it, popping it with a loud snap. "Why you sleeping now? It's early."

"I worked all day. Painting."

"Painting? Painting what?"

"Houses – an old house down on Inglis Street. What do you want?"

She bit at her fingernails. "Do you get paid a lot to do that?"

"No. Jeez, what do you want? I've got to take a shower and get going."

"How much?"

"It doesn't matter."

"Holy crap, don't be so cranky. I was just asking a friggin' simple question." She began pacing around the crowded space, blowing bubbles and flipping through his things.

"Patty, I've got to go. For the last time, what do you want?"

"Hmmph, one of these days you'll be sorry you're always snarky with me."

"Uh, huh. No doubt."

She stopped and faced him with her hands on her hips. "For your information, it wasn't my idea to come out here. Mom told me to come tell you not to come in the house because Dad's got a bitch of a hangover and he's uglier than a bull that got its balls whacked with a big stick. She says you should wait till he leaves before you come in. He's got to work tonight, even if he's sick as a dog." She looked up and whistled. "Holy frig, he's even mad at me – like he's always with you – and just because Mom told him I went out looking for him. I just didn't want him to wreck the car so's I'd to be able to drive it when I get my license. But he was really pissed off at Mom."

"I heard about it. Thanks for letting me know."

"You owe me."

"Uh, huh."

She sat next to him. "Will you teach me how to drive?"

"Maybe. I'd have to get a car license. I only have a bike license."

Her eyes brightened. "You could teach me to ride your bike."

He smiled and shook his head. "I don't think so. We'll try for the car. If Sid lets me use it – which I doubt."

She crossed her arms. "I could ride a friggin' bike like that. Least as good as you can." She paused. "Maybe you could introduce me to your friends and one of them could teach me."

"That wouldn't be a good idea."

"Why not? I could join up and be one of them Dark Angels."

"Girls aren't allowed to be members."

"What! Why figgin' not?"

"Just the rules. I didn't make them."

She jumped up. "Shit. I can never do anything I want. And you're always so mean to me. I don't know why those cool guys let a dork like you join that gang anyway. There's nothing cool about you. You were a friggin' dork when you were little and you're still a dork – a *mean* dork."

"I know. It's a mystery to me, too, why they let me in."

"Smartass. I shouldn't have told you about Dad being ugly. I should've let you come in. I'd love to see him kick your ass. You deserve it." She stormed out, slamming the door behind her.

Will rifled through his bureau drawers and tossed a clean change of clothes onto his cot. He inched the side door of the garage open and studied the back of the house. He saw Sid through the kitchen window, moving in and out of view, dressed in his uniform. He turned off the garage lights and sat back down on his cot – waiting and listening.

Ten minutes passed. Fifteen. Twenty.

He heard Sid storm out of the house, cursing under his breath. "You in there?" he called, as he stomped toward his car.

Will said nothing.

"Hey – in the shed! Hey, you. Stupid!" He paused. "What'd I tell you about leaving this piece of junk parked in the middle of my driveway? Get it the Christ out of the way before I get home."

Will heard Sid open the car door and then slam it shut. He heard him start and gun the motor, then grind the transmission into reverse and spin the tires in the gravel as he backed out of the driveway. He took a deep breath, grabbed his clean clothes and went into the house.

He called from the kitchen for his mother, but there was no answer. He glanced in her bedroom, but she was not there.

He went into the bathroom and jumped into the shower. The steaming spray stung his face and chest like a thousand pin-pricks, reviving his body, reawakening his senses and making him smile within seconds. When he finished, he dressed and gathered up his dirty clothes. He found Patty sitting on the kitchen counter as he came out of the bathroom.

"If you're looking for Mom, she went up to Danny's restaurant," she said, drumming her fingers on the countertop. "To get the hell away from Dad." She pointed at a plate covered with tinfoil. "That's supper. She left it for you."

"Thanks." He took the plate and sat at the table.

"Want a knife and fork, or are you going to eat that meat and potatoes with your hands?" She slid open the drawer next to her leg and dug out the cutlery.

"Don't throw them!" Will said, standing up and holding out his hand to her.

She raised her eyebrows. "I'm not *that* immature, in case you didn't notice."

He smiled and began to cut into the fried ham on his plate.

She hopped off the counter and pulled out a chair across from him. She sat on the caned seat, placed her elbows on the table and cupped her chin in her hands with a dramatic flair. She sighed. "I guess I forgive you."

"Thanks. For what?"

"For being mean and snotty to me."

"All right. Sorry."

"And I'm sorry I called you a dork. I mean, you still are a little bit dorkey. It's just the truth, so that's not being mean, right? It's just saying what's true." She twisted the hair hanging straight to her shoulders tightly around her fingers. "But I guess you're cooler than you used to be – just no way as cool as your friends."

He laughed. "Yeah, I know. I'm working on it."

She sighed again. "I'm bored. Wanna watch TV later? I think *Get Smart* is on."

"Sorry. I'd like to, but I've got to meet the guys and pick up my pay." He got up and put his plate in the sink. "Maybe Mom will be back soon and you can hang out with her."

"She's no fun." She slumped in her chair.

He began to leave but hesitated. He reached into his pants pocket and pulled out a five dollar bill. "Tell you what, if you clean up my dishes, I'll give you five bucks to go to the movies. I think *Easy Rider*'s playing at the Oxford. You'd probably like that movie."

She shrugged. "I suppose. Better than nothing."

She snatched the bill from his fingers and turned to the phone on the countertop. "As long as I can find somebody to go with."

Will turned onto Granville Street. Cars and bikes lined the street in front of the clubhouse. He parked his bike in place at the end of the row of bikes and bounced into the building. He hugged each Dark Angels member he encountered and slapped palms with other friends and acquaintances. Laughing, he backed into Stumpy, who stood in a circle, drinking beer with Frenchy Jack, Frantic, and some others.

Stumpy turned and looked at him. "What're you so happy about?"

Will shrugged. "I don't know. Nothing. Just in a good mood."

"Ah *oui, salut, mon fils*," Frenchy Jack said, moving in next to Will and slapping him on the back. "Jacques happy, *aussi*. Mildred, she say you boy make good painting today. She like all you boy. Make you food, eh?" He reached into his pocket and pulled out his money roll. "Jacques make pay for you, *oui*? No forget." He began peeling off bills, handing them to Will. "*Cinq, deux, deux, deux. C'est ça – onze.* Okay?"

Will nodded. "Thanks." He slipped the bills into his pocket.

Stumpy furrowed his brow. "Where you been anyway? We were just sayin' that we'd better go lookin' for you."

"Just fell asleep at home." He shook his head, smiling. "Jeez, you're as bad as my mother. Got to know my every move."

Stumpy growled and slugged back a gulp of beer. "You'll be lookin' for me to save your ass before this is over."

Will smiled at Stumpy and shook his head. He made his way down the hall. Weaving his way through the crowd, he went past the kitchen and into the living room. There, he found Shotgun, Kay, and a few others standing together eating pizza.

"Sorry, lover boy, she can't be here tonight," Kay said to him. "She had to work. Bite of Pizza?" She held her slice out to him.

"No thanks."

"Lover boy?" Shotgun said, grinning at Will. "You two got something going? That didn't take long."

Kay elbowed Shotgun. "I told you before, stop teasing him about things like that. He's a sweetheart and I think they make a cute couple." She puckered her lips and blew a kiss in Will's direction.

Will shook his head. "I don't know what you're talking about. We're not a couple. I don't even know if she'll want to see me again."

"Well, *I* know," Kay said. "And I think you can count on it. She told me all about your bike ride and everything else. She likes you a lot."

"Ohhh, and everything else," Shotgun teased. "That calls for a beer." He pushed past Will, whistling on his way to the kitchen.

"Don't get too excited," Will called after him. "There was no everything else."

Shotgun glanced back. "That's nothing to be proud of, stupid."

Before Shotgun returned with the beer, Speedy rushed into the room followed by Stumpy.

"Where's Barry?" Speedy blurted out, approaching Will.

Shotgun pointed at Barry, standing off to one side in the middle of a group of girls. Speedy darted off toward him.

"What's up?" Shotgun called to him.

"Trouble," Stumpy said, slowing to a stop next to them. "Big trouble, looks like. Floyd's out front parkin' his car. He just told us there's a big bunch of them Devil's Claw guys a couple streets up lookin' for trouble."

"Devil's Chain," Shotgun said.

"What's the fuckin' difference? Devil's Claw, Chain, fuckin' Devil's Dick. Don't make no difference. Floyd says they're gearin' up to whomp us."

Floyd barrelled up the hallway, nudging people aside and pulling on the end of his pointed black goatee. He jerked to a stop facing them, breathless and wheezing.

"Gimme a second," he said, clutching his belly and bending at the waist. "Speedy tell you what's going on?"

"A little," Barry said. "What did you see exactly?"

"Just a sec," Floyd said, taking a tight, raspy breath.

"Jesus, Floyd, you only ran half a block from your car. You can't be that wore out," Speedy said.

"It's my asthma. The air's changing. It's acting up again."

"Hurry the fuck up, Floyd," Frantic said. "It's not your asthma, it's that 300-pound bag-of-guts you call a body."

"Okay, okay. Whoa – so there's a bunch of them up on Argyle Street. Devil's Chain guys and all kinds of greasers and punks. I don't know, I'd guess maybe 30 or 40 guys. Some bikes but most of them in cars and trucks. I got a call about an hour ago from their head guy – Sloper is what he goes by. I dealt with him before. Cool dude. So he wants me to deliver some grass and crystal meth." He took another breath. "I told him he'd have to pay top dollar, no breaks, because I don't deal out in the open like that. Was okay with him. Said he really needed it to get all his guys fired up." He looked up at Barry and Stumpy. "Looks like they mean business – flashing knives and chains. One guy popped his trunk and showed me a pile of steel pipes and baseball bats. Asked me if I wanted to come along and watch the show. I said, 'What show?' He said, 'We're gonna exterminate some angel rats, run that scum into the harbour'. I told him I had to run to do another deal over at Uniacke Square." He shook his head. "That's about it."

"What do you want to do, Barry?" Frantic asked.

Barry looked around the room. "Gimme a minute to think." He threaded his fingers through his hair and walked in a circle around the group. "So what's their move?" he muttered. He stopped and grabbed Stumpy's arm. "Come with me." He dragged Stumpy to an empty corner at the back of the clubhouse.

"Are we just gonna sit here and wait?" Speedy asked. "It'll look like we're scared if we don't do something. Could hit them hard right up front – whatever."

"Sounds right to me," Frantic said. "We're already one up on them. We know what they're up to. Might not take much. A few rounds here or there."

Shotgun shook his head. "Now's the time to be smart and not go flying off feeling provoked and crazy. Think about it. The ball's in their court.

What're they gonna do if we don't go chasing them? Bust in here?" He drew his finger across his throat. "I don't think so."

Stumpy barged into the middle of the room, creating space for Barry. Stumpy clapped his hands together, the sound piercing the jammed room "**SHUT UP!**" he shouted.

"Looks like there's going to be trouble," Barry said. "We got news the Devil's Chain are coming our way. So if any of you are allergic to senseless violence, you might want to push off and go get high somewhere else."

"Look at 'em go," Stumpy said, as the hangers-on and girlfriends scrambled to grab whatever they brought with them and hustle toward the front door. Brandishing their weapons, the Dark Angels congregated around Barry and Stumpy.

"Keep all that shit out of sight for now," Stumpy said. "It ain't show 'n tell time yet."

"Frantic, you and Shotgun take – let me see – Speedy and Will and go out front," Barry said. "Keep an eye out to see what happens." He paused. "Stumpy, you take four or five guys up the hall. Your job is to man the door and keep in contact with Frantic and the guys out front. I'll get the rest of the guys in place to charge out – if that's what it seems like we need to do. We might have to improvise, depending on what their play is."

Will and Shotgun repositioned the bikes out front so they were all parked close to the front of the clubhouse. Frantic and Speedy walked in opposite directions about a hundred feet up the sidewalk, looking around and tilting their heads, listening for telltale sounds of approaching trouble. A few minutes later, they rejoined Will and Shotgun near the front door of the clubhouse,

"Hey, Frantic," Stumpy said, standing in the open doorway. "You and Will stand on the step there." He pointed to the bottom granite step. "You go there on the right, and Will, you go over on the left. Shotgun, Speedy – you guys come up here on the top step." He reached out and moved Shotgun into place, a little to the right of the door, and Speedy a little to the left. "Okay, just stay there and keep your eyes peeled." He backed inside the clubhouse and closed the door.

Will and the others stood motionless on the steps. The dull life-beat of the downtown waterfront throbbed in their ears. The smell of pizza and deep-fried food snuck up on them in the breeze. A few cars slowed, drivers gawking at them standing at attention like hired muscle outside a bar.

Speedy's head and shoulders began to twitch. He started to shuffle his feet. "What're they waiting for?"

Frantic shrugged. "How am I supposed to know?"

Speedy blew out a loud breath and sat down on the step. "This is stupid."

Frantic followed, sitting down and resting his elbows on his knees. He looked back at Shotgun. "What're we supposed to be doing here anyway? Are we supposed to be standing guard or scouting things out, or what?"

"It's not that complicated," Shotgun said. "Just keep an eye out. Be patient. It's like fishing or torqueing a nut. You don't force it – you do it easy and let things move into place."

Frantic glared at him. "Did I just hear you tell me to be patient? Did you really say that to me?" He jumped up. "That's the same as telling me to relax." He stepped down onto the sidewalk. "You fools can stand there like dummies if you want but I'm goin' up around the corner to check things out."

"I'll go with ya," Speedy said.

Shotgun shrugged. "Suit yourself. We'll be here. Give us a shout if you get into shit."

Will and Shotgun watched Frantic and Speedy walk south down Granville Street and then turn right at the first corner to head up George Street.

Will looked up at the black sky. He felt at his waist, tapping the handle of his gun with his fingertips.

"Something's up," Shotgun said, pointing to his right.

Will looked over to see Frantic and Speedy scooting around the corner side by side, hurrying back with quick, heavy-heeled steps.

"What'd you see?" Shotgun asked, as they jumped back up on the steps, returning to their places.

"It's weird," Frantic said. "Looks like two of them coming this way – one with a chain, I think."

"Walkin' in slow motion. Like they're zombies," Speedy said. "Maybe they're not coming here."

"Shit, there they are," Frantic whispered, nodding in the direction of the corner.

Two figures rounded the corner at George Street. With slow, stiff steps, they began inching their way down the sidewalk toward the clubhouse.

Shotgun banged on the door – three loud thumps reverberating against the thick wood. Moments later, Stumpy opened the door wide enough to stick his head out. "What?"

"Two guys coming. Devil's Chain, maybe."

CHAIN REACTION

STUMPY OPENED THE DOOR AND stepped onto the top step between Shotgun and Speedy. He craned his neck to get a better view of the two approaching men.

"That's it? Where's the rest of them?"

Frantic shot a disdainful look back at him. "How the fuck are we supposed to know?"

"Okay, just get ready," Stumpy said. He backed inside the clubhouse and began to close the door.

"Ready for what?" Speedy asked.

Stumpy shrugged. "How do I know? Get ready for anything." He closed and locked the door.

Step-by-calculated-step, the two men inched closer to the front of the clubhouse. As they came under the glare of a streetlight, Will was able to see them – a bigger man in front with a motorcycle drive chain hanging limp in his right hand next to his leg, and a smaller man trailing about ten feet behind. They wore denim cut-off jackets, but their hair was short and their faces clean-shaven.

"Don't look like bikers to me," Frantic whispered to the others.

"Greaser punks," Shotgun said. "Cranked and wound up by the Devil's Chain to make a name for themselves or feel us out. Either way, stupid for them."

The two men continued to approach, keeping their eyes on the Dark Angels standing on the steps. When they were about 20 feet away, the bigger man stopped and pointed. "Look at this – the big bad Dark Angels." He laughed and looked back at the smaller man still lagging behind. He took a few more steps forward. "You four sure are a bunch of pansy-lookin' retards, now aren't ya? Where's the rest of your faggot friends hiding?"

Will looked across at Frantic and they both looked back at Shotgun and Speedy.

Shotgun shook his head. "Nuts or stoned," he whispered. They scanned the streets behind the men and looked to their left in the opposite direction, but there was no one else to be seen.

The two men now took one step at a time as they closed the final few feet to the front of the clubhouse – the larger man a few feet from Frantic and the smaller one still some ten feet behind.

The bigger man turned his back toward the Dark Angels and pointed over his shoulder at the crests on his back. "See this," he said, craning his neck to glimpse Frantic and the others over his left shoulder. "This means we can go anywhere we want, anytime we want in this fuckin' city." He turned back to face them. "And there's nothin' you can do about it. We got a freakin' army behind us – an army!" He looked down, shifted his weight and spat on the sidewalk. "See this sidewalk. It's ours now. We're gonna walk down it and there's not a damn thing you can do about it." He glanced over at the bikes. "And if we feel like it, we'll take a piss on them bikes. That's the kind of shit you fuckers like to do, right?"

He moved a few more feet to the side until he was standing facing Will. He glanced up at Will and then looked over at Frantic. He raised the chain in his right hand and grinned. "Like I said – *our* sidewalk."

Will glanced over at Frantic, whose dumfounded expression gave no sign as to what might happen next. He looked down at the man facing him, who now turned his gaze up to meet his. They stood frozen in place, neither moving, neither speaking – locked in a void embrace of no turning back, no backing down – on the precipice of an unknown darkness. Will stared into the man's eyes, the man with the Pompadour-style black hair that smelled of Brylcreem – the hair that looked and smelled just like Sid's.

The man leaned back and swung his chain with the full force of his body, cracking Will hard on the left arm and shoulder. He felt his body jolt backwards from its force. He stared into the man's eyes and saw nothing there – nothing but a vacant craziness. The man's sweat of arrogance, the stench of his malevolence and stupidity assaulted him more than the chain. He saw that the eyes of the man who now stood in front of him – waiting, looking for a reaction – were brown. Like Sid's.

Time slowed. He felt no pain, no fear, no anger. His mind became empty – no thoughts or emotions. No words formed in his mind. No voice whispered to him, telling him what to do or what not to do — nothing. He reached across his body and casually took his gun from his belt. He aimed it down at the man, at the middle of his chest, and squeezed the trigger. **BLAM**! The sound exploded with a bright flash from the gun's muzzle, echoing in an instant off the buildings and up and down the street. The man's body jerked back and he dropped the chain from his right hand. As from a distant shore, Will heard a soft cascading thud, as the chain crumpled onto the sidewalk.

"Awww, you're shooting blanks," the smaller man said, his words sounding more like a plea than a taunt.

Will pointed his gun at him and squeezed the trigger – **BLAM** – hitting him in the left side.

At the same time, Frantic whipped out his Magnum and fired six quick shots – **BLAM, BLAM, BLAM, BLAM, BLAM, BLAM** – around the feet of the smaller man, blasting up a shower of pulverized cement chips and concrete powder from the sidewalk.

"When's the last time you saw blanks do that?" Frantic asked.

The two men stumbled against one another and turned to hobble away from the clubhouse, heading back toward George Street.

The clubhouse door flew open and Barry, Stumpy, and the other Dark Angels spilled out around Will and the others on the steps.

"Holy Jesus! What happened?" Barry asked, swivelling his head wildly from left to right.

"Sorry, Barry," Frantic said. "We shot up a couple of those Devil's Chain guys." He pointed at the two men nearing George Street. "There they go."

Barry squinted in their direction. "How the hell are they still walking? We heard a lot of shots."

Frantic nodded toward Will. "It was only the .32. He – um – it was Will who looked after business." He opened his eyes wide and smiled. "Mine were for the hell of it, I guess."

Barry and Stumpy looked at one another, then at Will. "*You* shot them?" Barry asked, his eyes big as silver dollars.

"He hit me with a chain." Will paused. Looking down, he pointed at the crumpled chain at their feet on the sidewalk. "All I had was the gun. I just reacted."

"Don't worry about it," Frantic said. "They were way out of line."

"Asking for it," Speedy added. "What the fuck did they think would happen?"

"Okay," Barry said, shrugging. He turned and strode into the clubhouse.

Stumpy shepherded all the others back inside and barricaded the door. He remained there with Will and Shotgun, the three of them standing shoulder to shoulder without speaking – listening and waiting – while the rest of the Dark Angels scattered throughout the clubhouse.

Moments later, they heard the wail of sirens in the distance. Barry approached Will and tapped his right arm. "Gimme me the gun. We'll get rid of it."

Will held the .32 out to him by its barrel. Barry grabbed the gun and handed it to Stumpy. "Make sure it never turns up again." Barry stepped forward and hugged Will. "I'm proud of you. We'll get you through this." He glanced over at Shotgun. "Keep him close to you."

Shotgun nodded.

"I'm okay, Barry," Will said. "I don't need anybody to look after me."

"Yeah, you do," Shotgun said. "Before this night's over you're going to be the hottest property in the city. The Devil's Chain and the cops are going to be fighting over who gets to you first."

The sirens got closer, and closer, growing more urgent with each passing second – howling and reverberating through the deserted harbour-front streets like wailing banshees on cocaine. The inside of the clubhouse was as quiet as a crypt when the police cars screeched to a stop out front and the sirens wound down, the whirring still resounding between the buildings. The Dark Angels heard police scrambling outside, yelling to one another and talking over their radios. They heard them pound on the clubhouse door and felt the door shake. Inside, Stumpy and half a dozen others pressed their bodies against the door as the police ran up the steps in force and threw their bodies against the thick wood, resulting in a loud, jolting thud that rippled through the buildings timbers.

Then, it all stopped. They heard car doors slamming and cars screeching away with sirens again howling.

Stumpy opened the door a hair's width and pasted his eye to the sliver of exposed light from the street. "Think they're gone," he said. He opened the door wide enough to stick his head out and look in all directions. "Yup, gone. Sounds like they're up around the corner."

Barry pushed past him to get outside. "What the fuck? Why'd they take off?" He paced around on the sidewalk and plucked a cigarette from his pocket. He lit it with his lighter and took two quick puffs, sucking hard and deep and blowing out big clouds of smoke. The others joined him outside. He waved Frantic over.

"Is Floyd still here?"

Frantic nodded. "Think so. Last I saw, he was hiding in the back bathroom."

"Go tell him to drive up around there and see what's going on." He snapped his fingers. "Fast. I've got a feeling we haven't got much time."

Frantic disappeared into the clubhouse and emerged seconds later, dragging Floyd by the arm.

"Make it fast, Floyd," Barry said, as Frantic pushed him forward. "We want to see you back here before anybody else shows up."

Floyd nodded, gasping for breath as he scrambled toward his black Chevrolet Caprice. He flung himself into his car and roared away.

Barry rotated his arms in big windmill circles, directing everyone back into the clubhouse. "No sense hanging out here like sitting ducks," he called out. "Will, Frantic, Speedy, Shotgun – get ready to go."

Barry and Stumpy remained at the door, holding it ajar and taking turns looking out. Will, Frantic, Speedy, and Shotgun stood behind them in single-file, leaning against the wall. Minutes later, Floyd's Caprice swerved into view, screeching to a halt in front of the clubhouse.

"You four stay put," Barry said. He bounded down the steps followed by Stumpy.

Floyd stuck his head out the driver's side window. "You got a few minutes maybe. The cops are up on Argyle Street rounding up the Devil's Chain guys. Ambulance people are there. Two dudes down on the street. Don't look good for them." He took a few quick breaths. "I talked to some kid who saw the whole thing. Said it looked like the cops thought the Devil's Chain guys had shot the dudes, so they were arresting all the ones they could get their paws on. But they were putting up a fight, saying they didn't do it. It's a real circus."

Barry dragged on his cigarette and flicked the butt into the ditch.

"Floyd, we need a safe place for our four guys. Don't know for how long – a few days maybe. We've got to see how this shapes up."

Floyd tapped the long fingernails of his fat fingers against the steering wheel. "I think I can help you out." He looked around. "Okay, listen, I got these three apartments. Use them for different parts of my business. Nobody – and I mean *nobody* – knows about them." He winked at Barry.

"We'll talk later about how we can compensate you for your trouble," Barry said, smiling. "Maybe a little muscle or firepower at some time. Something appropriate, right?"

"I always got need for services like that." Floyd grinned and looked past Barry to the doorway. "We're wasting time."

Barry waved for Will and the others.

"Go – now!" Stumpy commanded, pushing them out the front door one by one.

Will, Frantic, Speedy, and Shotgun raced from the clubhouse and climbed into Floyd's Caprice, cramming their bodies low into the seats, the echoes of gunshots and sirens still ringing in their ears. Floyd clicked the stick-shift into 'Drive' and steered the Caprice up the street. It glided forward with the quiet gracefulness of a sailboat slipping away in the night on a glassy ebony sea.

"You guys gotta promise to lay low and stay out of sight," Floyd said. "If you get busted in my place, it'll be bad for me. Lots of incriminating shit around, if you get my drift."

"Relax, Floyd," Frantic said from the back seat. "You don't gotta worry about us."

Floyd adjusted the rear-view mirror so he could see Frantic crouched low in back. He scrunched his forehead against his eyebrows. "You're kidding me, right? You, of all people. If you were me, would you be able to relax about this."

Frantic laughed. "Christ, Floyd, if I was you, I'd be fuckin' committing suicide, then I'd be really relaxed."

Floyd reached and deflected the mirror upward and looked straight ahead. "Yeah, well, just don't forget who's doing who the favour here."

Two quick turns later, he was headed north on Barrington Street, putting distance between the Caprice and the turmoil of the Devil's Chain – and the police. Approaching North Street, they whisked past four police cars headed in the opposite direction, their sirens wailing. Floyd turned to the left off Barrington Street at Devonshire Avenue, then slowed to a crawl as he wound his way through tree-lined side streets. He stopped in front of a three-storey red-brick apartment building – hesitating and looking across at the building. As car lights approached from the front, Floyd shielded his eyes against the glare and pulled away. Circling the block, he returned to the front of the apartment building, this time turning into a narrow driveway to the right. He turned off the car's lights before backing in tight against a vine-covered chain-link fence at the rear of the tiny parking lot.

Floyd turned off the car. "Stay here," he whispered. He slipped out of the car, disappearing up the ink-black driveway with the awkward gait and focused attention of a Komodo dragon in pursuit its prey. A few minutes later, a darkened third-floor window slid open and Floyd's head appeared. "Psssst – up here. Take the fire escape."

Will, Frantic, and the others crossed the parking lot to the back of the building and crept up the wrought-iron fire escape. One after another, they slid into Floyd's apartment through the bathroom window. Once they were all inside, Floyd shut and latched the window, closed the curtains and turned on the lights. He led them from the bathroom into the adjacent kitchen.

"There's no food here, but I think there's some beer in the fridge," he said. He walked through the kitchen into the living room, continuing to switch on lights along the way. "Schooner or Alpine, I think it is." He pointed toward a room off to the left. "Bedroom – there's one double bed in there and the couch here, so you guy's will have to figure out how you're gonna bunk up."

Frantic and Speedy plopped down onto the couch, while Will and Shotgun circled the room looking at the posters pinned on the walls.

Floyd went to the front door and double-checked the deadbolt. "One good thing about this place is there's no windows facing the street, so as long as you lay low and don't make too much noise, you should be all right." He glanced around. "Stay here for a minute." He headed back into the kitchen.

Will and the others heard him unsnapping locks and opening the kitchen cupboards. He returned with a pizza tray holding a dime bag of marijuana, some cigarette papers, a small pill bottle filled with white powder, and a hypodermic syringe. He placed the tray on a low glass-topped coffee table in the middle of the floor.

"Demerol," he said, holding up the pill bottle. "I'm gonna spot you guys with all this shit, but the deal is you gotta stay out of my business. No snooping around." He paused looking at each of them. "We cool about this?"

"It's all cool," Shotgun said.

"Man, I hope so. My neck's way out there on this one." Floyd shook his head. "I'll have to talk to Barry to figure out what he wants to do about feeding you. Probably get one of my delivery guys to bring something up. Don't want too much traffic coming here." He gestured toward a wall phone. "I'll call ahead of time. Otherwise, don't open the door for no one."

He walked to the front door and leaned against it. "What else?" He stared at them, clicking the points of his fingernails against the hardwood door. He shrugged. "Can't think of anything. You?"

"Food," Frantic said, getting up from the couch and moving forward to kneel in front of the coffee table. "Don't forget the food. Like tonight, right?"

"Might take a while."

Frantic nodded and reached for the bottle containing the Demerol. "Got a spoon?"

Floyd laughed. "Yeah, all kinds of utensils and pots and pans. Stove works, too. Just never used any of it for cooking food." He unlocked the door, opened it and peeked into the hallway before stepping out. "Oh yeah, TV works, too. But keep it low."

Frantic and the others shared the syringe to shoot up most of the Demerol. By the time Speedy switched on the 13-inch black-and-white TV that sat on a steamer trunk across from the couch, they had guzzled their way through half of Floyd's beer. Speedy moved the rabbit ears around, trying to erase the fuzziness and sharpen the grainy images.

"Shh! Listen," Shotgun piped up. "I think it's about us! Turn it up."

Speedy found the volume knob and twisted it to the right.

"Holy shit, it's on the CBC news," Frantic said.

They all leaned toward the TV.

"Gunshots shattered the calm of a late-summer evening tonight amidst some derelict buildings in Halifax's downtown." The news reporter paused and adjusted his dark-rimmed glasses. "The Devil's Chain motorcycle

gang reportedly went looking for the Dark Angels, another gang, and –
unfortunately for the Devil's Chain – found them. Sources at the scene
report that two Devil's Chain members are in the Victoria General
Hospital in serious condition. Several more of the gang's members are in
police custody, arrested on weapons and resisting arrest charges. Police are
refusing comment on the involvement of the Dark Angels in the shooting,
saying only none of that gang has been arrested but that the investigation
is continuing."

Shotgun looked at Frantic and raised his eyebrows. "Wow."

"What? That's good, isn't it?" Speedy asked, his shoulders twitching. "I
mean, what that guy said. Sounds good for us, right?"

"Yeah – sounds good," Will said. "Couldn't have been better if we had
written it ourselves."

The telephone rang, startling them to attention. Frantic lunged toward
the phone. "Maybe it's food."

"Yeah?" he said, speaking into the phone. He was silent as he listened.
Then, he looked over at Will.

PART 4

PART 4

A PLACE IN THE COUNTRY

"WHAT'S GOING ON?" SPEEDY BLURTED out, jerking away from the TV and sending a wash of frothy beer across the soiled shag carpet. "Frantic?"

"Shh." Frantic held his hand up toward him. "Yeah, bad luck. Okay, I'll let them know."

He hung up the phone and began to tug at his hair. "Floyd said they're sending some food up soon. Uh, one other thing, those guys are in the hospital – not doing so great. The smaller one's not too bad, but they don't know if the bigger guy's gonna make it." He scratched at his chin whiskers and looked at Will. "Guess I should've given you an even-smaller gun."

Will swallowed. "That's not good, is it?"

Frantic shook his head. "Not usually. There'll be more pressure on the cops for sure. And if you get arrested, yeah, it's a different ball game. But ..." He shrugged. "But, if you think about it, it's one less witness. It'll all depend on what other evidence they got."

At that moment, they heard a tentative tapping at the door. They froze in place, looking at one another.

"Floyd sent me," a voice on the other side whispered.

Shotgun eased the door open and a man with an acne-scarred face stepped in, struggling to carry two large pizza boxes and a case of Ten-Penny. He stopped short, almost falling over, as his eyes fell on Frantic.

"It's okay, man. We're all cool here, right?" Floyd's man said.

"Are we?" Frantic asked.

Will and the others glanced over to see Frantic still standing next to the phone, with a gun trained on the man.

"Cool as hell," the man said, bending at the waist and placing the pizza boxes and beer on the floor. He straightened up again and adjusted the Yankees baseball cap that covered his scraggly blond hair.

Frantic laughed.

"Where'd you get that thing?" Shotgun asked Frantic. "I thought you ditched your gun at the clubhouse."

"Did you hear that idiot?" Frantic said, ignoring Shotgun and waving his gun at the man. "Cool as hell? Hell ain't cool, man. It's hot." He paused. "You nervous or something? What're you so nervous about?"

"Uh, because you're pointing a big fucking gun at me?"

Frantic glanced over at Shotgun. "This is my back-up Magnum," He tilted it to the right and spun the barrel with his thumb. "You didn't really think I'd be doing this hide-out shit without a gun, did you?" He again looked at the man. "What's your name?"

"John."

"John what?"

"John Boudreau."

Frantic cocked the gun and aimed it at him. "John, if anybody finds us here, you know you're a dead man." He paused. "You know that – right, John Boudreau?"

"Right on, I do."

Frantic smiled. He lowered and uncocked his gun. "I like that hat you got there, John Boudreau."

"It's the real deal," Boudreau said, exhaling hard with a whistle. He took the cap off his head. "Got it on a run to New York picking up some merchandise for Floyd." He tossed it to Frantic.

Frantic pulled it on his head. "How does it look?"

"Like a cool hat on a dunce's head," Shotgun said.

"Anything you guys want me to tell Floyd?" Boudreau asked, inching back toward the door.

"Yeah, tell him and Barry not to leave us here long," Speedy said. "I get cabin fever real quick." He hardly had the words out before the door clicked shut behind Boudreau.

Will pulled himself from the couch in the morning. His head was heavy and felt like it was filled with glue. Stumbling to the bathroom, he saw Frantic and Shotgun out cold on the bed in the bedroom and Speedy flaked out on the carpeted floor, with a plaid throw-cushion under his head.

As Will returned from the bathroom, Speedy groaned, sat up and looked around. "Hey, we were supposed to switch places halfway through the night."

"Not my fault. I tried to wake you up, but you just snorted and told me to go to hell."

"Yeah, sure."

"It's true. Wouldn't have mattered to me. I couldn't sleep anyway."

Speedy laughed. "Serves you right. I slept like a log. Love that Demerol and beer."

They heard Frantic and Shotgun stirring in the bedroom.

"What time is it?" Frantic asked, as he and Shotgun dragged themselves into the kitchen. Frantic slumped onto one of the kitchen chairs and looked down at his hands. "Okay, so what the fuck are we supposed to do now?"

"Must still be morning," Shotgun said. "Feels like it anyway."

"There ain't even anything to eat," Speedy said.

Shotgun opened the refrigerator. "Still four cold Schooner left."

"Gimme one," Frantic said, gesturing for Speedy to toss him a bottle.

The others nodded, and Shotgun snapped off the caps on a wall-mounted opener next to the refrigerator and passed the beer around.

Frantic took a long, loud gulp. "I've had worse for breakfast." He began to wipe beer from his beard – then froze. He waved at the others to get their attention, bringing his finger to his pursed lips. He looked toward the door and tapped a finger to his left ear.

The others stiffened, motionless in their places.

Hearing the unmistakable sound of a key being inserted into the lock, they flung themselves against the wall next to the kitchen doorway. Frantic pulled his gun from the waist of his tattered jeans and cocked it. The door squeaked open and the bikers readied themselves. They heard slow footfalls on the shag carpet.

"Where the hell are they?" someone asked.

"HEY, you guys here?" another voice called out.

"Floyd," Frantic mouthed in silence to the others. He jumped into the middle of the doorway, flung his gun out and screamed, "BANG!"

Floyd screamed and fell backward, sending Barry flat on his ass behind him.

"Holy Jesus!" Floyd said. "Why'd you do that?"

Will, Shotgun, and Speedy pushed Frantic into the living room.

"You pervert, Floyd – you screech just like a little girl," Shotgun said, the words tumbling out on laughter.

Barry popped to his feet, an exaggerated scowl etched on his face. "Real funny."

"Stupid move on your part," Frantic said. "Lucky you didn't get drilled." He slid the gun back into his jeans. "You were supposed to call first, Floyd. Remember?"

"Yeah, yeah – you're right. Slipped my mind. Me and Barry been running around all night for you guys. You ought to show a little appreciation."

"Well, I didn't shoot you, did I?"

"Okay, enough of that," Barry said. "You want to know the score or not?" He paused, staring at them. "Looks like both those guys are going to make it. They said it was touch and go for one guy through the night, but he improved a little this morning. He's still unconscious, but the other guy fingered the four of you. Now the cops are leaning hard on everybody. Trying to get somebody to rat you out."

"We think you're still okay here for a few more hours," Floyd said. "But I wouldn't want to push it past that."

"I called our lawyer, Dedrick, last night," Barry continued. "He called me back just before we left to come here. They already got warrants for all four of you, but they got Will pegged as the main shooter. Dedrick's trying to get a feel for what kind of evidence they got. So, for now, we still have to lay low."

"I ain't gonna lay low here for long, Barry," Frantic said. "This place is as bad as jail. I'd just as soon take my chances being out on the go."

"I'm with him," Speedy said.

"I'm working on another place right now – a place in the country," Barry said. "Way outta sight. You have to hang tight for a few more hours. Right now's the most important time in all this." He paused and thrust his finger at Frantic. "Don't screw it up by flying off like some dimwit."

Frantic looked away.

"What about breakfast? Can we at least get some freakin' food?" Speedy asked.

Barry crossed his arms. "Do I look like a waiter or an errand boy? Tell Floyd what you want his boys to bring."

Floyd fished in the pockets of his suede jacket and pulled out a small notepad and a ballpoint pen. He passed them to Speedy. "Write down what you want. I'll see you get it." He grinned and twirled the point of his goatee between his thumb and fingers. "You boys are gonna have a pretty big tab to clear up by the time this is over."

Speedy grabbed the pen and pad and sat down at the kitchen table to write. "I want some eggs and bacon, and some bread. You know, regular groceries." He glanced over at Will.

"I can eat anything," Will said. "Doesn't really matter."

Speedy looked at him. "Jesus, this isn't that hard. Friggin' pick something."

Will hesitated. "Well, okay, if we can ask for whatever we want, put me down for some fresh peaches. They should be out now. My grandfather used to work in the Annapolis Valley years ago picking them."

Speedy shook his head, a disgusted look on his face "I'm not gonna write down fuckin' peaches for a fuckin' one-percenter shopping list. Let alone I don't know how to spell it."

"Coffee and milk," Shotgun said. "And peanut butter to go with that bread."

"How about some potatoes and steak?" Frantic joined in, his eyes getting big. "Man, I ain't had meat and potatoes for ages. And some of them cookies like Mildred gave us," he added. "I loved them things."

"How do you spell potatoes?" Speedy asked.

Barry reached down and snatched the notepad away from him. "You guys are nuts. You're only going to be here a few more hours. We'll bring you some hamburgers and Coke. Maybe some more beer."

"That Demerol was the cat's ass," Shotgun said. "More of that would be nice – and a clean needle."

A half hour later, John Boudreau arrived at the apartment with a dozen hamburgers and a case of Ten-Penny. Before they had finished eating, Floyd arrived again. He passed out rain jackets with large hoods, then hustled them out of the apartment and into a Casino taxi waiting at the curb.

"Leave the hoods up 'till we're out of the city," Floyd said, as the taxi pulled away.

"That's kind of stupid, Floyd," Shotgun said. "It's not even raining out and it's, what, two in the afternoon? That'll attract more attention than Frantic's rat's-nest head."

"Jesus, I just know I'm gonna end up getting busted with the rest of you," Floyd said, shaking his head and scanning the streets in all directions. "Well, stay as low as you can. And, if we get stopped, I don't know you. We just got picked up in the same cab."

"Wow. That's original, you bonehead," Frantic said. "You sure do look like an innocent bystander."

While Floyd's head swivelled around constantly, Boudreau drove west out of the city, continuing on to the Bedford Highway. Slumped low in the back seat so close together they could hardly breathe, Will and the others bantered back and forth.

"Where the hell are we going, anyway?" Shotgun asked, as they passed through Sunnyside and continued on toward Lower Sackville.

Floyd put his arm over the back of the seat and turned toward him. "Some place you know. In the Rawdon Hills." He paused. "Old guy with a farm."

"Al's place?" Shotgun asked, screwing up his face. "I should've known."

Floyd grinned and nodded.

"Who's Al?" Will asked.

"Kay's old man," Shotgun said. "He's a cool old character. Does he know what's gone down, Floyd?"

Floyed chuckled. "You're kidding, right? Everybody in freakin' Nova Scotia – probably even Canada – knows what's gone down. Nothing like a biker war and some shootings to juice up the news."

Moments later, Boudreau pulled onto the shoulder of the road and hopped out of the car. He reached across the roof and removed the Casino sign, anchored in place by four suction cups. "Not something we want there now," he said, jumping back into the cab. "Stands out once you're in the country."

Frantic eyed the back of Bourdeau's head, then shifted his gaze to Floyd. "We're puttin' our trust in you to get us where we're supposed to be goin', Floyd." He leaned forward. "And I'm not the trusting type. You hear me, Floyd?"

Floyd took a shallow raspy breath. "Jeez, I'm in this as much as you criminals – accessory and all that. Worst of this little run is over. We're out of the city now."

Will felt his eyes becoming heavy as Boudreau drove on. He noticed a sign on the side of the road that said Mount Uniacke. Soon, he couldn't focus on anything without it becoming blurry. The air in the car was warm and stuffy. The smell of stale beer, of clothes worn too long, and of men's bodies unwashed and crammed together made him turn his face toward the door, hoping for a whiff of fresher air. He looked skyward and saw nothing but layered grey clouds. Heard only the thrumming lull of the car covering ground.

Frantic pushed him, jarring him awake. "I don't care if you sleep, man. But you can't be leaning on me like that. It's not cool."

Will straightened. "Sorry." He fought to keep his eyes open, leaning his head against the side widow. He watched the countryside stream by, rising and falling as the car crested and descended the swelling hills – fields and woodlands, beginning to look more like early fall than late summer, the occasional farm, marshes and bogs, a river.

"Be there in about ten minutes," Floyd said.

Under the same grey sky, Halifax Police detectives Frank Garrity and Jim Akerman neared the North Common, scanning civic addresses from their cruiser. Akerman, in the passenger seat, glanced down at his notepad and tapped his pen against his window.

"That's it there," he said, pointing at Sadie's Lodge.

"Big place. Looks pretty posh," Garrity said.

"Kid's mother owns it and runs it, far as we can tell. Apparently, an old lady willed it to her. Some Sadie woman from Lebanon." Akerman ran his finger down the scribbled notes on his pad. "Kid's old man works as a security guard at the Halifax Shopping Centre. Got kicked out of the army a few years ago. Got a younger sister. Nobody else there except the roomers."

Garrity slowed to a stop in front of the house. They sat in the car, looking up at it. "Nice leaded glass in that front door," Garrity said.

Akerman nodded. "Lots of windows like that in this part of town. Used to make it here in the city before the Halifax Explosion. Made it in a big place in the north end. All got wiped out in the 1917 explosion. Never reopened – far as I know."

"Well, aren't you just a Goddamn walking *Encyclopedia Britannica*," Garrity said, smirking at his partner.

Garrity turned the car off. He bent toward Akerman, looking up at the front of the house through the passenger window. He drummed the fingers of his right hand against his thigh. "You realize we got next to nothing, Jim."

"Yeah."

"No guns, slugs, casings – no physical evidence. No witnesses. Just holes in a couple of drunken punks who went looking for trouble. That one that almost died – what was his blood alcohol level? Twice the limit or something like that?"

"Yeah – more than twice."

Garrity sucked air in between his front teeth. "Shit. No charges are going to stick. I don't know how they were able to get warrants. I heard those bikers already got that hotshot Jew lawyer Dedrick working on it."

"Yeah, but they don't know what we got." Akerman tugged at each shirt sleeve with the opposite hand until the cuffs jutted out below the sleeves of his tweed jacket. "If we can get our hands on any one of them – especially that young kid – we might be able to shake out some information or a confession. It happens. I mean, under the right circumstances, of course." He grinned. "Let's lay it heavy on his old lady. See what happens."

Garrity shrugged. "Worth a try." He opened his door and put his foot on the pavement. "But still feels like a fishing expedition to me."

Garrity and Akerman crossed the sidewalk and climbed the wide brick steps that led up to the verandah and the front door. With stubby fingers attached to his thick hands, Garrity smoothed back the wisps of black hair that grew around the sides of his bald head. He pulled in his belly and buttoned his navy blazer, bulging out in layers around his torso. Akerman looked down his bony nose at him and snickered. He brushed dandruff off Garrity's shoulders with his rakish fingers. "No wonder they call us Abbott and Costello," he muttered. "Jesus, where does this dandruff come from? You got no hair, Frank."

He stepped closer to the door and rang the bell. A few seconds later, Celeste opened the door.

THE MYSTERIES OF THE UNIVERSE

GARRITY FLASHED HIS BADGE AT Celeste. "I'm Detective Garrity, ma'am, and this is Detective Akerman. Are you Mrs. Alexander?"

Celeste wiped her hands nervously in her apron and smoothed back her hair. "I was – I mean, Alexander is my maiden name. I'm, um, I'm Celeste."

"We're here to speak with a William Alexander," Akerman said. "He lives here, doesn't he?"

"Yes, he's my son." She clasped her hands together to steady them. "Why are you here? Is he all right?"

"We think so," Garrity said. "But we need to talk to him. He could be in serious trouble, but if we can talk to him as soon as possible, we might be able to help him out."

"What kind of trouble?"

"Can we come inside, Celeste?" Garrity asked. "Is it okay if I call you Celeste?"

Celeste looked over her shoulder. She nodded. "But you'll have to be quiet. My husband's sleeping. He worked all night."

They stood in the front hall near the bottom of the stairway leading to the second floor. "What kind of trouble?" she asked again.

"Have you been watching the news?" Garrity asked.

"The news? No."

Garrity looked at Akerman, then back at her. "Um, well, two young men were shot last night. Seems there's a biker war that's broken out between the Dark Angels and another club."

Akerman flipped through his notepad. "Devil's Chain – that's what the other gang's called. It was two of them that got shot."

Celeste wiped at the tears beginning to trickle down her cheeks. "Why do you think Will might be in trouble?"

Before Garrity could answer, Akerman nudged his arm and moved his eyes past Celeste to the end of the hall. Sid stomped toward them in his boxer shorts, rubbing his eyes. "What in Christ's name is going on here?" He barged past Celeste, bumping her aside, and stopped in front of the detectives, glaring at them. "Who the hell are you?"

"I'm Frank Garrity. This is my partner, Jim Akerman," Garrity said, extending his hand to Sid.

Sid crossed his arms. "Good for you. What are you doing in my house?"

"We were just telling your wife that we need to talk to your son about the shootings last night," Akerman said. "You know – the skirmish between those two bike gangs. We think your son may be in trouble and we can probably help him out if we can talk to him."

"Hmphh, that's no surprise." He glanced at Celeste. "He's not here is he?"

She shook her head. "He didn't come home last night. But that's not unusual."

Sid looked at her. "What're you bawling about?"

"We think he's all right," Garrity said. "Word is that he got hit by a chain but wasn't hurt bad."

"My God! A chain!" Celeste said, her face suddenly blanching.

Akerman reached into his jacket pocket and pulled out a paper. "Like we said, we think he's okay, but a warrant was issued this morning for his arrest, along with three other Dark Angels. We really need to talk to him to clear this up. Do you have any idea where he might be?" He held the warrant out to her, but Sid snatched it away.

"You might as well talk to me," he said, straightening up and waving the warrant in the air. "No surprise to me. I knew it was coming to this. That little bastard's been bucking me for years. Every time I try to straighten him out, mother hen here steps in and undermines me." He turned to Celeste, the veins in his temples bulging.

She backed away trembling and lowered herself onto the lowest step of the staircase.

"Do you know where the hell he is?" Sid demanded.

She shook her head.

Sid turned back to Garrity and Akerman. "What'd the little shit do, anyway?"

"It's in the warrant," Garrity said.

"Two counts of assault with a deadly weapon, one of attempted murder," Akerman added.

Celeste gasped. "NO! They must have made a mistake." She began to weep into her hands.

"Holy shit," Sid said, brightening up. "You sure?"

Garrity glanced at Akerman. "One of the men that got shot identified your son as the shooter. The other one's still unconscious. It was close for him – shot right through the chest. A few more inches to the left …" Garrity's voice trailed off.

"So, bad as it is, it could've been a lot worse," Akerman said.

"No," Celeste said. "It couldn't have been him. It had to have been one of those other boys." She dabbed her eyes with her sleeves. "Will couldn't shoot a rabbit, let alone another human being. I've seen him pick up worms from the sidewalk and put them in the grass so they wouldn't die in the hot sun." She paused, looking at them through bleary eyes. "It couldn't have been him."

"Oh, for Christ's sake, Celeste – shut up," Sid said. "What a bunch of crap. Saying sappy things like that isn't going to help him now. If he wasn't guilty, he wouldn't be on the run – assuming he is." He turned back to the detectives. "Right?"

"Right," Garrity said.

"Or maybe he's just scared. He's how old – 18, 19?"

"Yeah, something like that," Sid said, with a sneer. "Nineteen going on 13 – if you ask me. Oh, and by the way, he's not *my* son. He's hers. Bad enough he's my stepson."

Garrity stepped around Sid and sat on the step next to Celeste. He put his hand on her forearm. "We understand how you must feel. We see this kind of thing all the time. No mother wants to hear anything like this. But it would be a whole lot better if he came in and talked to us, Celeste. We might be able to work out a deal." He winked at her. "If he's a good kid, like you say, maybe we can find a way to work with him to nail whoever's really responsible."

He reached into his breast pocket and pulled out a small billfold. He took a business card from it and held it to her. "Can you help us do that?"

"He's in with a bad crowd," Akerman said. "And sooner or later, all those characters end up in trouble, or dead. It's inevitable. So if you think of anything, like where he might be, or if he contacts you, please call us. If we can get to him soon enough, there might be chance for him."

Sid reached down and snatched the card from Celeste's fingers. "I know some of the places where he hangs out. I'll go nosing around. There's no way she's going to be any help to you."

"We'd appreciate any kind of help," Garrity said.

"Don't try to do anything yourself, though. Just call us," Akerman added. "These are dangerous men we're dealing with."

Sid pulled his shoulders back and cocked his head from side to side. "Who do you think you're talking to? Some kind of civilian jerk-off? I've been to war and back. I figure I've seen and done a whole lot more shit than either of you two – cruisin' around in that cushy dick car."

Garrity glanced at Akerman. "Right, sir," he said, rising from the step. "I don't doubt that." He and Akerman turned to leave.

"We'll be in touch if there are any developments on our end," Garrity said, as he closed the door behind them.

Once in the car, Garrity unbuttoned his jacket, leaned back into the seat and crossed his arms over his belly. Akerman again flipped through his notepad and began to scribble notes.

"What're you writing?"

Akerman shook his head. "Nothing important. Impressions, I guess. Let's see – no useful facts. Stepfather – arrogant, belligerent asshole. Mother – soft, out of touch with reality. Typical good-boy story. Same old thing."

"Like I said, we got squat to work with." Garrity started the car and tapped the steering wheel. "Unless we can get our hands on that Will kid."

Akerman looked at him. "Or *create* some useful evidence somewhere along the way."

Boudreau began to slow down just past the South Rawdon sign. "Much farther?" he asked Floyd.

"Got to be right around here."

"Second road to the left," Shotgun said, pointing. "Just after that mailbox."

Boudreau turned onto the narrow dirt road – a long driveway running between rows of high corn, leading to a farm house a quarter mile away on a hill of golden grass. Dust from the powdery soil billowed up beneath and behind the car and its suspension bottomed out over deep ruts and gearbox-sized bumps. As they neared the end of the driveway, Will saw a large man wearing a plaid shirt and bib overalls emerge from a barn across from the house and turn to face the car, his hands on his hips.

"That's Al," Shotgun said.

He didn't move as the car jerked to a stop few feet in front of him.

"Looks like an old-man version of Stumpy," Will said.

"Fuckin' hillbilly Santa Claus," Frantic said.

They all laughed as Al lumbered around toward the driver's window.

"You guys better not let him hear you," Shotgun said. "Or you'll be going to the hospital to have your heads removed from your asses."

"You in there, Buckshot?" Al asked, bending at the waist and tapping on the window. Boudreau rolled the window down and Al peered inside. "There you are, you scrawny goat. What're you all doing scrunched up in there? Get the hell out." He stood back as they pushed the doors open and crawled out stiff-legged, one after the other.

Al waved for Shotgun to come closer. "Get over here Billy Goat Buckshot and give me a hug." He laughed and pulled Shotgun to his chest, slapping him hard on the back with a bear-paw of a hand. His wispy white hair and long beard rippled as he shook his head. "Well, you boys went and got yourselves into a big pile of manure, now didn't you?" He moved from one to the next, hugging each and slapping their backs.

"Frantic, Will, Speedy, Floyd, Dave," Shotgun said, pointing at each of them in turn.

Al nodded at them. "Now, you turn around," he said to Shotgun.

"What?" Shotgun asked, looking back at the house.

"Never mind what. Turn around and face the house."

Shotgun hesitated, then turned his body to face the house. Al swung his right leg back and kicked Shotgun in the ass, exploding dust from his jeans and sending him hurtling forward into Frantic.

"There you go, Bucko. You know better than to be getting into shit if you expect to be hanging around my little girl."

Shotgun clutched his ass with both hands as the others burst out laughing. "Christ, Al, too hard! Unlike you, I'm short on ass-padding."

"He didn't really do anything wrong," Will said. "He was just there – if you know what I mean."

Al stepped up to Will and stared down his nose at him. "Yeah, that's what I heard. What'd they say your name was?"

"Will."

Al gave him another measured look. "No nickname?"

Will smiled. "Well, Will is more or less a nickname. Short for William."

Al grinned. "Will? That's it?" He shook his head. "Nothing like Gunshot here, or Animal, or Comanche, or Lucifer, or Killer? Nothing cool or scary? Just Will?"

Will shrugged.

"I suppose we could call you Will He." Al chuckled and threw his arm around Will's neck. "Like – Will He get caught or Will He get away? Will He pass me that wrench? Will He figure out the mysteries of the universe? It's like Willie, right?" He paused. "Nah, that's just weird, still not scary or cool enough, eh?"

"Most likely not," Will said.

"I tried to warn you guys about him," Shotgun said. "But, man, how do you explain somebody like that?"

Al lunged at Shotgun, laughing. Shotgun ducked out of reach behind Speedy and held him out by the shoulders toward Al. "Here – pick on somebody of your own roundness."

"We'll have some fun while you boys are here," Al said, taking a breath. "Just because you're on the run doesn't mean you have to curl up and die. Nobody'll find you here. It'll all work out. Way back in the old days when I was bootlegging booze and running smokes, there was many a time the cops were chasing me. Had some close calls, but they never did catch me."

"He used to ride an Indian," Shotgun said.

Al smiled. "Scout, 1934 Sport Scout. Best bike ever made. Better than them fat, ugly Harleys you boys ride. Mmm, mmm – what a motorcycle." He shook his head. "We'll have plenty of time to talk bikes. And I got some fine home brew." He nodded in the direction of the barn. "We'll tip some back tonight. Maybe go jack a deer. You like fried deer steak, eh Buckshot?"

Shotgun nodded. "That shine," he said to others, "Better than over-proof navy rum. It'll dissolve aluminum, I swear."

"Come on. I got a big meal on for you boys," Al said, turning toward the house. "Sausages and baked potatoes with creamed corn. None of it from a store."

"We're gonna head back now," Floyd said, turning back to the car, where Boudreau remained sitting in the driver's seat.

"Hey, you tell Barry not to forget us here," Frantic called after him. "He knows I got a short attention span."

Al bustled around the cramped kitchen, banging the cast-iron and nickel stove, clanging pots and pans and clinking dishes and utensils – the noisy hoopla of a too-big man in a too-small space. He scooped food onto plates and clunked them down onto the top of a rough pine table. "Don't be standing there drooling. Dig in. No ceremony around here when it comes to food." He leaned back against the cluttered counter and wiped his brow, smiling at them.

"You gonna eat?" Shotgun asked him.

"Not right now." He fished inside his overalls and hauled out a pipe. "I'll relax a bit and have a puff. I'll eat when you fellas are all done. You can clean up afterwards."

He pulled a pouch of tobacco from another pocket and packed his pipe. He lit up and meandered around the kitchen, puffing on the pipe and piling on more food when any plate was empty.

After supper, he gave them a tour of the house, pointing out where they could bunk down. He showed them the bathroom, tucked in a dark corner on the second floor. "Now boys, don't take offence, but you gotta introduce yourselves to this old tub, real soon. I can tell you been cooped up and wearing the same clothes for a while – if you get my drift."

"Is that copper?" Will asked, pointing at the high-sided tub.

"You bet," Al said, with pride. "Bet you never saw one like that before."

"Just in the movies."

"Well, this is the genuine article. Worth a pretty penny nowadays, I imagine. There's no shower. But I got a deep artesian well – so lots of water. My old stove heats it up lickety-split. Good thing is you boys won't have to use the same water. Can't beat that, right?"

Will, Shotgun, and the others looked at one another. "I go first," Frantic said, tapping his gun.

After they each scoured the grime and stale sweat from their bodies, they sprawled on old furniture facing the fireplace in the living room. Al knelt in front of it and struck a match. He reached into the mouth of the fireplace to light newspaper balled up under kindling and dried split hardwood already there.

"These stones were all taken from this land when it was cleared," he said, backing up to sit in a wooden rocking chair. He took a plate of food he had set down on a nearby table, placed it on his knees and began to eat.

"Looks like basalt and granite," Will said.

"What?" Al asked, wiping at his mouth with the back of his sleeve.

"The stones in your fireplace – I think they're basalt and granite. Lots of it in this part of Nova Scotia."

Al raised his eyebrows. "Could be. Never looked into it. Just know they been there for about a hundred years." He took a bite of food and waved at Shotgun. "Hey there, Birdshot, go in the fridge and get my jug of shine."

Shotgun got up and sauntered to the kitchen, returning with a gallon-size ceramic jug. He passed it to Al. He pulled the cork from the top with his teeth, spit it across the floor and took a swig. He held the jug out to Frantic, seated next to him. "Don't get too close to the fire with it. Damn flammable it is. Used to run my Scout on this stuff years ago. Better than the gas they had back then."

Frantic sniffed at the stubby neck of the jug. He squeezed his eyes shut and shook his head. "Sweet Jesus. Smells like ..." He paused and sniffed again. "Smells like Kentucky bourbon cut with – let's see – ammonia and formaldehyde." He took a drink and gasped. He held the jug out to Will.

"I think I'll pass," Will said.

"No, no!" Al said. "No passes. You know that saying – all for one and one for all."

Will took the jug and waved it beneath his nose, sniffing the air. "Don't know if it applies to this. Jeez, what is it exactly?"

Al laughed. "What difference does it make? I don't know, I just make it up with whatever I got on hand at the time – corn, barley, rye, whatever. It all ends up tasting about the same and having the same kick. Drink up. Like they say, it'll put hair on your chest."

Will took a sip. And then a bigger drink. He swallowed, grimacing – then his face became expressionless. "Not as bad as I thought it'd be."

"There you go! Not bad once it's past your throat, eh?" He motioned for Will to pass the jug to Speedy. "You'll feel a little aftershock in about ten seconds. But, after a few drinks, you won't notice that no more."

By the time the jug came around to Will for the third time, the talking around him had become indistinct, fused-together sounds nestled in a cloud of hazy consciousness. He studied the flames dancing in the fire. He leaned back in his chair and stretched his legs out straight, resting his heels on the coarse softwood floor. "Is that Douglas fir?" he mumbled to Al. He glanced up and saw Al heading toward the front door, his back to him.

"Gonna close up the barn for the night, boys," Al said.

Will watched him open the door, then stop in mid-step framed by the black night that filled the open doorway.

"Al?" Shotgun muttered, trying to find his feet.

Al remained frozen in place, staring into the night.

He turned to them. "Got company, boys. Lots of it – looks like."

Will, Frantic, and the others scrambled to the door.

ANCIENT GREEK PHILOSOPHERS

"Y**OU EXPECTING ANYBODY?**" A**L ASKED**.

"No," Shotgun said.

Al looked at them. "Me either."

Jammed together in the open doorway, they saw headlights of three cars already in the driveway and two others turning in off the highway.

"Shotgun, go now!" Al said. "Take them down to the cellar!"

Al stepped outside and slammed the door behind him. Shotgun dashed toward the back of the house, leading the others through the kitchen and into the pantry. He jerked open a trap door in the floor and pointed the way down the narrow opening to the cellar.

"Hurry up," he said, as they clunked down the wooden stairs leading to the cellar's dirt floor. When he stepped down himself, lowering the door above his head, they found themselves in complete darkness. "Keep moving along so we're not right at the bottom of the stairs," he whispered.

They stumbled forward, bumping into one another until they reached the far wall of cool interwoven stones. Shoulder to shoulder, facing the stairs they couldn't see, they stood in silence and listened.

"I don't like this," Frantic said, standing next to Will. "We're fuckin' trapped down here. We should've headed into the woods."

"Shh," said Shotgun. "Why don't you just yell out and tell them were down here?"

Will felt Frantic moving around. Then heard him cock his gun.

"Put that gun away!" Shotgun whispered.

"You can let them haul your ass away if you want. Go peaceful-like and all that. Not me."

They heard cars skid to a stop one after another, many doors open and close, and the voices of many people. Then, they heard footsteps – many hard-heeled footsteps stomping in all directions – slammed down with authority on the wooden planks of Al's floor inches overhead.

"Fuckin' army!" Speedy whispered.

"Nah, probably just a bunch of cops," Frantic whispered. "Maybe SWAT."

"Shut up, you idiot," Shotgun whispered. "Where do you think you are? Los Angeles? There's no SWAT in Nova Scotia."

"Says who?" Frantic persisted.

Their bodies stiffened instantly when the trap door to the cellar opened and light spilled down the stairs. Able to see more of the cellar, they jostled one another, their eyes searching in desperation for another way out.

"Shotgun? Frantic?" a female voice called down the stairs.

They looked at one another.

"It's a set-up," Frantic whispered. He aimed his gun at the stairs.

"Wait," Shotgun whispered.

"KAY?" he called out. "Everything okay?"

"All clear," she said. "You fools going to stay down there all night or are you going to come up for some air and party with us?"

"Don't know," Shotgun said. "We were just getting comfortable down here. What's in it for us?"

"Umm, Dad is standing right behind me, you asshole, so you'll have to use your imagination about that one."

"It's no set-up. Let's go, guys," Shotgun said.

They clunked back up the stairs, one after the other, and emerged into the brightness of the pantry and kitchen, jammed tight with Dark Angels and many friends – who set upon them, hugging and kissing them, hollering out their names with happy exuberance.

Stumpy bulldozed people aside to reach Will and Shotgun. He wrenched them away from the others and dragged them into the kitchen. "You doin' okay?"

"We've had a little cabin fever," Will said. "But we've been good, considering everything. People have been taking care of us – Floyd, Al, a few others."

"Can't complain," Shotgun said. "What's happening with the cops?"

"Barry and that lawyer guy been meeting with them off and on all day. Barry told me to tell you things are lookin' better. Whatever that means. It's been one big friggin' deal for sure." He draped his arms over their shoulders.

"Man, you four are like famous gunfighters or something now." He grabbed Will by the hair. "Remember how when you first came around and I had you figured for some kind of straight little jerk, some pansy choirboy? And now look at what you done. It's like you might become almost as big a legend as me."

He pulled Will close to him and threw him in a headlock, pretending to punch him in the forehead with his free hand. With his head twisted to one side, Will glanced toward the doorway leading into the living room and saw Gloria standing there. By the time he was able to pull away from Stumpy, she was at his side.

"Hello you," Gloria said, smiling. "So, what do I call you now?"

Will took her hand. "What do you mean?"

"Well, I thought with your new-found fame, they might have come up with a catchy nickname for you."

He laughed. "Funny, I had a similar conversation earlier with Al about nicknames. You two seem to think alike." He led her into the living room. They sat on the old sofa in front the fireplace. "I have to say you're the last person I expected to see here tonight. We were sure it was the cops coming to bust us."

"I suppose I could frisk you," she said with an impish smile.

He laughed again, stumbling for words. "You always surprise me. I'm glad you came."

She twirled a strand of hair around her finger. "So does that mean you still like me a little? I mean, assuming you did a few days ago."

"No – I don't, actually." He hesitated, watching her face. "I like you a lot."

"Oh, you charmer." She poked her finger into his chest. "Flattery will get you everywhere, you know." She hugged him and kissed his cheek. "Oh! Guess what. I brought you something." She began rummaging through her cloth handbag. "Books – two books. You know, in case you get bored while you're – now what's the right expression – on the run, hiding out, on the lam, evading apprehension, exploring alternatives to life behind bars? I'm not up on the best choice of words for your activities."

"Funny."

She grinned. "Well, don't sound so excited. I've been carrying these heavy suckers around in my bag all day. And I didn't even know if I'd get to see you." She pulled out one thick hardcover book, then another. She held them out to him in both hands.

He took them and looked at the covers. "You're kidding me – *Plato's Collected Dialogues* and the *Basic Works of Aristotle*! I don't believe it. Where did you get these?"

"Some professor guy who comes into Ginger's." She paused, then laughed. "Just kidding. I bought them at the bookstore at Saint Mary's."

He pushed the books back at her.

"What are you doing? Don't you want them?"

He looked around. "No, it's not that. It's just that the other guys wouldn't understand why I'd have books like these. Most of them already think I'm strange."

She rolled her eyes, took the books and stuffed them back into her bag. "Well, if you don't want them, that's fine. But I'm not dragging them around until you get out of jail, or whatever."

"Don't be mad at me. Really, I do want them."

"You sure? I can take them back. I kept the receipts."

"I want them. Thanks. It was a sweet thing to do."

She smiled. "I was thinking about how you were talking about that old Greek philosopher the other night, and I said to myself, 'I bet he'd like to read some stuff by some other old Greek philosophers.' The guy who works at the bookstore said these two dudes are the most famous. So, if you keep them, you have to promise to read them."

He held his palm up toward her. "Promise. I'll take them before you go and keep them out of sight." He laughed. "But, you know, they're not actually *old* Greek philosophers – they're known as *ancient* Greek philosophers. You know, as in *lived a long time ago*." He paused. "Though, I suppose they were each old at one time."

"Ohh – you mean like *really, reealllly* old? Like *ancient*?"

"Umm, well, not exactly."

She frowned at him, then burst out laughing. "Oh my God, you're way too anal. I was joking. Of course I know the difference."

He shook his head. "Okay, I give up. You win. Every time we have these kinds of conversations, you get the better of me."

"Poooor baby," she cooed, squeezing his arm. "And it's so easy." She took his hand and led him to a quiet corner. "What are you guys drinking?"

"Some of Al's moonshine – nasty stuff. You probably wouldn't like it."
She stared at him.

"Sorry. I'll get you some."

They sat off from the others, sipping Al's brew, making faces, laughing, talking, and moving closer and closer together. She again took the philosophy books from her bag and he looked through them, flipping from page to page and glancing around. As the logs on the fire burned down to glowing embers, and the party around them grew wilder, they never took their eyes from each other.

"This is a really old house, isn't it? Big, too," she said.

Will nodded. "It's got to be 150 years old."

"Do you think Al would mind if you showed me around? I like old houses."

"Al seems to be easy about almost everything, except for Shotgun screwing up when it comes to Kay. I doubt he would mind." He leaned to the side and looked her up and down, smiling. "But you're not dressed quite right for a tour of farm country."

"What?" she said, with mock surprise. "You don't think so?"

"Well, those high heels might get stuck somewhere and trip you up."

She uncrossed her slender legs and wiggled to pull down her black leather miniskirt. "Sorry, Kay picked me up from work and I didn't have time to change." She smiled. "These are my work clothes." She reached down and pulled at the top of the knee-high leather boots that clung to her ankles and calves – first one boot, then the other, with playful, confident joy – each leg outstretched in turn. "I usually don't wear clothes like these very often – or very long. They're meant to be removed more than worn." She giggled. "Kay teases me about this outfit."

"Why?"

"She calls it my CFM outfit."

"CFM? What does that mean?"

She looked at him. "Think about it, genius."

He shrugged and shook his head. "Is it the name of some brand?"

She shook her head.

"Leather company? Store?"

She shook her head, laughing. "Maybe if you show me around, it will come to you."

He took her hand and led her from room to room downstairs, weaving in and out among people, exchanging a few words with many they passed. He led her up the stairway to the second floor, empty of people, to where the bedrooms were – and to the bathroom with the high-sided bathtub of tarnished copper. He led her into the bathroom and closed the door behind them.

"That copper tub is something isn't it?" he said, turning to face her.

"It must be really old."

"It is. *Ancient*, actually."

She smiled and stepped closer to him. "Uh, huh. So did you figure out yet what CFM means?" she whispered.

"Possibly."

He pulled her against his body and kissed her lips. She kissed back with the driven, grinding passion of there being no tomorrow – devouring more than kissing. His breath caught in his throat and he pulled back, gently kissing her on the forehead and on each closed eyelid. "You're so beautiful," he whispered.

"You say that to all the girls you're about to fuck," she murmured.

"Not true. Only the ever-so-beautiful ones."

He slid her skirt up and ran his fingers up the inside of her thigh, continuing to kiss her face. His body quivered.

"What's wrong?" she whispered.

"You're not wearing any underwear."

"So observant. I told you I came in my work clothes."

He pulled her skirt completely up over her hips, and her satiny silver top over her head. Her hair cascaded down over her shoulders and to the top of her bare breasts. He lifted her onto the countertop of the enamelled bathroom sink, perching her on the edge. She tore off his shirt and wrapped her legs around his waist. He lowered himself to his knees and guided her calves to his shoulders. She grabbed him by the hair and drew his mouth to her body.

As starlight fell upon them from the sky outside, and as the purpose of the entire universe came alive in the hot, primal, glistening connection of their bodies, they made love – wildly and tenderly, roughly and gently, with abandon and with intimate attention – lost in the rapture and bewilderment of their hearts and souls dissolving into one.

He heard footsteps on the hallway floor and knocking at the bathroom door, but these seemed as distant from what was true and real as footfalls of the ghost of Socrates on the steps of the Parthenon. They collapsed against one another – breathless, aglow, kissing, swimming in a warm ocean of love.

"Where did you learn to do that?" she whispered into his ear, her breath hot and raspy.

"What?"

"What you just did. All of it." She paused. "Never mind. I don't think I want to know."

With his fingertips, he stroked her hair where it fell against her chest. "Nowhere – I didn't learn it anywhere. It's all you. I didn't know it was there." He smiled. "Or maybe I read it somewhere."

"Oh really! Must have been *some* book. Maybe it was that Sexy Piricus dude."

"Sextus Empiricus."

"Exactly. Of course." She kissed him. "That's exactly what I said."

"I did it again, didn't I?"

"Uh, huh." She laughed.

"We better get back downstairs before they send a search party for us."

"I know." She kissed him. "What you did tonight – if it's really from something you read somewhere – will you do me a favour?"

"Anything." He cupped her face with his hands and kissed her lips. "Anything."

"Keep reading. That's all. Just keep reading."

He laughed.

She laced her fingers in his hair, then moved her hands down to his shoulders, then to his arms. She squeezed his arms as if testing fresh fruit for its firmness. She sighed – a deep soulful sigh.

"What's wrong?"

"It's going to be hard to give you up."

"Why would you say that?"

"I don't know." She touched his cheek. "It feels inevitable. Too good to be true – or stay true."

"Why would you even be thinking that right now?"

She brushed a tear from her cheek. "Because I'm a woman."

"I don't understand."

She began to put her clothes back on. She fluffed her hair with her fingers. "I know," she said, taking his hand.

DADDY HUGHIE

UNDER AN INDIA-INK SKY FILLED with sparkling stars, the visitors began piling into the cars. Will and Gloria moved away from the others and stood pressed together near the barn.

"I don't want to leave," she said.

"I know." He brushed a few strands of soft hair from her cheek. "Stumpy wants to get everybody away from here before daylight. It's not too far off."

She nodded.

"Umm, I hate to say this, but Frantic says we might have to get away from here for a while – until this is settled or the heat dies down. Maybe go to Hamilton and stay with the Grim Reapers." He kissed her cheek. "I don't know. Maybe not. Things are happening so fast right now."

"I'm not going anywhere. I'm a patient person."

He smiled, taking her hand in his. "I hope so." He began to walk her toward the cars. "Can you do something for me?"

"What?"

"Maybe you and Kay could go and check on my mother? Just talk to her and tell her I'm okay."

"Sure."

"Barry said we couldn't call anyone because the phones might be tapped. Tell her I'll call as soon as I can. She's probably pretty worried."

"Okay."

"Go to Sadie's Lodge on Robie Street – across from the North Common. She's always there."

She nodded and hugged him. "If you go away, do you promise to find some way to contact me?"

"Uh, huh."

She stared at him.

"Yes, I promise."

"If you do, I'll find some way to come see you – no matter where you are."

Kay waved at her from one of the cars. They went over and she climbed into the back seat next to her. Gloria slammed the door shut and rolled down the window. Will leaned in through the open window and kissed her. She smiled and tugged at the bottom of her leather skirt, which had ridden up high on her thighs.

He waved his finger at her. "Don't do that."

She giggled and blew him a kiss as the car pulled away.

He followed the car's glowing taillights down Al's driveway. "I love you," he whispered to the red dusty wake.

"You guys want one last drink?" Al asked Will and Frantic when they were back inside the house. "I'm too wound up to sleep right now. May as well stay up, anyway. Soon be time for my morning chores."

Will and Frantic nodded and they all plunked down in the living room. Al took a swig from the jug. He pushed himself up and passed it to Frantic before tossing a few more logs on the fire.

"Getting cold these nights." He took a deep breath and rubbed his rough hands together. "You two got any interest in trying to jack a deer? Not much time before it's light."

"Seriously?" Frantic asked, sitting up and tousling his hair with both hands.

"Yeah. We'll go down by the orchard. It's not far. Might get a shot."

Al disappeared into the hallway and returned with a hunting rifle that had a long flashlight taped against the stock next to the scope. He held the rifle out to Frantic.

Frantic grabbed it and pulled the stock to his shoulder, aiming into the fire. "Why not? If it goes bang, it talks my language." He glanced at Will. "You coming?"

Will hesitated. "I suppose."

"Buckshot and Speedy must already be upstairs snoozing," Al said.

They went out the back door of the house and headed north through fields of waist-high grass and wildflowers, Al leading the way.

"Wow," Will said, pointing up at the starry sky.

"Something, eh?" Al said. "And there's people who think there's no God. I figure how can there *not* be a God?"

Al stopped every few minutes and flicked on the flashlight, shining it into the darkness that surrounded them.

"Is this all your land?" Will asked.

"More or less. Don't really matter where mine ends and somebody else's starts. We're all just visitors, the way I look at it."

Will laughed. "You remind me of my grandfather. He had a camp on an island right in the middle of Yarmouth Harbour. He didn't worry much about stuff like that, either. He built his camp there because that's what he wanted to do. Didn't ask anybody. Just rowed everything over in his rowboat – all the wood and materials for the camp, big old stove, furniture. Everything."

"Not enough people like that around nowadays." Al chuckled and shook his head. "Worst thing about civilization is people making up rules about how other people ought to live." He stopped once more and shined the light to his left. "He still got that camp?"

"No. He was killed a few years ago. Drove his pickup truck into the back of a fish truck that had broken down in the middle of the road. It was dark." He paused. "His camp's still there on the island. But nobody goes there anymore – at least as far as I know. I haven't been there since I was 12."

"Too bad. What was his name?"

"Hughie." Will laughed. "I used to call him Daddy Hughie because we lived with him and my grandmother until I was almost five."

Al put his finger to his lips. "There – under the tree," he whispered. He trained the light on a young buck, his head down in tall grass. "Apples ..."Al whispered. At that moment, the buck twitched. It snapped its head up and stared in their direction, its amber eyes lit up like glowing embers. Keeping the light's beam in the deer's eyes, Al cocked the rifle and passed it to Frantic. "Take a shot," he whispered.

The deer continued to stare into the light, still as a statue. Frantic took aim and pulled the rifle tight against his shoulder. Will breathed in time with Frantic, moving closer beside him. He felt Frantic's body relax and watched his finger begin to squeeze the trigger. When Frantic became perfectly still, he nudged him with his shoulder. The rifle's explosion flashed from the barrel and echoed like thunder off the sleepy hills. The deer vanished from the beam of the flashlight, leaving only tall parted grass illuminated in its place.

"Sorry, Frantic," Will said. "Lost my balance."

Frantic lowered the rifle. "No big deal. Think I had him, though."

Al looked at Will. "They're right spooky at the best of times. Surprised he stayed put that long." He took the rifle from Frantic. "We better head back."

They followed the path they had made in the grass back to the house. Once inside, Al stood in front of the fireplace with his back to the flames.

"Aren't you going to bed?" Frantic asked him.

Al shrugged. "I might have a little snooze right here. Too late for bed now – or too early, depending on how you look at it."

"You?" Frantic asked Will, as he headed toward the stairs.

"If it won't bother you," Will said to Al, "I'll stay here, too."

"Long as you don't snore louder than me."

"Doubt I'll sleep, so I won't likely snore."

Al waved at Frantic. "See ya."

Will slouched in the big chair. Al stretched out on the sofa with his hands clasped on his belly. The wood in the fireplace blazed, snapping and sparking from time to time and sending wisps of smoke curling up into the chimney.

Will felt his body twitch.

"You asleep?" Al whispered.

"No. Almost, I guess."

"Can I ask you a question? If you want to sleep, that's okay. It's nothing important."

"No. It's okay. What?"

"Well, I was wondering – why are you here?"

"What do you mean?"

Al smiled. "Not here as in hiding out here. I mean *here* as in why are you part of all this?"

"You mean the shooting?"

"No. I mean the Dark Angels." Al rubbed his eyes and pulled at his whiskers. "Don't take this wrong, son, but you're different from the rest of them – even Shotgun. And he's one of the good ones."

Will straightened. "My mother asks me the same kinds of questions and I never know what to say to her." He sighed. "I mean, it seems like I never really fit in – anywhere. Like, I'm always the one who's different. But I think I'm more part of this than most things." He shrugged. "But, as for why, that's harder to explain."

"Yeah, you're different from the rest of them all right."

"But we're *all* really different from one another, Al. That's what makes the club what it is – makes it interesting."

Al shook his head. "You don't understand."

Will looked at him.

Al took a deep breath. "I might be all wrong, son, but it seems to me you're with this bunch, but you're also not with this bunch. It's like you're taking part in it but, at the same time, standing back somewhere else and looking at it all – like you're studying it for some reason." He paused. "Like you're looking for something else – searching – and I can't help but wonder what it is."

Will shook his head. "Never thought of it."

Al laughed. "Well, like I said, I'm probably all wrong about it." He rubbed his belly up and down with his right hand. "Yeah, we're all searching for something, right? Whether we know it or not – money, sex, power, fame, happiness – *something* we think we ain't got at all or ain't got enough of. I figure if a man doesn't know what he's searching for, he won't know whether or not he's already got it, or on the right path to find it, or just wandering around goin' nowhere."

"Makes sense. Guess I've never thought about life that way. But it's like I've told my mother – this is the road I have to be on right now." He paused. "Even if I don't know where it's going."

"Yeah, I get it. I was like that once – about your age. You gotta do what you gotta do, right? But ..."

"What?"

"Oh, nothing." He paused. "Well, I was just thinking that *right now* is a passing kind of thing. But the things you do or that happen right now have a way of following you around – or pushing you around – forever. That's all."

Will nodded. He stared into the flames.

Soon, he was riding his bike along Water Street in Yarmouth. He felt someone on back and glanced over his shoulder. Gloria smiled at him. He stopped across from his grandfather's island. He saw the rowboat he had sat in as a little boy on the island's shore.

"Do you want to ride over and see Daddy Hughie?" he asked Gloria. "Tide's out."

"Yes." She looked in the direction of the island. "But how can you ride over there, across the rocks and in that black muck?"

He laughed out loud. "Don't worry. This bike will take me anywhere."

He turned the bike toward the harbour, facing the steep bank leading down to the shoreline. He cracked the throttle wide open. They shot down the bank and bounced over the big rocks and fishtailed across the mudflats, with muck and spray spewing everywhere, both of them laughing and screaming with delight. In no time, they flew up over the bank at Daddy Hughie's island and slid to a smooth stop in the clearing in front of the camp.

"See," he said, looking at his arms and legs. "We didn't even get dirty."

His grandfather came out of the camp. "Well, I'll be damned. I wasn't expecting to see you today, son."

"Actually, I wasn't planning to come. It just happened that way." He noticed that Gloria was now standing next to him. "This is Gloria. But I forget where we were going. Where were we going, Gloria?"

"It's up there, I think," she said, pointing up at the sky. "Oh. They're all gone now."

Will looked up at the blue sky. "The stars?"

"Yes."

"You know how to read the stars?"

"No." She paused. "I thought you did."

Daddy Hughie laughed. "Aw, don't worry about them things. It don't matter anyway. The main man for the government has it all figured out – the one that runs the island, and the water, and the stars – even the damn fisheries officers. He'll make it all happen just the way he wants."

Will looked to his right and saw all kinds of animals beginning to emerge from the woods around them – rabbits, a red fox, deer, a lynx, a black bear. A huge grey wolf with glowing eyes. Dozens of animals.

"Wow. Look at all the animals, Daddy Hughie."

"I was wondering when you'd notice them. Do you have your gun?"

Will felt at his waist. "Why? We're not going to shoot them are we?"

Daddy Hughie laughed. "Why else would they be here, son?"

"But what are we going to do with them? We don't have to kill them, do we?"

Daddy Hughie scratched his head. "That's about the only way I know we can mount them on the wall. Otherwise, they'd do whatever they want and then they'd take over. That's what the man said about me. So I said 'Suit yourself. Don't matter to me. Mount me on the Goddamn wall'. So he did. I'm in the camp if you want to go look."

Will began to sob. "No! It can't be like that!" He looked at his grandfather and saw that his face and head bore deep red scars and that his skin was sallow. "I thought you were dead. They told me you were dead and gone. It feels like you've been gone for a long time. Where have you been if you haven't been dead?"

Daddy Hughie laughed and put his arm around his shoulder. "I been right here. Where else would I be?"

Will could hear the timbre of Daddy Hughie's voice exactly as he had heard it from infancy – could smell the smoky wildness of his skin – could feel the warmth of his muscled body as if he were huddled in it against a dark, stormy gale from the east. He leaned for a long time into Daddy Hughie's body, feeling him breathing, hearing the air move in and out of his lungs.

"I've got a present for you," Daddy Hughie said, after a time. "Here." He held out a small telescope. "It'll help you see where you have to go or find what you're looking for up ahead."

Will took the telescope and extended its brass body until all three sections clicked into place. He held the eyepiece to his eye and looked out, away from the island. Then, he moved it from left to right.

"I can't see anything."

"What do you mean?"

"It's all just foggy. All I see is fog."

Daddy Hughie shook his head. "I could never get the damn thing to work either."

Will began to hear an intermittent ringing. He looked behind him. "It's coming from the camp, Daddy Hughie." He paused. "It sounds like a phone. When did you get a phone here?"

"By the Jesus, I didn't do that! Must be your grandmother's work. She's always got to be checking up on me."

"Nana knows you're here, too?"

Daddy Hughie looked at him and scratched his head again. "Goddamn it, she must."

THE BIG QUESTIONS

THE RINGING BECAME PERSISTENT AND more intrusive. Daddy Hughie and the island began to dissolve into the thick fog.

"Yeah, it's me," he heard Al say. "No, I was awake."

Will stretched his body out in the chair, then stood up and headed to the bathroom. When he came back downstairs, Al was hanging up the telephone.

"That was Kay calling to check on things."

Will nodded. "What time is it?"

"Around nine. You get any sleep?"

"Doesn't feel like it, but I was dreaming, so I must have."

Al laughed. "You were sure doing some talking, I know that."

"Really?" He rubbed his eyes and yawned. "Say anything interesting?"

"Just the odd word. Something about fog."

Will laughed. "I think I was dreaming about being on my grandfather's island. It was all pretty strange."

Al nodded. "Makes sense." He went to the refrigerator and opened the door. "You hungry?"

"Yeah."

Al swung the door shut. "Come on. We'll go get some eggs."

They walked toward the barn with the morning sun shoulder-high on the horizon to their left, the dew still lingering on the grass. "The coop's around back of the barn," Al said. "I used to let them run loose, but the coyotes started taking too many, so I had to close up the coop with chicken wire to keep them in and the coyotes out."

Inside the coop, Al put feed down for the chickens and began collecting eggs, placing them in a tin bucket lined with hay. "Not bad – eight today." When he finished, he passed the bucket to Will. "Like bacon?"

Will nodded, looking down at the brown eggs nestled in the bottom of the pail.

They returned to the house and Al rinsed off the eggs. He layered strips of thick bacon in his big cast-iron frying pan. His banging and clanging roused Frantic, Shotgun, and Speedy.

On Rainnie Drive, in Halifax, Detectives Garrity and Akerman sat waiting on hard wooden chairs in the hallway outside the office of Police Chief Everett Middleton.

Garrity stood up and began pacing the hallway. Hearing the office door open, he pulled in his belly and did up the dull brass buttons of his crumpled navy blazer.

Crown Prosecutor Robert Simms stuck his head out the door. "Good, you're here. We'll be a few more minutes." He closed the door.

Garrity looked at Akerman and shook his head. "I don't get it. What the hell they got to say to those two that we can't hear?"

Akerman shrugged. "Nothing good, you can be sure of that. Guess we need one of those smartass lawyers of our own."

Garrity nodded and sat down again.

Minutes later, the door opened again and Simms waved for Garrity and Akerman to come in.

"Have a seat, boys," Chief Middleton said, nodding to them from behind his desk. He pointed to two chairs to his right, the same as those in the hallway. "You all know one another other?" he asked, nodding toward Barry and Dedrick, seated to his left on mismatched armchairs of cracked and peeling vinyl.

Garrity and Akerman glared at Barry and Dedrick. "More or less," Garrity said, drumming his fingers on his thigh. "Never been introduced."

Dedrick stood up and crossed the room. He shook hands with Garrity and Akerman. "Frank, Jim. I'm Martin Dedrick."

Barry remained seated.

"This is Barry," Middleton said, tilting his head toward him. "Barry, um – damn if I know your last name."

Barry raised his hand. "Not necessary."

Simms sat on the front corner of Middleton's desk. He pulled at the creases in his grey dress pants, positioning the creases in the center of his legs. "Well, let's get to it, shall we?" He cleared his throat. "Detectives, we wanted to update you about this case. We've been meeting with Barry and Mr. Dedrick off and on over the past couple days – ever since the unfortunate events of the other night."

"We talking about the same thing, Bob?" Akerman asked. "Those Dark Angels degenerates trying to murder a couple other bags of shit? *Those* unfortunate events?"

"Okay, Jim. That's enough," Middleton said.

Simms took a pair of black-framed glasses from the pocket of his starched white shirt and placed them, with precision, on his face. He glanced at his reflection in the glass of the office door and ran his fingers through his blond wavy air. "Call it what you want," Simms said, turning his head back to Akerman. "We're not going to quibble over words. What we want to discuss with you is that we've reached a deal. And we need your cooperation to make it work."

"A deal!?" Garrity blurted out, almost choking on his words. "What a surprise."

Simms adjusted his necktie. "Yes – a deal."

"My clients, the Dark Angels, have agreed there will be no more gunplay," Dedrick said, clasping his hands together on his crossed leg and interlacing his fingers. "And they will lend support to the police to get rid of the Devil's Chain – within the law."

Akerman sighed. "And exactly how does that bring those fugitives to justice or make anything better? Wow, we get rid of one bunch of sewer rats. What about the other bunch?"

"One half of a big bunch is better than no half of a bunch, wouldn't you say?" Barry interjected, grinning.

"The fact is the investigation has not uncovered enough evidence to support charges at this time," Simms said. "We've agreed with Mr. Dedrick that the warrants should be withdrawn. The focus now has to be on how to make things better down the road."

"You backing this, Chief?" Garrity asked.

"They wouldn't be telling it to you if I wasn't. We gotta make the best of a bad situation." Middleton took a deep breath. He opened the center drawer of his desk and began picking though its contents.

Simms turned to him. "Chief?"

"Got a cigarette, Bob?" Middleton asked.

"No. Gave it up. Thought you did, too."

"I did."

Barry jumped up and pulled a pack of cigarettes from his pocket. "Peter Jackson okay?" He opened the pack and held it out. Middleton hesitated, then leaned across his desk and slid a cigarette from the pack. Barry lit it with his Zippo and sat back down, smiling. Middleton drew on the cigarette and sank back into his chair.

Smirking, Barry glanced at Garrity and Akerman, then looked back at Middleton. "I assume you're fine with a little marijuana in your tobacco, eh Chief?"

Middleton jerked upright and shot a furtive look at Barry. Garrity and Akerman burst out laughing.

Barry winked at Middleton and lit a cigarette for himself. "Just pulling your leg, Chief." He looked at Garrity and Akerman, blowing a cloud of smoke across the room in their direction.

"I'm curious, Bob," Akerman said. "How exactly do you plan to get rid of that other gang? I can't believe they're gonna lay down and play dead."

Simms glanced at Middleton, then turned to the two detectives. "Nothing too complicated. The Chief will be issuing orders to the force to ride the Devil's Chain hard. They won't be able to ride their bikes more than a half mile without being pulled over. They'll be ticketed or searched every time they're stopped. We'll squeeze them so hard they won't be able to take a breath. We've already charged several of them from the other night. It won't take long before most of them are before the courts or in jail for one thing or another." He paused. "And Barry will have his guys stay clean and keep clear of them. No violence – right, Barry?"

"As you wish, *mon capitaine*," Barry said, dragging on his cigarette. "The bottom line is my guys will do whatever I tell them to do."

"The other part of it," Simms continued, "is the Dark Angels will begin talks with the Devil's Chain to determine if they can recruit any of them to their club – closing the loop, or the noose, so to speak."

Akerman shook his head. "And you think that's a good deal, Bob? We get rid of the Dark Angels' rivals and help them get stronger in the process. You're telling me that's a good deal? What the hell am I missing here?" He shook his head. "Why don't we just set them up in a big field somewhere and let them kill one another off? Now, that's a deal I could get excited about."

Dedrick raised his hand.

"Yes, Mr. Dedrick," Middleton said.

"Detectives, you appear to be operating on the mistaken assumption that the Dark Angels are in a position where they *have* to make a deal. The truth is, they can simply walk away, or ride away – whatever suits them. You have no court-worthy charges. My clients are trying to cooperate with you in the interests of bringing this all-too-public conflict to a peaceful resolution. It's clear the Devil's Chain instigated this trouble. They went looking for the Dark Angels." Dedrick stood up. "Think it through, gentlemen, this is a reasonable deal for the police and a responsible direction for the city." He turned to Barry. "Come on, we should let our friends give this more consideration."

Barry stood up and dropped his cigarette on the tile floor. He crushed it out with his boot. "You know how to get in touch with us." He and Dedrick left the office, leaving the door open behind them.

"Nothing worse than a Goddamn smart-mouth Jew," Garrity said.

"Talks like he's reading from a Goddamn textbook. What a pompous asshole," Akerman added.

"Never mind, Jim. Close the damn door," Simms said.

Akerman took two steps toward the door and swung it shut. He looked at Garrity, then at Simms and Middleton.

"There's more," Simms said. He rolled his head from side to side, stretching the taut muscles at the sides of his neck.

"Yeah, like what?" Garrity asked, rolling his eyes.

"We didn't want to tell you two the whole deal ahead of time," Middleton said. "We wanted you to react the way you did – the way they'd expect you to." He took a puff from his cigarette. He held it out and looked at it, then sniffed at the smoke. "You don't suppose that bastard really put some kind of shit in this, do you?"

Simms raised his eyebrows and shrugged.

"Go ahead, Chief," Akerman said. "What's the rest of it?"

"Well, we're not going to back off from those Dark Angels. We're gonna be smarter about it, that's all – while they're feeling smug and letting their guard down."

"And helping us get rid of that other bunch," Simms added.

"Right," Middleton continued. "I want you two to disappear. Pick some other plainclothes men to work with you. Think smart. Our short-term strategy is to settle things down and get rid of that other club. But the long-term strategy is to bury the Dark Angels – bury them deep. Do whatever you have to do to bring those bums down – one at a time, or in bunches. Doesn't matter. Just get it done."

Garrity and Akerman straightened to attention. "You serious, Chief?" Garrity asked. "You're giving us that kind of leeway?"

Middleton looked at Simms.

"Detectives, as you know, the Chief always expects his men to carry out their duties within the law," Simms said. "However, should this special assignment lead you into – umm – circumstances where the limits of the law are, shall we say, stretched, the Chief and I will do our best to give you our full support and the protection of the law. That is, assuming you are careful enough not to leave any tracks on your hunting expedition that lead back to this office."

Akerman took out his notepad and pen. "Who would we report to?"

"Put that away," Middleton said. "This is off the books."

"What we're interested in is results," Simms said, walking to the door. "If there are any points of law you want to know about, you can check with me. Otherwise, we really don't want to know exactly what you're doing."

Middleton held his cigarette out to Simms. "Here take this."

Simms shook his head. "No thanks, Chief"

Middleton coughed. "Just *take* the Goddamn thing and get rid of it, Bob. I'm feeling light-headed."

Simms took the half-smoked cigarette and looked around the office. He dropped the butt to the floor and ground it out, twisting the sole of his shoe against it. "You might as well get an ashtray back in here, Chief."

Middleton coughed again. "We're going way out on a limb with you two on this one. There'll never be another opportunity come your way like this again." He rubbed his forehead. "Any other questions?"

"What hours do you want us to work?" Garrity asked.

"What hours do the Dark Angels work?" Middleton shot back.

Garrity looked at Akerman. "Okay, Chief. We'll get this done."

"In a couple years, nobody will even remember the name of that bunch," Akerman said.

"Dark Angels! That's it!" Al said to Will, as they walked back to the barn after breakfast. "You need some kind of nickname that goes along with Dark Angels. Something catchy. Memorable."

Will smiled. "I don't know. It's not that the guys haven't been trying. It's just that nothing seems to fit. Stumpy says it's because I'm a 'blah' kind of guy."

Al laughed and patted him on the shoulder. "I'll ponder it some more."

He opened the big front doors of the barn, allowing sunlight to spill into its cavernous interior. "Follow me. It's way in the back." He picked his way through a narrow jagged path, among cob-webbed farm implements, tools, machinery, and tons of nondescript junk that stretched from the planked floor up to the huge rough-hewn beams overhead. "Best not to disturb anything," he said, looking over his shoulder at Will and chuckling. "I know where everything is."

"Don't go too fast. I don't know if I'd be able to find my way out if we get separated."

Al nodded, smiling. "It's over there." They approached an object covered with a dusty patchwork quilt. "Haven't even looked at it for about five years. Don't believe I ever showed it to Shotgun."

Al peeled off the quilt from front to back, being careful not to stir up too much dust. "There she is. Haven't ridden her in about 20 years."

"Still in good shape," Will said, running his hand along the contour of the gas tank. "Will it run?"

Al scratched his chin. "She was working last off. But hasn't been running for a long time. Never put her away right, so she'd have to be rebuilt, I guess." He placed his hand over the throttle with a tender touch, as might a burley old man taking a young girl's hand, and rolled it toward him. "Only bike I ever had. Couldn't imagine there could ever be a better one. Stopped riding her around the time my Eleanor – Kay's mother – died. Same idea. Only woman I ever loved. Couldn't imagine someone like me could ever find another one like her." He paused. "Go ahead. Sit on her. You'll feel her soul right off."

"No, I shouldn't."

"Go on. I want you to. Gimme them books you been half-hiding under your arm there. What are they anyway?"

Will hesitated. "Philosophy books – Plato and Aristotle." He held the two books out to Al.

Al took the books and examined their covers, as Will threw his leg over the Indian Scout and settled into the dished-out saddle. He reached forward and gripped the handlebars, smiling at Al. "I've never sat on a bike this old."

"Or famous," Al said, beaming. "So do you feel her soul?"

Will looked the bike all over from where he was sitting and moved it from side to side to feel its weight. "Yeah, Al, I do."

Al leaned back against a rusty drill press and began thumbing through the pages of the books. "Plato, eh? Named a planet after him, didn't they?"

Will smiled. "That was Pluto."

Al grinned. "Oh, yeah. I was just testing you. They named that planet after that dog, Pluto, right?"

"No doubt."

"So these here Plato and Aristotle characters – is that what they did? Write philosophy books?"

"Yeah. Write and teach."

"And they made a living doing that?"

Will laughed. "It was a long time ago – more than 2,000 years ago. They lived in Greece and things were different back then. They were from the upper class, so they didn't work at regular jobs." He got off the bike. "They had a lot of spare time."

"Like me – or all them folks on welfare."

"Uh, huh. Quite similar."

Al stroked his whiskers. "So what did they write about?"

"Well, I haven't actually read these ones yet, but philosophers usually write about things like … um, well … they try to answer questions like 'Where did everything come from?' or 'Does God exist?' or 'Is it possible to know anything?' or 'What is justice, or beauty, or goodness – or the soul?' Things like that."

"Why?" Al asked, straight-faced.

Will paused. "Well, I suppose they wanted to know the answers. And explain things to other people."

"Why? What difference does it make if they know the answers to big questions like that?"

Will shook his head and smiled. "I don't know, Al. That sounds like one of those big questions itself. I guess some people just like to think about things and know the answers to questions like that."

"And you're telling me they can make a living doing that – even old Plato and Aristotle here made a living doing that? Other people would pay money to buy their books or to listen to what they have to say?"

Will nodded. "More or less."

"Man, that's right slick, it is. I got lots of ideas and people like to listen to my stories. Do you think I could get me one of them philosopher jobs?"

"There'd probably be a line up for your classes."

Al slapped him on the back. "Yeah, right." He paused. "Though, I suppose I could truck my Indian in and set her up in front of the class and lecture about her soul."

"You could."

Al grinned. "Want something to put these books in? Seems you don't want to advertise you got them."

"Okay."

Al looked around and grabbed an old wooden toolbox. He opened it and emptied its contents of assorted hand tools onto a nearby table. He placed the books inside and handed the toolbox to Will. "Room for more if you get some."

Al patted the Indian's gas tank and pulled the quilt back over it. He turned and zig-zagged his way out of the barn with Will following. As they came back into the sunlight, Shotgun waved at them from the back door of the house.

"Barry called," he said. "They worked out a deal. They're sending Stumpy out to get us. He's coming in a hearse."

PART 5

ELECTRIC WINDOWS

"A HEARSE?" AL ASKED, AS THEY came up to Shotgun.

"Barry said Stumpy got it from Floyd for doing some enforcer work for him. Wants to show it off to us, apparently."

"What did he say about the deal?" Will asked.

"Not much. Just that he and Dedrick got things worked out with the cops. They're pulling the warrants. Guess we can go back anytime."

"That's it?" Will asked. "Seems too easy."

"That's what I was thinking," Frantic said, coming out the back door. "I'm not going too public just yet."

"Those city cops are real slippery," Al said. "You boys better get the full story from Barry and that lawyer before you go riding into town like Gene Autry, singing *Back in the Saddle Again*."

"Stumpy will probably fill us in," Shotgun said.

"Yeah," Al said. He kicked at the dirt. "Damn. I'm gonna miss you fools." He put his arm around Will's shoulder. "We'll have to have us a big party out here when all this blows over. All you Dark Angels and all your friends."

"Sounds good," Frantic said.

"We'll do it before the cold weather sets in," Al said. "Maybe a Hallowe'en party." He chuckled. "You guys are always in costume – right, Gunshot?"

"You, too, you old hillbilly," Shotgun said.

Al lunged at Shotgun.

"HIDE THE SHEEP!" Shotgun shouted, jumping to the left and darting toward the barn, covering his head with his hands and ducking rocks Al threw in his direction.

They were still standing around outside an hour later when they saw a long black hearse with a grey vinyl top turn into the driveway. The hearse's horn blew off and on as it bounced up the driveway. It skidded to a stop near them and Stumpy jumped out.

"Something, ain't it?" he said, looking at the hearse. He smiled at them. "Bet you assholes never thought you'd ever be so happy to see me."

"Yeah, it's *something*," Frantic said. "Something ugly."

The passenger door opened and Floyd threw his right leg out, pulling the rest of his body out after it. "Hey, watch it. It's a DeVille," he said, shuffling over to stand beside Stumpy.

Stumpy looked at him. "I thought you said it was a fucking Cadillac?"

"It is, Stump," Floyd said. "A Cadillac DeVille."

"It's nothing but a dressed-up coffin-hauler," Frantic said, walking up to it.

"It's a Cadillac to you, you low-life freak," Stumpy said. "Something you ain't never had." He ran his hand along the vinyl top. "It'll hold a shit-load of stuff. It's even got a trailer hitch on back."

Frantic laughed. "Why the hell would they put a trailer hitch on a hearse?"

Stumpy moved between him and the Cadillac. "Why the hell not? To pull something with. Why else, stupid? Anyway, I don't give a shit what you think. I think it's real classy. I figure I'm way ahead of you four who got no other way back to the city."

"He's got you there," Al said, laughing.

"Damn right," Stumpy said. "So shut the hell up and get in if you're coming."

"I suppose you need something this big and ugly to drag you and lard-ass here around," Frantic said, nodding in Floyd's direction.

"Gives me the creeps. I know that," Speedy said.

"Let's just get in and go back without them," Floyd said to Stumpy.

"Yeah, let's fucking do that," Stumpy said, reaching for the door handle.

The others scrambled to throw their few things in the back of the hearse and climbed in after them, as Stumpy started the hearse and pulled away. They waved at Al from inside, then swung the back door shut.

"You didn't have to do that, you idiot," Frantic said. "We were just riding you."

Stumpy scowled at him in the rear-view mirror.

"I think you rode a little too hard," Floyd said, gripping the Cadillac's dash, as Stumpy hurtled down the driveway.

They turned onto the highway – tires squealing as Stumpy tramped hard on the gas pedal.

"Feels good to be on the open road again," Will said. He held his hand up to feel the air rushing in through the side window.

"I have to admit, it runs pretty good," Shotgun said.

Stumpy nodded and smiled a little. "What'd you expect? It's even got air conditioning. Close all the windows. I'll show you."

"Electric windows!" Floyd added.

"It's loaded," Stumpy said, grinning from ear to ear.

They drove on through the rolling hills with the windows closed tight and the Cadillac's air conditioning pumping cool air throughout the hearse.

"Gives me the creeps," Speedy said. "It's worse with the windows closed."

"Yeah, weird in here," Frantic said, lying on his back on the floor with his hands clasped behind his head. "Why would anybody think a guy's last ride on earth should be inside a refrigerated coffin-on-wheels like this?"

"Don't make no difference once you're dead," Stumpy said. "Least you'll be goin' out in style."

"What's that smell? Smell that?" Speedy asked.

They all sniffed the air.

"Yeah, I smell it," Shotgun said. "Something smells bad." He kicked the back of Stumpy's seat. "You got your boots off?"

"No. I don't smell nothing."

"Yeah. It's definitely something," Frantic said, sitting up.

"Jesus Christ, I bet it's all them dead people that's been in here," Speedy said. "Probably leaked that antifreeze shit out of their bodies onto this carpet. Fuck, you been laying in it, Frantic!"

Frantic pushed himself onto his haunches, staring down at the carpet. "You think? I don't see any stains or anything."

"What do you think you're going to see?" Shotgun asked. "They pick the colour of the carpet to match the embalming fluid. That's why all hearses have the same colour carpet."

Frantic and Speedy moved away from the middle of the floor and pressed their bodies against the sides of the hearse. "Don't you be messing with my head," Speedy said. "You know this kind of shit freaks me out."

Frantic whacked the back of Floyd's head. "Is that true?"

Floyd laughed. "How do I know? But I doubt dead bodies leak like that. Even if they did, it'd stay in the coffin, right?"

"Well, something stinks," Shotgun said, holding his nose.

Speedy jerked his head from side to side, looking at Frantic and the others. "Open those damn windows, Stumpy!"

"Bunch of pussies. I think you're all just jealous," Stumpy said. He groaned and opened the windows. "Satisfied now?"

"I'll be satisfied when I get out of this thing," Frantic said. "Where we going exactly?"

"Clubhouse," Stumpy said.

"After the shootings, we had to get your bikes away from the clubhouse," Floyd said. "I got a little warehouse down on Lower Water Street. That's where they are. We figured you'd want to pick them up soon as you got into town."

"Me and Barry and a few other guys pushed them there," Stumpy said. He looked at them in the rear-view mirror. "One more thing you owe me for."

"Do you really think the cops are going to leave us alone?" Will asked.

"Barry says that's part of the deal," Stumpy said.

"*Part* of the deal? What's the other part?" Shotgun asked, leaning toward the front of the hearse.

"Sounds a little crazy, but Barry says we gotta help the cops get rid of the Devil's Chain."

"You're fucking kidding me!" Shotgun said. "Barry made a deal like *that*?" He tucked his hair behind his ears. "Good for us, I guess. But what do the cops get out of that?"

Stumpy shrugged. "I don't know. I wasn't there. I'm just telling you what Barry told me."

"I think it's so they can at least get one club off the streets," Floyd said. "Public relations kind-of-thing maybe."

"I think they're still gonna pick us up," Frantic said. "Try to shake something out of us. They'll do their favourite little routine and haul a couple of us in at the same time and put us in separate rooms. They'll say something like, 'Shotgun, you tell us what we want to know and we'll cut you a deal. Frantic Fred's in the other room and he's ready to talk, so you better talk before he does. If he spills his guts, you get the rap, buddy.' That's what they'll do."

Floyd laughed. "They've done that with me so many times, I wrote out a script for them to follow. When they pull me in for questioning, I take it out and give it to them. I got the damn thing laminated."

Shotgun looked at Will. "If it happens, you'll be the one they'll try to work on. You know what to say?"

"Nothing?"

"That'd be okay. Or you can say, 'Am I under arrest?' or 'I want to talk to my lawyer.' If you're not under arrest, you can just walk away. No matter what, you don't have to say anything."

"Or you can say you heard me or Shotgun already told them what they wanted to know, so they don't need to hear it from you," Frantic said. "That pisses them off because then they know *you* know they're jerking you around."

Will nodded. "Sounds pretty simple." At that moment, he caught a glimpse of an animal moving through a field of tall grass on the opposite side of the road, its belly scrunched low to the ground. "Hey, look," he said, pointing past Shotgun's head and beyond the side window of the hearse. "See it?" The others craned their necks to look.

"I don't see anything," Speedy said.

"What was it?" Shotgun asked.

"Not sure," Will said, scanning the field. "It's gone. I think it was a wolf. It was big and grey."

"More likely a coyote," Shotgun said. "I don't think there's any wolves around here. Too close to civilization."

Will shrugged. "Maybe."

Once back in the city, Stumpy headed south, cruising down Barrington Street as though leading a parade. Head held high and looking all around, he drove to the waterfront. He stopped the hearse near the Halifax-Dartmouth ferry terminal. Floyd opened his door. "Follow me. And try not to be too conspicuous," he said, looking back at Will and the others. "Keep back a ways."

After climbing out of the hearse, Floyd scanned the area, then hurried down Lower Water Street. Stumpy gave two quick taps on the hearse's horn, waved at them and drove off.

"Let's go," Shotgun said, as soon as Floyd was about a hundred feet away. Frantic shook his head. "You're as crazy as he is."

"What do you mean?"

"A 350-pound fancy-ass drug dealer everybody in the city knows, followed by four one-percenters wearing colours out for a stroll. And you think we're inconspicuous?"

Speedy looked at Shotgun. "He's right. Let's just hurry up and get rolling."

They all broke into a run and caught up with Floyd as he turned left down an alley, running at a right angle to the harbour. "Jesus Christ! What's wrong?" he asked, looking past them.

"Nothing. We just want to get going," Frantic said. "This the place?"

"Yeah." Floyd glanced down, jangling his key ring. "If I can remember which key it is." He turned to face the sliding door that fronted a low shingled building, a little bigger than a two-car garage.

"You ought to get Frenchy Jack to paint this place for you," Frantic said, picking at the peeling paint on the door. "What do you use this dump for anyway?"

Floyd wiggled a key into the heavy padlock. "Um, you know, storage." He turned the key and the lock popped open. "Wouldn't be good to paint it. Might attract attention."

Will and the others pushed their bikes out of the shed and wasted no time starting them.

"Damn it," Will called over to Shotgun and Frantic. "I forgot a toolbox Al gave me in Stumpy's hearse. Will you tell him to drop it off at my place if you see him before I do?"

Shotgun and Frantic nodded.

Will glanced down at his bike's vibrating gas tank. It startled him to see his father looking up at him. He touched the picture and took a deep breath, then pulled in the clutch, kicked the bike into gear and rode out of the alley. He rode up the steep hills from the waterfront, headed straight home at a relaxed pace, smiling up at the sun and shivering in the cool, clear air. When he neared the North Common, he looked across its broad, flat expanse of greenness and saw Sadie's Lodge, its lines and features crystal sharp. He closed the throttle and let the bike slow down. He pulled in the clutch and coasted to a stop at the curb on Cogswell Street, still staring at

Sadie's Lodge, now off to his right at two o'clock. He sat there, while the bike's motor ka-chugged beneath him – KA-CHUGG – KA-CHUGG – KA-CHUGG – turning over so slowly it seemed impossible it could keep running. Controlled fury. His to command at the twist of his wrist. "If only life could be like that," he muttered.

He looked long and hard at Sadie's Lodge, then found first gear and rode away. He rode through the lights at the Willow Tree intersection and went another block up Quinpool Road. He turned left onto Vernon Street and pulled into the small parking lot at the back of Danny's Restaurant. He slipped in through the back door and bumped into Steve, who was cooking at the grill.

Steve raised his eyebrows and nodded to him. "I heard through the grapevine you guys were heading back to town, but I didn't think I'd see you this soon." He poured some cooking oil on the grill and began to scour it with a wire brush. "Is everything going to work out?"

"As far as I know."

"Danny and I can put in a good word for you if you need it. You know, like how you did a good job when you worked here. Stuff like that." He smiled, and took a pumice stone to finish cleaning the grill.

"Thanks. I might need it." He walked to the swinging doors that led into the dining room. He looked through the small round window of one door. "I have to call my mother. Can I use the phone in here?"

"Go ahead. She's been here a couple times since you been gone." Steve ladled some fresh oil on the grill with a wooden spoon and smoothed it around. He placed two pork chops on the grill. They sizzled immediately. He put his hands on his hips and turned toward Will. "She's had a real hard time with what's been going on. Cops were there and everything. She's come here a couple times to get away from Sid – like she's always done."

Will nodded. "I know. I'm not looking forward to this." He paused. "Can you do me a favour? Call her and tell her I'm here. If Sid's there, tell her not say anything but just to come over." He paused. "I'm not sure I should go back there. Either way, be less of a scene if she comes here."

"Sure," Steve said, wiping his hands in his soiled white apron. "Don't worry about this kind of trouble, kid. Compared to the things I went through back in England during the war, what you're going through now is just a lark. All you have to do is don't hurt your mother. I've known her since way back when she met your father. And he was the kind of man who would never let anything hurt her."

While Steve went to the wall-phone in the kitchen, Will pushed the swinging doors open and sat in a booth at the back of the restaurant. From where he sat, he could see the front door and all the other booths. The restaurant was empty of people except for an elderly couple to his left and two waitresses chatting behind the cash at the front of the restaurant. Through the restaurant's plate-glass front windows, he could see traffic going by on Quinpool Road. He sat staring out the windows – waiting for his mother to come, wishing things could be easier.

THE CONTRITE CONSCIOUSNESS

H E WATCHED HIS MOTHER PULL open the heavy glass door and come into the restaurant. He saw Patty hurry in behind her before the door closed, pushing aviator sunglasses up to rest on the top of her head. He slid out of the booth and stood up, holding his hand up to get their attention.

Patty skipped up the aisle toward him with a big smile on her face. His mother followed, her face creased and puffy.

"Holy God! I didn't think you'd be coming back," Patty said, throwing her arms around his neck. She kissed his cheek, and then jumped back and looked him up and down. "They told us you got hurt, and everybody was saying the cops were going to get you and put you in prison for a long time. Or else that you were going to run away."

"Shh," his mother said, catching up to Patty and taking her arm. "There are people here." She hugged Will, burying her face into his shoulder.

"Well, it's true, Mom," Patty said, sliding down into the booth. "It's not like it's some kind of big friggin' secret. The whole world knows about it." She tapped her fingers on the top of the table. "God, let go of him. You're the one who's being embarrassing."

Will took her hand and guided her into the seat across from Patty. He sat next to her.

"So did you really do it?" Patty asked, leaning toward him. "What was it like?"

"Patty!" his mother said, wiping her eyes.

Will looked around. "I'm not allowed to talk about it," he whispered. "You know, the walls might have ears. But think about it. Do you really think the cops would let me ride back home free as a bird if I had actually shot anybody?"

Patty looked into his eyes. "I don't know. I guess not." She sat back in the booth. "Crap. How friggin' disappointing is that?"

"Anyway, it's over and done with. And I'm not on their most-wanted list any longer." He smiled at her.

She squinted at him. "Hmmph, you never were a good liar. Sometimes people just get away with things. That's what I think."

"I'm glad you two think this is something to joke about," his mother said, her voice hoarse and tight. "I can't find one thing to laugh or smile about. All I've done for the last few days is cry and be crazy with worry."

Will took her hand. "You're right. I'm sorry."

Patty looked at him and rolled her eyes.

"I should have left you home so your brother and I could talk," his mother said. "I should have known you wouldn't be able to be mature about this."

"Well, thanks a lot. You guys can talk if you want. I don't care. I won't say another friggin' word." She made a zipping motion across her lips. "Go ahead. Talk. Go on. Just ignore me. I'm used to it." She crossed her arms and stared up at the ceiling. "Oh yeah, one thing, though. Things aren't going to be all hunky-dory now that you're back. Dad says he's going to kill you."

Will nodded and glanced across at his mother. "Uh, huh. He's upset, eh?"

"Upset? Yeah, that's one way of putting it," Patty said, still staring at the ceiling.

He looked at his mother. "I was already thinking it would be better for everybody if I didn't go back. I can come get my stuff when he's not there."

His mother shook her head. "No. You have to come back – for me. I never ask you to do much, but you have to do this."

"It won't work," he said. "Too much has happened. Sid will never be able to get past this."

"Then, you'll have to find some way to make peace with him."

"Hah – good luck," Patty said, shaking her head.

"You can't go away now. Not like this," his mother continued, ignoring Patty. "It will kill me. You have to try to make peace with Sid and get things back to normal."

He took a deep breath. "Normal? Things have never been normal, not with Sid."

"You have to get away from that gang and get a regular job. *That* kind of normal. Normal like you used to be. Not doing crazy things and getting into trouble. It's going to be the death of me. Is that what you want to do – kill me with all this craziness?"

"Oh, God! Don't be so dramatic. *Ohh, poor me. Don't kill me,*" Patty mocked in a sing-song voice.

Will looked down and shook his head. "I'm sorry. I didn't mean for anything I did to hurt you. I just didn't think about how what I was doing might affect you."

His mother sighed. "Well, it did – it always does. You must know that."

The kitchen doors swung open and Steve bustled into the dining room, carrying a pizza on an aluminum tray. "Thought you might like a snack. It's got the works on it," he said, as he lowered it to their table. "On the house. What Danny doesn't know won't hurt him. Hold on. I'll get you plates and some pop."

They watched in silence as Steve hurried to the front of the restaurant and returned with three plates and some flatware, followed by one of the waitresses carrying glasses of pop.

"Is it Coke or Pepsi?" Patty asked, after the waitress had placed the glasses on the table and turned to leave.

"Coke, I think," Steve said.

Patty curled her lip. "Pepsi's better."

"Ignore her," her mother said.

Steve laughed. "They're all the same at that age. Hope you like the pizza." He pivoted away and headed back to the kitchen.

"That old bald fart. What does he know about kids?"

"You were being rude," her mother said.

"I was not. All I said was Pepsi's better than Coke. What's rude about that? It's a friggin' fact. Pepsi *is* better than Coke."

Will began to separate the pieces of pizza. He slid a slice on each plate. "Is Sid home now?"

"He's sleeping. He'll be getting up soon to get ready for work," his mother said. She pushed the slice of pizza around her plate with her fork, staring down at it. "You can't stay with that bunch, Will. That's the cause of all this trouble."

He took a bite of pizza, then a drink of Coke. "I understand how you feel. But I can't leave right now." He shook his head. "It's not time."

"What do you mean 'not time'?"

He shrugged. "It's hard to explain. I'm not ready."

"I know what he means," Patty said, perking up. "He wants to keep having fun. That's all. He's not ready to go back to being a momma's boy, prissy little jerk – like he used to be. That's all." She grinned at them.

"And how much more trouble are you going to have to get in before you *are* ready," his mother asked, her mouth quivering.

"I know, I mean, I know I have to be more careful. I promise you right now that I'll stay out of trouble, and I won't bring any trouble home. Barry has settled things with the police and that other club. I'll be going back to work at Saint Mary's before long. Everything's going to be okay, you'll see." He paused. "It's just Sid."

His mother folded and unfolded her hands. "Maybe you could wait and call him at work. Try to talk to him on the phone and break the ice that way."

Will looked down. "No, I think it would be better if I went there and talked to him man to man. He'd probably think I was being a coward if I called him on the phone."

"I could go with you," Patty said. "If I was there, he might not beat you too bad."

"I'm not worried about that."

"Haaahhh – you friggin' should be."

Will smiled. "I think I know what makes him tick. I'll tell him whatever I have to. Whatever he wants to hear. I think I can reason with him."

"At least he wouldn't be drinking yet," his mother said.

He took another bite of pizza and another drink of Coke. He slid out of the booth. "You two stay here, okay? It'll be better if it's only the two of us there."

"Hmmph. Have it your way, stupid," Patty said.

"Be careful," his mother said. "If he goes crazy, just get out of there."

He nodded and turned toward the kitchen. He waved to Steve as he breezed through. "Thanks, Steve."

Steve looked up from the grill. "Make sure you keep enough slack in your chain. Know what I mean? Most guys keep them too tight. Binds things up and saps power. One of the first things I learned working on Triumphs during the war." He smiled. "You had a Bonneville, didn't you?"

Will slowed at the back door. He nodded. "Yeah, before I got the Harley."

He rode straight to Sadie's Lodge and throttled up the driveway, spinning the back wheel in the dirt. He noticed the toolbox Al had given him sitting on the ground up against the big garage door. His legs felt stiff once he put them on the ground, and he prodded at the sidestand twice with his left foot before flicking it out and leaning the bike against it. He dismounted and stood facing the house, with the bike between him and the back door. He could hear thumping from inside the house. Then, Sid burst through the back door, barefoot in khaki pants and a white T-shirt. He charged toward him, wiping shaving cream from his face with a hand towel. He slowed when his feet landed on the gravel of the driveway.

"YOU LITTLE BASTARD! WHAT ARE YOU DOING HERE?" he screamed.

"I came to apologize to you."

"APOLOGIZE!?" He lurched toward the bike and threw the towel to the ground, breathing hard and shaking. "It'll take a whole lot more than an apology to make up for what you did!"

"I know. You're right. But I have to start somewhere, right?"

"Goddamn you. I should kick your ass right now and then call the cops. They'd thank me for it. What are you doing back here anyway? Shouldn't you still be hiding in a hole somewhere?"

Will nodded. "I came to apologize for all the trouble I caused – for making things hard for you and Mom. You've got a right to be mad at me. I'm sorry."

"Yeah, well … well …" Sid sputtered, his breathing slowing down. "You're Goddamn right you made things hard. It didn't surprise me that you got in shit. I could see it coming. I told your mother that a dozen times – a hundred times! You didn't hurt me. Just proved me right. But you broke your mother's heart. Big shot criminal, right? Getting all kinds of attention. You must be proud of yourself."

"No, I'm not proud of that. I didn't want to hurt her, or upset you, or cause any kind of trouble for our family. Things kind of happened that I didn't expect. I got caught up in it all." He shook his head and shrugged. "I made a mistake."

Sid put his hands on his hips. "More than a mistake, I'd say. You fucked up worse than even *I* thought you would."

"Yeah. I guess you're right."

Sid paused. "No guessing about it. I *am* right."

Will nodded and looked down at the bike. "Yeah, you're right, Sid. Sorry."

Sid stared at him, then cocked his head to the side. "You serious? Or are you jerking me around? Playing me for some kind of fool? Is that it?"

"I'm serious. I was in the wrong. You were right. I screwed up." He hesitated. "Will you accept my apology?"

Sid crossed his arms and looked from side to side. "Yeah, well, even if I do accept your apology – which I don't know yet if I will – there's no way you can come back here. Not doing what you're doing. And what about the cops? Why you bothering to apologize to me? They're going to throw you in jail soon as they get their hands on you. Don't expect me to help you with that."

"We heard there wasn't enough evidence for them to arrest anybody. They withdrew the warrants."

Sid shook his head. "That explains it – why you're back here sucking up to me. You must really be desperate for somebody to mooch off. Your mother must be behind this."

"No. It was my idea to come talk to you."

Sid looked down at the bike. "That'd be a first. You never talk to me. We don't communicate. Remember?"

Will nodded.

"It's okay. I know you think I'm a prick. Hate my guts, right?" He stepped gingerly around the bike until he was standing closer to Will. "You know, I tried as best I could to be a father to you. Most men in my position wouldn't have bothered to do anything with a kid who wasn't theirs. But I did." He shook his head. "But, by the Jesus, you pushed me away every time. Very first time I saw you, you ran your wagon into my shins. You probably don't remember any of that. But I kept trying. After a while, I just gave up. I couldn't turn you around and make you like me."

Will slid his hands into his pockets. They both stood still, looking down at the bike.

"I didn't realize I was doing that," Will said.

"Do you think I liked being around a kid that hated me. You couldn't hide it – not that you ever tried. It wasn't fuckin' easy, you know."

Will looked across at him. "I don't hate you. I never really thought about it. There were some good things." He hesitated. "But some things have just happened that shouldn't have, I guess."

Sid laughed. "You can say that again. I know you never thought about it. Kids don't usually know when they're being selfish. Your sister's no different. She's already started to run wild. Don't care about me or anybody else." He became quiet again. "So good for you – you're acting like a man for a change. Too bad we never talked like this before – before it was too late." He took a deep breath. "Okay, now you made your big apology, and my heart's bleeding all over the place. So what?"

"Um, well, do you think you can accept my apology? Maybe we can try to start over."

Sid crossed his arms again and looked at him, frowning. "Too little, too late, I'd say. You're already a long way down the wrong road. I don't see you turning things around, and I sure as hell don't got the energy to do it after all these years."

Will nodded. "I understand. It's no problem. I can find a place to stay. I'll get Frenchy Jack to come by with his truck and help me get my stuff out of the garage." He smiled. "You'll be able to park your car there again."

Sid continued to stare at him, not moving from his spot.

"I'll find some way to put Mom's mind at ease about not coming back. At least she'll be relieved to know we talked this out in a civilized way."

Sid uncrossed his arms and began to step lightly back toward the house. When he reached the top of the steps, he stopped and turned around. "Jesus H. Christ, I'll have to listen to her for the next 20 years harping at me about how I drove you away, and blaming me for anything that happens to you from here on – her *precious* little boy." He shook his head. "Goddamn it! I'm already blamed for everything that goes wrong."

He lowered himself and sat on the top step, leaning back against the door. He ran his fingers through his hair. "Remember how I used to say you should join the forces?"

Will nodded. "Yeah, I do. You used to show me those films about Royal Military College. And you showed me how to spit-shine your boots."

"You remember that, eh Joe?" He grinned. "Well, the way you fucked up, you can't go to RMC now. But you might be able to enlist and go through basic training – like I did. That'd sure help straighten you out. There's worse things than being a military man."

"I'd have to think about it more. I mean, I know it makes sense." He paused. "I just wouldn't want to screw up something like that."

"Well, thinking about things is all fine and good, but you also gotta start doing something with your life. Take my word for it, you're not *that* special and this ain't Disneyland. There's limits to how much time real men have to figure out what to do with their lives – besides blowing it away like you're doing now. We didn't *think* about it in my day. We just did what we knew we had to do."

Will shrugged. "What can I say? You're right."

"Aw, Jesus Christ, stop saying that. I can't believe how much of a sucker I am for swallowing all this." He hesitated and sighed. "You got two or three months to get your act together. If I don't see any improvement by then, you're out of here with my boot in your arse. And if you screw up again like you already done and bring your shit back here, you better not ever let me see your face again."

Will smiled. "Thanks, Sid. I won't let you down. I promise. You won't even know I'm here." He walked to the bottom of the step and held his hand out to Sid.

Sid looked at him, expressionless. "Let's not take this too far. It's not like we found Jesus and are gonna get all huggy."

Will grinned and began to turn back to his bike.

"Hey," Sid said. "Just a minute."

Will stopped.

"The way you got that picture taped on your gas tank – it looks stupid. Couldn't you find a better place to put your father's picture? Especially where he's in uniform. What the hell were you thinking? Jesus, do think he'd be proud of you right now, or happy to have his picture taped on the gas tank of some Goddamn hippie bike?"

Will looked over at his bike. "I don't know. You're probably right."

"Well show some respect and put it some place decent." He stood up and chuckled, shaking his head.

"What?"

"It's funny – least it makes you think. Here, somebody like me comes back from Korea without a scratch, and a man like him is still back there under that stinking dirt – even better men than him."

Will nodded. "Yeah, makes you think."

"Your mother never let go of him, you know. I've had to compete with a dead man all along. That's been a big part of the problem right from the start – all our problems, if you ask me. And, now, here you are dragging his picture out just to make sure I never forget it. Your big war-hero father. Got himself blown up trying to help some other Joe." He shook his head and turned to open the back door. "No way I can win," he muttered.

THE ART OF PERSUASION

WHEN HE AWOKE IT WAS dark. He sat up and looked around, trying to shake off the grogginess that clogged his mind. The open book that lay heavy on his chest fell to the floor with a thunk. He bent and picked it up, holding it to the faint light trickling in through the windows of the garage doors. He squinted to read the book's title – *The Collected Dialogues*. He placed the book next to him on his cot. He heard tapping at the side door, and realized it was the tapping that had just awaken him.

"Will? You there?" his mother asked. "Unlock the door."

He jumped up, switched on the light and opened the door.

"I thought you were here, but I didn't know if I should wake you up," she said, stepping inside.

He plopped down on the cot again. "I remember lying down after Sid left, but nothing else. I haven't slept much the last few days."

"I don't imagine." She smiled and pushed his hair away from his face. "You seem better. More relaxed."

She nodded. "I don't know what you said to Sid, but I guess it was the right thing. He was calm and quiet when Patty and I got back home. He said he figured you had learned a lesson and might finally be growing up."

"I just apologized and told him he was right about everything."

His mother took a deep breath. "He's not all bad, you know."

"Uh, huh."

She sat next to him, putting her arm around his waist. "Those two girls came here while you were gone to tell me what was going on. Kay and Gloria, I think their names were."

"I asked Gloria to come. I couldn't call you." He hesitated. "Was it okay? I mean, did it help anything?"

"A little. They put my mind at ease about you not being hurt. We were told you had been hit by a chain."

He shook his head. "It wasn't anything. I don't have a mark on me."

"And they said everything was going to work out with the police. I never asked how they knew." She paused. "Which one is your girlfriend?"

"The blonde one – Gloria. Well, I wouldn't actually say she's my girlfriend. I just met her about a week ago. I think it was a week. I've lost track of the days. The dark-haired one is Kay. She's Shotgun's girlfriend."

"That Gloria sure is a pretty thing. Seems nice, too." She glanced down at her hands. "But she dresses kind of trashy. Does she dress like that all the time?"

He laughed. "She was probably going to or coming from work. She works at a bar. But she also goes to university. She even gave me a couple philosophy books. Look." He handed her the Plato book, then got up and retrieved the Aristotle text from Al's toolbox.

"That's nice. Maybe she'll be a good influence on you." She examined the books. "What did you say they were about?"

"Philosophy – ancient Greek philosophy."

She shook her head. "Don't ask me what that is."

He laughed. "I know what you mean. Don't ask me either."

"Oh, I almost forgot. I got you something, too." She jumped up and hurried to the far corner of the garage. From the shadows, she grabbed two large garbage bags and dragged them back to the cot. "Take a look. I got all this stuff at a garage sale yesterday – just next door."

He reached into one bag, then the other, and pulled out all the objects, wide-eyed – a collapsed easel, a palette, canvases, watercolour paper, and dozens of tubes of paint and artists brushes.

"You got this for me?"

"Uh, huh. I know you don't know how to paint. I didn't even know if you'd be interested. But I was rushing to Danny's Restaurant yesterday and it caught my eye. The man next door had it all set up near his garage. For some reason, it made me think of your father when I saw it. He liked beautiful things and would always point out something pretty or interesting – flowers, trees, clouds, sunsets, people's faces – all kinds of things that I wouldn't even notice until he pointed them out to me. He had a way of seeing things that other people didn't."

"I like this stuff. Maybe I could learn how to paint."

"It doesn't really matter if you don't use it. I just got it because it made me feel good."

He smiled. "No, really, I like it. Maybe it can be part of my rehabilitation. You know, anything to help keep me out of prison – philosophy, art, the army. Something's got to work."

"Now you're making fun of me,"

"No, I'm only teasing. I think it's great." He hugged her, and she kissed his cheek.

"I wanted to tell you I'm going to bingo," she said. "In case you came in the house looking for me. There's leftovers in the fridge. You're probably hungry."

She kissed him again, jumped up and hurried back to the house. He stayed behind, examining the tubes of paint and brushes. He opened several tubes and squeezed small blobs of paint onto a palette. He felt their liquid-smooth texture, swirling the velvety paint between his fingers and thumb. He began mixing the blobs of paint together to produce different hues and tones.

By the time he went into the house, his mother had gone. He found a plate of baked chicken in the refrigerator and began to eat with one hand while he dialled the phone with the other.

"Hi, it's me," he said.

"Where are you?" Gloria asked.

"I'm home. We got back this afternoon, but I had to sort out a few things right away."

"How's your mother doing?"

"She's okay now. Better than I thought she'd be."

"She was really upset when Kay and I went there. I think it was more from what the police and everybody else were telling her than from what happened."

"I know." He paused. "I guess I've been pretty selfish in all this. I didn't think much about how everybody else might be affected – including you. I was just focusing on myself. I'll have to be more careful from now on."

"Yeah. It's been a strange experience, that's for sure. But I wouldn't want you to be *too* careful. That might be boring. A little risk is good. And a little bad behaviour can be interesting."

He laughed. "And just when I was ready to turn over a new leaf. So, even if I'm suddenly more boring, will you still like me?"

"I don't remember saying I did like you."

"Well, would you want to see me again? I mean, to help you decide?"

"Hmm, let me think." She paused. "Well, I have to go to work in a little over an hour. But my roommates aren't here right now. I suppose you could come over. Maybe you could talk dirty to me to persuade me that you're not too boring. Wait, let me rephrase that. Maybe you could come over and talk that philosophy talk to me – or whatever that talk is that you talk. It worked once before."

Within ten minutes, he had showered and changed. Ten minutes later, he backed into the curb outside Gloria's place on LeMarchant Street. And ten minutes after that, he was in her bed, lowering himself against her perfect naked body.

"I had almost forgotten how beautiful you are," he murmured.

"It hasn't been *that* long."

"Feels like it." He kissed her forehead, her eyes, her lips. "I think I love you."

"You *think* you love me. Love isn't something you think. Is it?"

"I love you."

"Maybe. Or maybe you're just saying that have sex with me."

"Um, experience would suggest I don't have to."

Forty minutes later, she stood before him naked, her body glistening with sweat, illuminated by the flickering, golden glow of a bedside candle. He lay on his back with his hands behind his head, watching her.

"What's that scent?" he asked.

"The candle? It's honeysuckle, I think. Do you like it?"

"Yeah."

"You can stay here if you want. I'll be back around four in the morning."

"Thanks, but I should go home. My mother would probably have a stroke if I didn't go home tonight, after all that's happened."

"Okay."

"Oh, by the way, I'm going to paint you."

She put her hands on her hips and faced him. "Paint me? As in finger-paint my body?"

He laughed. "Maybe that, too. But what I meant was to do a painting of your naked body – probably with watercolours."

"Sounds like fun. I didn't know you knew how to paint?"

"I don't. But I'll learn. My mother got me a bunch of supplies the other day. To help reform me, I think."

"What does she want you to become – if you end up being reformed, I mean."

He pushed himself up on his elbows. "That, I don't know. Just to be more normal, I guess – a lawyer or doctor maybe. Every mother would be happy to have her son become a lawyer, right?"

"Hmm. I'm not sure. You're probably smart enough to do it, but I don't know if you have enough of that shallow cleverness in you to be good at it. Anyway, sounds pretty dreadful to me."

He laughed. "I suppose I'll just go back to painting with Frenchy Jack – that kind of normal. By the time we finish the house on Inglis Street we started last week, it should be time for me to start work at Saint Mary's. That job should last about a year. After that, who knows?"

The heavy rain that pounded down on the garage roof through the night continued into the morning, keeping Will in the garage and away from Mildred's house on Inglis Street.

The wet wind-driven weather took hold, seizing the city tight in a dull, soggy grip.

"*Merde!*" Frenchy Jack exclaimed, spitting on the ground, as they stood on the sidewalk later in the day, looking up at Mildred's house. "*Tabernacle.* Shit on Goddamn *Nouvelle Écosse* rain. Soak all *de* shingle. No paint even if it not rain. Too wet, *oui*?"

"Friggin' *oui* is right," Speedy said. "If you ain't got no inside work for us, we're gonna have to get work somewhere else."

"Or get back to pushing hash," Frantic said, shrugging.

"I try find new job. Got idea for new paint job. You work, eh Willie? You good man."

"Sure," Will said, pulling the collar of his jacket up against the back of his neck.

"What about us?" Speedy asked, scowling.

"*Oui,* you okay. Maybe Frantic okay, too. *Mais non* Stumpy. *Gros cochon.* He too fat and slow. Break ladder. Laugh at Jacques."

"What the hell you sayin'?" Frantic asked.

"He was just saying Stumpy's a little slow. But he'll try to find work for us," Will said.

Frenchy Jack winked at him.

"Ah, I don't care anyway," Frantic said. "I got a line on a good deal for some hash through Floyd. You in Speedy?"

"Better than shivering in this damn fog."

A car's horn honked behind them, making them jump. They turned and saw Stumpy's hearse scrunch up against the curb. The electric window on the passenger side slid down.

"Will," Stumpy called, waving for Will to approach.

Will walked to the hearse, looking left and right up Inglis Street, then bent at the waist to jut his head in through the window. "No work today. Still too wet," he said to Stumpy.

"I'm not here for that." He looked past Will at the others. "Listen. Barry wants you to come to a meeting tomorrow with him and me. He set up a meeting with the Devil's Chain brass."

Will frowned. "Why me?"

"Beats me. All he said was for me to get you to come because you know how to talk. What the hell does that mean? We all know how to talk."

Will shrugged. "Only the three of us?"

"Yeah. And three of them. Floyd helped set it up. Will you be at your place?"

Will nodded.

"We'll pick you up a little before 12 o'clock. Meeting's at 12."

"Where?"

"Saint Agnes Church."

"You're kidding."

Stumpy shook his head. "Don't ask me. Be ready." He glanced over his shoulder and peeled way, spinning up wet fallen leaves and a fine spray of brownish water.

"What'd he want?" Frantic asked.

"Didn't say much," Will said. "You know him."

Garrity and Akerman looked all around before opening the big oak doors leading into the parish hall attached to the back of Saint Agnes Church, at the corner of Chebucto Road and Mumford Road. "Over there," Akerman said, pointing at a small shoulder-high rectangular window that faced the parking lot. They walked over and stood in front of the window. "What time is it?" Akerman asked.

Garrity tugged at the left sleeve of his jacket and glanced down. "Eleven-thirty."

"Think those clowns will actually show up?" Akerman asked, kneeling on one knee to place a brown leather briefcase on the floor. He unsnapped the locks and flipped up the top. He snatched up a small silver camera and two pair of binoculars, holding a pair out to Garrity.

Garrity nodded. "Barry knows his sweet deal will go sour if he tries to jerk us around. We've been keeping our end of the bargain riding that other gang hard. There aren't too many left on the street, right?" He strung the strap of his binoculars around his neck.

"Five at last count – seven or eight counting a few prospects."

Garrity raised the binoculars to his eyes and scanned the parking lot, adjusting the focus. "This part is almost done, Jim."

Akerman sighed. "It's the big game I'm anxious to bring down."

"Need big guns for that." He lowered the binoculars and turned to Akerman. "We gotta push the limits, Jim. Not this chicken-shit, deal-making, smooth-things-over crap."

A half hour later, a black Cadillac hearse turned off Chebucto Road into the Saint Agnes Church parking lot and eased toward the west end of its paved surface, stopping near the parish hall.

"Yeah, baby. Now we're talking," Garrity said, whistling through his teeth and nudging Akerman with his elbow. Akerman crowded against him and jerked his binoculars up to his face.

A few seconds later, a light-blue Ford Mustang, with yellow and red flames on the front fender panels, pulled into the parking lot from Mumford Road and slowed to a stop, facing the hearse. Barry, Stumpy, and Will climbed out of the hearse and walked toward the Mustang, from which three other men emerged and stepped forward to meet them.

"You the prez?" Barry asked the man who stood in the middle and slightly ahead of the other two.

The man nodded. "Sloper."

"Barry." He held out his hand.

Sloper shook it. "I know." He looked at Will. "He clean?"

"We're all clean," Barry said.

Barry, Will, and Stumpy pulled back their jackets.

"You?"

Sloper and the others did the same.

Barry took out his cigarettes and offered them around. Only Sloper took one. Barry lit the two cigarettes and dragged on his. "Okay, let's get down to business." He blew smoke out the side of his mouth. "Sloper, the way I see it, there's not much life left in your club. Don't get me wrong, I'm not saying that to provoke anything. I'm just stating the facts. The heat's on you guys like stink on a corpse." He glanced back at the hearse. "We got it on good authority they're not going to ease up."

"We'll ride it out," Sloper said.

"Maybe so. Maybe not," Barry said, scratching his temple. "But my bet would be maybe not."

Sloper puffed on his cigarette. "What's it to you what happens to us?" he asked, exhaling. "You worried about us or something? Like I said, we'll ride it out."

Barry smiled. "Things are never as simple as they seem, are they, my friend? See, the other problem, Sloper, is we don't want you around either. Although we've taken a little breather from all the waltzing around, nothing's changed. You guys were pushing your luck all along. This is like a case of how two objects can't occupy the same space at the same time. So we wanted to tell you face to face we'll be hunting you down one by one." He dragged again on his cigarette.

Sloper stared at him, then glanced at Will and Stumpy. "Something new about that?"

Barry shrugged. "We've been doing our own police work. If you think you got it bad now with the cops, wait till the Dark Angels start hunting you for real." He paused. "Close your eyes, Sloper. Come on, close them."

Sloper continued to stare at him.

"Picture this, Sloper. You go to your bike or your car, and – *Oh Shit* – it blows up when you start it. Or, oh man, you go home or wherever you hang out, and turn the doorknob and – *Fuck* – another explosion blows your arms off. Or you see your brains blow out through the front of your skull – *Oh Jesus* – and splatter on the ground in front of you just as you hear the blast of a Magnum behind you. Can you picture that, Sloper?"

Sloper chuckled. "You should write stories. You talk so fuckin' picturesque. Okay, I give up. What's the deal?"

Barry looked at Will, then Stumpy. "Do you know something I don't? You bring some kind of deal for Sloper and the Devil's Chain?"

Will and Stumpy shook their heads.

"There's no deal," Barry said solemnly. "We just wanted you to know we plan to kill whichever ones of you the cops don't put away. That's the proposition, which is not the same as a deal, Sloper. Look it up in the dictionary."

Sloper was silent for a moment. "Let's go, boys. We're out of here." They turned toward the Mustang.

THE DANCE

"Wait, Sloper," Will said. He turned to Barry. "I've got an idea that might save some trouble and blood, and let all of us come out ahead of the cops. It doesn't feel right letting the cops win any of this."

Barry flicked his cigarette away. "Not interested. I like my proposition."

Will shrugged. "Okay, you're right. Your plan is tight. But ..."

"But what?" Stumpy joined in.

"But it will be a lot of work – a lot of time and energy – tracking down and killing a half dozen guys. Probably taking some heat and losing a few of our guys. That's time and energy we could be using to ride our bikes and party. And build our club."

"So what's your idea?" Sloper asked. "We all kiss and make up? Pretend nothing's happened?"

Will smiled. "In a manner of speaking."

Sloper stepped forward. "What the hell you talking about, kid?"

"We could do what some other clubs have done. The Dark Angels could absorb the Devil's Chain."

"Absorb? What's that mean?" Sloper asked.

"It means we agree to give full membership to any member of the Devil's Chain who wants to join the Dark Angels. You'd have to come over as prospects, but that would just be a formality. We'd vote you in within a month. But your club would have to be finished – gone, forever. And you'd all have to come over at the same time. You'd be able to retire your colours. Put them away somewhere."

Sloper glanced at the other two Devil's Chain members. He looked back at Will and shook his head. "You know that's not how it works. When there's an offer like that, the members of club that gets taken in get full membership right away. No prospecting."

"There's a difference in our circumstances, Sloper," Will said. "The difference is that we're more or less at war, and offers of full membership would only go to friendly clubs that are already on good terms with the more powerful club. *Really* good terms – like if they've already done some good work for the bigger club. So being taken in as prospects straight off is a fair deal, don't you think? I mean, as compared to being murdered."

"Hold on, Will," Barry said. "Seems a little *too* generous to me. We've got some guys who're real keen to start shooting. It'll be hard to get the whole club to go along with this."

"We'd have to take it to our guys, too," Sloper said. He hesitated. "I'll think on it tonight. My guess is my guys will go in whatever direction I think is best. Twenty-four hours?"

Barry nodded.

"I'll get word to you through Floyd," Sloper said, turning away.

"Sloper," Barry called, just as the three reached the Mustang. He took a few steps toward the car and waved for Sloper to come back. "Just you," he said. They met halfway between the hearse and Mustang.

"If you can pull this off, there'll be no prospecting for you," Barry said. "You are the president, after all. You have to think smart now, Sloper." Barry took a Dark Angels' business card from his jacket and held it out to him. "My number's on the back. Call me directly. Don't bother with Floyd."

Sloper took the card and slipped it into his pocket as Will and Stumpy approached them. He looked at the three of them and nodded.

"Your name," Will said. "Is it Sloper as in BSA Sloper from the thirties?"

"Yeah. My old man got one from England after the war. He was in the Canadian Merchant Navy. It was the first motorcycle I ever saw."

"Does he still have it?" Barry asked.

"No. My old lady got rid of it once he was gone. He survived the war and all the trips back and forth across the Atlantic and all them Nazi U-boats, then goes and drowns in a lake on a damn fishing trip." He shook his head. "I can still picture that bike like it was right in front of me now."

"Bad shit about your old man," Barry said.

"Yeah, too bad," Sloper said. "But I got over it."

Will stared at him. "You got over it? How do you get over something like that?"

Sloper shrugged and looked down. "I don't know – you just do. Not like it makes any difference today anyway. It's all in the past."

The Dark Angels watched in silence as Sloper walked back to the Mustang. They watched as it pulled out of the parking lot and headed west down Mumford Road.

"Solid guy," Stumpy said.

Will nodded.

"Maybe we should really let him in and let him stay," Barry said.

"Only him, though," Stumpy said. "We don't need no more of them."

"Yeah, he'd be good," Will said.

Leaving the Saint Agnes Church parking lot, they drove east up Chebucto Road, toward the downtown.

"Where you headed?" Will asked Stumpy.

"Clubhouse, I guess."

"Can you drop me off on Spring Garden Road? I have to meet Gloria."

Stumpy nodded.

"You did good, Will," Barry said. "We'll have to make you one of our main negotiators from now on – whenever that kind of thing is called for." He looked at Stumpy. "David and Goliath – Will and you. Right, Stump?"

Stumpy frowned. "Who're they?"

Barry laughed. "Couple old dudes from the Bible days."

Stumpy shook his head in disgust. "Where on Spring Garden?" he asked Will.

"Down by Barrington, I guess – that end."

Will climbed out of the hearse when Stumpy stopped across from Saint Mary's Basilica. He waved at Stumpy and Barry, waiting until they drove away before crossing the street. He walked up Spring Garden Road, approaching the Halifax Public Library. He stopped in front of the library and looked all around. Like a thief worried about being fingered, he turned his collar up, lowered his head and stole inside the building. He spent an hour picking through rows and stacks of books, leaving with several hardcover books tucked in the crook of his right arm.

Around the corner from the library, on Doyle Street, he noticed a sign that said Zwicker's Gallery. He stopped, drawn to it. When he reached the front door, he shifted his load of books to his left arm and pulled the door open.

A middle-aged man stepped forward from around a high counter of polished mahogany. "Oh my, let me give you a hand with those books," he said, with a thick British accent. He took hold of half the books and thumped them onto the top of the counter, while Will glanced from side to side.

"Are you looking for anything in particular?"

"No. Would it be all right if I just looked around?"

"Of course. We're a private gallery and most of the paintings are for sale, so we're happy to have people come through. Take as long as you want. Do you know anything about Zwicker's?"

"No. I didn't even know it was here until a few minutes ago."

The proprietor smiled. "You can certainly be forgiven for that. We moved up here from Granville Street a short time ago. We're one of the oldest private galleries in Canada – possibly the oldest. We've been in operation since 1886."

Will placed the rest of his books on the counter. For half an hour, he inched his way throughout the three levels of the gallery, absorbing its atmosphere and studying the paintings. On the main level, he came upon a studio flooded with natural light from opaque windows set in the back wall. A young man with thick curly hair worked over a large wooden table, overflowing with canvases, frames, and supplies.

"You can come in if you want," he said, glancing up at Will.

"No, it's okay. I don't want to interrupt what you're doing."

"Don't worry about that. People are in and out of here all the time. This is a working gallery. We do restorations and framings. A couple artists use the studio to paint."

"It's great," Will said. "Everything looks right and smells so good. It's all really peaceful."

"I find the whole place vibrates with some kind of creative energy. I keep hoping I'll be able to plug into it at some point, or get electrocuted by it." He laughed.

Will nodded. "Maybe that's what I'm feeling."

He walked home with his heavy load of books under a bright sun, amidst leaves that swirled down from the tress and rustled under his feet.

"All my clothes?" Gloria asked, her eyes widening.

"Yes, please."

She removed the last of her clothing and lay back down on his cot, tossing her bra at him. "Well, at least you're paying a little more attention to me. You've had your nose in those books and have been playing with those paints so much the last two weeks, I was starting to think you'd lost interest in me."

"Sorry. I've just been preoccupied." He knelt in front of the cot and kissed her. "And I just wanted to have enough confidence to do it." He reached to position her so she was facing him, leaning on her left elbow, her left leg straight and her right leg bent at the knee. He went back behind the easel and looked at her. "Can you tilt your head up and to the left a little so I can see the shape of your jaw better? That's it. No, don't smile. Now, turn your left shoulder a little to the left. Good."

He began to sketch the shapes on the rough Arches paper with quick strokes, glancing back and forth from the paper to her body.

"How long will it take?" she asked.

"This part shouldn't take too long – half an hour maybe. The watercolours will take a lot longer, but I won't need you to pose for that. Unless I get stuck on some of the tones or highlights." He paused. "In which case, you might have to stay naked for a few days."

She smiled. "Well then, you'll have to fire up that old stove over there because it's rather cool in here for a girl to be naked and unattended. Although, I imagine you could also take breaks every so often to warm up your subject, or model, or whatever it is I am. I'm sure you wouldn't want big goose bumps to ruin your painting."

"That would be bad. Um, about your breasts – would you like me to do them as they are, or would you prefer them bigger or smaller?"

"Hmm. Up to you. Might be interesting to see what you choose."

He nodded and kept sketching. "And what about your nipples – current placement okay, or should I make an adjustment?"

"Suit yourself. You could experiment. Try one on my forehead, Pablo."

"And what about their prominence, their, um, protuberance?"

"That might depend on that old stove." She shook her head. "You're funny."

He smiled. "I try."

"I know. You're only funny because you're jokes are so corny, and you think you're quite witty."

"I know. I do it on purpose."

She laughed. "Now, *that's* funny." She was quiet for a moment. "But what about those watercolours? It must get cold enough in here to freeze water in the winter. What're you going to do then? You'll have to use oil paints."

"It won't get *that* cold. Besides, I really like watercolours so far. It's the water that makes them interesting." He caught her eye and winked.

"Okay, tell me." She shook her head. "I know, you're waiting for me to be surprised and exclaim 'Oh, Will, whatever do you mean? How could water make something interesting? Pray, enlighten me, wonder boy'."

He laughed. "Well, if you insist. You see, it's like a motorcycle. You can never completely control a motorcycle. You just dance with it and persuade it to do what you want it to do. You have to understand it and anticipate what it's going to do in itself and in how it moves over the pavement – the surface – and you try to make it more of an extension of yourself than you are an extension of it. But you can never dominate it. It's the same with how you have to deal with water when you paint in watercolour. If you try to make the water do something that it doesn't want to, that's not in its nature, well, you might just end up with a back run into your nipple and that could be disfiguring. It might look bad, but then again it might not. You never know. It's the unpredictability I like."

She looked at him with a flat expression. "You're so strange."

"That's why you like me, right?"

"That's one of the reasons." She paused. "So when can I see it?"

"When it's finished."

"Why not sooner? I'm excited. Can't you tell?"

"For one thing, it's only started and it's probably not going to be very good." He smiled at her. "I'd rather you be disappointed only once, instead of many times before it's finished. For another, you'll probably point out something you think isn't quite right, or that could be better. And then,

I'll be trying to paint you as you see yourself instead of the way I see you. I have to learn to be my own critic."

"You're silly. I would like it because you did it, not because it's perfect."

He awoke the next morning and smiled to see the day had dawned clear and dry. He strapped his work gear on the back of his bike with bungee cords and rode straight to Saint Mary's at the end of Robie Street – shivering all the way. He found Harry in a plywood trailer on the job site, the word 'Office' stenciled above the door in black.

"I'm not going to put you back on the concrete crew. They're all black guys from Preston and Cherry Hill," Harry said, shaking Will's hand. "We already tried one white guy with them. He didn't last a day. They hang real tight together and they've got their own pecking order."

"It'd be fine."

"Nope. Especially if they get wind of the fact you're with that bike club." He shook his head. "Besides, I thought you might like a chance to pick up some carpentry skills, so I'm going to pair you up with Jean – Jean Bourque. You'll work with him as a carpenter's helper. He's from Wedgeport. Good man. He's been with us a long time."

Will shrugged. "It's up to you."

"Well, I can't picture you shovelling concrete all your life." He turned and waved for a wiry middle-aged man with a head of thick grey hair that looked like an industrial-grade Brillo pad to come over.

"I think you two are from the same neck of the woods," Harry said, introducing Will to Jean Bourque.

"I was born in Yarmouth," Will said. "Harry said you're from Wedgeport." Jean nodded. "Been here a few years." He patted Will's arm. "Ready?"

"He doesn't waste time," Harry said, chuckling.

"Or words," Will said.

It was almost as cool at the end of the day as it had been in the morning when Will rode back home, this time headed north on Robie Street. He sped down the far-right lane, squeezing between parked cars and cars in the nearest lane to his left, scattering dry leaves and road dust in his wake.

"Mom?" he called out as he walked through the back door at Sadie's Lodge, heading to the bathroom. "Gonna shower, okay?" He peered into the darkened bedroom. "Mom? You there?"

"Just having a rest," she said from the bed.

He hesitated at the bedroom door. "Everything all right?"

"Uh, huh. Not feeling too good that's all." She remained lying motionless on the bed, her back to him.

He glanced around, then walked to the bed and sat at her back. "Where's Sid?"

"Not here."

"Why don't you feel good? What's wrong?"

"Nothing serious."

"What does that mean?"

"It's Patty."

He could feel the bed begin to shake as she started to cry. "What about Patty?"

"She's – she's gone. He caught her drinking with a boy in the basement a few hours ago. He dragged the boy upstairs and threw him out the back door." She began to sob. "Patty got mouthy with him and he turned on her. Turned on his own daughter and beat her with his fists. I tried to stop him. But I couldn't." She rolled over toward him, and he could see her swollen cheeks and eyes, and the bloody Kleenex she held against her nose. "He was like a crazy man. Worse than I ever saw him. Patty took off. Said she was never coming back."

"Jesus, Mom!" He jumped up from the bed. "We've got to get you to a doctor. We'll find Patty later."

She shook her head. "I'm not going to a doctor like this. It's not that bad. I'll call Danny and Maria later to come get me. I'll stay with them tonight in case he comes back."

"Where is he now?"

"I don't know. It doesn't matter. He's supposed to work, but he's been drunk for the last three days. Probably went to the liquor store." She looked at his face. "You stay away from him. He'll calm down eventually."

Will looked away.

She sat up. "Will, promise me you won't do anything stupid."

He took a deep breath. "I promise I won't do anything stupid."

He showered in a daze, going through the motions of cleaning his body and drying off. He wrapped a towel around his waist and hurried to the garage, carrying his dirty work clothes under his arm. He dressed in the encroaching darkness, putting on layers of riding clothes to fend off the fall air that spiked through anything but leather like hundreds of frigid needles. Lost in thought, he started his bike and rode downtown – down to the Dark Angels' clubhouse.

He walked up the hallway, finding Barry near the kitchen. "Is Frantic here?" he asked.

"In the basement. Why?"

He pushed past Barry and headed to the door leading down to the basement.

"Hey! What's up with you?" Barry asked, following behind him.

He took the stairs two at a time and found Frantic and Stumpy at the far end of the basement, filing the serial numbers off the crankcase of a Harley-Davidson motor. "I need your gun," he said to Frantic.

THE REASON IN MEN'S SOULS

"WHAT GUN?" FRANTIC ASKED, WITHOUT looking up from filing the crankcase.

"Your Smith and Wesson."

Frantic stopped filing, and he and Stumpy looked up at Will as Barry came up behind him. "You want my Magnum? My .44?"

"I'll only need it for a few hours."

Frantic laughed. "You're joking, right?"

Will shook his head. "You've got to trust me on this."

Frantic leaned back against the workbench. "That's like telling me to relax." He studied Will's face. "You think I'm going to give you my favourite gun? Just like that? And you can't tell me what you want it for?" He tapped the file against the palm of his hand. "Forget it. Go get your own gun someplace else." He turned back to the crankcase, which Stumpy still held tight on the bench.

"What's going on, Will?" Barry asked, stepping forward.

"It's no big deal, Barry. I need to have a conversation with someone. I have to make him see reason." He paused. "I think the gun will help. That's all."

Barry hesitated. He moved forward and stood next to Frantic. "You got three of those things. Why can't you lend him one for a few hours? He's a big boy."

Frantic sighed. "What's wrong with that .32 I lent him before? Seems to me that gun did the trick."

"We got rid of it. You know that," Barry said.

"Never mind," Will said to Frantic. "If it's a big problem for you, I'll get one somewhere else." He turned to leave.

"Ah, Jesus fucking Christ – come back here," Frantic said. He reached inside his jacket and pulled out his gun. "Here, cowboy. It's loaded." He gripped the barrel and held it out to Will. "There's six slugs. Do you think that'll be enough? Or will you be needing more? You know, to have a talk with somebody, or whatever you're gonna do."

Will grabbed the gun by its handle and shoved it inside his belt at his left hip. "No. I don't think I'll need more."

"Need any help?" Stumpy asked.

"No." He turned and headed back toward the basement stairs.

Barry, Frantic, and Stumpy looked at one another. When Will disappeared from sight, Barry nodded in his direction. "You two go follow him and see what's going on. Don't interfere, but don't let him do anything really stupid."

It was dusk when Will rode toward Sadie's Lodge. He slowed on Cogswell Street, on the south side of the North Common, and parked his bike near the same spot he had stopped when getting back into town from Al's farm. He walked with measured steps to the middle of the Common, from which point he had a direct line of sight to the front door of Sadie's Lodge. He sat cross-legged on the cold ground. He watched. He waited.

After a half hour, he saw Danny and Maria's red Pontiac Grand Prix stop in front of the house. The car horn blew and, a few moments later, his mother hurried out the front door, down the steps and into the back seat. The streetlights all around began to blink on just as the car pulled away.

He continued to watch and wait, without stirring – except to scrunch his shoulders up against the cold.

He watched a Ford Falcon come up Robie Street and swing into the driveway at Sadie's Lodge. He saw the car's brake lights blink on at the end of the driveway in front of the garage.

He saw the light come on in the living room's big bay window at the front of the Lodge. He stood up and began to walk across the grass toward the house. He hadn't noticed until then that his legs had fallen asleep. They tingled and prickled as he walked. He noticed that the wind had picked up, gusting now from north to south and blowing leaves across his path. He glanced to his left and caught a glimpse of what looked like an animal, a big dog in the street-light shadow of a tree. He squinted, trying to see the animal more clearly but the shadowy shape disappeared.

Parked in Stumpy's hearse on Robie Street near the Willow Tree intersection, Frantic and Stumpy leaned forward, straining to see Will. "What's he doing now?" Frantic asked.

"Looks like he's headed to his house," Stumpy said. "I told Barry way back I wasn't gonna be that boy's babysitter, and here I am doing it. I need my head examined."

Frantic shook his head. "Must be something real bad. I never seen him like this before." He opened the passenger door. "Let's go."

Will walked up the driveway and entered the house through the back door. Before he could close the door, the wind took it and slammed it shut behind him.

"Celeste? That you?" Sid called from the living room.

Will walked down the front hall and turned into the room. Sid looked up at him from where he was sitting in a big reclining chair, an open quart-bottle of Canadian Club whiskey in one hand. "Oh, it's you."

Will stood motionless, separated from him by the width of a red and gold oriental carpet, in the middle of which sat a low walnut coffee table.

"What?" Sid asked, clunking the bottle down on the top of the table. "What the hell you looking at? Jesus, if all you're gonna do is stand there and look stupid, you can make yourself useful and go get me a glass with some ice cubes."

"No," Will said, shaking his head.

Sid frowned at him. "What'd you say, Joe? Am I slurring my words or not making myself clear? Get your ass in that kitchen and get me a Goddamn glass with some ice cubes in it. Now!"

Will felt every muscle in his body tighten. His ears began to ring. A now-familiar vacantness crept into his body. "No, Sid. What I said was 'No'." He stepped onto the carpet, bent down and slid the coffee table off to the side. "I have a different idea about what's going to happen. You're going to leave here now and never come back."

Sid sat bolt-upright up in the chair. His eyes bulged out. Then, he threw his body back in the chair, laughing into his hands. "Oh, that's rich. Momma's boy acting all tough. That biker shit's gone right to your head." He lowered his head into his hands and pushed his fingers through his hair. "That's got to be the funniest thing anybody ever said to me."

Will stood facing him.

Sid stared at him. His face flushed. "You worthless little shit! You better get your ass outta here while you can still stand up. You been asking for a shit-kicking for a long time, and I'm in just the right mood for it today." He looked down at his knuckles. "I set that douche-bag mother of yours and that slut kid of mine straight today. Might as well finish the job."

Will stepped closer to him. "Sid, I don't think you understand. I'm trying to reason with you. The time has come for you to go away and never come back." He paused and took a deep breath. "It's for the best, and I want to give you a chance to do the right thing."

Sid jumped up. "You arrogant little bastard. You'll be the one leaving – in an ambulance!" He lunged at Will, reaching for his throat. Will stepped to the side, grabbed Sid's arm and slammed him onto the oriental carpet on his back. The air burst out of Sid's lungs with a thud-crunching wheeze and spit flew from his mouth.

Will jammed his left knee into the middle of Sid's chest and whipped the Magnum from his belt. He placed the end of its six-inch barrel in the middle of Sid's forehead, forcing the back of his head down onto the carpet. Sid, gasping for breath, stopped struggling.

"It's time for you to leave." He cocked the gun. "Do you understand, Sid?"

"You crazy bastard! You treat me like this after all I did for you and your mother?" He cleared his throat and spit up into Will's face. "Go ahead, big man. Go ahead. You might as well do it because I'm not going anywhere." He paused. "Go ahead. You ain't got the guts anyway. You were always just a little coward."

Will inched the gun from the center of Sid's forehead until the end of its barrel was pointing an inch to the right of Sid's left ear.

"I knew it," Sid said, grinning.

Will squeezed the trigger twice – **CRACK, CRACK**. The gun's deafening explosions and Sid's screams pierced the air at the same time.

"OH JESUS! OH JESUS!" Sid screamed. **"YOU SHOT ME IN THE EAR! YOU BLEW MY EAR OUT!"**

Will brought the barrel of the gun back to the center of Sid's forehead. "Are you ready to listen to reason?" He said calmly. "It's time to move away. Right, Sid?"

"MOVE? WHERE? WHERE THE HELL AM I SUPPOSED TO GO! I GOT NOWHERE TO GO!"

Will nodded. "You'll find a place. A place far away."

Sid began to sob. "I can't believe you're doing this to me. Don't you care what happens to me?"

"**WILL!**" Stumpy screamed, as he and Frantic burst through the front door.

"In here," Will said.

They stormed into the living room, with Stumpy breathing hard and Frantic holding a Magnum in each hand.

"It's okay," Will said. "Everything's under control. Sid and I were just having a talk, and he's decided to move away." Will pulled the gun away from Sid's forehead and stood up.

Sid moved up on all fours, then found his feet. "Crazy fool tried to kill me," he blubbered, cupping his hand over his left ear. The blood that had drained from his face flushed back again. He stiffened his body toward Will. "This isn't over, you bastard. You wait."

As Frantic cocked both his guns, Stumpy stepped forward and grabbed Sid by the hair with one hand and the throat with the other. He bent Sid's head back and pulled his face toward him. "If he says it's over and you're hauling ass, that's the way it's gonna be. No ifs, ands, or buts."

"But – but I got nothing ready," Sid sputtered. "No clothes. Nothing."

"That there sounds like a but to me," Stumpy said, staring into Sid's eyes, inches from his own. "How about you, Frantic? You hear that?" He yanked Sid's head back farther and tightened his grip on his throat.

Frantic raised his two Magnums and aimed them at the center of Sid's chest. "Uh, huh."

Will turned and picked up Sid's jacket from the recliner. "I'm sure you'll get by." He placed the jacket in Sid's flailing right hand. "Your car keys in there?"

Sid tried to nod against Stumpy's crushing hold on him.

"When you get wherever you're going, write to me and I'll ship your things to you. One more thing." He moved closer to make eye contact with Sid. "Do not ever, ever call my mother or bother her about any of this."

"You finished?" Stumpy asked Will.

Will nodded.

Stumpy dragged Sid to the open front door and flung him outside. Sid tumbled down the steps and landed on his back on the sidewalk. He jumped to his feet and staggered toward the driveway. A few seconds later, they heard his car start and the motor race.

"You gonna tell us what that was all about?" Frantic asked.

Will shook his head. "Probably not. It's a little complicated."

Stumpy frowned at him. "That was your old man, right?"

"Stepfather."

"And you had a gun to his head!" Stumpy continued. "What'd he do?"

Will un-cocked the Magnum and slid it back in his belt. He sighed. "It's a long story – 15 years long. But this afternoon, he beat up my mother and sister."

Stumpy looked at Frantic, then back at Will. "Shoulda said so right away, you asshole. We let him off way too easy. Goddamn woman-beater scum."

"No," Will said. "This was perfect. We just applied some logic to his soul."

Stumpy again furrowed his brow and squeezed his eyelids almost shut. "Why the fuck does he talk like that?" he asked Frantic, without taking his eyes from Will.

Frantic shook his head. "Don't know. But don't worry about it. He doesn't know either. He's just babbling."

Stumpy nodded and relaxed his face. "Thought so."

Frantic stepped toward Will. "I'll have my gun now."

"Can I keep it until tomorrow"? He paused. "You never know, right?"

"No. I don't trust you with it. I want it now."

Will laughed. "Umm – let's see. You got a Magnum in your right hand and a Magnum in your left. And you want this one, too?"

Frantic looked down at the guns he was still holding. He un-cocked them and holstered one under his left arm and put the other in his belt. He held his right hand out to Will. "Come on. Pass it over."

Stumpy chuckled. "He's got a point."

"How about tomorrow?" Will asked.

Frantic glanced at Stumpy. "I can't believe you're siding with him on this." He stared at Will. "Tomorrow. No later. And you fucking better call me if anything comes up and you feel the urge to *talk* to somebody." He took a deep breath. "You're taking to this whole gun thing *way* too good."

"I'll behave myself."

Danny's Pontiac came to a stop front of Sadie's Lodge at the same time as he pulled up on his bike from work. He glanced over, seeing his mother and Patty climb out of the back seat. By the time he got off his bike in front of the garage, they were walking up the driveway toward him. He noticed that the swelling in his mother's face had gone down, but that both she and Patty had purplish bruises and red marks on their faces.

"Have you seen Sid?" his mother asked, hugging him. "Nobody's seen him anywhere for a couple days now."

"I saw him leave here in a hurry two nights ago. He jumped in his car and took off. Didn't say where he was going."

"Probably dead in a ditch somewhere," Patty said. "It'd serve him friggin' right."

"Don't talk like that," Celeste said. "He's still your father."

"Hmmph – according to you. But I'll never talk to that prick again."

"He'll probably show up again," Will said. "He always does, right?"

His mother nodded, and Patty rolled her eyes. "Unfortunately," she said.

The next night, at the end of his first week back at Saint Mary's, his mother met him at the back door when he went into the house to shower, a pensive look on her face. She hugged him with stiff limbs, following him with her eyes as he walked past her toward the bathroom.

"Will," she said.

He stopped and turned toward her. "What?"

"It's about Sid."

"Oh? What's going on?"

"Sid's brother, Cal, called this afternoon – from Toronto. He said Sid's staying there with him." She stared at him. "He said Sid wasn't coming back."

"That's interesting."

"Uh, huh. He said Sid told him he couldn't come back."

"Really?"

"You shouldn't be surprised," she said. "You knew that, didn't you?"

Will shrugged. "I wasn't sure he wasn't coming back. You know him."

"What did you do to him, Will?"

"I persuaded him to leave. You know, reasoned with him."

"You persuaded him? Cal said Sid told him you tried to shoot him in the head and barely missed. That you and two of those Dark Angels told him to leave town and never come back. Is that true?"

"Well, I did tell him to go far away and never come back. That's true. But I didn't try to shoot him. If I *had* tried, he wouldn't be in Toronto with Cal."

She slumped onto a chair at the table, shaking her head. "My God! I can't believe you did that. What were you thinking? How could you do something so crazy?"

He approached her and put his hand on her shoulder. "It had to be done. Something had to be done. You know that. Think about it, Mom – with everything that's happened over the years and the way he is, and with Patty and everything, it would only have been a matter of time before something worse happened. There's no other way he would have left."

"But it's such a – such a crazy thing to do. To use a gun like that. And after you said you would settle down and things would be normal."

He nodded. "I know it seems that way. I'm sorry." He pulled a chair over and sat next to her. "But, really, what's crazy is the way we've lived all these years. Putting up with his craziness and abuse. Always being on edge. Never knowing when he's going to be drunk, or blow up, or be okay. And thinking that's normal. *That's* what's crazy."

They sat in silence. She looked around the kitchen, then stood up and went to the sink. She put in the drain plug, loaded the dirty dishes in and turned on the water. She stared out the window as steam rose and began to fog it up.

"Do you really think he'll stay in Toronto?" she asked.

"I think so. Even if he comes back this way, I doubt he'll come around here."

She began to wash the dishes. "You should move into the house now."

He hesitated. "Maybe. But I do like being in the garage."

"I thought you just stayed there to be away from Sid."

"In the beginning – when I was 15. It's different now. It's kind of like my own place."

She nodded. "I should have thought of that." She paused. "What if he does come back, Will?"

He smiled. "I'll have to reason with him again."

PART 6

THE INSCRUTABILITY OF CHANCE

FRANTIC RAPPED HARD ON THE side door of the garage. Stumpy stood behind him. "He's gotta be here," Frantic said, nodding in the direction of Will's Harley leaning against its sidestand in front of the big front door.

Will opened the door as he pulled a sweatshirt over his head. "Hey, guys. What's up?"

"Don't play dumb with me," Frantic said, pushing past him to go inside. Stumpy followed. "Where is it?" Frantic asked.

"What?"

"Will – don't push him," Stumpy said.

"You know what. My fucking gun, that's what. You were supposed to give it back to me two weeks ago and you been dodging me ever since."

"I've been working."

"Yeah, working and hiding from me."

"Christ, it's cold in here," Stumpy said. "Ain't you got no heat?"

Will headed to the cast-iron stove. "I just got here a few minutes ago." He opened the door, stirred the still-orange coals and threw in three pieces of split hardwood. "Doesn't take long to warm things up once it gets going."

"So where's my gun?" Frantic asked again, beginning to look around.

"It's here."

"You got it on you?"

"No."

Frantic stopped moving and crossed his arms, facing Will. "Get it."

Will hesitated. "I want you to sell it to me."

Frantic dropped his arms to his sides. "No. No fucking way. That's my favourite gun and you know it."

"I know. But it's my favourite gun, too. I've been saving all my money since I started working. Just tell me much you want for it and I'll pay you. No haggling."

Frantic jerked his head from side to side and grabbed a fistful of hair at the right side of his head. "It's not for sale, Will." He turned to Stumpy. "You tell him."

"You don't need no gun. Especially that one," Stumpy said. "Every time you get one of those things in your hand, you end up in shit. Why do you want it, anyway?"

"I'm not sure. It just feels right. Like it will bring me luck. Plus, I haven't really gotten into trouble with it. Not really." He paused. "It's made things happen that should have happened anyway – like with Sid, right? When everything gets all fuzzy and confused, it helps me make things clear and set them right."

Frantic began to pace around the garage, looking in boxes and kicking at anything in his path. He stomped over to the stove and stood in front of it with his back to Will and Stumpy. He didn't speak.

"You better back off," Stumpy whispered to Will.

"I'll sell you one of my other Magnums," Frantic said, without turning around. "No – tell you what – I'll *give* you one." He spun around and walked back to Will and Stumpy. "But I want the one you got."

"Five hundred cash. Right now," Will said. "Don't get me wrong, I really appreciate your offer. But it wouldn't be the same. It's not just any gun that's lucky, it's the one I've got." He paused. "I know you know what I mean, Frantic."

Frantic took a deep breath. He grabbed a wooden box containing a Harley transmission case and a bunch of other parts. He tipped the box over and scattered the parts across the floor. He placed the box upside down and sat on it. "I heard Gloria told Kay you been carrying it every day. That's what Kay told Shotgun. That true?"

"Yeah, except when I'm actually working. It's too big for that. Get's in the way." He bent to his cot and flipped the pillow back. "Otherwise, when it's not on me, it's here."

Frantic looked at the gun. "Any plans to use it?"

Will shook his head. "No plans. But no promises I won't if it makes sense to."

Frantic put his elbows on his knees and leaned forward. He sighed. "It would be like I'm giving up my first love, you know."

"I know."

Frantic sat still. His breathing slowed. "I would only do it because it's you. You know that, right?"

Will nodded.

"You got the money?"

Will turned toward his workbench. "It's here."

"Never mind. I don't want it right now. Wouldn't feel right. Give it to me some other time – in a couple months, maybe. Right now, we'll just say that I'm extending your loan period."

Will nodded. "Thanks."

Frantic stood up. He headed toward the door. "Don't talk to me about it again. Okay?"

"Okay."

It was dark, the garage was warm and the cast-iron stove was ticking and clicking when Gloria arrived. She slipped her leather jacket from her shoulders and her scarf from her neck, dropping them on the cot. "Everything all right?" she asked Will, as she hugged him, and then skipped over to stand in front of the stove.

He walked over and stood next to her. "Yeah, fine. Why?"

"Well, Shotgun told Kay that Frantic was really mad because you hadn't given his gun back to him and that he was coming over to get it from you."

"He was here."

"What happened?"

"I talked him into selling me his gun."

She crossed her arms. "I see."

"That's okay with you, isn't it?"

"I guess. If you think it's necessary." She turned, went back to the cot and sat on it. "I also heard about what happened with Sid."

Will shook his head. "Doesn't surprise me. These people can't keep quiet about anything."

She pulled at her bottom lip. "Well, I'm not sorry he's gone. He gave me the creeps. Seemed like he was always sneaking around and leering at me whenever I was here."

"You should have told me."

She shrugged. "Men like him are like that."

He sat beside her and put his arm around her waist.

She squeezed his forearm. "Can I ask you something about that gun?"

"Go ahead."

"Why do you need it now? Seems like all the trouble is settling down – like with the other club and now Sid. It's up to you, but aren't you worried it's going to bring you more trouble?" She stared across at him. "From what I hear, even some of the guys are thinking you're going over the edge."

He leaned back on his elbows. "Is that what *you* think?"

She repositioned her body so that she lay straight on the cot with her legs draped across his body. "It seems kind of – I don't know, what's the right word? Extreme, I guess."

He nodded. "I can see why you'd think that." He hesitated. "If I tell you something, do you promise you won't think I'm crazy? Or tell anybody else?"

She looked at him. "I promise."

"I keep seeing things – things like wild animals. But they're just fleeting images, always just out of sight. And it feels like somebody or something is watching me. Following me." He paused. "Weird, right?"

"Uh, huh, kind of, to be honest." She turned on her side toward him. "You're not hearing voices, too, are you?"

He laughed. "No. I knew you'd think I was crazy. It's probably just my imagination running wild because of everything that's gone on."

"Probably."

"Anyway, I'm not sure I'm out of the woods yet. So I thought it wouldn't hurt to keep the gun a little longer."

"But not forever, right?"

He smiled. "Only as long as it makes more sense to keep it than to get rid of it. Unless I get sloppy and shoot myself in the foot first."

"Hmm. Seems to me you might hit something a little more delicate than that. Considering the way you stick it in your belt."

He winced. "Oww. That wouldn't be good."

"Let's just say you'd be finding yourself another stripper-girl passenger for the back of your bike."

He smiled and squeezed her calves. "Are you going to be able to come to the party tomorrow night at the clubhouse? Sloper's getting his colours."

She nodded. "You're in luck. I got one of the other girls to cover for me. What time should I be ready?"

"I'll pick you up after I get cleaned up from work – around eight, I guess. I'll have to work late because they want to get the slab poured before the weekend."

She nodded.

A cold wind whistled through the open upper floors of the Loyola Building on the grounds of Saint Mary's University the next morning. Will and Jean Bourque moved from one framed-up column to the next. They checked all the fastened joints holding the plywood in place for each column, making sure each was secure for concrete to be poured in.

"Cement trucks are supposed to come after lunch," Jean said, bending his neck to look down half a dozen floors from the exposed edge of the building to the rough ground below. "Should be finished by six if they keep coming regular all afternoon." He paused. "That your bike over there?" he asked, pointing at Will's Harley parked near the Student Union Building.

"Yeah."

"Getting a little cold to ride, isn't it?"

"Sort of. But it's not bad if you're just cruising around town. Another story if you're out on the open road at highway speed."

Jean laughed. "I bet. That girl of yours go on it in this weather?"

Will nodded. "Uh, huh. We'll be on it tonight."

"You better hang on to that one." He nudged Will. "Look at that little sweetheart down there." He pointed at a tall brunette, wearing bell bottoms and a pea jacket, hurrying along the walkway below.

"Nice."

Jean shook his head. "Sweet Jesus, what I'd do in a place like this – if I was 30 years younger, that is. I heard you used to go here."

"Yeah, for a while."

"Why'd you quit? Seems like a good deal to me – compared to what you're doing now."

Will shrugged. "It didn't seem relevant to anything important to me at the time. You know, things like bikes and being with the Dark Angels. I knew I'd always regret it if I let those things pass me by."

"That's the name of your gang, eh?"

Will nodded.

Jean stared off, then looked down at his boots. "Funny. I was just thinking how when I was your age, I had a chance to go work with my Uncle Henri in Florida. He was a little older than me and we were close – like brothers. He had shipped out as a deck hand a couple years before when this big yacht came into Wedgeport to ride out a storm. He went on the spur of the moment. Didn't take nothing, just the clothes on his back."

Jean turned his back against the wind. "We might as well head back down. Everything's good here."

Will looked at him. "Is that it? What happened to him?"

"Well, he's down in Florida learning about sailboats and boat charters, and he manages to get an old sailboat of his own. He calls home and wants me to go down and help him out and try to set up a business. But my father was dead-set against me going. Said it was a crazy idea and that I should get a trade and settle down. Of course, I listened to him. By the time I get out of vocational school, my girlfriend was pregnant, so we got married. Built a house next to my father's on his property." He paused and cleared his throat. "And that was it – the kids came along and I never left Wedgeport, till five years ago when I started with Maritime Formworks."

He stopped walking and turned to Will. "Now, get this. All this time down in Florida, Uncle Henri gets one boat, then another, and another, and more and more. He ends up a multi-millionaire, selling sailboats and yachts and operating a big boat charter out of Miami, Fort Lauderdale and Key West – Turquoise Water Cruising and Yachts, he called his business." He shook his head. "See what I mean? That could've been me. Can't you just see me there on a swanky yacht, all tanned up, with beautiful women in bikinis hanging off me."

Will laughed. "Yeah, I can picture that. Maybe you could still do that. Why not? You could go down and work for him or whatever."

Jean shook his head. "Nah, we're not on the same wavelength anymore. We haven't kept in touch. He's in a whole different world." He paused, looking off. "Besides, there's the wife and kids, right?"

It was dark and frosty when Will helped Gloria squeeze her leather jacket on over extra layers of clothes. "At least there's no wind," he said. "Want to ride around town a bit before we to go to the clubhouse?"

"Yeah. We can see how it is. Let's get outside, it's hot in here."

They left the garage through the side door and went to the bike. While Gloria stood to the left side of the bike with her arms crossed, Will kick-started it and sat on it as it warmed up.

"I don't know," she said. "Who's to say he would have been better off going to Florida?"

"What?"

"That carpenter guy you were telling me about. Who's to say he'd have been better off? He might have fallen overboard and drowned. Or, if he had lots of money, maybe some criminals, or some bikers, might have bumped him off. Or, who knows, he might have married some gold-digger bitch who took him for all he was worth. And then he took to drinking because he lost everything and became an alcoholic and drank himself to death." She raised her eyebrows. "Think about it. There are all sorts of possibilities."

"Just negative ones in your mind, I guess. That's how his wife would think."

She frowned at him. "I'm just saying you can't assume he made the wrong choice. Maybe his family life here and his work give him more happiness that he appreciates – or more than he would have had in Florida. Who's to say?"

"Right. And what would *you* rather be doing?"

She closed her eyes and tilted her head to one side. "I'd rather be on a sailboat in Florida," she said, swinging her leg over the back of the bike and climbing on. "Let's go." She wrapped her legs around his waist and clutched his shoulders with her gloved hands. "This thing must be warmed up by now."

Shivering, they wriggled through the crowd at the clubhouse until they stood next to Barry and Shotgun. The music was already pulsing and a haze of smoke from hash, grass, and tobacco swirled in the air. Barry leaned forward and kissed Will on the forehead.

"Haven't seen much of you in a while. You still working at that shit construction job?"

Will smiled. "It's an okay job."

Barry laughed. "Yeah, and I'm the Pope. It's beyond me why you work like that. A kid with your head could make good money dealing. Or, you know what would be really cool? You could become a lawyer or a shrink." He slapped Will on the back. "It'd be great for the Dark Angels to have their own home-grown lawyer or shrink. I could probably even arrange for the club to pay for your education."

Gloria smiled, nudging Will with her elbow. "Sounds like a good idea to me."

"Barry's philosophy is that a real one-percenter shouldn't have to lower himself by doing actual work," Shotgun said. "Just one more part of his charming, psychopathic, warped personality."

"Ooooo, that's mean," Barry said. He turned to Gloria with a hurt look on his face. "You gotta stick up for me. Say something nice about me."

Gloria studied his face. "Okay. Well, you've got nice white teeth. And, when you smile, you look quite striking. And I think your face is very expressive."

Barry stared at her. "I *love* this girl," he said to Will. He reached out and pulled Gloria to his chest. "Is it all right with you if I sleep with her?"

"You'll have to ask her," Will said.

Barry looked at Gloria and made his eyebrows jump.

"Umm. Not right now," Gloria said, pushing him back.

"That's fine," Barry said. "Great. 'Not right now' means you will, but not right now. Some other time, right?" He flashed his white teeth. "I can wait. I'm a patient person. Sometime before tomorrow morning would be just fine."

Gloria and Will laughed. Shotgun grinned and shook his head. "He's so deranged, it's even hard to insult him now. He thinks it's a good thing to be crazy."

"My shrink would be proud of me," Barry said. "I play mind-games with him about being paranoid. Helps my ego and makes me feel good. I'm still paranoid and twisted, but I let him believe that I think people are really saying good things about me and just want to do me good. Anyway, my shrink, he says human beings should have goals." He poked his finger in Will's chest. "So you should take my advice and plan to be a lawyer or shrink. Look around at all these assholes." He waved in a circle around him. "They haven't got much to work with. Not like me and you – and Shotgun here, to a lesser extent. They got nothing else to do and no place else to go but to be here, in this club. They've reached the end of the line. Do you think they'll all be around doing this in 15 or 20 years? No way. They'll all be dead or in jail. Extinct."

"Maybe," Will said, "But all those straight and self-righteous people who follow the rules and worry about getting to heaven, they don't necessarily have any better luck. The good people get hit with life's crap just as much as anybody else. They get cancer, their kid gets hit by a car – they get killed in war. Doesn't matter if they have plans or goals."

Barry nodded. "You're right. But the part you're missing is the odds. It's all about the odds." He grabbed a lit cigarette from Frantic as he walked by and took a drag. "The odds aren't good when you do all the shit we do. You can dance with the devil and waltz away a hundred times, a thousand times, but you have to get away *every* time and he only has to get you *once*."

"What're you saying about odds?" Frantic asked, turning around. "I want in if you got some kind of bet on the go."

"No bet," Shotgun said. "Barry was lecturing Will about how us one-percenters take too many risks and all that shit. We're doomed."

Frantic took a big swig of dark navy rum from a quart bottle. "Who gives a shit about that?" He passed the bottle to Will and patted his sides. "My friends here – Mister Smith and Mister Wesson – always been good at shifting the odds in my favour. Fuck, who'd want to live a boring life and not take any risks. Let's you know you're alive. Right, Will?" He gave Will a thumb's up. "He knows what I'm talking about."

Will nodded. "Can't argue with that."

Frantic snatched the bottle back and took another drink. "Watch, I'll show you what I mean." He pulled his .44 out and flicked open the cartridge chamber. He took five cartridges out, leaving one still chambered. He spun the chamber, held the gun straight out in front of his face and squinted to look in the chamber. Then, he snapped his wrist, flicking the chamber closed. He looked around the room.

THE SENTINELS OF ZEUS

FRANTIC FIXED HIS EYES ON Stumpy. He raised his gun and pointed it at him. Speedy, standing next to Stumpy, nudged him and pointed in Frantic's direction.

"PUT THAT THING AWAY, YOU IDIOT!" Stumpy shouted across the room.

The people standing near him began to scramble aside.

Frantic laughed and pulled the trigger – CLICK. "It's okay, Stump. You live." He spun the chamber again, and once more pointed the gun down, looking into the chamber. He flicked the chamber shut, raised the gun and aimed it at the circle of people, swinging it in a slow arc from left to right. He jerked it to a stop, aimed at Sloper. Sloper sat motionless and without expression on an old sofa. He stared at Frantic. Everyone near him lurched away.

Sloper looked at Barry. "This some kind of final test?"

Barry shook his head. "Afraid not. He's on his own."

Sloper began to get up.

Frantic pulled the trigger – CLICK, the gun went again. He smiled. "Hmm, your number wasn't up, Sloper. Guess you get to be a Dark Angel after all."

"Okay, Frantic, that's enough," Barry said. "You hear me?"

"Oh relax, Barry. Isn't that what you're always telling me? Just two more tries, okay? I'm doing everybody a favour by making them happy they're alive." He spun the chamber, checked it at a glance and pointed the gun at Speedy. "BANG!" he said. "Sorry, Speedy. You're a dead little troll."

He lowered the gun and looked around at the circle of people. He took another drink of rum. "Jeez, you can put the music back on and stop being so serious." He looked at Barry and Shotgun. "See it makes you love life a lot more when you face down death."

"Idiot," Shotgun said.

"Whew. I need something to drink," Gloria said.

Barry winked at her. "I'll get you one. Think of it as foreplay, sweetheart."

As they headed toward the kitchen, Frantic called after Barry. "Hey, Barry, I wasn't finished. Remember, I said there were two more left."

"Forget it," Barry said, waving him off. "Your roulette freak-show is over."

Frantic laughed. He raised the gun and loaded another bullet into the chamber. He spun it with the fingers of his left hand. He began to tap his right foot and sing – "Born to be wi…iiild, hmmm, mmmm, Born to be wi…iiild." He jammed the muzzle of the gun up under his bearded chin. He began to sing again as he pulled the trigger, "Born to be" – **BANG**! The gun boomed and the top of Frantic's skull exploded upward, splattering blood and chunks of his skull and brain to the ceiling and all over the people standing nearest him. His body crumpled to the floor like a limp ragdoll.

People screamed and bolted for the outside as pandemonium fell upon the clubhouse like a demonic tornado. Others cried and clung to one another, recoiling from Frantic's body and the gooey mess all around him. Will glanced at Gloria and saw her wiping blood from her vacant face and picking unrecognizable bits of flesh from her jacket. He took her by the hand. "Come into the kitchen with me. Come – now!"

He left her in the kitchen and ran back into the living room, where Stumpy, Barry, Shotgun, and several other Dark Angels were standing over Frantic's body.

"Holy Jesus!" Stumpy said. "I fuckin' knew some kinda shit like this was gonna happen. Holy Jesus. I knew it, I just fuckin' knew it!"

Shotgun knelt on one knee and picked up Frantic's left wrist. "I can't feel anything ticking," he said, his voice tight.

Will knelt next to Shotgun and placed two fingers against the side of Frantic's neck. Then, he put his ear to his chest. He shook his head. "He's gone."

"Before he hit the floor, if you ask me," Shotgun said. "What're we supposed to do now, Barry?"

"Stop talking and let me think," Barry blurted out, beginning to pace in a quick circle around Frantic's body. "They'll try to pin this on us, you know. He'd probably want us to get rid of his body. So the cops wouldn't get it and order it chopped up."

Stumpy gagged. "What? Why would they do that? It's already half blown to shit."

"It's called an autopsy, stupid," Shotgun said. "A whole lot worse than what you're looking at now."

"It won't work," Will said, shaking his head. "There were too many people here. It'll look worse if we try to cover it up than if we just deal with it straight. It was an accident. Everybody saw it."

"I'm not that optimistic the cops won't find some angle to work against us," Barry said. He stopped pacing. "But you're right. We've got no choice." He waved his hands over Frantic's body as if casting a spell. "All of you – move back and don't touch anything. Not one thing." He turned to Stumpy. "You get everybody out of here except –let me see – you, me, Will, Shotgun, and maybe Speedy."

Gloria came from the kitchen, wiping her hands in a dish towel. "What about me? I can be a witness."

Barry looked at Will.

Will nodded. "She'd be believable." He took her by the arm when she came beside him. "Are you sure you're okay?"

She nodded. "I'm okay now."

"All right," Barry said. "Stumpy, as soon as the place is cleared out, you call the cops."

"What about an ambulance?" Stumpy asked. "Shouldn't we get one of them, too?"

Barry stared at him. "For what?" He paused. "The cops will decide what they need once they get here. It'll all take some time. Might as well hunker down for the night."

When Stumpy stomped off, the others joined closer together around Frantic's body.

"Poor bastard," Barry said.

"It feels like we should do something for him," Gloria said. "Cover him with a blanket or something."

Barry shook his head. "Better not."

Will stared at the pool of blood that spread out in an irregular pattern from Frantic's head and shoulders. It grew larger and looked more black than red. Will again knelt beside Frantic, this time in the pool of blood. He put his hand on Frantic's heart. "Almost looks like he fell in a big puddle of dirty oil."

"Yeah. Except that half his head's gone," Speedy said. "But I see what you mean about how it looks like oil. Creepy."

Will felt the warm blood soak into the knees of his jeans, sending a tingling wave up through his spine to his neck and into his head. All his senses vibrated to attention. He leaned down and kissed Frantic's cheek. He smelled blood and rum and flesh, and other things he had never before smelled. It confused him that he would feel so much horror and so much excitement at the same time.

It was four in the morning before Garrity and Akerman left the clubhouse. They sat in Garrity's unmarked police car and watched as two heavy-set attendants brought Frantic Fred's body out on a stretcher, jostled it down the granite steps and loaded it into the ambulance. Akerman sighed and rubbed the back of his neck. "Christ, I'm tired."

"Frustrating, isn't it?" Garrity said, squeezing the steering wheel. "The way we keep drawing blanks with these guys. At least the Chief gave this one to us right away."

Akerman chuckled. "That poor asshole didn't draw no blanks now, did he? Would've rather nailed the fucker myself."

"Had kind of a blank expression on his face, though, wouldn't you say?" Garrity said, rolling his eyes back in his head and letting his head flop to one side.

Akerman laughed and shook his head. "Even without the top of his head, he still had more hair than you."

When the ambulance pulled away, Garrity started the car and looked up at the front door of the clubhouse. "The Chief and Simms will probably be disappointed we couldn't get any more out of this. Nothing but one less cockroach on the streets."

"One less is one less. I like to think we're on a roll."

As they pulled way, Stumpy latched the big front door of the clubhouse and headed back up the hall to the kitchen. "They're all gone," he said to the others.

"The cops didn't seem too happy," Will said.

"What'd you expect?" Shotgun asked, passing bottles of Ten-Penny around. "They're pissed because the only one they got to haul away was Frantic."

They stood in a circle. "Jeez, it's too fucking quiet now," Barry said. He held his beer out. "To the death of a one-percenter."

They clinked their bottles together solemnly.

"The best," said Shotgun.

"We should clean this place up," Gloria said. "It looks awful – the blood and everything."

"Nah, leave it," Barry said. "Cops scooped up most of the big pieces as evidence, anyway. I'll get a couple prospects to clean the place up tomorrow."

"What about his family?" Will asked. "Shouldn't we call somebody?"

"He's got nobody," Shotgun said, flicking his hair back. "He joined the navy after his old man kicked him out back in Toronto. His old lady died when he was little. Not something he ever talked about much."

"Better that way," Barry said. "Won't have to fight with anybody to bury him as a one-percenter – with his colours and everything." He took a drink of beer. "If he's got any relatives who give a damn, they'll find out eventually. If not, who cares? He wouldn't care about that shit."

"So we'll get to decide what to do with him?" Stumpy asked.

"I don't expect anybody else to claim him and pay to bury him," Barry said. "I'll call Cruikshank's when they open. They did a good job with Trigger's funeral. They get it about us and the one-percenter stuff."

"Trigger?" Will asked.

"Joey Triggs," Shotgun said. "He was a member a while back. Died before you joined the club."

"Died?" Barry said, becoming agitated. "You mean fucking taken out by the cops."

Gloria's eyes widened. "Are you serious? What do you mean the cops took him out?"

"He had a boat – more like a little barge," Barry said. "He lived on that thing and dove from it. Kept it anchored in the Bedford Basin. The cops had been hounding him for one thing or another – drugs, assaults, breach of probation." Barry took a gulp of beer and smiled. "You could say Trigger cut a wide path through the city. Anyway, one night, his boat blew up with him on it. They fished his body out of the water but said he was dead from the explosion first. They said it was an accident – propane. But he told me he was being followed by a couple of cops all the time. He knew they were going to try to take him out."

Gloria looked at Will. "Would they really do that?"

Will shrugged and glanced across at Barry.

"Trigger never kept any propane on his boat," Barry said. He tipped his beer up and finished it off. "Cruikshank's pieced him back together. Even though he was in the water overnight, we were able to have an open casket. They're *that* good. I'll bet they find a way to let us have an open casket for Frantic."

"Maybe they can put a hat on his head or something," Stumpy said. "You know, to cover the top."

Barry nodded. "Is that priest you know still at Saint Patrick's over on Brunswick Street? What was his name?"

"Father MacPherson."

"Can you talk to him? Get him to do the funeral?"

Stumpy nodded. "I think he's still there."

"How do you know him?" Will asked.

Stumpy blushed. "He was a character witness for me a couple years ago, when I got charged with crackin' a cop on the head with a two-by-four. I used to go to church there when I was a kid."

"He was a freakin' altar boy," Shotgun said, laughing.

"That was a long time ago," Stumpy said, scowling at him.

"Was Frantic a Catholic?" Gloria asked.

"Who knows?" Barry said. "Doesn't matter. We just need some kind of clergyman and a place to bury him. You tell him he's Catholic, okay, Stump?"

Stumpy nodded. "Might be a good thing, anyway. You know – might help him get into heaven or whatever. At least stay out of hell. Maybe go to that other place. What's it called?"

Barry stared at him. "Stumpy, we're talking about Frantic." He shook his head. "It's purga-fucking-tory, and he'll be doing real good if he ends up there."

Barry, Will, and Stumpy stood over Frantic's open casket in front of the altar at Saint Patrick's Church, staring down at his body. "Told you they'd do a good job," Barry whispered.

"Yeah, he even looks peaceful," Will said.

"Uh, huh," Stumpy said.

They stood in silence. Then, Barry shook his head. "No, he doesn't look right."

"Why do you say that?" Will asked.

"He looks *too* good – peaceful. Know what I mean?"

"Oh, yeah," Stumpy said. "That ain't good."

"He should be frowning a bit, and his mouth should look meaner. You know, like snarling," Barry continued.

Will and Stumpy nodded.

"Maybe we can change it," Will said.

Barry and Stumpy looked sideways at him. "How you gonna do that?" Stumpy asked, his brow furrowed.

Will shrugged. "We could try to push his skin around. See if it works."

Barry nodded. "Yeah, why not? Worth a try, right?"

"Are you sure it's okay?" Stumpy asked, still staring at Will. "Ain't that considered a sin or something? You know, messin' with a dead body."

"No, it's okay, Stump," Will said. "You're allowed to touch dead people. You can even ask Father MacPherson. He'll tell you the same thing." He reached inside the casket and pushed down on Frantic's cold waxy skin at the sides of his eyebrows, then at the corners of his mouth. "How about that?"

"Better," said Barry.

Stumpy nodded, glancing around with a guilty look on his face.

Barry reached inside the casket and pulled the black woollen toque that covered Frantic's head down lower on his forehead. "Got that pin?" he asked Will.

Will passed him a chrome one-percenter pin. Barry again reached inside the casket and pinned it to the middle of the toque. He leaned back and gazed into the casket. "Now, it's all perfect," he said, patting Will and Stumpy on the back.

"Yeah, he'd like that," Stumpy said. "Bet he's up there lookin' down at us and smiling."

Barry looked at him and shook his head.

"Look at all them vultures gawkin' and takin' pictures," Stumpy said, thrusting his middle finger out though the open window of his hearse as he drove south from Saint Patrick's Church through the narrow downtown streets. He glanced in the rear-view mirror at Frantic's bike, being pulled behind the hearse on a flat-iron trailer. "Told all you guys this thing would come in handy." He threw a smug smile at Will, Barry, and Shotgun, who rode in the hearse with him. "Is it still running?" he asked, nodding back toward the bike.

"Yeah, I can hear it," Shotgun said.

"He'd like that, right?" Stumpy asked.

"Yeah, he'd like that a lot," Will said. "It was a good idea you had there, Stump."

Stumpy nodded, smiling and staring ahead.

"Here they come," Garrity said to Akerman, crouching behind Our Lady of Sorrows Chapel, sitting high on the grounds of Holy Cross Cemetery. He switched on his camera.

"Why you bothering to film them?" Akerman asked.

"Never know what might come up. Might see some new faces or get some evidence of some kind."

"Besides, it's a new camera – a Super Eight. I want to see how it works."

"Maybe we should let them see us. Fuck with their heads."

Garrity grinned, stood up and stepped away from the chapel.

The procession turned into the cemetery and moved slowly along the gravelled roadway, downhill to an open grave.

"Look at them bastards," Stumpy said, pointing at Garrity and Akerman. "They got no respect. I'm gonna go talk to them soon as we stop."

"Forget it," Shotgun said. "Let's just do what we came for and get out of here."

Once all the vehicles had stopped, they slid Frantic's casket out of the hearse – with Barry, Stumpy, and Will on one side, and Speedy, Shotgun, and Frenchy Jack on the other. They carried it to the graveside and placed it on straps over the open grave.

Father MacPherson moved from person to person shaking hands, looking solemn and providing whispered condolences. He stood at the head of the casket and offered incantations in Latin in a weary monotone, concluding with a louder, more-energetic recitation of the *Pater Noster* and a jerky sign of the cross.

"Well, that's it," he said to the 50 or so people crowded around. "If anyone wishes to say anything before the casket is lowered, please do."

Shotgun stepped forward. He placed a .44 calibre slug on the casket. "Relax, Frantic," he said, smiling.

Speedy stepped forward and placed a drive chain on the casket. "See you soon, brother."

Others took turns leaving objects on the casket or tossing them into the pit.

"We'd like some time alone with him, now," Barry announced. "Members only." He nodded to Stumpy.

Stumpy ushered Father MacPherson away, along with all the other guests. "What about them?" he asked Barry, as he returned, looking in the direction of Garrity and Akerman.

"We'll wait a few minutes. If they don't leave, fuck them. We'll do it anyway."

They milled around the casket, waiting – glancing over occasionally at Garrity and Akerman.

"They're not going to leave," Shotgun said. "They haven't stopped filming us since we got here."

"Having too much fun," Will said.

Barry looked at him. "Still got his gun?"

"Yeah, his holster, too."

"Want to take the lead in this?"

Will nodded. He reached inside his jacket and slipped the Magnum from its holster. He aimed it skyward. Then, one by one, the others did the same with their guns.

Will glanced at Barry. "Any special way to do this?"

"No. Just let it rip. But don't empty your guns."

The guns exploded into space – 40 shots, 50 – echoing off Our Lady of Sorrows Chapel, bouncing off a thousand gravestones in all directions, scattering screeching blue jays and squawking crows from the bare-bone branches overhead.

Will lowered his gun and slid it back in the holster under his left arm. His ears rung and the acrid smell of gunpowder stung his nose. He looked up the hill in the direction of the chapel and saw Garrity and Akerman running at full speed toward them, their guns drawn.

They skidded breathlessly to a stop at the perimeter of the circle of Dark Angels surrounding Frantic's casket.

THE MOIRAI

"YOU'RE ALL UNDER ARREST!" GARRITY shouted. "PUT THOSE WEAPONS ON THE GROUND! NOW!"

None of the Dark Angels moved.

Akerman weaved through them and positioned himself in front of Barry. "Come on, do it, now!" He stared at Barry. "We got no choice, Barry. I can't believe you guys would do something so stupid."

Barry patted his jacket pockets. He turned to Shotgun. "You got a smoke?"

Shotgun raised his eyebrows. "You know I don't smoke."

Barry looked at Akerman. "That's not good. I was already in a shitty mood." He reached out and lowered his hand over Akerman's gun. He eased it toward the ground as Garrity pushed through the crowd to stand next to them.

"Get your Goddamn hand off that gun!" Garrity exclaimed. "That's obstructing a peace office, on top of what you idiots already did."

Barry continued to stare into Akerman's eyes, ignoring Garrity.

"It's okay, Frank," Akerman said. "I got it under control."

Barry sighed. "You gotta be the two biggest dickheads in the universe. You confront us on *this* day? You really think you're in control here?" He glanced around. "Take a look. You see any cavalry here to rescue you?" He turned to Will. "Will, do you see anybody around – somebody like Superman – you know, some character with super powers to swat a hail of bullets away from Dickless and Tracy here?"

Will shook his head. "Not one, Barry."

"You got superpowers, Fatman? I mean, Batman?" Barry asked, turning to Garrity.

"He ain't even got human powers," Stumpy said. He moved in close behind Garritty and looked down onto the top of his sweaty bald head. "Pig-powers maybe. Fat, slimy pig-powers."

Will reached in under his jacket and took out his gun. He held it down against his leg, and cocked it. The other Dark Angels with guns all did the same.

Akerman looked at Garrity. "We're going to stand down. Okay, Frank?"

Akerman slid his gun away from under Barry's hand and put it in his holster. Garrity straightened up and thrust his gun into its holster at the back of his left hip. He pointed his stubby finger at Will. "So you're going to be the next big hotshot that takes over from your dead asshole buddy here? The next young gun to blow his useless brains out?" He chuckled. "Send us an invitation. We'd like to see it. Right, Jim?"

Akerman nodded. "More than anything I can think of, right now. Christmas is coming. It'd be a nice gift for us."

Will shrugged and smiled. "As long as you both take turns spinning the barrels of your guns, too."

"You two have to settle down and put things in perspective," Barry said. "You see, it really doesn't matter to us if we kill you right here and now. We'll deal with the consequences, whatever they are. But you two – well, you'll just be dead. Forever." He paused. "And if you don't die in the next few minutes, you're both going to have heart attacks if you keep up all this anger stuff."

"And you should learn some fuckin' respect for the dead," Stumpy added.

"That sounds good," Garrity said. "We'll be happy to respect all you losers – when you're all dead."

Barry put his hand on Akerman's shoulder. "Jim. Frank. I'm crushed. I thought we were friends, or at least friendly enemies. Now, here you are speaking harshly to me like this. It leaves emotional scars when you talk to sensitive people in that manner."

"He's insane," Garrity said to Akerman. "They all are. Let's get out of here." He pushed Barry aside and barged through the crowd, with Akerman following close behind.

"Yet *more* verbal abuse. Keep it up and I won't have any choice but to report you, Frank," Barry said after them. He looked at Will. "You can put that away now."

Will nodded and again slid the gun into his holster.

Will opened the side door of his garage and found the ground and his bike blanketed with fluffy snow. "It's snowing," he said to Gloria, rushing back inside and opening the big front door. "I hate it. It's come early." He brushed the snow from his bike and pushed it inside.

Gloria got up from the cot and looked out the front door. She wrapped her arms around her body and held herself tight. "It's definitely cold enough." She blew out and watched her breath rise into the black air as a wispy, grey cloud. "You have to admit it's pretty."

"No. It's not pretty. There's *nothing* pretty about it. It just means I can't ride my bike." He pushed the sidestand out and leaned the bike against it. "Guess I'll be taking the bus back and forth to work now."

"Maybe it won't stay on the ground."

He shook his head. "Not with my luck. Might as well take my bike apart and start working on it."

"What's wrong with it?"

"Nothing."

"So why are you going to take it apart?"

He closed the big door and began to wipe the bike off with a rag, not looking at her. "So I won't expect to be able to ride it till spring. Fix it up. Whatever. Something to occupy my mind."

She looked at him. "Well, aren't you Mister Negative. What's wrong? You've been acting weird lately."

"Nothing."

"Nothing?"

He continued to wipe the bike off.

She returned to the cot and sat on it. She watched him. "I think it's dry now. Maybe you could put some more wood in the stove. That wouldn't be too upsetting for you, would it?"

He tossed the rag aside and went to the stove. He jerked the door open and jammed the firebox full of wood. "Think that'll do it?"

She stared at him. "Why are you so angry? Are you still upset because of Frantic? It's okay if you are, you know. It's only been two weeks. It's normal."

He crossed the floor from the stove to his bike and sat on it. "I'm not angry."

"You're something."

He put his hands on the handlebars. "I don't know what's wrong." He hesitated. "I've been having this dream – almost every night."

"The same dream?"

He nodded. "I'm walking down this narrow path in the sun, and I feel as if someone's coming up behind me. And I look back and see I'm leaving a trail of splattered red blood behind me. Then, I see some kind of strange shadow – just a dark shape – hiding among these dying trees and sickly, colourless bushes. So I keep walking but I can feel that it's getting closer. I keep looking back and I can only see a dark shape moving like a phantom from place to place." He took a deep breath. "And it gets bolder and bolder. As it gets closer, it feels like it's all around me and its presence starts to block out the sun and everything starts to get black and cold. I remember my gun and I reach for it. But I can't seem to get it out. Or, if I do, I can't focus on that thing. Or it's not there."

She pulled her knees together and leaned forward with her elbows on her thighs. "Sounds scary."

"Yeah, mostly because I know it's evil, but I can't make out what it is. Sometimes the surroundings are a little different, or the thing looks different. But it's always the same feeling."

"What happens in the end?"

"It doesn't really end. I wake up." He got off his bike and sat next to her. "But that's not all." He swallowed. "It's starting to happen even when I'm awake."

"What do you mean? You're seeing things again?"

"No. I don't mean like before. Not like with the wolf." He took her hand. "It's more a feeling. Like a presence. Like something bad is going to happen – a foreboding. Nothing seems the same and I feel all cold inside."

She raised his hand to her mouth and kissed it. "Well, what do you expect? You're living a pretty dangerous life. Lots of crazy, wild things have happened to you in the last few months. It'd probably be abnormal if you didn't feel strange – out of sorts."

"I suppose."

She paused. "But, if you're really worried about it, maybe you should talk to Barry and see if you can see his shrink. Or talk to Shotgun. He might have an idea about what to do."

"I don't know. Maybe." He pushed himself up and went to his bookcase.

He stood facing it, his back toward her. "Have you moved anything around in here? Rearranged things?"

"No." She looked around. "Like what? I pick your clothes up once in a while."

"You haven't touched any of my other stuff – my books, or tools, or bike parts?"

"Why would I?"

"Never mind."

"What? Now, you're starting to scare me."

"Nothing. It's nothing." He sighed. "I think some of my things have been moved around – more than once in the last couple of weeks."

She folded her hands and looked down at them. "Maybe it was your mother. Or Patty."

He nodded.

"I think he's depressed," Gloria said to Shotgun. Crossing her arms, she leaned her back against a wall, still spattered with droplets of blood, in the living room of the clubhouse.

"I'm not depressed," Will said. "I just don't like Christmas."

She put her hands on her hips and tapped her foot. "It's a whole lot more than that, and you know it."

"It's no big deal," Shotgun said. "We can get you some drugs."

"Jesus, I'm *not* depressed."

Gloria turned to Shotgun. "He's been seeing things and having bad dreams. Hasn't touched me in three weeks. All he does is mope around and stare off into space. If that's not being depressed, what is?"

Will stiffened and frowned at her. "Why did you have to say all that? It's more complicated than that. Plus, I've been tired. I do work all day outside in the cold. It's *real* work. Some kinds of work are a little harder than prancing around and flashing your tits."

He swished the beer around in his bottle. "You have to admit, it's all pretty pointless. Meaningless. We go down one path or another. Doesn't really seem to matter which one. Maybe we're in charge of what happens to us. Maybe not. Maybe it's all part of somebody else's big plan, or just a stupid game, and we get moved around like pawns on a big chess board. Either way, we don't know where it's all headed or what it all means – if anything. It's all pointless."

"Whoa," Shotgun said. "I think I better get us some more beer. I'll be right back."

Gloria crossed her arms. "Who do you think you are?"

"Like I said, it's more complicated than you think."

"Of course it is." She rolled her eyes. "With you, it's *always* more complicated. Nothing is ever simple, or just what it is. Everything's got to be a 10,000-word deep problem that only you understand." She grabbed his arm. "You drive me crazy with your arrogance. What makes you think you're so different from everybody else? Why can't you just be depressed, like other people? It's quite common. There's treatment for it." She paused. "Oh, wait, maybe that's the problem. It's *too* common for you. If it was some kind of rare problem with special meaning that only very special, extraordinary people get, well, for sure, that'd be the problem *you'd* want."

"Thanks. That helped a lot. I feel much better now."

Shotgun returned and passed beer to each of them. "Get that settled, did we?"

Gloria shook her head. "Tell him to go see a doctor."

Shotgun clinked his bottle against Will's and then Gloria's. "My advice would be to take the drugs. If it's not depression, it won't hurt anything. If it is depression, it might help. Besides just taking drugs might cheer you up. Does me."

"I don't need drugs for depression. Thinking you have to take drugs like that would be enough in itself to make you depressed."

Shotgun laughed.

"It's not funny," Gloria said. "If he's not depressed, he's going crazy. Seeing things, imagining he's being followed, acting like a completely different person. It's weird shit, Shotgun."

Shotgun picked at the label on his beer bottle and peeled it off. He glanced up at Will. "You hearing voices too?"

"No. Not voices."

"What then?"

"It's nothing." He hesitated. "I just thought I heard some noises outside the garage. Probably just cats. I'm a little on edge, that's all."

Shotgun looked at Gloria. "Could be those Devil's Chain guys. They've been out of the hospital for a while now. Lots of guys would like to have his ass."

"That wouldn't be as bad," Gloria said. "At least I'd know he's not crazy. Real things don't scare me. But ghosts and craziness do."

"You still carrying your gun?" Shotgun asked.

Will patted the bulge under his left arm and smiled.

"That's freaky," Shotgun said. "You look just like Frantic when you do that."

Gloria shook her head. "Even if those guys are after him, that doesn't explain how he's acting."

"I'm standing right here while you talk about me like this. I'm not an inanimate object, you know."

"You might as well be. The way you're acting. Wrapped up in yourself – in your little cocoon." She waved her hands in front of his face. "Hi there. See me? I'm here. I exist. I'm real."

He turned away from her and walked into the kitchen.

The next day, after work, he had to shovel snow from the steps and landing to get into the back door at Sadie's Lodge. Once in the back porch, he kicked his boots off and brushed snow from his jacket before going into the kitchen.

"Mom said for me to tell you to clear off the front steps, too," Patty said, sitting at the kitchen table. She pressed a copy of *Seventeen* onto the table top with one hand and flipped noisily through the pages with the fingers of her other hand.

"Where is she?"

"Don't remember. Gone out somewhere. Bingo maybe." She reached across the table and pulled the telephone closer. "I'm supposed to be gone out, too. But that dork boyfriend of mine hasn't called yet."

He glanced around. "Did she cook supper?"

Patty pointed at the refrigerator. "Oh yeah, talkin' about dorks. Some dorky old guy with a whacko accent called for you."

He went to the refrigerator, looked inside and took out a plate wrapped in tinfoil. "An accent?"

"Yeah. From that artsy-fartsy place you go to. Said your painting was ready to be picked up and you better come tonight to get it."

"Zwicker's?"

"Yeah, that's what he said. What painting do you got there?"

"It's a watercolour of Gloria. I painted it a while ago. I got it framed to give to her for Christmas."

"You painted a friggin' picture? When did you learn to paint?"

"I'm teaching myself."

She snickered. "Must be a friggin' gross painting."

"No doubt."

"What're you gonna get me for Christmas?"

"I don't know. How about a book about manners or one about English grammar? Your choice."

She glared at him. "You're friggin' kidding me."

"No. You're rude and you don't know how to speak English, so you could put either to good use."

She bit at her fingernails. "You're such a mean prick-of-a-brother, you'd probably do that."

He reached for the telephone.

"Hey, I'm using that!" she said, grabbing for it.

"I'll just be a minute." He dialled the phone. "I just want to make sure they're going to be there." He paused. "Busy."

She jerked the telephone away from him as he hung up. "I told you I was waiting for a call. You can go to that stupid place and get that stupid painting anytime."

He picked at the cold fish sticks and fries his mother had left for him, then left the plate beside the sink and headed into the back porch. He threw on his heavy work jacket. "If Gloria calls for me, tell her I'll be back in a half hour. Sooner if I take a taxi back."

"Mmm, hmm," Patty said, without looking up.

"And don't tell her anything about the painting."

"Maybe so, maybe not. It'll depend how I feel at the time."

"I wouldn't expect any less." He slammed the back door as he left.

The snow was tapering off, and he noticed the full moon encircled by a frosty, glowing halo between scurrying clouds. He hurried toward Zwicker's with the north wind at his back. When he turned onto Doyle Street, he saw only one car parked at the far end of the street. As he neared the front of Zwicker's, everything was in darkness, except for a faint light coming from inside. He went to the glass door and peered in, noticing that the light was coming from the studio. A piece of watercolour paper was taped to the inside of the door. He moved his head to the side so the light of the moon could illuminate it. 'In Studio' was printed on the sign in rough strokes of a ballpoint pen. He pulled the door open and stepped inside. The warm stuffy air and the smell of paints, and canvas, and old woodwork rushed at him.

"Hello," he called out.

"In here," someone called from the studio.

He stepped toward the doorway and the light that spilled into the hallway. "I didn't know if you'd still be here. You didn't have to hang around for me. I could have come tomorrow."

He sensed something – someone, a presence – move behind him. At the same moment, a short round man stepped through the studio doorway and backed into the shadow behind the wedge of light. Will glanced over his shoulder and saw the tall figure of a second person leaning against the wall in the shadow to the left of the front door.

THE MYTH OF ER

"I'LL BE DAMNED, CHRISTMAS HAS come early," Garrity said, stepping into the light.

"I can't believe he went for it," Akerman said, chuckling. He pushed himself away from the wall and stood straight, silhouetted against the moonlight streaming in the front door. "I had you figured for being smarter than this, kid."

Will saw he held a gun down low against the side of his right thigh. He looked back at Garrity and saw that he, too, had his gun drawn.

"These poor merchants," Garrity said. "They're getting ripped off all the time by break-and-enter scumbags."

"The druggies and the bikers are the worst," Akerman said, tapping the gun against his leg. "Breaking into legitimate businesses to steal whatever isn't nailed down to feed their drug habits. Owners of places like this are more than happy to take us up on an offer to do a little stakeout now and then. Especially when there's been a rash of break-ins, like around here in the last few weeks. It was probably you, right kid?"

"Probably was," Will said.

"Well, well. Listen to how he talks, Jim. Just what we like – a real smartass biker punk." He stepped closer to Will. "You have no idea what you've just walked into, do you? Your time has come."

"It doesn't matter," Will said.

Garrity looked past Will to Akerman, then back at Will. "You whacked out, or what? We got you for break-and-enter and attempted theft. And a few other charges with a little arranging of things here and there. Just for starters."

"But, aw, it was too bad," Akerman joined in. "If that's all it was, no big deal, right?" He laughed. "But that fucked-up, Dark Angel asshole, well, he had a gun. And those two hard-working detectives – the head guys of the city's anti-biker task force – who got tipped off about him and caught him in the act … well, they didn't have any choice, now did they? That punk looked like he hadn't slept in days, and he turned on the detectives."

"Yeah, too bad," Garrity said. "Just a young kid. But, you know, they had to defend themselves. They didn't intend to kill him. But he shouldn't have pulled that big gun on them." He paused and sighed. "Yeah, too bad. They just wanted to stop him. Give him a chance to be rehabilitated and turn his life around."

Will laughed. "You two must really be desperate to be doing this kind of shit – having to resort to setting me up for a phoney rap."

"Yeah, well, you've been too lucky a few times, but your luck's run out," Akerman said. "You've used up the last of your worthless lives."

Will sighed. "I guess that means you don't think I have the upper hand right now. You don't realize it would be better for you just to give me my painting and let me leave."

Akerman shook his head and laughed. "Jesus, Frank, you're right. He *is* crazy." He raised his gun and pointed it at Will. "Okay, I'm missing something. You wanna tell me how *you've* got the upper hand here?"

"You're obviously more afraid of me than I am of you. There's two of you, one in front of me and one behind. You've both got your guns out. Looks like you spent a lot of time working out this plan to set me up. And now you want to snuff me out and make it look like self-defence. So, really, it all means you're both cowards. You have no respect for the law you're supposed to be upholding. You lie, you connive, you sneak around like little boys – little misguided boy scouts pretending it's all about doing what's right."

"You smart-mouthed bastard," Garrity said. "Let's get this over with, Jim. I don't care if he's crazy or not."

Will held his hand up. "It seems to me it would be more interesting if you actually took a little risk yourselves here. Why don't you at least put your guns away, and we'll all draw at the same time? I mean, it'd give you more of a sense of accomplishment. More of a rush. Don't you think?"

"That would make us as whacked out as you are," Garrity said.

"Frank, come on, how exactly do you want to do this?"

"Doesn't matter. I'll just shoot the fucker. It'll be better if it looks like something that just happened. Let's not over-think it."

Will looked past Garrity down the hallway and noticed his portrait of Gloria leaning against a side table behind and to the right of Garrity. He saw that someone had smeared a black moustache and goatee on her face and had pressed black handprints on her breasts and hips. A black arrow running the length of her thigh pointed to her pelvis. Beneath the arrow, the word 'Enter' was scrawled. Will felt his face flash hot. He took a step in Garrity's direction.

"**GUN!**" Akerman screamed. He and Garrity dove to opposite sides of the hallway, opening fire with their .38 Police Specials. Will felt a slug tear into his chest – high and to the left. An image of a grizzly tearing into his chest with three-inch canines flitted into and out of his mind. The impact spun him back, as two more slugs from Akerman's gun slammed into the wall somewhere behind him. Clutching his chest, he thudded onto the floor near the front door, landing a few feet from Akerman.

"DON'T MOVE!" Akerman yelled. "GET YOU HANDS IN THE AIR WHERE WE CAN SEE THEM! NOW!"

Will raised his right arm. He tried to raise his left but couldn't move it.

"You okay, Frank?" Akerman asked.

"Yeah. Least I think so." Garrity got up on all fours, then stumbled to his feet. "I hit that Goddamn floor hard." He trained his gun on Will. "THE OTHER HAND, TOO!"

"I can't move it," Will said, clenching his teeth against the searing pain that paralyzed his chest and shoulder.

"Roll over on your stomach," Akerman said.

Will rolled to his right and Akerman and Garrity pounced on top of his back, grinding their knees into his back and twisting his arms behind him.

"You got cuffs?" Garrity asked, puffing hard through pursed lips.

Akerman shook his head. "Didn't think we'd need them."

Garrity moved off Will and grabbed his wrists, now jerking his arms out in front of him. He placed Wills' hands on the floor and stood up. He stood on them, while pointing his gun at Will's head. "Get that Magnum," he said to Akerman.

Akerman felt at Will's hips, at his sides up to his armpits and at the small of his back. He shot a furtive look up at Garrity and shook his head.

"What?" Garrity asked, frowning. "Jesus, it's big enough. Check the front of his body."

Akerman rolled Will a little to the right and frisked the front of his body. "Not there, Frank. He's clean."

Garrity dropped to his knees next to Will's head. "Where's that Goddamn bazooka of yours, kid? Why don't you have it on you tonight? We know you been carrying that thing all the time."

Will felt something warm and wet starting to soak the front of his chest. He was beginning to see pinpoints of light dancing in front of his eyes. "Forgot it home," he muttered.

Garrity sat back on his haunches and looked at Akerman. "This isn't good, Jim. He has to have that gun."

"Shit!" Akerman said. "Doesn't matter. We can still finish him. We just gotta say he reached for a gun, right? We had him under surveillance. We caught him in the act of committing an indictable offence. We had reasonable and probable grounds to believe he was armed and was going to shoot at us. It's tight, Frank."

Garrity shook his head. "How we gonna do it, now? We should've just shot the shit out of him as soon as he moved. That was our chance." He paused. "He's got no gun. They'll do ballistics and everything."

"Don't be getting soft on me, now, Frank. I'll do it, right now – no problem. Let's stand him back up over there and I'll pop him in the forehead." He began to pull on Will's right arm.

"Wait. How bad is he hit? Maybe he won't make it anyway if we stall for a while." Garrity leaned over Will's face, his eyes bulging. "Where you hit anyway?"

"Chest. Up high," Will said, grimacing.

Akerman rolled him onto his back and tore at his clothing until he had his bare chest exposed. He wiped the blood away with his hand and found the bullet hole. "Nah, that's no kill-shot. Look, it's just below the collar bone."

"Unless it got the top of his lung. Like I said, we should wait."

"No. Let's do it. Help me get him up."

Garrity didn't move. "I got a bad feeling about this, Jim. It's too risky. You know the Chief won't go out on a limb for us. It's gotta be squeaky clean." He ran his hand over the top of his bald head, shiny with sweat.

"And those bikers will go after this with that lawyer of theirs. It won't only be internal. Think about it. We got lots on him. He'll be going away for a while. You can count on that." He paused. "Think about it, Jim – you got 20 years in, right? Do you really want to put your career on the line for this punk?" He pushed himself up. "It's not about going soft. It's about being smart. We got him, Jim, we got him. It's not perfect, but it's good."

Akerman stood up and began to pace back and forth. "It galls me to let him off again this easy. You know this one's got a horseshoe up his ass. I just have a feeling it's gonna slip away from us again."

Garrity shook his head. "Not this time."

"Well, we're going to fucking wait a while. If he's not dead in a half hour, we'll call it in. Do him good to suffer, the way I see it."

Garrity nodded.

Akerman knelt on one knee next to Will. He pointed his gun at Will's forehead. "You so much as twitch and I'll ventilate that crazy head of yours." He grinned at Will. "On second thought, go on and twitch. Or, better yet, try to grab my gun. Come on, Quick Draw, reach for it."

Will's breath caught in his throat and he coughed, spraying blood on the front of Akerman's sports jacket and shirt.

"Fuck!" Akerman said, jerking back. "Another jacket ruined."

Will laughed. "It was ugly anyway, Jim. You can steal another one somewhere. Or whatever it is that cowards and crooked cops do to get their clothes."

Akerman cocked his gun and jammed it against Will's forehead. Will could feel his hot breath pulsing down against his face. Akerman's face began to blur.

"No, Jim!" Garrity said.

Akerman glanced at Garrity, then drew his gun back and smashed its handle down against the left side of Will's head.

Will heard a sharp CRACK, saw a bright flash of light and felt a quick spike of pain, as everything went black.

It felt as if he had been travelling for a long time. But he couldn't remember the beginning of the journey, how he got where he was, or what his destination might be. He looked all around and saw the sky was low and grey and the landscape featureless. It was a place he didn't recognize.

He walked in a circle around his motorcycle, studying it, and felt a wave of relief his bike was here. He mounted it and worked through his starting ritual, step-by-step. He threw himself up and kicked down on the kick-start pedal, but the motor didn't start, didn't even sputter. He kicked it again, and again. But, still, it would not bark to life as it always did.

He dismounted and began to push it forward on the surface of the black asphalt. He felt the hardness of the asphalt through the soles of his boots. He pushed until he was running – faster and faster. He jumped on the bike, kicked it into first gear and let out the clutch. The back wheel locked up and the bike skidded to a stop without starting. He tried once more to push-start it – running and running and running. Again, it shuddered to a stop, its motor dead. His body began to feel heavy and tired. It became difficult for him to move his legs.

He heard a noise coming up behind him. It sounded like a galloping horse. He looked back and saw Frantic approaching him, riding a black horse. Its long mane was whipping about in the wind. Frantic pulled back on the horse's mane with both hands, and the animal pranced to a stop in front of the bike.

"What's going on?" Frantic asked.

"It won't start. I've got to get going."

"Where?"

"I don't know. Some other place." He glanced around. "Look there's nothing here. No signs or anything. I can't stay here."

Frantic laughed. "Me either."

Will looked at his face and head. "How can *you* be here? I thought you were dead."

"I am. For now." The horse continued to twitch and step up and down under him, pawing at the asphalt with its front hoofs. "Whoa," he said, reaching down to pat the side of the horse's neck. "This guy doesn't like to stand still at all." Holding the horse's mane with his left hand, he slid off its back and stood next to Will. "I need my gun back."

"I don't have it." He held his jacket open. "Look for yourself. Besides, it's mine, now. You sold it to me."

"Not really. You can never sell something like that. Anyway, I need it back. It's my lucky gun. I've got one more bullet." He held a .44 calibre cartridge up in front of his face. "So I'm going to try again. They say I can try as many times as I want – till I get it right. If I'd had my favourite gun that night, I wouldn't be here just yet. And you wouldn't either. If you let me have it, I'll get you out of here. You don't need it now anyway."

Will looked around. He felt the cold wind blowing through his clothes. "Okay. But I don't know where it is."

"I do," Frantic said, reaching under his jacket. He began to pull out a length of rope that was coiled around his body.

Squinting to see more clearly, Will watched as Frantic uncoiled the rope – gold in colour and finely woven, like satin or silk, and about as big around as the barrel of a .44 Magnum. As Frantic pulled it away from his body, it began to glow. He walked to the bike and tied it around the upper triple clamp at the front forks. He walked back to the horse and looped it around its neck three times. He jumped back up on the horse's back. "It's made of memory and hope – the past and the future. So it's stronger than it looks. Get on your bike if you're coming."

The horse reared up on its back legs and lunged forward. Will leapt on his bike just as it started to be pulled away. The bike glided forward under him in silence, as on a silken highway. He felt the cool wind against his face and heard it whooshing as it blew past his ears.

They rode on for what seemed like a great distance and felt like a long time. Then, an image of his gun appeared in his mind. "FRANTIC," he called up to him. "I REMEMBER WHERE IT IS. IT'S UNDER MY PILLOW!"

Frantic looked back and laughed. "I KNOW. IT WAS MY IDEA. I GOT YOU TO LEAVE IT THERE."

Will watched as Frantic took his right hand from the horse's mane and unsheathed a long sword from a scabbard at his left side. He leaned forward and with one slicing swing severed the golden rope near the horse's neck. "YOUR BIKE WILL START NOW," he shouted back to Will.

Frantic and the horse disappeared into the distance. The golden rope fell from the front forks and blew away. As the bike began to slow, Will tapped it into second gear and released the clutch. The motor fired. He opened the throttle and accelerated through the gears. He rode on looking for road signs, but there were not any to be seen. It began to get dark. Soon the darkness enveloped him and he could not see where he was going.

He felt the bike still moving and vibrating beneath him, heard the exhausts booming and smelled the hot gasses. He sensed objects and danger on all sides. He felt he had to stop. He pressed his right foot down against the back brake pedal and squeezed the front brake lever. But the bike would not stop. The harder he tried to brake, the faster the bike moved forward. He felt the bike lose contact with the ground and fly through the air. He landed with a huge splash in a body of water, and he and the bike went down, down under the water.

He watched his bike sink out of sight beneath him, light from somewhere shimmering off the chromed surfaces. He looked up and saw the blue-green surface of the water high over his head. He kicked with his legs and feet and pulled at the water with his arms and hands. He held his breath as long as he could, then began to breathe under the water. He felt the water inside his mouth, salty and warm.

His head burst above the surface and he saw that Daddy Hughie's island lay right before him. He smiled when he saw Daddy Hughie at the shoreline, waving to him to swim ashore. He reached the shore and rolled onto his back on a thousand small pebbles, which molded themselves softly to the contours of his body. His body felt so heavy. He was so tired. He could not open his eyes, but could feel the warmth of the sun on his face and smell the sharp salty air that rose off the harbour. He could feel sleep coming.

He felt his grandfather's rough hands reach under his head and cradle it. He felt him pat his cheek. He could smell wood smoke, and seaweed, and mudflats, and Turret tobacco, and all the woodsy, manly smells of the island and of his grandfather. Nothing bad could happen to him now. Daddy Hughie, the toughest, strongest man in the world would protect him.

He felt another hand, a soft hand, take his hand and squeeze it. Another voice, near but sounding far away, spoke his name. "Will. Can you hear me, Will?" But it wasn't Daddy Hughie's voice.

PART 7

THE KEEPER OF THE WINDS

H E BEGAN TO FEEL PAIN in his head and chest. He felt his hand being squeezed again. He began to sense he was no longer lying on the shoreline of Daddy Hughie's island, that he was somewhere else. He fought to open his eyes.

"Come on, Will. You can wake up now," someone was saying.

He opened his eyes and saw a man with a narrow face and gold wire-rimmed glasses, looking down at him. Long blond hair framed his face. "It's okay. You're in the hospital. I'm Doctor Stewart. Do you understand what I'm saying?"

Will nodded. He glanced past Stewart and saw a uniformed police officer, sitting on a metal folding chair next to the door that led from the room.

"Good." Stewart smiled. "You're in the Victoria General Hospital. You've been here three days. Do you remember what happened?"

"Umm – I think – yeah. I got shot," Will mumbled.

"And you got a nasty fractured skull. You've been unconscious until just now."

Will tried to raise his head to look down at his chest.

"It hit you in the upper part of the chest, a little below the clavicle. Grazed the top of your lung and made a messy exit hole in your upper back. You were lucky. It should heal without leaving any permanent damage or impairment. You had the angels on your side that night."

Will moaned. "My head."

Stewart nodded. "I know. Must hurt like hell. Apparently, after you were shot, you fell and hit your head on the metal door frame. It's that fracture that's had us most concerned."

"I don't remember that."

"Skull fractures and concussions are like that. It's not unusual for patients not to be able to remember events right around the time of the mishap. It might come back to you in time."

The police officer seated by the door got up and came to the opposite side of the bed. "He going to be okay?"

"It's looking better than it did two days ago," Stewart said.

The officer took his handcuffs from his belt and grabbed Will's right wrist. He snapped one end on Will's wrist and the other to the bedrail. "I'll let them know at the station. Detective Garrity told me to call him if the kid ever woke up."

"Is that really necessary?" Stewart asked, pointing at the handcuffs.

The officer laughed. "It sure is. I guess you don't know how dangerous this little prick is." He rattled the handcuffs against the bedrail. "When will he be ready to go?"

"I'm not sure. That might depend on where he's going."

"Oh, that's easy. His ass is going to jail, for sure."

"I'll take that into consideration then when I talk to Detective Garrity."

"Got a phone I can use here?"

"Nurse's station," Stewart said, nodding toward the door.

"Don't you be going anywhere, boy," the officer said, chuckling. "I'll be right back."

Stewart crossed his arms and looked down at Will. "I patched up those two other bikers who got shot up last summer, and I did the autopsy for the medical examiner on that fellow from your club. I did trauma work in Detroit before coming here – to get away from all that craziness – so now I get all the shootings and stabbings whenever I'm on duty."

Will nodded. "You don't look like any doctor I've known."

"Yeah, the police aren't too impressed with me." He paused. "It's none of my business, but I've heard them talking when they've been here. Sounds like they've got a strong case against you, though it was quite obvious they were hoping you'd never come around." He adjusted his glasses. "I think I can hold them back for four or five days, a week possibly. But, after that, you'll be in their hands. You've got a long road ahead of you, my friend."

"I think I've just come from there," Will said, trying to smile. "My mother?"

"I'll call her right away. No one has been allowed to see you. But she's been here every day – your girlfriend and other friends, too."

The room began to spin in front of Will's eyes. "I've done things. But not at Zwicker's. They set me up." He shrugged. "But I guess it doesn't matter. You get away with some things you do, but get nailed for some things you don't do. It all balances out in the end, right?"

Stewart grinned. He took a small penlight from his breast pocket and shined it in Will's eyes, first one then the other. "How are you feeling now?"

"My head hurts. My chest hurts."

"On a scale of one to ten – one being no pain, ten being unbearable pain?"

"Eight and a half. Nine."

"You allergic to anything?"

"No."

"Have any preferences in narcotics?"

"No."

"Okay. We'll start you with Demerol. With your head injury, we'll have to be careful not to sedate you too much."

Stewart squeezed Will's hand again with his soft smooth hand. "You're going to be okay."

Will nodded.

An hour later, Garrity and Akerman breezed past the nursing station and slipped into his room.

"He was awake a while ago, but they gave him some dope and he conked out again," the officer at the door said, standing up and shaking out his legs. "Jesus, we need a better chair in here if we're going to be watching this fool 24/7."

"What'd he say?" Akerman asked.

"Nothing really. Didn't seem to remember much. I cuffed him right away." He yawned. "You bring coffee or anything?"

"No," Garrity said. "Go down to the cafeteria if you want. We're good here. What's your name?"

"Mark Avery. Constable."

"Thanks, Mark," Garrity said. "You're doing a great job here. I'll mention your name to the Chief."

"Really?" Avery said, straightening up. "Doing my duty, that's all. Just another pensionable day in my books."

Akerman shook his head. "No, not when we can get one of these biker bums out of circulation. Then, you're performing a real public service. That's valuable police work, Avery."

"Right, sir. I never thought of it that way. Just felt like long, boring hours the last few shifts."

"Think of it as time well-spent, helping to get rid of a cancer eating away at the city's innards," Garrity said.

Avery nodded and strode through the doorway with his shoulders high and square.

Garrity and Akerman went to the side of the bed. Akerman took Will's right wrist and shook it back and forth, rattling the handcuffs against the bedrail. "Hey, Sleeping Beauty, wake up."

"Wakey, wakey," Garrity said, pushing Will's bandaged left shoulder.

"Arrgghhh," Will groaned. He opened his eyes and looked up at the two detectives. His eyelids felt as if they were glued to his eyeballs, as if leaden weights were attached to the upper lids. He struggled to focus on Garrity and Akerman.

"Come on, sunshine, perk up," Garrity said. "We know you're happy to see us. We got good news and bad news. No, shit, I lie. We really just got bad news for you." He laughed. "The first part of the bad news is you're still alive. The second part is that soon as you get out of here, you're goin' to jail."

"We got you nailed tight, kid," Akerman said. "But – like if you get any funny ideas about going through a big court circus and getting that Jew layer to make this harder than it has to be – think about this …" He leaned over the bed until his head was next to Will's head. "You know what? We did some digging and found out that your old lady's got no insurance on that Sadie's Lodge place." He pushed himself back. "Be a damn shame if anything was to happen to it. You know, by accident of course. So you'd be smarter than you've been so far to plan on pleading guilty to everything."

"Sounds like you're worried," Will said.

"You arrogant little shit," Garrity said. "I suppose you think you still got the upper hand?"

Will nodded.

Garrity stepped closer to the bed, but stopped short as Stewart came through the door. "Sorry, gentlemen, he's not supposed to have any visitors."

Garrity bristled. "You know we're not visitors. When are we going to be able to take him in?"

"Perhaps in five to seven days – at the earliest. It will depend on how he progresses."

"We're not much for coddling dangerous criminals, Doc, so the sooner the better."

Stewart looked over the top of his glasses at Garrity and Akerman. "It's not black and white. It could be five days, it could be two weeks. It will depend on how quickly his condition improves. His injuries are serious – life threatening. I'm assuming you don't want the liability of taking him out too soon and having things go bad in jail."

Garrity glanced at Akerman and rolled his eyes. "We'll be waiting to hear from you," he said, brushing past Stewart. "Don't forget, we've got an officer here round the clock. So we'll hear about it if you try to jerk us around. I'm not above charging your uppity ass with obstruction of justice."

Stewart looked at Will after they left the room. "Pleasant pair."

"They're consistent, I'll give them that."

"How are you doing now? Has the pain diminished?"

"It's quite a bit better."

"I'll see if I can persuade that police officer to sit in the hall. It's really better if you can rest without unnecessary disruption." He turned to leave but stopped in mid-stride. "Oh, actually, I came in here to see if you might feel up to talking to your lawyer tomorrow. He has asked to talk to you as soon as you are able to do so. He and that Barry fellow from your club have been calling regularly about it."

"Tomorrow?"

Stewart nodded. "At ten, I think he said."

"Yeah. I guess so. But I don't think I have a lawyer."

"He said his name was Dedrick."

Will nodded.

"I'll call him, then."

The cold from winter's frigid air still clung to Dedrick's long black overcoat when a nurse ushered him into Will's room the next morning. "Dedrick," he said to Will, holding out his hand as he approached the bed.

Will moved his right wrist, rattling the handcuffs.

Dedrick lowered his hand and smiled. "How are you doing, anyway?"

Will shrugged. "Okay, I guess. Better than yesterday. I mean, considering I've got a bullet hole in my chest and a cracked skull, and that I'm handcuffed to a hospital bed and going to jail when I get out of here."

Dedrick laughed. "Sorry. Dumb question. Doctor Stewart says you're doing well."

"I sat up a little this morning. My head still hurts a lot."

"Do you feel well enough to talk about the charges against you? Doctor Stewart says your cognition is fine."

"Yeah, but I don't know what there is to talk about."

"I know. That's why I'm here. It's not as straightforward as you might think. Or as what the police might have told you. I heard you had a couple visitors yesterday." He unbuttoned his coat and removed his scarf, tossing it on the foot of the bed. "They've brought charges against you for three indictable offences – break and enter with intent, resisting a peace officer, and possession of a weapon, a gun. I know they think they have a strong case against you on all the charges." He paused. "What we have to talk about is how you want to plead to the charges."

"The only thing I'm actually guilty of is having the gun."

Dedrick smiled. "Unfortunately, the way it works is that it doesn't much matter what you did or didn't do. What matters is the evidence they have against you. I don't know all of what they have, but my prediction would be that if we let this go to trial by your pleading not guilty, you could end up with substantial prison time. It's not just the evidence itself, it will be hard for the court to ignore the fact you're in the Dark Angels when it comes to sentencing. And there's been a lot of publicity, to say the least."

"It doesn't seem right to plead guilty to something I didn't do."

"I understand that. But I'm a lawyer not a miracle worker. If I thought we could go to court and create reasonable doubt and beat those charges, I'd tell you that's what we should do." He shook his head. "And, if we try that and lose, you could be looking at maximum time of 10 to 14 years. Not that you'd necessarily get that much time."

"And if I plead guilty?"

"We'd bargain with the Crown to end up with a sentence that would be closer to a minimum than a maximum."

"What do you think that would be?"

"Three to five. You'd be out in two perhaps." He shrugged. "Considering everything, that would be a very favourable outcome – in my opinion."

"In other words, I've got options but they all include going to prison. It's just a matter of for how long."

Dedrick smiled. "That's a nice succinct way of expressing things. But, if we're both thinking along the same lines, I'll go have a chat with the Crown Prosecutor. Bob Simms has this case. We were in law school at the same time. I know how he operates." He reached for his scarf and draped it around his neck. He began to button up his coat. "I know it sounds bad, but I've got an angle or two. I'd rather you have low expectations and have me exceed them, than have high expectations and have me disappoint you. A step at a time, that's how we'll do it."

"What kind of angles?"

"Ah, that's a trade secret," Dedrick said, shaking his head. "Another thing, don't be too athletic in here. As soon as they can move you safely, they'll take you to the police lock-up. Probably try to do it on a weekend or over the holidays. Then, you'll go before a judge to enter your pleas. Do you know how that works?"

"More or less."

"Well, I'll be there, but the main thing by then will be whether or not we can get you released on bail. If not, you'll be remanded in custody, which means you'll stay in jail until your sentencing. But the Crown has to show cause why you shouldn't be released. The burden's on them. Anyway, we can talk more about that as things progress. For now, work at getting better, but don't do it too fast. The longer you can stay here, the better."

"Doctor Stewart thinks maybe a week or so."

"If that's what it is, that would give us a few days this side of Christmas to finish with your show-cause hearing. That could work." He walked around to the far side of the bed and shook Will's handcuffed hand. "Anything else?"

"How could they charge me with possession of the gun when I didn't even have it?"

"They got a search warrant to search your place. They found it in the garage under a pillow. I guess you sleep there?"

Will nodded.

"Doesn't actually have to be on your body."

A few hours later, Dedrick knocked on the door of Simms' office. The door opened and Simms stood facing him with a blank expression. He pushed his glasses closer to his eyes. "Come in, Martin," he said, shaking Dedrick's hand. He nodded toward a wooden armchair off to the left of his desk, which faced the door. "Have a seat."

Dedrick glanced to his right and saw Garrity and Akerman seated on straight-backed wooden chairs. Once back behind his desk, Simms butted out his cigarette in a heavy amber-coloured ashtray, overflowing with butts and ashes and positioned within easy reach of his right hand on the top of the desk.

Dedrick sat down and placed his black leather briefcase on the floor at his feet. He crossed his right leg over his left and folded his hands on his thigh. "You're looking well, Bob. Still playing tennis?"

"Yeah, once in a while. Can't seem to stay away from these damn cigarettes, though."

"Well, you're doing something right. You don't look a day over 30." Dedrick smiled. "Interesting case, isn't it, Bob?"

ALEXANDER, WILLIAM H.

"*INTERESTING*? I DON'T KNOW ABOUT interesting, Martin. This kid is past due. He's a menace."

Dedrick chuckled. "You're right. He's been pushing the limits." He paused and looked across at Garrity and Akerman. "But he's not the only menace on the loose, right?"

Garrity leaned forward in his chair, but Simms held his hand up, palm toward him. "That's uncalled for, Martin, and you know it. Are you trying to inflame this situation?" He picked up a Bic pen and tapped it on a pad of lined yellow paper. "Let's cut to the chase, Martin. What are you looking for?"

"Two years on the weapon's charge. You eat the other two charges."

Garrity and Akerman burst out laughing, and Simms grinned. "You can't be serious. We'd be willing to settle for seven, maybe six. He pleads guilty to all the charges and it's over just like that."

"He thinks he's got the upper hand, just like that kid always does," Akerman said.

Dedrick raised his eyebrows. "Well, now that you mention it, we're offering you a chance to save yourself and the Halifax Police Department the embarrassment of having this case go to trial and receive a lot of exposure in the press. You have to allow that we would be doing you a favour by pleading guilty to the weapon's charge. The other two charges are a joke. What we're really talking about here is at best entrapment, but more accurately police criminal misconduct – which we will obviously pursue as actions in civil court. You'll want to tell Chief Middleton that the Police Department and the city are going to need a good defence lawyer. So, really, what we're offering you is an opportunity to withdraw these charges to avoid embarrassment and messy litigation."

"He's riding you, Simms," Garrity said.

Dedrick looked at Simms, ignoring Garrity. "My client was a regular visitor to the gallery. He was on good terms with the proprietor, who, by the way, is prepared to testify on his behalf. He has an interest in painting that can be easily established. He had brought a painting in to be framed earlier in the week, as the gallery's records can verify. The painting, however, mysteriously disappeared the night he was shot. Clearly, *he* didn't remove it from the gallery. Someone called and left a message at his home that he should come pick up the painting that very night. There were no signs of forced entry. He was not carrying a gun or any other weapon."

He paused and looked over at Garrity and Akerman. "I'd be happy to have him take the stand and tell his story. I think a jury would find him to be very articulate and convincing under oath. I'd look forward to calling other witnesses – law-abiding people – who would testify to his character. Did I mention – you'd know this – he has no criminal record. But most of all, I'd look forward to examining Detectives Garrity and Alkerman on the stand." He looked back at Simms. "You'll have to spend a lot of time helping them get their stories straight, Bob. And firming up the evidence."

Simms looked down at the yellow pad. "I know you can't help being full of yourself, Martin, but I would think you'd be less deluded about guys like this, by now." He looked up at him, tapping the pad with the pen. "He was a regular visitor because he was casing the place. So what if he's artsy, that doesn't mean he isn't also a thief. We both know it's often the quiet, innocent-looking ones that are the most dangerous criminals – the serial killers, the psychopaths that just snap and do the worst shit. Jesus, Martin, word is he drove his stepfather out of town at the end of that Goddamn Magnum. And that kid sister of his, sure she's going to lie to save his skin. You think *she's* a reliable witness. She's running wild, too, from what we hear. Shit, we could probably even bring his old man back to testify against him."

"You should go and talk to people who know him," Garrity said. "They'll tell you he's strange upstairs. Always talking weird psycho-babble shit. Acts like he's from another planet. The only defence you got that might make sense is that he's a mental case."

"Think about it, Bob," Dedrick said, continuing to ignore Garrity. "It won't be difficult for me to create doubt about the evidence. It will be even easier to drive a bus through the holes in the lies these two will be telling. A lot of this will revolve around credibility – the credibility of the evidence, the witnesses, and the story itself." He paused. "You must know you will not be able to prove these charges beyond a reasonable doubt. Your reputation will take a hit, Bob, a bad hit. Especially, when we take this to civil court and sue for damages, including punitive damages."

Simms leaned back in his chair and took his glasses off, dropping them on the note pad. "He's a loose cannon, Martin. These detectives have had him under surveillance since the end of the summer – after he shot those other two bikers. I'm sure you know he was the one. I guess you think that's okay. And that it shouldn't be anybody's concern he's been carrying that gun, or that he used it against his old man." He leaned forward. "Martin, I know you can see the pattern here like the rest of us. If he gets off easy again, you and I will be sitting here the next time talking about a murder charge against him. He's a walking time bomb – just itching for an opportunity to explode."

"I understand your concern, but that's not my impression. More importantly, none of that has anything to do with these specific charges. If you're going to nail him, do it right."

"Smartass prick," Akerman said to Garrity, under his breath.

Simms sighed. He looked at Garrity and Akerman. "Five years," he said, looking back at Dedrick. "And I have to swallow hard to do that."

"Come on, Simms!" Garrity said. "Don't cave in to this. It's all a big bluff. We're not afraid for this to go to trial. Right, Jim?"

Akerman nodded. "This is no chess game, Dedrick. This is real life."

"Three years. And only the weapon's charge," Dedrick said to Simms, retrieving his briefcase from the floor and resting it on his knee. "And we won't pursue litigation."

As Simms sat motionless in his chair, Dedrick rose and approached his desk. He held his hand out to Simms. "I'll write this up and get it back to you by four today. This will be an easy case for you after all, Bob." Simms slowly extended his hand. Dedrick grasped it and pumped it up and down twice.

Garrity and Akerman looked at one another. Garrity hung his head.

"What do you have in mind for bail?" Dedrick asked.

"No. No way. He's high-risk," Simms said. "We can put something together to keep him locked up until sentencing."

"On the basis of a guilty plea to a weapon's charge? I don't think so. Twenty thousand sounds about right, don't you think?"

"He could disappear like smoke into that maze of biker connections. He's got nothing to keep him here." He paused. "Forty thousand."

"Twenty-five – and I'm out of your hair."

Simms tossed the Bic pen onto his desk. Dedrick smiled and turned to leave.

"Close the door behind you," Simms said.

As soon as Dedrick closed the door, Garrity jumped up and slammed the palm of his hand down on Simms' desk. "Christ, are *you* on their payroll, too? I don't know why we break our asses to bring these guys in, just so you can take the easy way out."

"Forget it, Frank. You're wasting your time," Akerman said. "I could've told you it'd turn out like this." He winked at Garrity. "We'll get it right the next time."

"Spare me the dramatics," Simms said. "You bring me your sloppy shit, then complain that what we end up with smells bad." He pointed his finger at them. "He's right. You're both lucky this isn't going to trial."

Garrity and Akerman burst through the door into Will's hospital room and rushed up to his bed. "Vacation's over, princess," Garrity said. "Glad to see you're dressed. I guess you were expecting us." He went around to the far side of the bed and unlocked the handcuff holding Will's wrist to the bedrail.

"My lawyer told me you'd be here today."

"I bet the shyster did," Akerman said. "Well, where you're going isn't going to be this cozy." He joined Garrity and grabbed Will by the right arm. "Let's go."

They jostled Will out of the hospital and pushed him into the back seat of the unmarked police car parked at the front door.

"Watch out for his boo-boo head and his sore shoulder," Garrity said. "We wouldn't want him to sue us for police brutality."

"It would be understandable if you wanted to make a run for it right about now," Akerman said, standing at the curb and holding the car door open. "How much of a head start could we give him, Frank?"

"I don't know. What's fair – 15, 20 minutes?"

"What do you think? We got a deal?" Akerman asked Will. "You and your lawyer friend like to wheel and deal, right?"

Will sat in the back seat, looking up at him.

"Not sure?" Akerman continued. "Okay, half an hour?" He paused. "Tell you what, I'll leave the door unlocked. If the mood strikes you, we'll look the other way."

"Too cold out," Will said.

Akerman slammed the door and climbed in the front seat.

In the morning, two uniformed police officers appeared outside the bars of the lock-up in the basement of the police station. "Alexander, William H.," one of them called, reading from a clipboard.

Will got up from the steel cot on which he had been lying. The officer unlocked the cell door and the other stepped inside. "You're to be in court in an hour," he said. He looked at Will, then back at the other officer. "How are we supposed to cuff him with his arm in a sling like that?"

"Frank Garrity sent word not to bother."

With one officer in front and the other behind, they led Will out of the police station.

"Where's the court house?" Will asked, as they pulled out of the parking lot and headed south on Brunswick Street.

"Spring Garden Road," the officer driving said. "It's the Provincial Court building."

"You're quite the celebrity," the other said. "Made a big splash on the news." He laughed. "That's probably why Garrity's got such a boner on for you." He glanced at Will in the rear-view mirror. "You don't look so tough to me. You trying to be a cop killer like they say?"

"No, I wouldn't be interested in that," Will said, smiling. "Sounds like a dead-end plan."

The officer glanced at him again. "You got a sick sense of humour."

Minutes later, they whisked him into the Provincial Court building and into a crowded holding room. "When they call your name, you go into the courtroom through that door," one officer said, nodding in the direction of a closed door at the other end of the room. He pushed Will down onto a low wooden bench and sat next to him. Every so often, the door opened and a bailiff thrust his head around its edge, calling out the name of the next to appear before the judge.

"Alexander," he called out, after what felt to Will to have been about half an hour. Before he could move, the officer jumped up and pulled at his right elbow. He led him to the doorway and showed him through as the bailiff opened the door wider. "Take a seat at that table," he said, pointing to a wooden table at the front of the courtroom behind which sat two empty chairs.

Will glanced up at the judge as he crossed the front of the courtroom, and then noticed Simms seated at the same kind of table on the other side of the courtroom. He stole a glance toward the back of the courtroom and saw Dedrick arise from a bench at the back wall. Will pulled a chair out and sat at the table. Moments later, Dedrick arrived at his side and sat next to him. He leaned toward Will. "Judge MacIsaac," he whispered. "Be careful what you say. And be polite."

Behind the bench, Judge MacIsaac rustled through papers. He adjusted his reading glasses below bushy grey eyebrows. He glanced over his glasses at Will and Dedrick. "You're representing the accused I take it, Mr. Dedrick?"

Dedrick stood up. "Yes, Your Honour." He nudged Will. "Stand up," he whispered.

MacIsaac glanced at the document in his hands, then looked at Will. "William H. Alexander. Is that you, sir?"

"Yes, Your Honour."

"Is your client ready to enter a plea, Mr. Dedrick?"

"Yes, Your Honour."

"Mr. Alexander, is that so?"

"Yes, Your Honour."

"You understand do you, Mr. Alexander, that this court is not bound to accept any plea arrangement you may have agreed to with Mr. Dedrick and Mr. Simms?"

Will glanced at Dedrick, who nodded at him. "I didn't realize that, but that's fine, Your Honour."

MacIssac cleared his throat and again looked down. He read from the document in his hands. "Mr. Alexander, you are charged that, on or about December tenth of this year, you did have in your possession a weapon for a purpose dangerous to the public peace, namely a .44 calibre Smith and Wesson revolver, an indictable offence contrary to section 85 of the *Criminal Code* of Canada." He paused and looked up at Will. "You do understand this charge, do you Mr. Alexander?"

"Yes, Your Honour."

"And how do you plead then?"

"Guilty," Will said.

MacIssac looked at Simms. "Mr. Simms would you read the pertinent facts of this matter into the record."

Simms stood up and snatched a legal-sized sheet of paper from the table top in front of him. "My pleasure, Your Honour." He glanced across at Will and Dedrick. "Your Honour, Mr. Alexander came to the attention of the police as a member of the Dark Angels motorcycle gang and as someone suspected by the police of having engaged in various criminal activities over a period of several months. As a consequence, he was placed under surveillance by Detectives Frank Garrity and Jim Akerman of the city's special biker task force. These detectives had reasonable grounds to believe the accused had the weapon in question in his possession, and so conducted a lawful search of the defendant's garage, where they found the weapon." Simms paused. "Mr. Alexander here was arrested at Zwicker's Art Gallery."

MacIsaac tilted his head down and looked over his glasses at Will. "At an art gallery?"

Simms glanced across at Will and Dedrick. "Umm, yes, Your Honour. He was there after hours."

"I assume we're not going to go into that today," MacIsaac said, shifting in his seat.

"Uhh, no, Your Honour," Simms said.

"Your Honour?" Dedrick interjected.

"Yes, Mr. Dedrick."

"Your Honour, in light of the fact this is my client's first criminal offence – in fact the first time he has been charged with an offence – we would like to request that a pre-sentence report be prepared."

"Yes, Mr. Dedrick, that would be my plan. This court would be interested in what that might reveal. Is that acceptable to you Mr. Simms?"

Simms shrugged. "As the court wishes, Your Honour."

"As to conditions of release, have you and Mr. Dedrick reached some agreement about that as well, Mr. Simms?"

"We're requesting that bail be set at $25,000."

MacIsaac frowned. "That seems excessive. Why so high for a single weapon's charge?"

Simms shifted in place. "There are compelling reasons, Your Honour. Because of Mr. Alexander's biker connections, the Crown is concerned that strong measures must we taken to compel his appearance back in court for sentencing. Shall I go into the details?"

MacIssac shook his head. "No, that won't be necessary. My interest is not sufficiently piqued. All I need to know is that defence is in agreement."

"We are, Your Honour," Dedrick said.

MacIsaac leaned back. "Now, then, Mr. Alexander, you will be released on bail as soon as the arrangements are made. And you are to appear back before me for sentencing on … hmmm … let us see." He began thumbing through a thick notebook. "Would the first of March work, gentlemen? Nine in the morning? That's a little over eight weeks from now, allowing a little extra time for the holidays."

"Yes, Your Honour, we can make that work," Simms said.

"Likewise," Dedrick said.

"So, again, Mr. Alexander, you are to be back here before me for sentencing on March first. In the meantime, you will be contacted by a probation officer, who will complete a pre-sentence report to help the court decide what to do with you. You would be wise to cooperate fully with him. Do you understand all this?"

"Yes, Your Honour. Thank you."

MacIsaac bent his head and looked at him over his glasses. "Don't thank me, young man. Just be sure to be back here on March first. Someone is putting up a considerable sum of money to guarantee your appearance back here – probably someone who cares about you. That money will be forfeited if you fail to appear." He dropped his book on his desk with a heavy thump.

Will nodded.

MacIsaac continued to look at him. "I'm curious, Mr. Alexander – what happened to you that you are all bandaged up in that manner? Have you been in an accident?"

Will glanced at Dedrick, while Simms rushed to clear the papers off his table. Dedrick smiled. "Tell him the truth," he whispered to Will. "Politely."

PATHWAYS

"WELL, YOUR HONOUR, I GOT shot at Zwicker's Art Gallery about two weeks ago." He paused. "One of the detectives Mr. Simms spoke of – I think it was Akerman – shot me. I also ended up with a fractured skull. They said I hit my head when I fell. But, in my dreams, I keep seeing Akerman hitting me in the head with his gun. I'm not completely sure about that part."

"Your Honour!" Simms blurted out. "You can't allow the accused to make inflammatory, unsworn comments like that. With respect, Your Honour, that's extremely prejudicial!"

MacIssac leaned back and removed his glasses from his face. He placed them on the papers on his desktop. He shot a glance at Simms, then fixed his gaze on Will. "Yes, I assumed it might have been more than a slip on an icy sidewalk. See you in eight weeks, Mr. Alexander." He looked back at Simms. "And, Mr. Simms, I think you've been before me often enough to know better than to advise me as to what I *can* or *cannot* do in my courtroom."

Simms shuffled his feet in place. "Yes, Your Honour. I was only …"

"Tread lightly, counsellor," MacIssac interrupted. "Tread lightly."

The bailiff signalled for Will to return to the holding room. Looking back as he crossed the courtroom, he saw Dedrick walking down the aisle, and then saw his mother, seated next to Barry and Stumpy at the back of the courtroom. She waved at him, a weak smile on her strained face. A sudden pang of guilt and sadness overcame him, leaving him feeling sick to his stomach and making his legs feel wobbly.

Minutes later, Dedrick bustled into the holding cell. "We're all set. Come on, I'll drive you home." He flashed the bail papers to the officer who had brought Will to court. He led Will out through the side door into a cold hallway and then to the outside.

Will saw his mother, Barry, and Stumpy, standing on the front steps of the building. They rushed to meet him. "I'll get my car," Dedrick said, heading off.

As they approached, Will saw that his mother looked very thin and pale. Barry and Stumpy were smiling. His mother reached him first and threw her arms around him. Will pulled back, wincing.

"*Ohh, sorry!*" his mother said. "I didn't mean to squeeze so hard."

"It's okay," he said, turning his body and hugging her with his right arm. "It's a lot better."

"Friggin' invalid," Stumpy said, grinning. "You ain't much use to anybody now, are you?"

"That went okay," Barry said. "Dedrick's been working hard on this one. It's not often he gets to defend any of our guys who are actually innocent."

Will nodded. "How'd you get the money for bail?"

"Mr. Dedrick helped me take out a loan against the house," his mother said.

"Are you sure that's a good idea? What if something goes wrong?"

His mother pulled her coat tighter around her neck. "What choice did we have? Anyway, it's done." She paused, looking into his eyes. "I'm counting on you to make sure nothing does go wrong. Too much has already gone wrong."

"More likely that something would've gone wrong if they'd remanded you in custody for two months," Barry said.

A car horn sounded from the street. Will turned and saw it was a black Mercedes sedan parked at the curb.

"Dedrick," Barry said. "Let's go."

"Nice car," Will said.

Barry laughed. "Should have a bumper sticker on it that says Dark Angels. He's made enough money off us the last few years to pay cash up front for it."

They all climbed into the car and Dedrick pulled away. "What are your plans for the next eight weeks, Will?" he asked, turning onto Brunswick Street.

Will shook his head. "I don't know. Lay low. Maybe work on my bike if I can."

"You could read and paint," his mother said. "You like to do that. And Doctor Stewart said you'd be going to physio."

Stumpy, sitting in the front seat, looked back at Will with a puzzled expression. "Paint? How you gonna paint this time of year? And with one good arm?"

"She doesn't mean painting houses. She means painting pictures. You know, like an artist paints pictures."

Stumpy frowned at him. "You're shittin' me, right?"

"No."

Stumpy laughed. "That's freakin' crazy. What do you paint?"

"Portraits of people. Different things. Usually watercolours."

Stumpy faced front again.

"I'd be interested in seeing your work sometime," Dedrick said.

His mother smiled. "I always said he'd be famous for something, someday."

Stumpy again looked at him. "Maybe you could paint a picture of me. You know, sitting on my bike."

"Maybe. After I get out of jail. Although, I don't know."

Stumpy frowned. "Don't know what?"

"Well, it's just that it's a lot harder to paint big ugly hairy people."

Stumpy scowled at him. "You're still an idiot. I thought that smack in the head might've smartened you up." He turned away. "I knew you didn't really know how to paint."

"Please don't talk about going to jail," his mother said. "I can't even imagine that happening, let alone being able to deal with it."

"He'll be out in no time," Barry said. "We'll make sure he's taken care of in there."

Will stared out the window of the Mercedes. He saw the North Common come into view over the banks of dirty snow that lined Bell Road. "It feels nice to be back among the living," he said to no one in particular. "Even the snow looks good."

His mother smiled. "In case you're wondering, Gloria couldn't come today. When school finished for Christmas, she had to go to Grand Pré. Her mother got sick."

"I was afraid to ask where she was."

"She told me to tell you she'd be back after Christmas – and something about needing a philosophy lesson."

"Freakin' egghead," Stumpy muttered from the front, shaking his head.

Will heard his mother call his name from the back door of the house. He opened the side door of the garage and stuck his head out. "I just got off the phone with Mr. Dedrick," she said. "He said he didn't have to talk to you but wanted to remind you about court tomorrow at nine."

Will nodded, pulling his head back from the water dripping from melting snow on the roof. He closed the door and sat on a wooden stool, with Gloria circling him, a pair of scissors in her right hand.

"It's already too short," he said. "I don't see why you think it's important for me to cut my hair and get dressed up. It's not like there's a trial. Even the sentence has already been determined."

"You never know," she said, snipping at his hair. "At least if you look presentable and make a good impression, he won't be as likely to give you a longer sentence. It happens sometimes, you know. And who knows what that probation officer wrote in his report."

"LaRue? He was okay. He just asked basic things – like about my background, and school, and if I was ever in trouble, and what my plans were."

"Yeah, but you can be sure he talked to other people and you don't know what they said."

"What am I supposed to do about that?"

"Nothing. But you can cut your hair and put on dress pants and a sports jacket for court, and stop giving me and your mother a hard time about it. You'll look very handsome, too. Kind of like a preppy college boy." She kissed his cheek.

"I think I'm on the other side of that equation."

When Stumpy's hearse pulled up in front of Sadie's Lodge at eight-thirty the next morning, Will, his mother, and Gloria hurried down the front steps and piled in. Stumpy stared at Will and whistled. "Holy smokes. Ain't you the prettiest little thing this side of the Dorchester pen."

"Keep your pants on, Kong," Will said to him, reaching to hold Gloria's hand. "I'm not your type, remember. Not primitive enough."

"Jeez, why d'ya keep saying stuff like that? I'm just messing with ya."

"Ignore him," Gloria said, blowing a kiss to Stumpy. "It just means he likes you."

Without speaking, Stumpy whisked them to the Provincial Court building. When he slowed in front, Will saw that Dedrick, Barry, Shotgun, Speedy, and a few other Dark Angels were already there, standing in the open doorway.

"You're up first," Dedrick said to Will, patting his shoulder. "You look a lot better than the last time I saw you. MacIsaac may not recognize you."

"Am I going to have to say anything?"

"He will certainly ask you if you have anything to say. Have you thought about that?"

"No, not really."

"You may want to say something. But sometimes it's better to take a pass on that when things are straightforward – as they are now. It depends on what kind of mood he's in."

"It's better if he don't talk," Speedy said. "The way he talks that judge will lock him up for good and throw away the key."

Dedrick grinned. "My advice would be to keep it short – very short. MacIsaac doesn't suffer fools kindly. And, if he asks you a question, just answer the question. Stay on track and don't embellish. It should all go fast."

"I don't think I have anything to say that would make a difference."

Will felt a heavy hand on his back. He spun around. Al stood there with a big smile on his face. He grabbed Will and crushed him against his chest.

"What are you doing here?" Will asked.

"I came to see you, what else? Kay and Shotgun have kept me posted on what's been happening. Who knows, I may not be around by the time you get out."

"Jeeez, I hope it won't be that long."

"The courtroom is open," Dedrick interrupted. "We should go inside now."

With Dedrick leading the way, they filed into the courtroom. Dedrick directed Will to sit beside him at the defendant's table, while the others jammed into the benches behind them, shoulder to shoulder.

Moments later, Simms hurried into the courtroom without looking at anyone and took his place at the Crown's table. Garrity and Akerman followed and sat in the first bench directly behind him. While Simms was still organizing papers on the table in front of him, MacIsaac bustled into the courtroom from a door behind his bench.

"ALL RISE," a bailiff standing to the right of the bench said with authority. "Supreme Court of Nova Scotia now in session, Justice Andrew MacIsaac presiding."

MacIsaac took his place behind the bench and waved for everyone to sit down. He dropped a large stack of files on his desk and took the first from the top. He began to thumb through the papers in the file, occasionally looking up over his glasses at Will.

"What's he waiting for?" Stumpy whispered to Shotgun.

Shotgun shrugged. "Who knows? Cat and mouse game, I guess."

"Mr. Alexander, stand up please," MacIsaac said, finally.

Will stood up.

"Well, Mr. Alexander, I see you've made it back here. And looking much better since the last time I saw you. Your injuries are improved as well, I take it?"

"Yes."

MacIsaac paused. "That would be 'Yes, Your Honour', Mr. Alexander."

"Yes, Your Honour."

MacIsaac looked at Simms. "What is the Crown seeking for sentence, Mr. Simms?"

Simms stood up, as did Dedrick. "Crown and defence are jointly recommending a sentence of three years, My Lord."

Dedrick nodded when MacIsaac looked his way.

"You may be seated, gentlemen. Mr. Alexander, you can remain standing."

MacIsaac again picked through the papers in the file. He held up a legal-size document. "Have you seen this report, Mr. Alexander? It's the three-page pre-sentence report prepared by Mr. LaRue. You remember him, I'm sure?"

"Yes, Your Honour. I've seen it. Mr. Dedrick showed it to me."

"And you read it, did you?"

"Yes, Your Honour."

"What did you think of it?"

"What did I think of it?"

MacIsaac sighed. "Yes, Mr.Alexander, that is what I asked. To repeat myself – What did *you* think of it, sir?"

"I thought it was good."

"You thought it was *good*. What do you mean by that?"

"Um, well, I thought it was well-written."

MacIsaac grinned momentarily. "Well-written? You thought it was well-written?" He cast a finger in Simms' direction. "Mr. Simms. How long have you been serving as Crown Prosecutor in these courts?"

"Ah, 18 years, Your Honour."

"Tell me, then. When was the last time you heard a defendant describe his pre-sentence report as well-written. Is that something you have *ever* heard, Mr. Simms?"

Simms chuckled and cleared his throat into a cupped hand. "Never, My Lord. I think that's a first."

"Does that strike you as unusual, Mr. Simms?"

"Well, no, not really," Simms said, rolling his eyes and shrugging. "Not knowing the defendant as I do."

MacIssac turned toward Will. "Mr. LaRue will no doubt be pleased to hear your evaluation of his report-writing skills, Mr. Alexander. But what about the content of the report?"

"I thought it was fair and accurate."

MacIsaac paused. "How old are you now, Mr. Alexander?"

"I'll be 20 in a few months."

"So that would make you how old *now*? This will all go much better if you answer my questions in an exact manner. Shall we try again? How old are you now, sir?"

"Nineteen."

"Very good. Now, tell me, Mr. Alexander, why are you here in my court?"

Will glanced at Dedrick, who did not stir. "Ah, it's for sentencing, Your Honour – for possession of a weapon."

"I KNOW THAT!" MacIsaac bellowed. "The offence tells me *what* you did to get here, but it doesn't tell me *why* you are here." He paused. "Is it your goal to be a criminal, to spend time in prison, Mr. Alexander? What I want to know is why you are so determined to be a criminal."

"No, Your Honour. That's not my goal."

"So say you, Mr. Alexander. But your actions scream out the opposite."

He drummed his fingers on the top of his desk. "I suppose you assumed you could simply waltz in here and have me assent to a deal these two lawyers worked out for you – to save everybody a lot of time and trouble. Is that what you assumed?"

"Yes. Well, I mean, I thought it was an agreement."

"Ah, yes. That it was, Mr. Alexander – an agreement. An agreement about charges and sentencing negotiated by Mr. Dedrick and Mr. Simms. A cozy deal you all thought you could live with. But, as I think you've been advised, this court is not bound by any such deals, and I have to tell you frankly, Mr. Alexander, I am unconvinced I should accept this agreement – this deal for your sentencing."

Dedrick stood up. "Your Honour, may I?"

"No, counsellor, you may not. I do not wish to be interrupted at this time. Sit down."

Simms smiled, as Dedrick sank back down.

"As I was suggesting, Mr. Alexander," MacIsaac continued, "it appears to me that you are determined to be a criminal and to go to prison. I don't see any other explanation as to why you are standing before me. And this report," he said, waving it in the air, his voice rising, "it just adds to my confusion. Let us review the high points, shall we?"

He held the report out and moved his glasses lower on his beefy nose. "It tells me you had a difficult childhood – your father killed in action in Korea, growing up with your mother and an abusive, alcoholic stepfather, moving from place to place. It says you were in 12 different schools by the time you got to high school. A lot of instability in your early years. A sad story, indeed – right, Mr. Alexander?"

Will looked straight ahead at MacIsaac.

MacIsaac shook his head. "No need to answer. It's the kind of story we've all heard hundreds of times, and most of those hundreds or thousands of other people don't choose to show the blatant disregard for the law you do. Most of those other unfortunate souls don't seem intent on becoming criminals." He stared down at Will over his glasses.

"But, then, Mr. LaRue writes that you were a good kid – in his words. Never gave your mother any trouble. Were good at sports. Got good marks in school – even had the highest average in all of grade 10 when you were at Saint Patrick's High. Were twice president of your class in high school and on the student council. Says you have a very high IQ – near genius level, if we are to believe the test results." He paused, turning the page.

"But, then, your marks start going down and down. You squeak into Saint Mary's University, but flunk out your first year there. Within a few months, you're running with this so-called Dark Angels motorcycle gang and working at menial jobs." He paused. "Does this all sound right so far, Mr. Alexander? Well, yes, it must be. You already said it was accurate. Shall I go on?"

Will nodded.

"So, then, Mr. LaRue notes there was a warrant issued for your arrest last summer in relation to some gang shootings, but no charges. And, while you are pleading guilty to this one charge for possessing a weapon, there were other charges of break and enter with intent and resisting a peace officer. And I see there was also an alleged altercation with your stepfather, involving your use of a gun. Now, I grant you, none of these allegations has been proven, but they are all in the report as information – as alleged criminal misconduct – for me to consider, as I may wish."

He tossed the report down on the desk and took off his glasses. "It appears to me, Mr. Alexander, that you are a young man who is basically out of control – for whatever simple or elusive reasons there might be. And that it is incumbent on this court to control you for society's sake and for your own sake. So, Mr. Alexander, what do you think, is that not a reasonably close summary of things?"

"Yes, Your Honour."

MacIsaac scratched his head. "Is that all you have to say? What in God's name does all this mean, young man? What sense am I to make of a story like this that I may know what to do with you?" He stared at Will. "There aren't enough clichés in the English language to describe the degree of rash and irresponsible behaviour you have demonstrated. And that gang," he said, shaking his head, "no more than a vehicle for your recklessness."

Will shook his head. "I'm sorry, Your Honour, I wish I knew what it all means. I do think about it. I try to figure out what's happened and why, and what it might mean. But, before I can understand what's already happened, new things, more things, happen that also have to be figured out, and it feels like I can never quite catch up or understand how all the pieces fit together – if they do – and where it's all headed."

MacIsaac leaned back and folded his hands on the desk. "Well, then, Mr. Alexander, congratulations, you have finally uttered something reasonably intelligent." He looked past Will, scanning the courtroom. "You have many friends here today. Mostly motorcycle friends, it would appear. Tell me, beyond this interest you have in motorcycles, and presumably your motorcycle gang, is there anything else in this world that interests you? Something that gives your life focus or meaning?"

Will hesitated. He glanced at Dedrick. "Go ahead," Dedrick murmured.

"Yes. I'm not very good at it, Your Honour, but I like to paint – watercolours mostly. And I like thinking about things and reading books about philosophy and religion."

MacIsaac looked at Simms. "Were you aware of that Mr. Simms?"

"Somewhat, Your Honour," Simms said, snickering.

Dedrick stood up again. "Your Honour, with respect, is this really necessary? I don't understand where the court is going with this. I would reiterate that we believe the recommended sentence is appropriate under the circumstances."

"Thank you, Mr. Dedrick. I know you don't understand. You may be seated." He shifted his gaze back to Will. "One more question, Mr. Alexander, and then I will speak to the sentence. I want to be sure you are being honest and not simply trying to pull the wool over an old man's eyes." He glanced at Dedrick. "Now, then, tell me in your own words what philosophy is and what art is. Since these are things you say you spend time pursuing, you must know something about them."

Will wrinkled his brow. "You mean like a definition?"

"No, I mean like a brief explanation."

Will looked down. "You want to know what I think, Your Honour? I've never tried to explain it to anyone actually – in simple terms."

"Now's your chance."

Will shifted in place. He grabbed the edge of the table. He hesitated. The seconds ticked by with excruciating slowness.

MacIsaac shook his head and cleared his throat. "Yes, well, that's as I thought. If you …"

"If I had to answer briefly," Will interrupted, "I guess what I might say is that philosophy is the way we can try to know the answers to all the important questions that have ever been asked about existence and about the meaning of all things – like Siddhartha or Plato did. Philosophy is about how we can think God's thoughts. And art? I'd say art is what ordinary things and everyday experiences look like when we can see them the way a child does, or the way God does." He stopped short, becoming aware of the eerie stillness in the courtroom.

MacIsaac tapped the desk top with the palm and fingers of his right hand, as if applauding. "Very good. Yes, Mr. Alexander, very good, indeed." He smiled at Simms, then Dedrick. "So where does all this leave us?" He paused. "Young man, you like to take chances, don't you? Risks – calculated or otherwise?"

"Yes, Your Honour."

"And you appear to like deals. Otherwise, we would not be here right now going through this exercise. You weigh the odds and are open to being persuaded by logic – like Aristotle perhaps?"

Will nodded.

"Excellent. Well, then, here is *my* deal – and your chance. I am prepared to offer you a choice, Mr. Alexander. You face two paths. On the one hand, you may choose to have me sentence you right here and now to five years in a maximum security prison." He paused. "On the other hand, there is another other path." He paused again, staring at Will. "You see, I am prepared to offer you a conditional discharge. You would not have to go to prison, but you would have to accept and abide by the conditions I impose and you would be on probation. Are you with me so far?"

"Yes, Your Honour." He hesitated. "But what would the conditions be?"

"Ah, that's what's coming next. So you will be on probation for three years, the same length of time you were prepared to spend in prison. Who knows, you might end up with Mr. LaRue as your probation officer. As for conditions, first, you will leave the Dark Angels motorcycle club and sever all ties with them. Second, you will return to university as a student within six months and remain in university throughout the period of your probation, achieving good marks, not scraping by. You will also have conditions such as not possessing weapons, remaining within the jurisdiction of this court, and so on – regular kinds of conditions of obvious relevance."

MacIsaac closed the file. "There you have it, William Alexander. That's the deal. Quite simple – black or white – it seems to me. This is your chance to be serious about studying philosophy or art and making something of your life, having a goal to be something other than a criminal. However, if you would rather go to jail than to university, I will bow to your wishes and send you there – for five years, not three years." He tapped the desk with his hand. "So what's it going to be, sir?"

Will stared at him, finding it hard to breath. "I don't know," he muttered. "I mean, I don't know what to say, Your Honour. I wasn't expecting to have to decide anything like that on the spot."

Dedrick stood up. "Your Honour, given this unexpected direction, we respectfully ask for a recess so my client can come to a more-considered decision."

"Ten minutes, Mr. Dedrick. No more. I have already invested more time and energy in this case than good judgement would support."

MacIsaac pushed himself out of his chair and disappeared through the door behind his bench. Everyone in the courtroom with the exception of Simms, Garrity, and Akerman jumped from their seats and swarmed around Will and Dedrick.

"Oh man, tough spot," Shotgun said.

"You wouldn't have to serve all that time," Barry said. "Five years is way too much on a charge like that." He looked at Dedrick. "We could appeal the sentence, right Martin?"

Dedrick nodded. "Yes, we could probably get less jail time. But that's what it would be – less jail time. When you think about where we started from with these charges, a conditional discharge is a superb result." He put his hand on Will's shoulder. "He's trying hard to do you a favour."

"Yeah, isn't that great," Barry said, scowling. "But he would be out of the club."

Dedrick shrugged, turning to Will. "Right. That's the question. Can you live with the conditions?"

"No one-percenter could," Barry said. "Right Will?"

Will nodded. He felt a tug at his other arm. He turned and found his mother standing next to him, with Gloria at her side. His mother took his hand in hers. "All you have to do is say 'Yes'. None of your friends would blame you," she said, her eyes pleading and her voice quivering. "If they send you away, you might never come back."

He turned to Gloria. "Sit with me," he said, pulling her down into

Dedrick's chair as he lowered himself into his. "I feel like I'm drowning," he whispered to her.

"Just breathe." She smiled at him and squeezed his knee.

He sat, staring ahead at MacIsaac's bench. "What should I do?"

"I don't know. I can't tell you that." She looked at the side of his face. "I brought something for you. I thought you might want it in prison. You said before that you kept it where you could see it – for luck." She reached into her bag and pulled out a small clear-plastic envelope containing a photograph. She passed it to him.

He sat still and took a deep breath, peering down at it.

"Maybe you could ask yourself what *he* would want you to do," she said.

ROAD TO RAWDON

IT HAD TO BE THAT he was dreaming. *How could real life feel so good,* he thought? The sun of the mid-May evening shone on him from the right, warming that side of his body, while the cool onrushing air sent shivers up his back and ripped tears from his eyes, tears that were instantly blown away at his temples.

He smelled something sweet for a brief moment. *Apple blossoms? But where were they? In someone's backyard,* he decided. *Somewhere in a backyard, or more than one, on Edward Street or Marlborough Avenue, one of the shaded side streets off to the right.*

He rolled the throttle on, going faster, heading south on Robie Street – revving the big motor until the fury of the vibrations in the handlebars threatened to shake his fingernails from his fingertips. The thrill of going so fast on city streets and all the familiar hair-raising sensations made him smile.

He reached back and patted Gloria's left leg. "TOO FAST?" he shouted back to her.

"NO," she yelled back, squeezing his hips between her knees. "I LOVE IT!"

"NICE BOOTS," he said, grabbing her calf.

He began gearing down as he neared the stop sign on Inglis Street. Once there, he turned left on Inglis, but didn't get out of first gear before he swung hard right to head into the campus of Saint Mary's University. He found a place to park his bike in the parking lot north of the McNally Building, away from any other vehicles.

He steadied the bike while Gloria dismounted, then leaned it against the sidestand and swung his leg over, cutting the motor at the same time.

"That was fun," he said.

She ran her fingers through her hair as she looked at her face in the mirror mounted on the left side of the handlebar. "I hear there's going to be a new law in Nova Scotia that you have to wear a helmet when you're on a motorcycle."

"That would be a drag. Are you sure?"

"I read it in the newspaper. Next year, I think."

"That will ruin the whole experience."

She nodded, pulling lipstick from her bag and making a stiff oval shape of her lips to apply it. "Maybe that's something you can discuss in your philosophy class – the protection of people and the public good versus the freedom to choose and take risks. Seems like something that would be right up your alley." She puckered her red lips at him, then smiled.

He laughed. "Probably not. This is an introductory Greek philosophy course. I doubt we'll talk much about helmet laws or motorcycles."

"You never know. You're supposed to be smart. You should be able to find a way to make it relevant."

"Thanks, but I've had enough conflict for a while. This is supposed to be my new start, remember? A little summer course, a couple hours each night for six weeks. Ease back into studying, into straight life. That's what you said when you registered me. I could have waited until September without violating my probation."

"The sooner you start, the sooner you'll finish. It's not like you had anything exciting lined up."

He looked up at the buildings. "This feels a little weird. Being back here. It's hard to know whether the dream was being here or being in the Dark Angels."

She looked him up and down. "Well, in terms of feeling weird, you're going to stand out a little from the jocks and preppy types – dressed the way you are."

"What's wrong with the way I'm dressed?"

"Uh, nothing, if you're into black leather and faded blue denim. The leather around here is maroon and the pants are, like, corduroy, or khaki. You know, collegiate stuff. How soon we forget."

"I'll think about it," he said, turning away.

"Do you know where you're going?"

"I think so." He reached into his pocket and pulled out a schedule.

"Introductory Greek Philosophy. It's in auditorium 'A', in the library building. Over there," he said, pointing to his left. "You don't have to babysit me like this, you know. I'm really going to go."

"I know." She took his hand as they began walking across the parking lot. "I'll only stay for the first 20 minutes or so to keep you company. Then I'll sneak out and walk home. It's such a nice night. Besides, I want to make sure there aren't too many pretty girls hovering around you."

He laughed. "You don't have anything to worry about. They'll probably leave their clothes on. Unlike certain other pretty girls I know."

"Girls?"

"Well, one girl."

When they reached the library building, he stopped. "I just thought of something. Today is May fourteenth."

"Uh, huh. So what?"

"It's my father's birthday. He would have been 41 if he was still alive. It's also the same month and day I joined the Dark Angels."

She nodded. "Yeah, it's funny how certain numbers keep coming up, isn't it? For me, it's been the number 11."

"I wonder if it means anything?"

"Who knows. Coincidence, I'd say. But, there you go, something else for you to philosophize about." She winked at him.

It was twilight by the time his class finished. As he started his bike, he glanced skyward and saw there were no clouds and that the first faint sparkling stars were becoming visible. He turned onto Robie Street, heading north, and then noticed a heavy haze high in the sky straight ahead. By the time he passed University Avenue, he could see and smell that it was smoke – rising up and bending in his direction from the wind – about a mile straight ahead. He rode faster.

Cresting the small hill approaching the Willow Tree intersection, he saw fire trucks and police cars crammed in front of Sadie's Lodge with their lights flashing. His heart began to thud in his chest. He caught a red light at the intersection but blasted through, dodging cars coming at him at right angles. He screeched the bike to a stop on the North Common side of the street and ran toward the Lodge.

"NO! NO! Get back!" a policeman shouted, rushing to meet him and grabbing him by the arms.

"I live here!" Will said, pushing back against him. He looked past the policeman up the driveway and saw that the garage was burned to the ground, a smoldering heap of blackened timbers and unrecognizable debris. A half-dozen firefighters moved back and forth, streaming water onto the back of the house.

"You can't go there, son. There's nothing you can do."

"My mother! Is she out?"

The policeman hesitated. "Ambulance guys took a woman to the hospital about 15 minutes ago. They said she was the owner. Is that your mother?"

Will nodded. He stopped pushing against the policeman. "Is she okay?"

The policeman straightened up. "Come get in my car. It'll be easier to talk there." He took Will by the arm and began to lead him up the street and away from the front of the Lodge – up toward a police car parked near the corner of Welsford Street.

Will shook his arm loose. "It's okay. You don't have to hold on to me."

The policeman climbed into the car and leaned across the seat to open the passenger door. Will climbed in. "I can't tell you a whole lot about her," the policeman said, wiping his brow with the back of his hand. "You'll have to find out from the hospital. But ..."

"I want to know."

"I saw her when they put her in the ambulance. She was burned pretty bad." He paused. "They found her outside. Out back by the garage. They figure she may have gone out there to try to put the fire out or see if anybody was inside. People who saw it burn said it went up real fast – almost like it blew up. The firemen said there must have been a lot of flammable materials in there. That so?"

Will nodded. "Yeah. Some gas and other things."

"Yeah, started big time in that garage, they figure, and jumped to the house." The policeman shook his head. "Damn fires. I hate fires. Only thing worse might be drownings. Ever see somebody who's been in the water for a few days?"

Will shook his head. "Was anybody else hurt?"

"Don't think so. I heard everybody else got out of the house. There were a few guests there, apparently."

"What about my sister?"

"I don't know. I saw a young girl – 15, 16 – get in the ambulance with your mother. Could that've been her?"

Will nodded.

"I was also talking to the people next door. They were worried their house might go up, too. They said they saw somebody come out of your driveway shortly before the fire broke out. A short man, kind of heavy, bald. You don't know who that might've been?"

Will stared out through the car's windshield. He noticed there was a film of soot on it.

"Do you know who that might've been?" the policeman asked again, looking across at him.

"No. I don't know."

"Maybe a guest. Somebody staying there."

"Maybe."

The policeman started the car. "You cold? You're shivering. Here – I'll turn some heat on. It's still chilly in the evenings this time of year."

Will sat motionless in the car, staring straight ahead.

"Do you want me to drive you somewhere? The hospital maybe?"

Will shook his head. "No. I've got my bike." He pointed across the boulevard. "Over there."

"Nice bike. It's a Harley, right?"

Will nodded and opened the door. "Thanks for everything," he said, pushing himself out of the car and swinging the door shut.

With Patty glued to his side, Will watched the clock on the wall in the emergency department waiting room at the Victoria General Hospital – minute-by-minute, hour-by-hour. At midnight, Gloria rushed in.

"Why on earth didn't you call me?" she blurted out, hugging him and then Patty.

"Sorry," he said, shaking his head. "I just wasn't thinking. It's all been a blur since I got here."

She took off her jacket and draped it over the back of the chair next to his. "I thought you might come by after class, but, when you didn't, I thought you'd gone for a ride or something – just to celebrate your first day. When ten-thirty rolled around, I called your place, but the line was dead. So I took a cab over and saw what happened." She paused, looking into his eyes. "They wouldn't tell me anything, except that they took your mother here."

"She's going to friggin' die, I just know it," Patty said between sobs.

Gloria knelt next to her and took her hands in hers.

"She's conscious, but she's got second and third degree burns over a lot of her body, especially around her arms and chest and shoulders," Will said. "They think she shielded her face from the fire with her arms. A doctor was just here again. He said they were trying to stabilize her breathing and were treating her for pain. She might have some lung damage. He said the other big concern was for infection. So they've already started her on antibiotics."

"Have you seen her?" Gloria asked.

"Not me," Patty said, biting at her nails. "I don't want to see her looking like that."

Will nodded. "Only for a minute." He shook his head. "I'm not a doctor, but it looks bad to me. They said we should know how it's going to go within the next 24 to 48 hours – at least for the first part of dealing with things. It's going to be a long road back, if she makes it."

They sat side-by-side in silence, watching other people come and go, watching the clock.

"What's going to happen with the Lodge?" Gloria asked after a while.

Will shrugged. "I don't know. I'll have to call Martin tomorrow. I don't think she had insurance. Maybe he'll know what we can do."

"Do they know what caused the fire?"

"I don't think so. They say it started in the garage and spread to the house. Apparently, the people next door saw somebody around the property before the fire broke out."

"Somebody will investigate it, won't they? I mean, if it's suspicious."

"I'm not sure. I suppose so." He paused. "I'm going to look into it myself."

She looked at him, frowning. "What does *that* mean?"

"I don't know." He glanced up at the clock again. "I don't really know what anything means. But I have to do something."

Time ground on. Will watched Patty sleep, slumped over in her chair.

"Poor thing, she's like a little girl," he whispered to Gloria. "Can you take her to your apartment? She's got no place else to go."

Gloria nodded and nudged Patty awake. "Come on, kiddo. We're going to my place to get some rest." She helped her to her feet. "There's nothing we can do here right now." She turned to Will. "Call me if anything happens."

Will nodded. "If things are the same by daylight, I'll probably leave then."

"Leave for where?"

"I don't know. For a ride to clear my head. Think about what I have to do next. Talk to Martin. Things like that."

Gloria stopped. "Are you sure there isn't something you're not telling me?"

"I've told you all I know."

He followed Gloria and Patty to the exit at the end of a long hallway whose floors looked to be made of polished granite. After watching them leave, he began pacing back and forth in the hall, watching and waiting for the first light of day. When it came, he left the hospital and rode to the Ardmore Tea Room on Quinpool Road.

He sat in a booth along the windows facing the street and picked at a breakfast of ham and eggs and hash browns, sipping hot black coffee and watching the truckers, students, and change-of-shift people come and go – laughing and talking, waking up or winding down.

Soon, he was motoring through Bedford, then Sunnyside and on to Lower Sackville. Near Windsor, and turned right onto Route 14. *Fourteen, that number again*, he thought. His mind flitted back to covering this same route months earlier – 'on the run', as Gloria had said.

The air was fresh and cool, but he felt no chill. All around him, everything he saw and felt and smelled told him life was triumphing – everything so vibrant and sweet. Tears came to his eyes. Inside, he felt only a nauseating, churning emptiness.

He turned into the long driveway leading up to Al's place. He stood on the footpegs as he navigated among rocks, loose dirt, and potholes. He saw Al walk out the back door and wave at him. He stopped the bike and killed the motor at Al's feet.

"You're the last person I expected to see come up my driveway today." He looked hard at Will. "But I'm glad you decided to."

Will hopped off the bike and looked around. "I know what you mean. I just started riding and ended up here."

Al stepped forward and hugged him. "I just heard about what happened. Gloria called Kay early this morning."

Will nodded. "I've got to call Gloria soon."

"Want some breakfast?"

"No thanks. I already ate."

"Do you want to walk over to the chicken coop with me? I was going to get some eggs."

Will nodded and they began to amble toward the barn.

"What do you think's going to happen now?"

Will shook his head. "I don't know. I can't seem to focus on much or concentrate enough to sort it out."

"It'll come. You can't rush it."

"Al?"

Al stopped walking. "What?"

"Could we take a look at your bike before getting the eggs? Would that be okay?"

Al shrugged. "Sure."

They made their way into the barn and moved among its jumbled-up contents, back to Al's Indian Scout. "Beautiful as when you last saw her, I bet," Al said, peeling off the dusty coverings.

"More beautiful."

They stood in silence, staring down at the bike.

"It's all been my fault," Will said. "All of it. Everything I've done has gone bad. No matter how right it's seemed, or whether I've tried to think it out or it's just happened, it's all ended up bad."

"Maybe. But the story's not over till the very end. You don't really know where the story is just yet. Might be over, or might be the middle. Who can say?"

Will laughed. "Sure feels like it's over and that it's all bad. It's my fault my mother's hurt. Who do I hurt next? Gloria? No? How about Patty? No? How about you?"

"You ain't that powerful, son."

Will ran his hand along the gas tank. "Could you do me a favour?" He paused. "No questions."

"Sure."

"I want to borrow your hunting rifle."

"I got more than one hunting rifle. Any particular kind you want?"

"One with a scope. A high-powered one – for big-game hunting."

Al nodded. "I see. I never took you for much of a hunter." He nudged past Will and sat on the bike. "You *really* want to be a hunter, Will? Somebody who can take aim and shoot a living breathing creature? Kill it dead."

Will stared down at the bike. "I can do whatever I have to do."

"Yeah, I know what you mean. Me – I learned that about myself in the war. *Whatever* you have to do." He paused. "I'm a little worried, though. From what I hear, you don't got a great reputation when it comes to borrowing firearms."

Will smiled. "That would be true. But I'd promise to give it back to you."

"So when exactly would you be needing this rifle? It's a while yet before hunting season in these parts. October would be the earliest."

"No rush at all. Maybe not even for a year or two. I have to think things through."

"Well, that might be different." He smiled. "You'd likely want to come out here from time to time and get taught how to use it. Practice up till you're right good."

Will nodded. "I would."

Al chuckled. "Yup – all about patience, right? My Eleanor always used to say, 'Al, you can be tame without being tamed'. That was some woman."

"I wish I had known her."

"I wish you had, too." He hesitated. "You know what, if you're going to be coming out here to learn to hunt and shoot, we should do another project. Something you could help *me* with."

"Like what?"

"How about if we get my bike running? You know, tear the motor down, change up all the fluids and the tires. Paint her up. She should run. Might have to track down some parts. But we'd have some time, right?"

Will nodded, feeling a warm tear trickle down his cheek.

"Jeez, we could even get into some of them philosophy talks you like."

"We could."

Al swung his leg over the bike and got off, groaning as he did. "I don't know, I might not even be able to ride it in a few years. My arthritis is getting some bad." He covered the bike over again and began to lead Will out of the barn.

"You gonna stick around for a while or head back?"

Will shrugged. "I'm in no rush. I have to call Gloria and check on my mother, soon. That's about it for today." He looked out over Al's back field. "Oh, and I guess I have to get back in time for class tonight. I started summer school at Saint Mary's yesterday."

"That's right good, it is." He put his arm around Will's shoulder. "You'll probably change your mind about hunting. Ain't a lot of them college types that hunt."

"No. I won't change my mind." He shook his head. "I'll never change my mind, Al."

ECCLESIASTES

AL ROLLED HIS INDIAN SCOUT out of his cluttered barn. He circled it, smiling at it from different angles, as the sun glinted off flowing curves and gleaming surfaces of rich paint and deep chrome. He bent forward and stroked the new tan leather of its seat with his fingertips, as a lover might caress the cheek of his beloved.

He left it parked in front of the barn, then went to his pickup truck, lowered the tailgate and backed the truck up against the sloping hill that fell away from the left side of the barn. He wheeled the bike over and pushed in onto the bed of the truck without having to lift it, still smiling to himself. He tied the bike down with a nylon rope and leather straps, jostling it from side to side and front to back to make sure it was secure.

He returned back to the barn and grabbed a blue Toronto Maple Leafs hockey bag sitting on the floor to one side. He returned to the truck and tossed it into the cab in the narrow space behind the driver's seat. As he navigated his driveway at a crawl, he kept glancing at the bike in the rear-view mirror. At the end of the driveway, he turned right, in the direction of Windsor. He looked all around at the greenery and began to whistle. At the end of Route 14, he turned left, in the direction of Halifax.

"William Alexander!" his mother said. "Please hurry up! I told you I wanted to be early so we could get a good seat."

He came out of the bathroom, brushing his teeth. "Don't panic. We've got at least an hour. Besides, it's no big deal."

She put her hands on her hips. "No big deal? What are talking about? *You* might not think your graduation is a big deal, but I do."

Gloria, sitting at the table, smiled as she brushed foundation on her face and glanced up from the small mirror in her makeup compact.

"You do, too, don't you, Gloria?" his mother asked.

"Absolutely." She paused, then frowned at Will. "But are we really going there with Stumpy and Barry in that damned old hearse? I didn't think that thing was still running."

He laughed, turning back to the bathroom to rinse his mouth. "It's important to them, I guess. Stumpy even put seats in the back for us. Being in that hearse was part of quite a few momentous events. Besides, I think they're trying to recruit me back to the club now that my probation's going to be over."

"Momentous?" Gloria said, rolling her eyes.

He came back in the kitchen, smiling. "They were momentous to us."

"What do you mean *recruit* you?" his mother asked, the colour draining from her face.

He shook his head. "Don't worry. That's in the past. I'm a reformed criminal now."

His mother sighed. "Hurry up and finish getting ready. I hope nobody sees us getting out of that thing. We could have gone in Mr. Dedrick's nice car. I think he was disappointed we weren't going to go with him."

"I love that Mercedes," Gloria said.

Will laughed. "What difference does it make if somebody sees us in an old hearse? I think it can only add a little character to the event."

His mother stopped fidgeting and looked at him. "Well, do you think those two will at least be dressed respectably?"

"God, I hope not," he said.

"Stop! You stop that right now." She turned to Gloria. "Tell him to stop it, Gloria. He's just doing that to get me worked up – as if I'm not a bundle of nerves already."

At a little before one o'clock, Stumpy swung the old black Cadillac onto the boulevard in front of Saint Mary's University. Will and the others looked in all directions.

"No place to park around here," Will said, shaking his head.

"I told you we should have come earlier," his mother said, exasperated. "I knew something like this would happen. Let me out right here."

"Don't fret, Celeste," Barry said. "We'll get you there."

Stumpy circled around and stopped in front of the big oak doors at the main entrance to the McNally Building. "What now?" he asked, as the DeVille's engine huffed and chugged and blue smoke rose up in thickening columns all around the car.

"Jesus, hurry up," Barry said. He pointed to his left. "Pull in behind that Volvo. We gotta get out of this gas chamber."

"That's the president's spot," Gloria said. "See the little sign? You know, the president of Saint Mary's. And that's probably his car."

Will laughed. "Yeah, that's perfect. Pull in close behind him, Stumpy. He's not going anywhere."

"I'd say it's my spot, anyway," Barry said. "Doesn't say on the sign president of what."

Stumpy eased up to the Volvo until they heard a clunk, felt a little jolt and saw the Volvo move forward a few inches. He threw the shift lever up into 'Park'.

"You two going to wear your colours inside?" Gloria asked.

Stumpy glared back at her.

"No offence. Just asking."

"What do you want us to wear?" Stumpy asked. "We ain't got none of them satiny outfits and funny hats like Mister Bojangles, here."

"Give it a try," Will said. "Worst thing that can happen is they'll ask you to leave."

They all climbed out of the car. Barry patted his pockets. "Have I got time for a smoke?"

"No," Gloria said, grabbing his arm and twisting him toward the stairs.

In the same hour, an unmarked police car slowed to a stop in the shadow of a terminal building on the most-southerly pier jutting into Halifax harbour.

Garrity unbuttoned his sports jacket and rubbed his belly. "Shit, I shouldn't have eaten that chilli for lunch. My stomach's been giving me fits lately." He moaned. "Look in the glove box, Jim. I think I left some Rolaids there the other day."

Akerman stopped tapping his notepad with his ballpoint pen. He shook his head. "You need a Goddamn stomach pump, not Rolaids." He leaned forward and opened the glove box. He fished around inside. "Here," he said, tossing half a package of Rolaids to Garrity.

"How much longer?" Akerman asked.

Garrity glanced at his watch, then shoved all the Rolaids into his mouth. "Not long. A half hour, maybe less. You got somewhere to go?"

Akerman shook his head. "This heat's getting to me. It's hot even in the shade. Did you get them to look at the air conditioning in this thing yet?"

"It's the humidity – not the heat. It's not that hot. This is Goddamn Halifax, Jim." He reached and turned on the air conditioning to 'Cold'. "I put a requisition in but I don't know if they touched it yet. We'll know in a few seconds. Close your window."

They rolled up the windows and sat, waiting.

Akerman wiped his brow. "How much coke is supposed to be moving out of that ship?"

"Ten kilos."

"That's it? Ten kilos?"

Akerman frowned. "Why would they bother shipping only ten kilos in an ocean-going ship?"

Garrity shrugged. "Okay, yeah, it's small potatoes. But drug dealers aren't geniuses. The information was there's a biker connection. It's worth some surveillance."

"Well, I don't see any boats heading this way. Who called it in?"

"I don't know exactly. We got it second hand from one of our snitches – one of Floyd's runners, I think."

Akerman sighed. "If you ask me, it's a waste of time. Bet the action's happening somewhere else. We'll hear about it later – wait and see." He laughed. "What'd you say the name of that tub was? Funny name, wasn't it?"

Garrity reached into his shirt pocket and pulled out a slip of paper. He squinted to read it. "Jesus can't read my own writing. Hold on – it's spelled E – c – c – l – e – s – i – a – s – t – e – s ... Ecclesiastes. Yeah – *The Ecclesiastes* – that's it. Out of Jerusalem."

He slid the gearshift lever down into 'Drive'.

"Still too hot in here. They didn't fix that damn air conditioner," Akerman said, rolling down his window and looking out. He laughed and shook his head. "Do you realize what you just said? *Jerusalem*. Jerusalem is a land-locked city. There's no fucking ships out of Jerusalem, Frank."

Akerman heard a sharp, precise **crack** from the rear, like the tip of a bullwhip snapping against the back window. At the same instant, he felt the back of his head buffeted by a quick concussive jolt. He ducked his head instinctively, then glanced up and to the left. He saw that the inside of the windshield in front of Garrity was splattered with blood and fleshy matter. He looked at Garrity and saw that the right side of his bald head was missing. Blood gushed out of the hole, as Garrity began to slump toward him.

A hot spasm of horror pierced Akerman's stomach and choked air from his lungs. As he thrust out his left arm to stop Garrity from falling against him, a second bullet ripped through the back window of the police car and exploded through his head.

The car crept forward, gaining more momentum the farther it went. At the end of the pier, it bumped up over a low concrete ridge and plunged into the harbour. It bobbed on the surface of the water, its nose pointed down and its trunk above the surface. Gurgling brown-green water swirled and hissed and frothed all around the car until it disappeared beneath the surface.

The sun was beginning to kiss the peak of the roof at Sadie's Lodge when Stumpy pulled up to the curb in front of the house. They all sat in the hearse, no one stirring to get out.

"I don't think I want this day to end," Celeste said. She looked pensively out the window and up at the house. "I was just thinking. Maybe we should rename it."

"Rename what?" Will asked.

"The lodge – a new name. You know, maybe something that has to do with making a fresh start."

"That's a nice idea," Gloria said.

Will nodded.

Barry lit a cigarette and blew the smoke out his window. "So what's next, Will? Remember what I said a long time ago about you being a lawyer or shrink?"

Will smiled. "How can I forget?" He took Gloria's hand in his. "I don't know about law school. That might be too hard to swallow. I'm thinking I might stick with philosophy and get a PhD."

"What can you do with that?" Stumpy asked.

Will laughed. "Nothing particularly useful – talk about truth and absolutes. Maybe teach philosophy." He opened the door.

Stumpy frowned. "You're gonna be a *teacher*?"

Will shrugged and smiled. "Not sure. Maybe. What do you think?"

Stumpy stared straight ahead. "Yeah, I can see you doin' that – better than being a lawyer." He glanced at Barry and Will. "Know what? I didn't think I'd like all that graduation stuff today, but it was kind of cool – kind of." He paused and took a deep breath. "Do you think I could go to a school like that and learn important stuff? You know, get some real schooling and be a – you know, a college graduate?"

Will glanced at Barry. "Sure. Why not?"

Stumpy narrowed his eyes. "Are you jerkin'me around?"

"No. I really mean it."

"See," Stumpy said to Barry. "I told you."

Will, his mother ,and Gloria stood on the sidewalk and watched as Stumpy and Barry pulled away and drove up Robie Street, with Stumpy nodding his big head up and down in time to music from the radio and blue exhaust smoke swirling in the hearse's wake.

"I forgot the front-door key," his mother said.

They took a few steps down the sidewalk and turned into the driveway.

"Somebody's here," Gloria said, pointing at a motorcycle parked near the end of the driveway.

"That's strange," Will said. "It's Al's Indian."

They walked up to the bike, staring at it every step of the way.

"It's pretty," his mother said. "I don't know anything about motorcycles, but I love that paint. It looks thick and creamy – like butterscotch."

Will nodded. "It's really old. Al and I have been working on it off and on for the last three years. But I didn't know he'd gotten it running."

"Is he here?" Gloria asked.

Will looked around, feeling his skin crawl. "Something's not right," he said, shaking his head. "He wouldn't do this. Leave his bike here like this."

"Maybe he's inside," his mother said. She turned toward the back of the house. "Look," she said, pointing. "There's an envelope on the back door."

Will walked with stiff legs to the back steps, then up them. He pulled at the piece of electrical tape holding the envelope to the glass of the screen door and took the envelope in his hands. He tore it open and pulled out a piece of paper.

"What does it say?" Gloria asked.

Will read in silence.

"Will?"

"He says 'Sorry I missed your big graduation today. Take care of your new motorcycle. I can't ride it no more so you may as well have it. Time you had a real bike – ha, ha. By the way, no hunting this year. Got rid of all my guns. – Al."

"He's giving you his bike?" his mother asked.

Will nodded, staring at the bike.

"What's wrong? You look like you've seen a ghost," Gloria said. "You don't seem too happy about it."

He nodded. "I think I *have* seen a ghost."

"Almost ready?" he asked Gloria.

"Uh, huh," she said. She slid her lipstick tube into the breast pocket of her leather jacket. "Look okay?" she asked, puckering her lips.

He smiled. "Yup. They're red enough that cars will be screeching to a stop all around us."

"Jerk," she said, grinning, as she zipped up her jacket.

They left the garage through the side door and walked slowly to his bike, its motor lopping along with a low guttural growl – sending shock waves through every metal part, every nut and bolt, making everything shake and quiver. Gloria smoothed down her hair and pulled her helmet over her head. "Hate wearing this thing," she said.

He nodded, pulling on his helmet.

"Can we take the Indian sometime?" she asked, swinging her leg over the back of the Harley and climbing on behind him.

He nodded. "Soon as I get it registered and get a back seat on it for you." He stretched his arms forward and grabbed the high handlebars.

"You never used to be so concerned about following all the rules."

He glanced back at her and shrugged. He gave the throttle a quick snap, making the motor bark.

"Guess you've really decided against rejoining the club." She pressed her body against his back. "I hope you're not going to get all boring on me now that you're a good boy."

"Don't know what I'm going to do. Haven't decided." He smiled at her. "Guess you'll have to take your chances." He kicked the transmission down into first and eased the clutch out.

He rode at an easy pace out of the city, headed west, with the morning sun warming their backs. Once past Lower Sackville, he began to gear down. He stopped in the gravel on the shoulder of the road.

"What's wrong?" Gloria asked, looking around.

"Nothing," he said. He took his helmet off and rubbed his forehead with his fingertips. "Give me your helmet."

She looked at him, narrowing her eyes. She undid her helmet and eased it off her head. "What're we doing? Why are we stopping here?"

"We're not." He took the two helmets and latched them to the sissy bar with their chin traps. He hopped back onto the bike and revved the motor.

"Really?!!" she said, her voice rising with delight. "Where are we going?"

He shook his head. "I don't really know. There are lots of roads. It doesn't matter. They're all good, right?"

The back wheel spun in the gravel and chirped when it hit the asphalt. He rolled the throttle on. The road up ahead undulated and snaked left and right. Grass and bushes and trees began to whiz by – faster and faster – becoming a green blur on each side. He pinned the throttle wide open – smells of spring flowers and apple blossoms and farm animals – the bike's booming exhausts – Gloria's ecstatic screams – the blast of road wind – the skin on his face stretched tight against his cheek bones.

Frantic's crazy laughter echoed in his head, his father's calm face looked up at him from the surface of the crimson gas tank. He felt Daddy Hughie's big arms and rough hands squeeze him tight. He was *alive*!

It didn't matter what happened next. It would all be as it had to be.

AUTHOR BIO
HUBERT E. DEVINE

Hubert Edward Devine lived for a time in Germany and Ontario before returning to his hometown of Yarmouth, Nova Scotia, where he now lives. He graduated from Saint Mary's University with a Bachelor of Arts (*summa cum laude*), majoring in philosophy and languages, and later from Dalhousie University with a Master of Arts in classical philosophy. While at Dalhousie, he was a Killam Scholar and the recipient of a Canada Council Fellowship.

A lover of words, ideas and beauty, Hubert has been quietly writing for many years. *Dark Angels* is his first published novel.

www.ingramcontent.com/pod-product-compliance
Lightning Source LLC
Chambersburg PA
CBHW020958120726
47905CB00009B/2748